GIOVANNI

Titles available in this series

Yannis
Anna
Giovanni

GIOVANNI

Beryl Darby

ISBN 978-0-9554278-2-4

Printed and bound in Great Britain by
Biddles Limited, King's Lynn, Norfolk

First published in the UK in 2008 by

JACH Publishing
92 Upper North Street, Brighton, East Sussex, England BN1 3FJ

website: www.beryldarby.co.uk

For Janine, my photographer, personal assistant, critic, and above all for being my daughter who has continually supported and encouraged me.

Reviews for *Yannis* – the first title in the series

The Daily Mail (National Newspaper)

Yannis makes for a most interesting and enjoyable read.

Evening Argus (Local Newspaper)

Brighton based Beryl Darby is a compulsive writer and *Yannis* is the first of five novels she has written about the same Cretan family. Her saga is built around actual events in the island's history, although the characters are fictitious.

Essentially Worthing (Local Magazine)

A gripping read. You'll get hooked into the atmosphere of this exciting and sometimes harrowing tale, based on actual happenings at the leper colony of Spinalonga near Crete.

C.M.P.C.A (Local Area Magazine)

This is a chilling story, and even more disturbing because it all actually happened. But while everything certainly doesn't end happily ever after, you are not left sad. In fact, after living through the many triumphs and tragedies of these people for 700 odd pages, you are sorry to bid them farewell. Beryl has a comfortable style, an acute ear for dialogue, and total mastery of her subject. *Yannis* works on many levels: it tells a story too long untold, depicts a Greece few of us know at all – with human emotions at their most intense. I promise, once you've been drawn into this close Cretan community you'll be hooked.

Written by D. Shorley FCLIP Sussex University

Uckfield Lending Library (Michael Hollands)

I asked the library to buy *Yannis* and finished it at Easter. I thought it was absolutely wonderful how you got into the minds and situations of the characters and brought it all so vividly to life. There were moments that were really moving.

Ian Rees – Elektros Bookshop, Elounda

A remarkable read, I was unable to put the book down.

Reviews from readers

I started to read *Yannis* at 9.00 p.m. and when I lifted my eyes from it the time was 3.00 a.m.!!

* * *

Thank you so much for such a lovely story. I don't have a lot of time to read, but I couldn't put *Yannis* down.

* * *

Have only this morning closed *Yannis* with regret. There are moments in life when words seem so inadequate to the occasion – and this is another. A massive story – full of the keenest observation of the human condition and the compassion that strings us all together.

* * *

I just had to write to tell you how much I loved your book. It was compulsive reading and beautifully written – I read every single word! I found that whilst I was reading I was also seeing all the characters, places and situations in my mind and I think that is the sign of a great author. You are up there with the best of them and I can't wait to read *Anna* when it is published.

* * *

I just wanted to say how much I enjoyed the novel – if enjoy is the right word to use for such a tragic subject. I didn't realise leprosy was still a problem in this century, particularly the way the lepers were treated so thank you for opening my eyes to this subject. I kept imagining it as a film. It's got all the ingredients. Such a mixture of emotions and human conditions.

* * *

I have just finished reading *Yannis* and really enjoyed it.

* * *

I have read *Yannis* during my holiday and thoroughly enjoyed it. Wonderful! It made me cry.

Family Tree

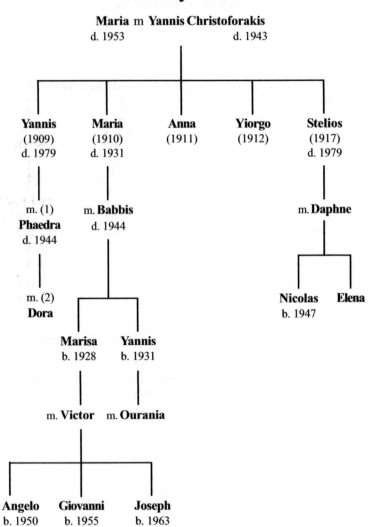

Maria m **Yannis Christoforakis**
d. 1953   d. 1943

Yannis   **Maria**   **Anna**   **Yiorgo**   **Stelios**
(1909)   (1910)   (1911)   (1912)   (1917)
d. 1979   d. 1931   d. 1979

m. (1)   m. **Babbis**   m. **Daphne**
Phaedra d. 1944
d. 1944

m. (2)   **Nicolas**   **Elena**
Dora   b. 1947

            Marisa   **Yannis**
            b. 1928   b. 1931

            m. **Victor**   m. **Ourania**

Angelo   **Giovanni**   **Joseph**
b. 1950   b. 1955   b. 1963

Family Tree

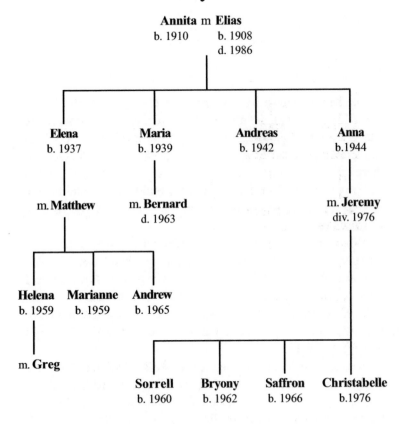

Annita m **Elias**
b. 1910   b. 1908
           d. 1986

Elena   **Maria**   **Andreas**   **Anna**
b. 1937   b. 1939   b. 1942   b.1944

m. **Matthew**   m. **Bernard**   m. **Jeremy**
               d. 1963   div. 1976

Helena **Marianne** **Andrew**
b. 1959 b. 1959 b. 1965

m. **Greg**

Sorrell **Bryony** **Saffron** **Christabelle**
b. 1960 b. 1962 b. 1966 b.1976

Author's Note

I visited Spinalonga in 1984 with my daughters, and Janine took a cine film as we walked around. We were the only visitors to the island at that time. Upon having the film developed and whilst showing it, I was asked who the girl in the house was. As I looked there appeared to be a girl, aged about ten to thirteen, dressed in white with long black hair, inside the building that had been a taverna. As the camera panned around she appeared to lean forwards to see us.

When I met my friend who had lived on the island as an exile for so many years, I asked if any young girls had lived there. He smiled sadly and said there was Anna, she had died over there. I felt a cold shiver go down my spine and goose bumps rise on my arms. Obviously I had to incorporate this somewhere in one of the books. I found it fitted rather well into 'GIOVANNI' when I wrote it in 1993.

At this time, and the subsequent times that I visited Plaka, the village was becoming more derelict as the original inhabitants abandoned it for various reasons. 1995 was the last time I visited Crete and to my amazement, lining the road to Plaka were self-catering apartments and there was once again a thriving community catering to the tourist industry.

1976 - 1979

Annita laid the finishing touches to the table. Each year there seemed to be more people to join them for the annual Thanksgiving dinner. She hoped she had ordered enough ice cream, crisps and coca-cola to satisfy Anna's younger girls. They always seemed to have such enormous appetites until they reached puberty and suddenly became weight conscious and worried her by not eating enough to keep a fly alive.

She counted the places again, Elena and Matthew, Helena, Marianne and Andrew, Maria she would put next to her father and he would stop her being maudlin, Andreas, Anna, Jeremy and the three girls, Sorrell, Bryony and Saffron. She hesitated. Maybe Helena would bring the young man from High School. She sensed there would be an announcement there eventually. Annita rolled a spare set of silver cutlery in a linen napkin and placed them on a plate at the end of the table. Either way she would have time to lay the place or remove the articles from sight when her family arrived.

Andreas arrived first, greeting her effusively before removing his overcoat and handing her a sheaf of flowers.

'For my favourite hostess. Only once have I missed Thanksgiving at home and I vowed it would never happen again. You're looking as young as ever, Mamma. I swear my current leading lady looks years older than you – and she claims she's not yet thirty.'

'Oh, Andreas, you always were a flatterer.' Annita caught the odour of alcohol on his breath as he kissed her. 'Come on in. I need your opinion on the table.'

Andreas surveyed the large, oval dining table with approval. 'I'll have to write a play that revolves around a Thanksgiving meal and use your table. It's magnificent as always. It's so delightful to have a proper napkin and not those awful paper things you get at most places.'

Annita smiled happily at him. He always knew how to please her.

'I'll have these arranged in a vase. Help yourself to a drink. Your pappa should be down any minute.'

'You mean he's prepared to give up an evening with his beloved microscope to spend it with the humble likes of his family?' Andreas raised his eyebrows in mock amusement. 'He'll spend the whole evening wondering what developments have taken place in his latest experiment and trying to think of a good excuse to return to the lab.'

'No, he won't.'

The voice from the door made Andreas turn. 'Pappa! It's good to see you. What's new on the lepromatus front?'

'Very little, I'm afraid. Last month I wrote a paper and...'

'Elias! You promised not to talk shop tonight and you know Andreas is teasing you.'

Andreas looked sorrowful. 'You always did see through me, Mamma. Now, I've helped myself, can I get either of you a drink?'

Elias eased himself into a chair. 'I'll wait until the others arrive.'

'Well, you won't have long. There's a car just pulled up. Oh, God, it's Anna and her tribe.' Andreas dropped the curtain back in place. 'We could pretend there's no one in,' he suggested.

'Don't be so silly.' Annita felt herself almost giggling. Andreas always had this effect on her and she refused to accept that the slights and gibes he made at and about his youngest sister were serious.

Anna swept into the room, Jeremy and her three girls bringing up the rear. Andreas watched as they dutifully greeted and kissed each other. That was a very flowing dress his sister was wearing. There was another on the way! He looked at his nieces, Sorrell, nearly sixteen, was a striking figure in her skin-tight dress. Bryony had obviously been influenced by her sister, wearing a scarlet evening gown and her plump, childish face looked ridiculous covered in make up. Thank goodness Saffron still looked like a child. He poured himself another drink and nodded towards Jeremy who smiled vaguely back at him. Maria crept in through the door and Anna turned her attention towards her, commenting on her wearing widow's weeds at a Thanksgiving and so many years after the death of her husband.

'I always wear black,' sniffed Maria, near to tears. 'If you lost someone you loved as much as I loved Bernard you'd know how I feel. It would be sacrilegious to wear anything else. He would still be mourning me if the position had been reversed.'

Andreas did not hear Anna's reply, but by the way Maria's eyes filled with tears and she tried to dab them away without ruining her makeup he knew it had not been kindly.

He helped himself to a handful of peanuts from a small glass bowl and topped up his glass. No doubt the evening would be spent with Maria alternating between tears and putting on her 'brave face'. Someone should rescue her from Anna, who would certainly not help the situation.

Andreas moved over to where Sorrell and Bryony stood, Sorrell grimacing over the coca-cola she had been given.

'Well, well, Sausage and Bacon, how are you both. Trying hard to grow up, I see.'

Sorrell glowered at her uncle. 'Actually I am grown up. Rather too old to be called by the childish name you seem to like to give me.'

'Oh, ho, touchy in our old age! Maybe it would be more fitting to call you Sage and Onion.'

Bryony giggled. 'That would make us sound like a stuffing.'

'So it would,' agreed Andreas. He raised his voice deliberately. 'And talking of stuffing, am I correct in thinking my dear sister is in an interesting condition yet again?'

Anna blushed. 'You may call it interesting.'

'Personally I call it fascinating.'

'I don't know what you're on about. Jeremy and I...'

'Jeremy?' Andreas raised his eyebrows. 'I thought his name was Rudi.'

Anna's face was scarlet and a hush seemed to have settled on the room.

'I don't know what you mean.' Anna spoke through clenched teeth, her eyes glittering dangerously.

Andreas swallowed the last of his drink. 'Come, come, my dear. He's quite a striking figure. What will you be calling this little addition? Something appropriate, I hope.'

'You bastard! You out and out bastard!'

Anna flung herself at her brother who fended her off easily.

'Now that I'm not – unlike some.'

'How dare you, you pervert.'

Andreas shook his head. 'I'm not a pervert. Perverts tend to corrupt the innocent. I am quite innocent of corruption, or population for that matter.'

Jeremy stepped forward, his face and neck a dull red. 'I think you should apologise to my wife. You have been most insulting.'

Andreas laughed. 'I'll not apologise for speaking the truth. Ask her about her friend Rudi. Accept what lies she likes to tell you, but don't start playing the innocent injured husband in a few months time when you find the truth staring you in the face with a pair of big brown eyes.'

Jeremy sucked in his breath. 'What's he talking about, Anna?'

'He's seen me a couple of times with Rudi. His nasty perverted little mind has worked over time.'

'Not my mind, but a certain piece of Rudi's anatomy has been, if his description is to be believed.'

Anna's face was as white as the napkins. 'You're disgusting. I'll not stay here and be insulted. Take me home, please, Jeremy. Girls, come along.'

Saffron looked up at her father's furious face. 'Do we have to go, Daddy? We've not had anything to eat yet.'

'I think it might be better. Your mother's not feeling very well.'

Sorrell looked at her mother and stepfather. 'Well, I'm staying and so is Bryony,' she spoke defiantly.

Jeremy shrugged. 'You and your sister can do as you please.'

Sorrell's jaw dropped. She had expected to be ordered home and was prepared to add to the scene by declaring that she was not a child to be told what she was going to do.

Elena and Matthew entered, their arrival unnoticed by those already in the room until they began to call greetings and make apologies for being the last.

'Just about everything went wrong. Elena was searching for her earring, Marianne had lost her gloves, Andrew couldn't decide whether to wear a bow tie or a cravat, the traffic was heavy, to name but a few of the crisis I've endured during the last hour. Still, we're here now, so the party may commence.'

'I think you've just missed the best bit,' murmured Andreas and refilled his glass.

'Andreas,' his father's voice cut across the room like a knife. 'I think it's time you left. You have an appointment, remember.'

Andreas gave a mock bow. 'How good of you to remind me.' He swallowed the contents of his glass. 'I'm so sorry not to be able to stay longer. Your party has been sadly depleted, Mamma, and that was not my intent.'

Annita shook her head sadly. Surely Andreas had been venting his spite on his sister unnecessarily. She would have to talk to Anna and see if she could smooth things over between them.

Andreas was at his parent's house early the next morning, contrite and full of apologies. 'I didn't mean to spoil your party, Mamma.

I shouldn't have come. I was in a filthy mood and I'd already had far too much to drink. I'd had a row with Laurence. I thought he was interested in Rudi, I'd seen them together number of times. I should have known better. Laurie isn't like that; he would have come straight out and told me. He just looked at me sadly and walked out. After he left I went straight round to Rudi's. He's an unpleasant character.' Andreas winced inwardly as he recalled the disgusting words Rudi had used. 'He told me about Anna, in graphic detail, I might add. I felt such a fool and I was frightened Laurie wouldn't come back. I didn't know where he'd gone. I trailed round all our usual haunts, then gave up and came here. I shouldn't have done so. As soon as I saw Anna I just had to vent my anger on her.'

Annita held up her hand. 'Now, Andreas, stop. I don't know what you're on about. Why should you be upset if Laurence meets people?'

Andreas looked at his father in despair. 'Mamma, sit down. Now, listen. Laurie and I are friends, very good friends, we have been for years. The thought of him and Rudi...' Andreas shuddered. 'I knew he'd had lunch with him – I saw them leaving, Rudi's arm across Laurie's shoulders and they appeared to be laughing and joking together. I was jealous and jumped to conclusions. It's as simple as that. The little green god sitting on my shoulder.'

'Why should you be jealous? What does it matter to you who Laurence has lunch with?'

A wry smile touched Andreas's lips. 'Mamma, I really have to spell it out for you, don't I? Laurence and I don't just share a flat, we live together, we share everything and we're happy to do so. We keep our private life very private, we're very discreet. We don't mince down the road together holding hands, occasionally we're seen in the company of a woman, and as far as any but our very close circle of friends know we are just flat mates.'

Annita's hand went to her mouth. 'You mean, you and Laurie, you're…'

'Yes, Mamma. Don't pretend to be shocked. I can't help my genes. When I realised I tried to be conventional for your sake, but then I met Laurie.' Andreas smiled. 'We're both very happy the way we are.'

'So when you saw Laurence with this Rudi you thought the worst. You stupid boy, why didn't you ask him?'

'If you'd seen Pappa with another woman giving the impression that they were more than casual friends would you have calmly asked him what he was doing? I doubt it. You would have lashed out the same as I did. Apparently Rudi has been seeing Anna for some months. He's not the first one since Jeremy married her. Her name is a byword in this town, has been for years. I was so furious with myself for causing a scene with Laurie that I took it out on her. I'm very sorry I spoiled your evening.'

'There can be other parties. I'm more concerned about you and Anna. Has Laurie come back and have you settled your differences?'

'Yes, Mamma. I've apologised and he's forgiven me. Rudi has a part in his current production and he was telling Laurie that he's been offered a film test. If he's successful he wants Laurie to release him from his contract early.'

'Then you'd better go over to Anna and apologise to her.'

Andreas shook his head. 'That I'll not do. She's a slut; has been ever since she was at High School.'

'Andreas.' Elias spoke for the first time.

'It's true, Pappa. The boys in my class used to snigger behind their hands about my kid sister. One even asked me if I used her! I knew what she was up to and it was degrading, degrading for her and the family. God knows how many abortions she's had. Sorrell and Bryony have no idea who their fathers are and I doubt if Anna knows either. At least Jeremy married her, but I doubt if he'll be able to pass this one off as his. Rudi's a very dark skinned Turk.'

Annita turned a horrified face to her son. 'You mean, Anna and a Turkish man?'

'I do. In itself that's no big deal, although I can't say I like them, but it doesn't look too good when your husband's white English. I'm not exactly looking forward to having a Turkish relative.'

'Andreas, are you sure of this or are you still feeling spiteful towards your sister?'

'Pappa, I can't swear that it's Rudi's child she's carrying, only time will tell, but it's far more likely to be his than Jeremy's. According to Rudi…'

Annita put her hands over here ears. 'I don't want to hear what this Rudi says. It was wicked of her to cheat on Jeremy. I'd wanted to talk to her. I knew there was something wrong. I was just waiting for an opportunity, but she never seemed to be here alone with me.'

'Why didn't you tell me?' Elias turned to his wife. 'I'd have talked to her, whether she was alone or not. Get her on the 'phone and tell her she's to come straight over.'

'In that case I'll go now.' Andreas picked up his coat. 'I am sorry, truly, for the scene I caused last night.' He held out his hand to his father. 'Thanks, Pa. I thought you would have told Mamma about Laurie and me years ago.'

Elias shrugged. 'The subject was never discussed. We're all made differently. I'm just sorry we didn't do a better job when we were making you.'

'Don't worry about it. I don't.' Andreas kissed his mother's cheek and let himself out.

Anna arrived, her face swollen with crying, but her eyes glittering with hatred. 'What was so urgent I had to come straight over? I'd just managed to get to sleep when you called.'

Elias looked at his youngest daughter sternly. 'I think we should have a little chat. We should have had it years ago, and I blame myself for being too indulgent towards you.'

Anna eyed her father warily.

'Sit down and tell me about this child you're expecting.'

Anna sat. 'What is there to tell? Andreas opened his big mouth last night and Jeremy's leaving me – and says he's taking Saffron with him,' she spoke petulantly.

'I can't say I blame him. I take it you don't deny the child you're expecting is not his?'

Anna eyed her father scornfully. 'I don't think Jeremy has it in him. He's useless; has been ever since Saffron was born.'

'Why didn't you seek advice? Many men have problems after the birth of a baby, the mother is usually tired, the baby interrupts your privacy; it's not easy to regain your old relationship. Jeremy also had the additional problems of two step-daughters.'

'If he couldn't cope he shouldn't have taken on the responsibility,' replied Anna mutinously.

'And what about your responsibilities? I'm not just talking about your daughters, I'm talking about the responsibility you have to yourself. You've had two abortions. Do you want another?'

Anna shuddered. 'I'm never going through that again, besides, Rudi loves me. He'll stand by me.'

'Will he?'

'Yes, and besides, it's too late to have an abortion. I'm more than six months.' Anna spoke defiantly.

Elias sighed. 'Then I think your girls should stay here with us for a while whilst you sort yourself out.'

Anna looked at her father in disbelief. 'Why? We shall be a family again when Rudi and I are married.'

Elias shook his head. 'Do you think you should marry this man?'

'I suppose Andreas told you Rudi is Turkish.' Anna spoke sulkily.

'Oh, Anna,' Elias shook his head sadly. 'I have patients and workers at the hospital of all nationalities. If it was just you and Rudi I would disregard the fact that he's a Turk. I am thinking of the two girls you already have.'

19

Annita wrung her hands. 'I should have talked to you earlier, persuaded you to give him up, or at least take precautions. What are you going to do?'

For the first time Anna's defiance seemed to crumble, then she tossed her head. 'We,' she spoke very deliberately and laid her hand on her stomach, 'are going back home to catch up on our sleep.'

Annita looked at the small baby lying in a crib beside her daughter. She was certainly darker skinned than Anna's other three girls. Annita felt a growing impatience with the irresponsible woman.

'How are you feeling?'

'A bit tired, otherwise I'm fine.'

'There's nothing wrong with her, I gather, despite being premature?'

'She's perfect and quite beautiful.'

'What will you call her?' Annita waited for another unusual name.

'Christabelle.'

'Hmm.' Annita considered. 'Christabelle Bartlett sounds quite nice.'

'She won't be a Bartlett. I'll register her in Rudi's name.'

Annita raised her eyebrows.

'Jeremy has filed for divorce.'

'Will you contest it?'

'I'm hardly in a position to! No, good riddance to him.'

'And what will happen to Saffron?'

Anna shrugged. 'She's his daughter. If he's determined to keep her he can do so.'

'She's your daughter too. Don't you care about her?'

'Of course. That's why I won't fight over her. She was always a daddy's girl and if she's happy with him we'll leave it that way. She can always visit during vacations.'

Annita shook her head. 'I despair of you, Anna. You were brought up as a good Greek girl, and you carry on like, like, well a tramp. It's been one man after another with you and none of them have lasted. All you have to show for your relationships is four children, all by different fathers, and you don't care about any of them particularly. You're selfish through and through. Did you care how you were hurting poor Jeremy when you were carrying on with that Rudi? Did you ever give a thought to what would happen to your family if you had his child? How do you think Sorrell and Bryony are ever going to hold their heads up again with a sister who is half Turkish and you not married to her father when she was born?'

Anna raised herself up in the bed. 'That's all you care about, isn't it, Mamma? What the family will think because Christabelle is partly Turkish.'

Annita shook her head. 'That's the last thing that would worry me. If it was a stable relationship between you and Rudi it wouldn't be an issue. What worries me is how this child will feel in a few years time, when her Greek sisters disown her and you've become tired of her or had another.'

'So what would you have me do? I could claim to have been raped by an unknown assailant.'

'What I would like to see you do is get married to Rudi and settle down. Make a proper home for your girls again, and be a stable family.'

Anna snorted. 'One minute you're saying Sorrell and Bryony won't accept her and the next you're asking me to marry her father and make us into a family. This is America, Mamma, or had you forgotten? You don't have to get married. More and more women are making a life for themselves and their children without wearing a wedding ring and being shackled to some man.'

'How does Rudi feel about you bringing up his daughter alone?'

'We'll talk about it when he gets back from Hollywood. He was offered a trial shoot for a part in a film and I insisted he went for it. I didn't need him here. He should be back by the time I leave the clinic and we can make arrangements then.'

'And what about Sorrell and Bryony?'

Anna shook her head. 'They can stay at school and visit us later, when we're settled.'

Annita rose from her daughter's bedside. 'I just hope it all works out as you envisage.'

Sorrell sat on the end of her bed in the dormitory. She hated this school with its rules and regulations. Nine more months and she would be able to leave and do as she pleased. She had plans for her future. She was practising her skills. On the weekly trip the girls were permitted to the town she wandered away on her own. It had not taken her long to become adept at picking a pocket, taking a handbag that had been left unguarded for a moment or helping herself from a shop to whatever she fancied. This enabled her to save her monthly allowance and add to it considerably.

Her grandmother wrote to her regularly and she would reply, saying how much she loved the school and appreciated their help with her education, always adding that she had found it necessary to purchase something essential and expensive. Her grandmother nearly always enclosed a cheque for the amount she had mentioned and Sorrell added it to her savings. There was no mention of her mother and Sorrell did not ask after her. She had heard the furious rows that had taken place between her mother and stepfather and knew exactly why the family had been split up, taking a malicious pleasure in telling her younger sister in graphic detail of their mother's dilemma.

Bryony had gazed at her, wide-eyed and wondering, hardly able to believe her sister's words. 'When will we see Mamma again?' she asked.

Sorrell shrugged. 'Who knows and who cares?'

'I care. I love Mamma and Saffron and Jeremy. We were a family. I don't see why we can't all live together still.'

Sorrell looked at her scornfully. 'You're just a baby who doesn't understand these things.'

'I'm not a baby. I'm nearly sixteen.'

'In that case you should act your age.'

Anna sat across the room from Rudi. He looked at her with distaste. What had made this woman seem so attractive to him? She was sulky, defiant and definitely stupid. He had assumed she would be using some form of contraception.

'What do you expect me to do about it?' he asked, pointing to the baby lying in a Moses basket at her side.

'Marry me, of course.'

'Marry you! Don't be ridiculous.'

'You said you loved me. I thought you would marry me.'

Rudi shrugged. 'I have no intention of marrying you, besides you have no proof that it's my child.'

'You know she's yours. You have a responsibility towards us.'

'Not me. I'm not as stupid as that husband of yours. I don't take on a child just because someone claims I'm the father.'

Anna's face crumpled. 'Jeremy's divorcing me. What am I going to do?'

'That, my dear, is your problem.' Rudi rose and looked at his watch. 'I really have to get ready to go out now. I have an appointment.'

Anna rose unsteadily from the chair. She approached Rudi and tried to place her arms round him, but he pushed her away. 'I suggest you leave now. As I said, I have an appointment. She doesn't appreciate being kept waiting.' Rudi smiled complacently.

Anna's face blanched. 'You've found someone else?' Her voice rose hysterically. 'You can't have. You can't leave me. I want to be with you. This is your baby, our baby. I have a right to be with you. If you go to Hollywood we can make a fresh start down there.'

'I have no need to make a fresh start, as you put it. I am quite happy as I am. If you insist on playing with fire you can expect to get burned.'

'This is your child,' Anna screamed at him.

Rudi shrugged. 'That's what you say. I deny it. I have my career and my future to think about.'

'What about my future?'

'Your future has nothing to do with me, and stop that screaming.'

'I won't stop. I'll scream until your neighbours come and ask what you're doing to me. Then I'll tell them. I'll....'

A slap across Anna's face sent her to the floor and she looked up at Rudi mutinously. He towered over her. 'Now get up and go before I really hurt you.'

Snivelling Anna rose to her feet. Her head was throbbing and her nose was dribbling blood. Rudi passed her a tissue with one hand and opened the door with the other. 'Goodbye, Anna. Don't bother to call again.'

Anna arrived on the doorstep of her parent's house unexpectedly. Her face was swollen and a purple bruise on her cheek bone had almost closed her eye. At first she had tried to blame Andreas for the breakdown of her marriage, finally bursting into tears and admitting that Rudi had refused to accept her or their child.

'Did he do that to your face?' asked Elias

Anna nodded. 'He almost knocked me unconscious.'

Elias poured himself a brandy and regarded his daughter dispassionately. 'You can stay here for a few days. Tomorrow we'll have a serious talk and make some arrangements for you.'

'Arrangements? What do you mean?' Anna eyed her father suspiciously.

'Anna, you need time to think sensibly about your future. I also need time to think about the situation. Obviously you cannot go back to this Rudi, nor can you afford to run the house we gave you when you married Jeremy.'

'But can't I live here with you? You have plenty of space.' Anna looked bewildered.

'You certainly cannot,' Elias replied grimly. 'We supported you with both Sorrell and Bryony, but we're considerably older now. We don't want a small child around all the time.'

'She's your granddaughter,' replied Anna sulkily.

Elias nodded. 'I think she's quite beautiful – when she's asleep. The trouble is she seems to spend most of her time crying. I know she'll grow out of it, but why should our lives be made a misery until then? No, Anna, you certainly cannot stay here.'

Elias looked at his daughter sadly. She was still wrapped in her dressing gown and she yawned widely.

'Christabelle had me up half the night,' she complained. 'She just wouldn't settle.'

'Are you trying to feed her yourself? Maybe the trauma you have been through has affected you and she needs a bottle supplement.'

Anna scowled at her father. 'I'll see how she goes through today.'

Elias pushed a cup of coffee towards her. 'Now, we need to talk. Did you make any decisions last night?'

'How could I, with Christabelle being a nuisance? Besides, there's no rush.'

Elias sighed. As usual his daughter had expected her problems either to go away or be solved for her. 'I think it could be better if you moved away, made a new start, somewhere where you are not known.' He held up his hand as Anna was about to protest. 'I can sell your present house and it should fetch enough to buy a smaller property in a less expensive area. Your mother and I will keep an eye on you, but you will have no contact with the rest of the family. They will be told you have gone away to live with Rudi.'

'What about my girls? I'll want to see them,' protested Anna.

'If Rudi had said you could go to Hollywood with him you would not have considered your daughters for a moment. They can stay with us during their school vacations. When they have finished their education we may have to think again.'

Annita looked at her husband. This was the first she had heard of these plans.

'What will I live on? I'll need some money,' muttered Anna.

'I want the address of this Rudi. If the child is his he must take financial responsibility.'

Anna sniffed. 'I doubt he'll do that. He says he'll deny he's Christabelle's father.'

'You leave that up to me. You are not to contact him. There is also another condition. You are to book into a clinic to be sterilised. You obviously have no idea about birth control or you would not have ended up in this situation. I am disgusted with you, Anna. Many fathers would disown you.'

'It sounds as if you have.' Anna spoke resentfully. 'It's all Andreas's fault.'

'Rubbish! I agree he spoke out of turn, but the truth would have come out as soon as the child was born and the situation would have been the same. You have no one to blame but yourself. Go back to bed. Think over my offer during the day and let me know what you have decided. This is the last time I'm prepared to help you get your life in order.'

'I think you're mean.' Anna's lip trembled. 'I could easily stay here with you.'

'I think I am being more than generous,' Elias snapped back at her.

'I've told you what I'm prepared to do and I'm not discussing it any further.'

'Was it necessary to be quite so harsh with her?' asked Annita of her husband when Anna had left the room.

'Yes. She has to grow up and be responsible for her own life. Every time she has landed herself in a difficult situation she has run back home. She can't rely on us always being here to solve her problems for her. You're not to go telling her that I'll relent in time. I've made up my mind. This is the last time I'll try to sort her life out for her.'

Annita sighed. She knew it was no good arguing with Elias once he had made a decision.

Elias arrived unannounced at the house Rudi had rented. The handsome Turk looked at him suspiciously. 'Yes?'

'I'd prefer to come inside and talk to you, if you don't mind.'

'What do you want to talk about?' Rudi blocked the doorway effectively.

'A small matter of finance. We can discuss it here if you wish, but I doubt that you would want your neighbours to hear and I have a very loud voice. Alternatively we could set up an appointment with my lawyer present.'

'What are you talking about?'

'Permit me to come inside and I will explain.'

'I think you're crazy and I'm going to call the police.'

'Fine. I can ask them to charge you with assault and battery when they arrive. I don't take kindly to having my daughter beaten.'

'I don't even know your daughter!'

Elias shrugged. 'As you wish, but if I leave now before we have reached an understanding I shall be consulting a lawyer and take action against you for assault causing actual bodily harm.'

'No, wait, what are you talking about? You've got the wrong man. I don't know your daughter.'

'My daughter is Anna Bartlett, the woman you made pregnant. Now, do I come in or do I raise my voice and alert the neighbours to the kind of ruffian they have living in the area?'

Reluctantly Rudi held the door open and Elias followed him through to the patio at the rear of the house.

'Very pleasant,' murmured Elias as he settled himself on a chair beside the small swimming pool.

Rudi shrugged. 'So I slapped your daughter when she was being a nuisance. She had become quite hysterical.'

'You did far more than slap her. She has a broken cheekbone, a black eye and will probably need some dental treatment.'

Rudi sat in the chair opposite Elias. 'It was an accident. I didn't mean to hurt her. How much does she want for the dental treatment?'

'You led my daughter to believe that you wanted to marry her.'

'I never told her I'd marry her. She knew there was nothing serious between us.'

Elias shrugged. 'She claims that it was serious, but I'll not argue over that point with you. I want a financial settlement on my grandchild, your child.'

'What kind of settlement? If I make a one-off payment that will mean I've admitted liability – and I don't.'

'I am thinking of a settlement that will last until such time as the child finishes her education. A regular monthly amount, shall we say a thousand dollars a month?' suggested Elias.

'You must be crazy. Where would I get that sort of money?'

'That is your problem.' Elias waved his hand around. 'You have managed to rent a very nice house here. According to Anna you have accepted the leading role in a film. You are obviously making a success of your career. You should be able to find that amount quite easily.'

'I have overheads, expenses.'

Elias shrugged. 'The choice is yours. Either we come to an agreement or I instruct my lawyer to take you to court. By the time they have finished with you it is pretty doubtful that you would have ten dollars left. Your reputation would be ruined; you'd probably not be able to work in the film business ever again.'

'That's blackmail. You can't prove I'm the father.'

'I'm a chemist. I know of various ways that paternity can be proved. The choice is yours. We reach an understanding or I shall be consulting a lawyer and take action against you for assault causing actual bodily harm. It is always possible that you raped my daughter, of course.' Elias rose from his seat. 'My lawyer will be in touch.'

Rudi bunched his fists and Elias wondered if the man was going to hit him.

'I'll not take up any more of your time.' Elias made to move towards the door where Rudi effectively blocked his way. 'I shall also ask my lawyer to check your papers. You could be in the country illegally. It could take some years to verify the legality of them.'

'No, wait.' Rudi eyed Elias suspiciously. 'So how do I know that after a year or so you don't ask me to contribute more? You could put the price up every year until I have nothing.'

Elias smiled. 'I am an honest man. I have an agreement here, already signed by my wife and myself and countersigned by my lawyer. If you care to read it and sign we will abide by the conditions it stipulates. All I have to do is insert your name.'

Rudi held out his hand. 'Let me see.' He read the typewritten sheet slowly. 'It says here the amount can vary due to inflation. You will be asking me for more.' He thrust the paper back towards Elias. 'It would never stand up in court.'

'On the contrary, I had it drawn up by a lawyer without mentioning you. If you read it carefully you will see it says a percentage increase due to inflation. If there is no inflation there is no increase. Bear in mind that in ten years time you could be earning twice as much due to inflation, but if the payment stays the same it would hardly cover the cost of a growing child's clothes.'

'I can't afford a thousand,' growled Rudi.

'How much can you afford?'

'Five – and that will be a struggle.'

'Eight,' replied Elias firmly. 'I'll not go lower than that.' He inserted the figures in the space on the paper and passed it to Rudi for him to insert his name and signature.

Elias sat in the lounge with his daughter. 'Now we need to have a very serious talk. Your mother and I have made some decisions and we will expect you to abide by them. As I said, Sorrell and

Bryony will spend their vacations with us until such time as they have finished their education and are mature enough to have somewhere of their own to live.'

Anna opened her mouth to interrupt her father, but he held up his hands. 'We are thinking of them and their future. You are not a good example to them, Anna. The house we gave you when you married Jeremy will be sold and the proceeds from that will be sufficient to buy you somewhere smaller out of the area. Somewhere where you are not known and you can start again. You can tell your new neighbours whatever you please regarding your child.'

'You are disowning me.'

'Of course we're not. We are doing this for you because we care for you and your daughters.'

'So who is going to pay for their education? I haven't any money now Jeremy has gone.'

Elias sighed. 'We are, of course, as we have done for the past few years. Whatever is left over after the sale of your present house and the purchase of your new one we will invest and each month your household expenses will be paid from it. I will send you a monthly allowance for your daily living costs and I expect you to budget and manage on it. I have also made an arrangement with Rudi. He will provide for your child until such time as she finishes her education.' Elias ran a hand through his thinning hair. 'When I have found a couple of houses that I consider suitable I'll take you to see them. I can't do any more for you, Anna. We're not getting any younger and won't be here for ever to sort out your problems for you.'

Anna eyed the second house her father had taken her to see warily. The first one she had rejected immediately, saying she would never feel safe living in a one level house and sleeping on the ground floor. After the large house she had been used to the rooms seemed cramped and dark.

Elias opened the front door and led the way into a hall with the stairs rising up at the side. Anna walked through the first door that led to the lounge which had patio windows leading to a veranda that ran the length of the house, the other door led to a well appointed kitchen. Beneath the stairs was a small toilet and hand basin, the basin taking up most of the space. On the upper floor were two bedrooms with a bathroom between them. Looking out of the window at the front she could see the lawn leading down to the side walk with a low white fence on either side, to the left the occupant had planted a hedge against the fence for greater privacy. At the back she looked out over a paved area, again with a hedge down the left hand side.

Anna felt resentful. It would have been so much easier if she could have just moved back into her parent's house. If Andreas had not been drunk and outspoken at the Thanksgiving party she was sure Jeremy would have accepted Christabelle as his child and there would have been no problem.

'Well, what do you think of this one?' asked Elias.

Anna shrugged. 'It will do, I suppose. There's no bathroom en suite.'

'You don't need a second bathroom, there's only you and the baby.'

'Suppose I decided to get married again, or the girls wanted to come and stay?'

'If you remarry this house can be sold and the money used as a deposit for somewhere larger.'

'You gave Elena and Maria a house when they married.'

Elias sighed. 'I put down a large deposit on their house and Elena and Matthew have paid back the outstanding mortgage. I did the same for Maria and Bernard. After Bernard died Maria no longer wished to live there and I sold up and bought her an apartment. You seem to forget that when you and Jeremy were married I put down the deposit for your house. You have no income so can't possibly keep up the mortgage repayments. It's only by selling that I can afford to provide you with somewhere else suitable and an allowance.'

Anna took a last look out of the lounge windows. 'I suppose it will do. There's nowhere to park my car.'

Elias looked at her in exasperation. Not once had she shown any regret for her actions or given either of her parents a word of thanks. 'It's within walking distance of a shopping mall and also a school. You don't need a parking space as you can't afford to run a car.'

Anna looked at her father in horror. 'No car?'

Elias shook his head. 'I'm repaying the mortgage on this house, all your utility bills and giving you a personal allowance of two hundred dollars a month. I can't afford another cent. If you want a car you must economise and finance it yourself. You could always try going out to work when Christabelle starts school.'

'Work! I'm not going out to work.'

'Then you won't be having a car.'

Sorrell looked round the dormitory room she had shared with three other girls for six years. At last she was free. There was one thing she planned to do before she finally left the hated school for ever. All her belongings had been packed into a large trunk and the janitors had collected the trunks from each room the previous night; she had only a small case with her night clothes, washing kit and dirty washing from the previous day.

She walked sedately down the two flights of stairs; then craned out of a window. There was her grandmother, waiting patiently in her car with Bryony already sitting in the passenger seat, chattering avidly.

'She can move herself from there,' thought Sorrell as she descended the next staircase. From that floor she could hear the noise from below, the staff were gathered, bidding farewell to the pupils and wishing them a good vacation, girls were calling to each other, promising to write or visit.

Swiftly she opened the door to the staff room and went to the wall of lockers where the staff left their personal belongings during the day. The keys left hanging in the lock of most of them as usual. Sorrell pulled open the first one and removed the purse, searching through it swiftly for cash before returning it. Within minutes she had raided twenty lockers and knew she had a profitable haul stuffed into her knickers.

Two doors further on was a staff rest room and she entered the first cubicle, removing the notes and placing them into two purses of her own. She flushed the toilet and hurried on down the stairs. There were still a number of girls milling around and she made her way to the door.

'Goodbye, everyone. I have to rush. My grandmother's waiting,' she called. One or two heads turned and a hand was raised.

She turned to the principal who stood by the door and shook her hand. 'Goodbye Miss Wentworth.'

'Goodbye, Sorrell. We will miss you. Good luck for the future.'

Sorrell managed to stop herself from snorting. The woman said exactly the same to every girl when they left. 'Thank you,' she murmured before running down the steps and tapping on the passenger window. 'In the back, Bryony,' she ordered.

Dutifully Bryony climbed out of the car and took a seat in the back. 'Do you want to put your case over here?' she asked.

'No, I can manage it, thanks. Hello, Grandma.' She gave Annita a dutiful peck on the cheek. 'How's Grandpa?'

'He's well, I'm pleased to say. Are you girls ready? Nothing left behind?' Sorrell and Bryony shook their heads. 'Then we'll get off.'

Sorrell looked behind her as the car drew away from the school. There were plenty of pupils still massing around on the front steps. There was no reason why any one should attribute the pilfering of the staff purses down to her.

Basic decoration had taken place and the carpets laid. Whilst Anna waited for the furniture to be delivered she took stock of her new surroundings. She had been unable to persuade her father to change the bathroom fitments and refurbish the kitchen. He had insisted that both rooms were clean and serviceable. If she wanted to update them she would have to save up and pay for the work herself. She would need to find someone capable of doing the work that she could use her charms on and have the labour free.

Two large men began to manhandle the furniture into the rooms and place it under Anna's directions. A third seemed to manage to bring in only the lighter pieces and disappear for considerable spells. When he was challenged he alleged he was sorting out the next items to be brought in. He winked conspiratorially at Anna.

She smiled back at him. 'I can offer you some coffee. I haven't really stocked up yet, so I haven't any beer.'

'Coffee would be fine for me. I'll take a rain check on the beer. How about if I call in next week and see how you're settled? Make sure there are no odd jobs that need to be done.'

'I'd be very grateful. You don't always realise the little extras that you need to be done until you've lived somewhere for a few days.'

'We'll make that a date, then.'

Davros launched his boat and waited whilst Giovanni and Nicolas placed the coffin on board. The two men climbed back onto Manolis's boat and he began to nose his way carefully out of the tiny harbour. During the drive from Heraklion to Aghios Nikolaos, Elena had prepared her mother and aunt for the unconventional funeral they were going to attend, but she was concerned about the effect it would have on Dora when the time came. Nicolas had orders to stand by her and watch for any sign of collapse on her part.

Davros reached the island as Manolis was helping the last of his passengers ashore. Giovanni and Nicolas removed the coffin from the rowing boat and Davros stood unsure whether he was expected to join the funeral cortege or stay with his boat. Giovanni took pity on him.

'The choice is yours,' he said in a low voice. 'Just don't tell the village when you return.' Giovanni pushed a wad of notes into the boatman's hand.

'I'd best stay with the boat.' Davros had an idea that there was going to be more than a service conducted on the island and he decided that the less he knew the better.

Giovanni and Nicolas, accompanied by Yannis and Doctor Stavros walked to the small house where the body had been laid prior to the funeral. Gently they placed the dead man inside and closed the lid.

Standing on the shore, waiting for them to return, Dora seemed quite composed. She looked around at the high Venetian walls curiously.

'It's just as Yannis always told me. I'm glad he's staying here. He loved this island. He wanted to fight the closure order and return here to live, you know.'

Father Andreas stepped forward. 'Do you feel quite up to this? It is most unorthodox and we're probably breaking the law. If you'd rather sit somewhere until we return we will all understand.'

Dora shook her head. 'My niece has prepared me. It's what Yannis would have wanted.'

The men returned bearing the coffin, walking slowly up the slight incline to where the church stood. Dora stopped.

'Is this where Yannis died?'

'Just up there. I'll show you as we go past.'

They filed into the small church and Father Andreas began to intone the service. Spiro felt the tears running unchecked down his face. This was how it had been during the terrible years of the war. He felt a hand in his and looked down to see Flora, her head buried in Manolis's chest, as she sobbed, but still trying to offer him some comfort in the midst of her own grief.

Marisa looked at Victor. She was trying hard not to think of her wedding day when the whole island had radiated happiness on her behalf. He squeezed her arm and nodded towards her aunt, who sat with a smile on her face, her fingers playing with something in her lap. Marisa frowned and nudged her brother, Yannis, who followed her gaze. He shrugged. He did not understand his aunt's reaction and hoped her mind was not affected. Giovanni found it difficult to concentrate as he should. He could hardly believe the scene before his eyes, there was so much grief, yet those who should have mourned his uncle most seemed almost happy.

The service over, they followed Father Andreas, still intoning, up into the graveyard.

'Just there,' said Elena, in a hushed voice to Dora. Dora stopped and looked at the spot, before crossing herself and moving on.

The tower came into view and Father Andreas waited until everyone had arrived. The coffin bearers placed their burden on the ground and opened the lid, lifting Yannis's body carefully, they placed it on the wide stone sill where Spiro held it and waited until Father Andreas said a last prayer before allowing it to fall into the depths.

Giovanni lifted a spade and began to shovel in copious amounts of lime to help decay the body quickly, but Anna stayed his arm. She leaned almost into the tower, making Giovanni hold her, as he feared she would topple in.

'Goodbye, Yannis.' She withdrew her head and threw some-thing down into the depths.

'What was that?' asked Giovanni.

'The good luck charm our mother gave to him when he went to Heraklion. He always wore it. I know he'd want it with him and the chain broke when he died. It was in his hand.' Anna turned away. Her final duty was done. Now she would have to face the conventional service in the village and weep and wail as befitted a bereaved sister.

She looked at Dora, white faced, but calm, and went across to her. 'I did do the right thing, didn't I?' she asked anxiously.

Dora managed to smile. 'You did. Yannis belongs over here. Nowhere else is good enough for him.'

The men picked up the much lighter coffin and walked back to where Davros was waiting with his boat. He made no comment as they placed it on board and then joined the other mourners aboard Manolis's boat for the return to Plaka.

Once again the group waited, then when everyone was assembled, the men shouldered the coffin and walked along the road to the church. Davros eyed them suspiciously. They were certainly carrying it very easily. He shrugged. It was none of his business, and he had been well paid to keep his mouth shut.

The service and burial over, the family returned to the farmhouse and Giovanni wondered how quickly he could escape. His mother and father were staying with Anna and Yiorgo for a few days, his two great aunts were returning to Aghios Nikolaos with Elena and Nicolas for the night before returning to Athens. Spiro was deep in conversation with Manolis and would probably spend a few days with him and Flora before returning to the hospital in Athens where he lived. Doctor Stavros would no doubt return by boat with them. Giovanni's gaze alighted on Father Andreas. The priest needed someone to take him back to Heraklion.

Relief spread over the elderly priest's face at the suggestion and he seemed as willing to leave the gathering as Giovanni.

They took the new road up over the hill and no more than an hour later saw them on the outskirts of Malia. Giovanni drew in to a taverna and grinned a little shame-faced at the priest beside him.

'I don't know about you, but I could do with a drink.'

Father Andreas nodded. 'A little wine would not come amiss.'

They sat together in the sunshine, contemplating the last few hours, until Giovanni leaned forward confidentially.

'Father, may I ask you something?'

Andreas nodded. 'I may not be able to answer your question.'

Giovanni hesitated. 'The funeral we've just attended, tell me about it.'

'What do you mean? You were there.'

'I know. I went to the island and I saw and heard the same as everyone else, but I didn't understand. Aunt Anna and aunt Dora seemed almost, well, happy, yet Flora and Spiro were heartbroken. My mother wasn't much better.'

Father Andreas smiled. 'I can't say I fully understand their reactions myself. I know your aunt felt very strongly that Yannis should be laid to rest on Spinalonga and Dora went along with her wishes. Anna said Yannis had come home to be with Phaedra, his first wife. As for Flora and Spiro, they were his two oldest and closest friends. They both owed a good deal to Yannis; in fact Flora owed him her life. To lose Yannis…' Father Andreas spread his hands; words could not describe the sense of loss he knew both people were suffering. He sighed. 'I must write to my sister tonight and tell her. She will be so sad.'

'Did she know him?' Giovanni had scant knowledge of his family history and had met Father Andreas on few occasions, despite being related and living in the same town.

Father Andreas regarded the young man in surprise. 'Of course she knew him. She was betrothed to him.'

Giovanni poured another glass of wine for both of them. 'Tell me. Tell me about the family.'

'There is little to tell. Yannis lived with us in Aghios Nikolaos whilst he attended the gymnasium and before he went to High School in Heraklion.' His eyes took on a far away look. 'The last time Annita saw him was the night of their betrothal party. She was so happy. We all danced in the street until the early hours of the morning.' Andreas shook himself slightly. 'That's not quite true. She saw him once more from my father's boat before she went off to America.'

Giovanni leaned forward eagerly.

'When Yannis returned to Heraklion after Christmas we heard no more from him and Annita made me promise to go to Heraklion and look for him. I met Father Minos and we saw Yannis being taken to the hospital ship bound for Athens. Breaking the news to your great-grandmother caused her to have a stroke.' Father Andreas shook his head sadly at the memory.

'So how did uncle Yannis get to Spinalonga?'

'He caused a riot in the Athenian hospital, helped by Spiro and many others who are long since dead. As a punishment they were sent to Spinalonga. They had no medicine, nowhere to shelter and their food was sent over from the villages. It was very difficult, particularly during the war when their supplies were cut off.'

Giovanni smiled. 'Pappa has told me about that, and how he and mamma were married on the island. I never met uncle Yannis. I wish I had.'

'He was a great character.' Father Andreas smiled at his own memories.

'Did your sister go to America because of uncle Yannis?'

'Indirectly. She became a nurse and went to Athens hoping to nurse him. She met a biochemist whilst she was there and agreed to help with his research into leprosy. He was offered a research scholarship in America and he asked her to marry him. It was thanks to him that Yannis ended up living in Athens.'

Giovanni's brow creased into a frown. 'But Aunt Anna said he wanted to come back to the island?'

'He did. He spent years writing to the government asking for a new medicine, which he knew more about than they did, thanks to Elias. They finally gave in to him and took tests. The tests showed most of them to be negative, so they took them all back to the hospital in Athens, closed the island and told them they could live where they pleased. Yannis wanted to return to the island, but it was out of the question, so he stayed in Athens, bought his own apartment and married again. If you really want to know more I suggest you write to his widow and ask if she will send you some of the articles that he wrote.'

'Tell me more about your sister. Is her husband still alive?'

'Yes, Elias is still working. He insists on going into the laboratory every day to check on experiments. He's done a tremendous amount, but he's still looking for a vaccine. He's convinced he'll find one soon.'

'Have they any children?'

Father Andreas nodded. 'Children and grandchildren; I suppose they must be about your age, bit younger, maybe.'

'Have you ever been over to see them?'

The priest looked at the young man in horror. 'Oh, no; I couldn't go over there. It's much too far; besides, they speak the English language. I wouldn't know how to talk to them.'

'Do you mean Americans generally or your relatives?'

'I don't expect they speak Greek. Why should they?'

Giovanni pursed his lips. 'It's their native tongue. They should speak it. I live over here, but I still speak Italian.'

'Yours is a somewhat different case. You lived in Italy as a child and it was the language you used at school. They would have attended an English speaking school.'

Giovanni shrugged. 'So what do they do?'

Father Andreas frowned. 'I'm not sure. Two of Annita's girls are married, the other is a widow and her son is a bachelor.' He did not wish to elaborate on the trials his sister had with her family. If their behaviour was the result of living in America he was very glad he had never been tempted to go to the country.

'And your sister's husband? What did you say his name was? Elias? Has he any family anywhere?'

'His mother died a long while back, but he has two sisters. One was a photographer for a magazine and the other is an actress.'

Giovanni raised his eyebrows. 'Are they famous?'

'Better to say well known, and I add to that very respectable, despite their professions.'

Giovanni grinned. 'I never doubted they would be otherwise.' He lifted the bottle of wine. 'Just enough left for a few mouthfuls each, then we should be on our way.'

Giovanni thought no more about the conversation he had shared with Father Andreas. He was far more concerned with ensuring that the accounts were in order for the past summer months and that his uncle Yannis would be unable to find fault. He was very conscious of the fact that he was a junior partner in the hotel and wanted to prove to his uncle that he was competent. When Yannis collected the ledgers Giovanni approached him tentatively.

'Could you spare a while to chat? I've had an idea.'

Yannis sighed. Usually when Giovanni said he had an idea it meant a good deal of money was needed to put it into practice, but he had to admit that so far everything he had suggested had shown a handsome profit.

'How much?'

Giovanni grinned. 'Come and sit down and I'll tell you.'

Giovanni waited until they each had a glass of ouzo, then from his briefcase he took a number of colourful leaflets. He raised his glass in salutation, and then pushed it to one side to make room on the table.

'When do most of our customers come to the hotel?'

'In the summer, of course.' Yannis frowned. That was obvious to anyone.

'And it's hot in the summer, isn't it?'

Yannis nodded. What was the boy getting at?

'It's all right for us, we're used to the heat, but many of our customers aren't. Suppose we put air conditioning in the rooms? It would be a selling point. I've done my homework.' Giovanni forestalled his uncle's question. 'There's only one hotel with any, and that's only in the dining room.'

Yannis sipped at his drink and considered. 'So what are you talking about? A fan in the ceiling of each room?'

Giovanni shook his head. 'A bit more sophisticated than that. Look, there's an illustration – before and after installation.' Giovanni pushed the brochure across the table.

Yannis studied the two pictures. 'There's no difference.'

'Exactly. Instead of a noisy, ugly fan in the ceiling there's a tiny grill. The fan is run from a motor and the cool air is pumped into all the rooms through a series of pipes.'

Yannis looked again at the picture and then over the page to the diagram. 'Very ingenious, but suppose some people thought it was too cool in their rooms?'

'They could use their control panel to switch it off and it wouldn't affect the room next door.'

'So what kind of money are we talking?'

'I can't be exact. The engineers would have to look at the building and decide on the size of the motor and the amount of piping necessary. At the outside I would say five hundred thousand drachma.'

'What! That's a monstrous sum. We could never afford that.'

Giovanni smiled and tapped the account books. 'I think you could be paying more than that amount in tax if you don't show a bit of expenditure. Besides, we could add a little to our prices for the additional comfort offered.' Giovanni drained his glass. 'Shall I get you another?'

Yannis shook his head. Five hundred thousand drachmas! The boy must be mad if he thought he had that kind of money to throw away.

'What are the running costs?' he heard himself asking.

'According to the brochure no more than a few drachma a day, but I always doubt their claims, so I've doubled it. If we charged an extra five drachma for every guest, we would not only cover our running costs, but have repaid the cost of the installation within three years.'

'And you think the accountants are going to come up with a big tax assessment?'

'If my figures are correct they have to. You've had a good year.'

Yannis looked at his empty glass. 'I will have another.' He waited until the waiter had placed two fresh glasses of ouzo on the table. 'What about the money I'm spending on the new house? Won't that be taken into account?'

'Not from the hotel profits. That's your personal money you're spending. The only way to avoid the tax man is to spend on the hotels. You could always do some redecoration and buy some new bed covers, but it seems a bit pointless to spend money unnecessarily.'

Yannis snorted. 'You're a fine one to talk about spending money unnecessarily.'

'My ideas have always brought you in money, uncle Yannis. You have to admit that.'

Yannis smiled. 'You're a good boy. Get the engineers to come and give an estimate; then we'll talk about it again. By that time the accountants should have sorted out the books and we'll know what kind of money we need to spend. I take it we'd be all right for a hundred thousand now?'

'No problem.' Giovanni knew his uncle was as conversant with the income from the hotel as he was.

'That's good. I'm planning a small investment.'

Giovanni raised his eyebrows.

'Your aunt Dora is finding things a bit difficult. Since Yannis died she has no income.'

Giovanni looked at his uncle in horror. 'She must have something.'

'Very little. There are a few royalties from Yannis's writing and he left a small sum invested in a savings account. His pension has stopped, of course, and she only has her own to live on. She's having a job making ends meet. Daphne has suggested she sell the apartment and move in with her, but these things take time. She's been turning out Yannis's belongings and there are four or five boxes of sketches done by that child who was on the island. She thinks they're quite good and has asked me if I'd like to buy them.'

'And you're going to, of course.'

Yannis nodded. 'One or two might be saleable. If I give her a decent price I can always put it against the profits made from Ourania's shop and if they don't sell I can tell the accountants it was a bad investment.'

Giovanni grinned. 'Has she anything else of Yannis's worth selling?'

'She only mentioned the sketches.'

'Do you think I could write to her?'

'Why shouldn't you? You're family.'

'You know I brought Father Andreas back up to Heraklion, well, we were talking and I really know very little about old uncle Yannis. I didn't even know he was betrothed to Father Andreas's sister! He suggested I wrote and asked Dora to send me copies of some of Yannis's writings about his life on the island. You don't think she'd mind?'

'I don't see why she should. A good deal has been published, so there's nothing private about it.' Yannis drained his glass. 'I'll be off.' He picked up the ledgers. 'Get that estimate for me and then we'll talk again.'

Annita read the letter from her brother and showed it to her husband.

'How sad, poor Yannis. To go back after all these years and then die.'

Elias shrugged. 'He was more fortunate than many of them. What do you think Andreas means? He says he conducted a service on the island and they placed Yannis in the tower; then went back to Plaka for the funeral.'

'I'm not entirely sure, but I have a feeling that Yannis stayed on the island. The tower he mentioned, that's where they used to place their dead, isn't it?'

'That's what he told me. His first wife was placed in there during the war. I wonder whose idea that was?'

Annita shook her head. 'Andreas doesn't say, but I doubt if it was his and Yiorgo wouldn't have enough imagination to think of anything like that.' Annita looked at the pair of sketches that hung on the wall, one showing Yannis walking along a row of vines, his head bent as he searched for pottery, and the other of two girls deep in conversation. 'I shall always remember him as he was that last summer we spent together. I could never picture him any other way.'

Annita's eyes were misty and Elias placed his arm round her shoulders.

'If Maria had lived and done more sketches you would probably have one of him as an old man now and have a job to remember him as a boy.'

Annita smiled shakily. 'You're right. I was no older than Bryony and thought myself so much in love with him.'

'I'm sure you were. Love goes very deep when you're young.'

Annita sighed deeply. 'I just wish Maria could find someone to take the place of Bernard. Two short years. It was so cruel for her.'

'I don't think Maria wants anyone to take his place.'

'But she's not happy. How can she be?'

Elias shrugged. 'Maria is her own worst enemy. She is determined no one can take Bernard's place and has developed such a hard exterior that no one can be bothered to take the time to pierce through. If she would only unbend a little and give people a chance she'd find out there were other decent men in the world who could make her happy.'

'Oh, Elias!'

'Don't 'oh, Elias' me. She's like you, and you know it.'

Annita felt herself redden. 'I've never had a hard exterior.'

Elias snorted with derision. 'You had an exterior like a concrete block when I first met you. You wouldn't even speak to me. If it hadn't been for uncle Lambros taking you to meet mamma you'd still be sitting alone in your room in Athens, growing old, bitter and twisted.'

'According to Sorrell I am that anyway.' Anna bit her tongue. She had not meant to mention her latest encounter with her granddaughter.

'That child needs a good slap. Pity I didn't give her mother one when she was young enough. Could have saved a good deal of trouble. What did she want this time?'

'She wanted me to pay her air fare to Europe.'

'You didn't give her the money, did you?'

Annita shook her head. 'I certainly didn't. If she wants to go off travelling she must save up for it herself. She told me I was old and didn't like seeing people enjoying themselves.'

'Rubbish. I suggest she gets herself a steady job instead of all this moving from one to another.' Elias smiled at his wife. 'If she did that and saved her money she could probably afford to go travelling next year.'

Annita smiled with him; then frowned. 'Do you think it would be possible to go over to Crete? We're neither of us getting any younger and I'd like to see my brother and cousins again.'

'I don't see why we shouldn't. We could go to Athens first to see Aspasia; then take the ferry over. I'll find out when her operation is due. There's no point in going if she's in hospital. I'll ask Andreas to look into the travel arrangements. He's always dashing off somewhere or other so will know what we have to do.'

'What about the girls whilst we're gone? There'll be no one to look after them.'

'Bryony will still be at college and I don't think we can be held responsible for Sorrell any longer. She is nearly twenty one.'

'What about Anna? Suppose she needed us?'

Elias snorted. 'Why should she? The bank pays her allowance each month. She never telephones and when you have tried to talk to her she's made an excuse and puts the 'phone down.'

Annita sighed. 'I would like to see her little girl.'

'So would I, but I think things are better left the way they are.'

Annita wrote a long letter to Anna. As she had surmised, Helena was betrothed to the young man from college and a wedding date had been set for the following September. Elena was already in a flurry of preparations and poor Matthew kept reminding her that he was not a millionaire. Everyone was so happy for them; even Maria had been able to put her own sadness aside for a short while to congratulate them whole-heartedly. Annita wondered if her improving attitude had anything to do with a certain Father Jerez with whom she spent one day a week and was very reticent about how they spent their time. She mentioned briefly that Bryony had just returned to college for her final year and Sorrell was hoping to travel to Europe when she had saved enough money. Finally she wrote of the proposed visit of Elias and herself.

Anna read the letter gleefully. She must write back quickly to her cousin and ask if she had any specific dates in mind. Maybe Marisa and Victor could visit from Italy at the same time.

1980 – 1982

Yannis unpacked the boxes that had been delivered to Ourania's shop and scrutinized the pictures carefully. The sketches were good. He could recognise Flora and Manolis, Yannis, Spiro and Father Minos; although a good many of the other people were unknown to him. He decided his money had been well spent and placed a couple of the most striking on the walls of the shop and left a box in the back room. He would see what response there was before he went to too much trouble.

Half a dozen he took with him to show Flora. She was enraptured, able to name each person and begged to be allowed to come and inspect the others.

'Anna was very talented. She could have been a famous artist had she lived. I'm surprised Yannis didn't use these illustrations when he wrote his stories about the island.'

Yannis looked at the one-armed woman and slapped his thigh. 'I think you've got it. You're a wonder, Flora.'

'What do you mean?'

'Why don't I suggest that the publisher collects the articles together, adds some of the sketches and issues the whole as a book.'

'Why would people want to buy a book like that?'

'Tourists will buy books on anything. I think most of them just take them home to impress their friends. When will Manolis be home? He could help.'

'Manolis couldn't write a book.' Flora giggled at the idea.

'I'm not thinking of that. He takes people out to Spinalonga to see where you lived, why not have sketches of the original inhabitants for sale as souvenirs?'

'You'd very soon run out of sketches if they proved popular.'

'No, we'd have reproductions of them. Not all, of course, maybe twenty or thirty.'

Flora looked doubtful. 'I'm not sure I'd want any pictures of me sold to tourists.'

'They wouldn't have to be. I'll come and talk to Manolis about my idea and if he agrees you could go through them and take out any of you and Spiro. We're not likely to offend anyone else.'

'What about Father Minos?'

'Is he still alive?'

'I believe so. I know Yannis went to see him at Ierapetra. Maybe you could go down and ask him?'

Yannis nodded. 'Is there anyone else we ought to ask?'

Flora shrugged. 'I think everyone else is dead now. Come and talk to Manolis if you want. He's always looking for ways to make money.'

Manolis was full of enthusiasm for Yannis's idea. 'It could really take off, and it's certainly different from your usual run of souvenirs. The Americans would probably fall over themselves to buy them. We could reproduce a few more each year, depending on sales, and if the publishers agree with your idea of a book I could try selling that as well.'

'You'd need somewhere to sell it.'

'I'll just have a box on the boat. When the trippers come aboard I'll give them a spiel about it and again on the way back. You hold the main stock and I'll come and collect books as I need them.'

'Now wait a minute.' Yannis could see Ourania's shop overflowing with books and pictures. 'Where am I going to store them?'

'You've got the flat below yours as a stock room and you're building a new house. You could use your present flat for storage when you move.'

'I'd planned to rent the flat out to help pay for the house. If I have it full of stock it's not bringing in any money.'

'Store them at your new house then.'

Yannis frowned. He had planned to get right away from his wife's business. For years he had stubbed his toes on boxes and crates of statues and ornaments that he had bought in quantity at bargain prices and been forced to store them in their living quarters. 'I don't know if I'll have the space. I'll have to think about it. Anyway, do you object to having your picture reproduced and sold to tourists?'

'Not a bit,' answered Manolis cheerfully. 'Good for business.'

Yannis wrote at length to Dora describing his idea and hoping she would approve. To his surprise she wrote back almost immediately, as full of enthusiasm as Manolis had been and even more help. Amongst her husband's papers was an almost completed manuscript of his life story. She had had no idea he had been working on it and had been on the point of writing to his publishers when her nephew's letter had arrived. Now she wanted Yannis to come to Athens, bring a selection of the sketches and they could visit the publisher together. Yannis put the idea before his wife.

'Fine,' replied Ourania. 'I think it's an excellent idea. There's one condition, though. I go to Athens with you.'

Yannis smiled at her. 'I don't see why you shouldn't come. In fact I was going to suggest it. You've never had a holiday in all the years we've been married, so it's about time.'

Ourania looked wistful. 'I'd really like to go to Turin to see Marisa.'

'No you wouldn't. You'd like to go to Turin to see the shops and spend a fortune on clothes. Be content with Athens this year and if things work out well maybe you could go back to Italy with Marisa next year.'

Ourania gave a happy smile. Whenever she had suggested a trip to Italy with her sister-in-law in the past Yannis had always found some good excuse that made the whole idea impossible. Maybe this time she really would be able to go.

Ourania was delighted with Athens from the moment they drove off the ferry. There was so much to see, everyone appeared to be terribly busy, yet they still had time to greet friends briefly before hurrying on their way. Once in the centre of the city she craned her neck first one way and then the other to view the fashions displayed in the shop windows.

'Stop, Yannis, stop!'

'What's wrong?'

'There's the most wonderful suit in that window. I want to see how much it costs.'

Yannis smiled grimly to himself. 'I can't stop on the main road whenever you want to look in a shop. You'll have to wait until we've booked into the hotel. We'll go for a walk this evening and you can look.'

Ourania pouted. It was hardly likely the shops would be open at that time. Maybe when Yannis had finished his business with Dora she would be able to walk around the shops with her and Daphne.

'Which hotel are we going to?'

'There's one in a side road near here which isn't too expensive. We'll stay there for a couple of days. Better than imposing on Dora.'

Ourania nodded. She was surprised that her husband had agreed to spend even one night in a hotel other than his own and rather dreaded the inspection he would give it to ensure it would come up to his standards. She was pleasantly surprised when they drew up outside an opulent building that looked far superior to anything she had seen in Heraklion.

She looked at Yannis in surprise. 'Is this the right place? It seems very grand.'

Yannis nodded. 'I have a bit of business I want to do whilst I'm here.'

'You're not going to buy it, are you?'

'I wish I could! No, I've heard they have this air conditioning that Giovanni's been on about and I thought I'd like to try it out and maybe talk to the manager. See how he feels about it.'

Ourania nodded. She should be used to Yannis always having an ulterior motive for whatever he did.

They moved inside and Yannis took in the décor. The gilt work was rather overdone and made the reception area look pretentious and crowded. The middle-aged man behind the reception desk was waiting for them with a fixed smile on his face and Yannis made a mental note to tell Giovanni not to look at his clients until they were actually at his desk; far better to look busy and pretend not to notice them as they walked through the door.

'I have a room booked. Mr and Mrs Andronicatis.'

'Yes, sir. Of course, sir. Number seven.'

'Is there somewhere I can park my car?'

The receptionist looked doubtful. 'Where is it now, sir?'

'Outside.'

'You can't leave it there all night.'

'I don't plan to. Where can I park it?'

'There may be a space in one of the side roads.'

'You mean you haven't got a car park for your visitors?'

'Very few people bring their car to Athens.'

'Ask the porter to bring the luggage in, show us to our room and then I'll see about moving it.'

Yannis waited impatiently whilst an elderly man took the key to the car boot and returned with their suitcases. He collected their room key from the receptionist and escorted them up two flights of stairs to their room.

'Don't you have a lift?'

The porter shook his head.

'Suppose we had more than two cases?'

'I would have to go back for the others, sir.' He opened the door on a pleasant room, placed the cases on the floor and drew back the curtains. 'Please ring if there is anything you need.'

Yannis shut the door and turned to Ourania. 'You unpack whilst I go and find somewhere to park the car. I thought they would at least have their own car park.'

Ourania shrugged. 'How long will you be?'

'I don't know. Why?'

'I thought I'd have a bath.'

'Good idea. I'll try to be quick so I'm in time to dry your back.' He squeezed her arm and she heard him running down the stairs.

Bathed and changed they went down to the restaurant and studied the menu. It was not particularly appetising and Yannis thought it definitely over priced.

'We'll go for a walk before we decide,' he said firmly. Ourania did not argue. She was hoping they would pass the shop where she had seen the suit in the window.

Yannis steered his wife well away from the main shopping area. 'There'll be plenty of time for you to window shop tomorrow. We ought to go down into the old area of Athens during the evening. I've heard that's where most of the night life is, and the best tavernas.' Yannis pointed to the Acropolis. 'We'll go up there tomorrow. I'm told there is a wonderful view. We could do that after we've been to Dora's.'

'How long are we staying, Yannis?'

Yannis shrugged. 'A couple of days should be sufficient. I'll talk to the manager tomorrow; then we'll visit Dora. After lunch we can go to the Acropolis, and back home on the ferry the next day.'

Ourania tried to hide her disappointment. 'If we went to see Dora first tomorrow I could stay with her whilst you talked to the manager. Maybe she could show me round the city.'

'You mean she could take you to the shops and you could try on that suit!'

53

Ourania smiled and squeezed her husband's arm. 'You know how long you are when you start talking business and you hate going shopping with me.'

'Just don't spend too much, 'Rani, or I'll never be able to afford a roof for the new house.'

Dora greeted them with enthusiasm when they arrived at her apartment during the morning. She limped backwards and forwards, bringing coffee and pastries, before producing the pile of exercise books her husband had filled with his small, neat writing.

'Have you read it?' asked Yannis.

Dora nodded. 'It's very personal and very sad in parts. It would need someone to go through and sort out what was relevant to a good story and what were just an old man's memories.'

'The publisher could do that. I've brought a selection of Anna's sketches with me, just to show him her work. He'll probably want to choose for himself if he thinks it's a good idea.'

Dora nodded. She seemed to be considering her next words carefully. 'Do you know who Anna was?'

'Not really. Uncle Yannis said she was the Mayor of Heraklion's daughter, the one who was shot when the Germans invaded, and he and Phaedra adopted her.'

Dora shook her head. 'Not according to what he has written in here.' She tapped one of the books with her finger. 'She was his daughter.'

Yannis opened and shut his mouth. 'But how? She couldn't be. He was on the island and she was taken over there just before the blockade. No, you must have misread it.'

Dora handed her nephew the book, and with Ourania peering over to read also, he studied the next few pages. A puzzled frown creased his forehead when he had finished and he turned back to the first page and began to read again. Finally he looked at Dora.

'Do you think this is true? Did he really have an affair with Pavlakis's wife? Sly old dog.'

Dora nodded. 'I'm not sure Yannis ever meant to write this as a book for publication. I think he wrote it to come to terms with his own feelings over the years, and to do so he had to write the truth.'

Yannis frowned. 'Are you saying you don't want to approach the publishers?'

Dora shifted uncomfortably. 'I don't want them to have all of it. What good would it do for anyone to know Anna was his daughter? There's another part, later on, describing how he felt when Phaedra died. It's too personal.'

Yannis felt unreasonably annoyed. Had he been brought to Athens on a pretext? 'Why did you first suggest publication, then, Aunt Dora?'

'I hadn't read it at that time. I thought it was going to be a straight forward account of his time in hospital and then on the island. Like the articles, but more detailed. I had no idea about Anna.'

'Is that why you don't want it published?'

Dora shook her head. 'It makes no difference to me. I just don't feel it's right to publish his innermost thoughts and feelings for everyone to read. How would you like it if it was you?'

Yannis shrugged. 'It wouldn't make any difference to me once I was dead.'

'Yannis!' Ourania looked at her husband in horror.

Dora smiled sadly. 'I'm not shocked, but I'm not prepared to have Yannis's name besmirched. He deserves to be remembered for all the good he did and if it's admitted that Anna was his natural daughter he'll only be remembered for having had an affair with the mayor's wife.'

'Dora's right,' agreed Ourania. 'It isn't necessary to tell everyone.'

'So what do we do?' asked Yannis. 'Forget the whole idea?'

'No, we can still see if the publisher is interested. We just don't give him that particular book.'

'Does it make sense without?'

'I'm not sure. We need someone to sit down and read it carefully. I was wondering if Elena would do it?'

'Why Elena?'

'Well, she's family, and she's a secretary so she can type. If she typed it out and then we took it to the publisher he wouldn't know if we'd left anything out or not.' Dora looked pleadingly at Yannis.

Yannis stood up. 'Aunt Dora, it doesn't belong to me. I think it should go to the publisher as it stands, but if you feel differently I'll not argue. How long do you think it will take Elena to type it and how much will she charge?'

'I don't know. I've not spoken to her yet. I wanted to talk to you first.'

Yannis nodded. 'Provided she doesn't want too much for the typing you do it your way. Now, I must get back to the hotel. I've asked to see the manager and I know Ourania wants you to take her shopping. We shall be going home tomorrow, but when you have something ready let me know and I'll come over again.' Yannis dug into his pocket. 'This is for you. Ourania sold a couple of Anna's pictures. This is your commission.'

'But, Yannis, you paid me for them.'

'I paid you one hundred thousand drachma for about four hundred sketches. The ones I sold fetched six hundred drachma each.'

Ourania permitted herself to smile. It was so like Yannis. She knew he had not sold any of the sketches, and when he did they would not fetch anywhere near that amount.

Dora looked at Yannis open mouthed. 'I never thought they were worth anything like that.'

'I thought I was buying them as a favour to you,' admitted Yannis honestly. 'With the ideas we have for them you could end up a very rich woman.'

Dora shook her head. 'It doesn't seem right, somehow.'

'Don't you worry; Yannis would be pleased to know he'd left you something of value – and they have no sentimental value for anyone. No doubt when Marisa and I are gone our mother's sketches will be sold. They won't mean anything to anyone then.'

The owner of the hotel approached Yannis with a worried air. 'How can I help you, sir? Do you have a complaint? I'm sure we can put things right.'

Yannis gazed at him in contempt. He had no idea how to treat his clients. Leaning back comfortably in his chair Yannis smiled easily.

'I have two complaints. One is the lack of car parking facilities and the other is the lack of a lift.'

The man spread his hands. 'I can only apologise and hope neither has caused you too much inconvenience. As you see, we are in the centre of the city; land is at a premium, where could we have a car park?'

'There is a derelict site almost opposite you. Surely the owner could be approached and the land rented for a small sum?'

The owner turned and looked out of the window, as if seeing the plot of land for the first time. 'I suppose so. I hadn't thought about it. You are the first customer who has expected us to have a car park.'

'I'm sure I won't be the last. Why don't you have a lift? Some people must find it difficult to get to the fourth floor, and I should imagine your elderly porter also has a problem.'

Embarrassed the hotelier looked down at the floor. 'These things take money.'

'Naturally. You could afford air conditioning, though.'

'That was put in by my predecessor.'

'And do you find it successful?'

For the first time the man smiled. 'Very. You were comfortable in your room last night, weren't you?'

Yannis nodded. 'How much does it cost to run?'

'I'm not quite sure. Not very much. It is the installation that is expensive.'

'How much was it?'

The man looked annoyed. 'What business is it of yours, may I ask?'

'I am considering putting it into my own hotels.'

'How many do you have?'

'Three.'

'Three! In Athens?'

'No, in Crete.'

The owner licked his dry lips. 'We have found our customers appreciative of the service.'

'I'm sure they are, but what I really want to know are the installation and running costs.'

'I can't help you there. As I said, my predecessor decided it would be a good investment. I have only been here for six months, you understand.'

Yannis frowned. 'Did you have a hotel before?'

'No, I was a shop keeper.' He leaned forward confidentially. 'I'd always fancied having a hotel. When Vasilis decided to sell I jumped at the chance. If I'd realised the state of the place I wouldn't have been so eager.'

'What's wrong with it?'

'It needs modernising. As you said yourself, there is no lift. The kitchen is in the basement and the dining room is on the first floor. Many of the rooms on the top floor are unusable if it rains due to the condition of the roof and everywhere could do with a coat of paint. I'm in a quandary. I could get a bank loan to pay for the repairs, but I'd have to close the hotel whilst they were being done. How do I repay the loan? If I try and save the money and make improvements gradually trade will drop off and they'll never be done.' The little man looked near to tears.

'So why did this Vasilis decide to have air conditioning instead of repairing the roof?'

'He thought it would attract custom, and it seemed to, according to his books, but when the engineers put it in they damaged the roof. That made some of the bedrooms unusable and he had no money for repairs.'

'Have you tried asking them for compensation?'

'Oh, yes. They said the roof was in a poor state of repair before they did their work and the damage wasn't their responsibility.'

'Didn't you ask for a property survey before you bought?'

The owner shook his head sadly. 'I only looked at his books. They showed he was making a profit. I'd known him for years and I took his word for it that all was in order.'

Yannis snorted. 'And where is your friend now?'

'I've no idea. He's left Athens.'

'And left you with a sinking ship. How much do you think the repairs to the roof would cost?'

'I'm not sure. It depends whether I patch it or have a new one, and if I repaired the roof I certainly couldn't put in a lift or move the kitchens.'

'Are you still making a profit?' asked Yannis.

'Very little.' He sighed deeply.

'So what do you plan to do?'

'There's nothing I can do. I can't hope to get my money back if I sell and unless the repairs and improvements are done we'll have to drop our prices. Once we start to go down hill there'll be no saving it.'

Yannis nodded sympathetically and looked at his watch. 'You will have to excuse me. I have to meet my wife. Maybe we could have a drink later and continue our chat.'

The owner nodded eagerly. It was not every day that he met someone who was willing to listen to his tale of woe and misfortune.

Yannis hurried from the hotel to the post office and for a further three quarters of an hour monopolised a telephone booth, finally emerging with a smile on his face. He drove over to Dora's feeling vey pleased with himself.

As he had guessed the two women had not returned from their shopping expedition and he spent a frustrating half an hour sitting in his car waiting for them. He swallowed his annoyance as they arrived, both with happy smiles on their faces, and asked Dora where she could recommend for lunch. Throughout the meal the women chatted together, but Yannis was hardly listening. As they hesitated between the choice of fruit salad or ice cream for dessert Yannis made his apologies.

'I've arranged to meet someone on business. You two spend the afternoon together and I'll pick you up at seven.'

'I thought we were going to the Acropolis?' protested Ourania.

'We can do that tomorrow,' Yannis promised rashly and Ourania smiled. Obviously Yannis intended to stay in this wonderful city longer than the two days he had originally planned.

Yannis returned to the hotel and sought out the owner once more. 'Would you care to come to my room and share a bottle of wine?'

The owner looked a little wary. 'It's not customary for visitors to entertain me in their rooms.'

Yannis threw back his head and laughed. 'I'm not suggesting anything improper. I wish to talk to you and I'd prefer to know our conversation was not being overheard. If you're so sensitive I'll take a bottle up to my room and you can join me when you're ready.'

'There is no need. I'll collect one from the cellar.'

The wine was surprisingly good and Yannis complimented the owner on his choice.

'At least Vasilis left me a good cellar, but even that is sadly depleted.'

Yannis raised his glass. 'To your future good fortune.'

Sadly the man smiled and joined in the toast.

'Now,' Yannis leaned forward in his chair. 'To business. When I left here I telephoned my bank and my business partners in Crete. I hope I shall be making a further telephone call to ask my nephew to join me. Subject to your approval, and subject to a full survey of the building, I am willing to back you.' Yannis held up his hand as the owner opened his mouth to speak. 'My nephew will come and assess the potential of the building. I have great faith in him. He has good ideas and they're usually profitable. Provided the structure is basically sound there will be no problem with raising finance from my bank. You could stay here as a salaried manager and have a controlling interest.'

Orestis scratched his head. 'I'm not sure what you mean.'

Yannis refilled his glass. 'I am offering to pay for the repair and modernisation of your hotel. In return I expect to have a free hand with whatever improvements I decide and also in the décor. The money will be secured as a loan, with the interest repayable at the end of each year. You cannot sell the hotel without my agreement. Should you decide to sell I must be given first refusal. If you decided to sell to an outsider, whatever figure you received, the loan would have to be repaid in full from that amount and the proportion of that year's interest as soon as the sale was completed.'

Orestis looked at Yannis with disbelieving eyes. 'You would do that?'

'I would. It's how I started in the hotel business years ago.'

'And if the hotel starts to make a profit?'

'As a partner you would have the same share as the rest of us. Now what do you say? Shall I telephone my nephew?'

Silently Orestis nodded. This man was obviously the answer to all his prayers.

Giovanni drew up outside the hotel. He was feeling extremely annoyed at the presumptuousness of his uncle. The girl he had been cultivating all week was on the point of capitulating to his charms and uncle Yannis had to call him to Athens with instructions to take the overnight ferry. It really was not good enough, he was a junior partner, but the way he was at the beck and call of his uncle he might just as well be a hired hand.

Yannis was waiting for him and cut short his complaints. 'There are plenty of other girls. I want you to have a look around and tell me what you would do with this hotel if it belonged to you.'

Giovanni raised his eyebrows. 'Are you making me a present, uncle?'

'No, I'm not. I just want your opinion.'

Giovanni's eyes swivelled round the reception area. 'Well, for a start, I'd get rid of all that hideous gilt rubbish. What's wrong with natural stone and wood?'

Yannis nodded. This was the kind of talk he had wanted to hear.

'There's no lift. Where would it be feasible to put one in?'

Giovanni walked to the end of the reception area and looked up the stairs. 'Can I go up? I need to see the layout.'

'Feel free. I want you to go up on the roof and have a look. They've got one of these air conditioning plants that you're so keen on and when it was installed the roof was damaged. Then we'll have a look at the bedrooms and you can give me your opinion.'

Together the two men climbed the stairs and Giovanni squeezed himself out onto the roof, wishing he was not wearing a decent suit. Whichever way he looked there were cracks and fissures, the whole area needing to be stripped and re-waterproofed. He grimaced as he returned to where Yannis was waiting for him.

'Forget the roof. It's a write-off. Let's have a look at the bedrooms.'

Yannis opened the door and revealed a fair sized room, but with dark water stains showing on the walls and ceiling. Giovanni moved over to the window and twitched aside the curtain. He whistled in appreciation.

'Have you seen the view?'

Yannis joined him and they admired the Parthenon buildings that looked almost close enough to touch. 'Americans would pay double for this view alone. Are all the rooms like this?'

'Near enough. Look at the bathroom.'

Giovanni opened the door. The white basin and toilet were quite acceptable, but the shower was no more than a patch of tiling on the floor with a drainage hole. He shook his head. 'That won't do.'

'So what do you think?'

'Are you buying?'

Yannis shook his head. 'Just investing. Do you think it would warrant having money spent on it?'

Giovanni nodded. 'I doubt if you'd find a better position in the whole of Athens. It will certainly cost an arm and a leg to make it 'A' class.'

'I'll have to call a halt to my house for a while,' observed Yannis ruefully.

'And the air conditioning for the hotel.' Giovanni's face fell.

'We can see how this works before we commit ourselves.'

'How does the owner feel about your proposals?'

Yannis grinned. 'He's a fool. He wanted to own a hotel so he bought this one from a so-called friend on the strength of looking at his books. Didn't examine the roof or have any sort of survey done and now he wonders why he isn't making money. Who's going to stay in a room like this?'

'What's yours like?'

'There are no damp patches, but there's definitely scope for improvement.'

'So what are you planning?'

'I wanted your opinion. You seem to think it could be profitable, so the next step is to get a decent property survey done If that's satisfactory I want your ideas down on paper, with the probable cost ready for me to present to the bank manager next Monday.'

'What?' Giovanni was aghast. 'I can never have it ready by then!'

'Of course you can. Show me your plans tomorrow and if I approve you can start to get the estimates.'

Giovanni shrugged. When his uncle was in this sort of mood there was no stopping him. 'I'll need some pencils and paper. Do you think there are any plans I could look at?'

'I shouldn't think so for a minute,' replied his uncle cheerfully, 'but you could try asking Orestis.'

'But, Yannis,' protested Ourania, 'I don't see how you can make money if you're going to take out a bank loan and give Orestis a share of the profits.'

Yannis smiled fondly at his wife. 'It's simple. I borrow an amount from the bank and give it to him as a loan. I pay the bank a sum each month with the interest. The amount I owe the bank lessens, so the interest lessens until it is finally paid off. Orestis pays me back three percent more in interest than I pay the bank and he has still not paid off any of the original loan. Once I've cleared the loan from the bank everything he pays me is pure profit.'

'Is that legal?'

'Perfectly, provided he is willing and an agreement is drawn up by a solicitor. I'm taking a gamble that he'll make enough profit to pay my percentage each year.'

'And if he doesn't?'

'He would probably have to sell me his hotel to pay off his debts.' Yannis drew his wife towards him and kissed her. 'Don't you worry about finance. Leave me to do that. What did you do with Dora today?'

Ourania blushed. 'You won't be cross, Yannis? I know it was terribly expensive, but I just couldn't resist it.' From the wardrobe she lifted out the suit she had admired as they drove through the city.

Yannis looked at the price tag and whistled. 'That could be two new bathrooms! What makes it so expensive?'

'It's an original model. No one else has one like it.'

'You could have bought two dozen suits in Athens for this price and no one in Aghios Nikolaos would have one similar.'

'I was thinking of when I go to Turin.'

'Any more suits like this and you'll be going nowhere!'

Ourania's face fell and Yannis was quick to comfort her. 'Enjoy yourself. You work hard enough in the shop, you deserve a treat.' He took a roll of notes from his pocket. 'Spend what you like; we'll only be here a couple more days so make the most of it.'

Ourania looked at the money. 'I don't need all that, Yannis. I've bought what I really wanted.'

Yannis shrugged. 'Take it whilst I have it. Put it in the bank, if you like, but it's yours.'

Ourania hugged him to her. 'You really are the most wonderful husband anyone could have.'

'I neglect you by dashing off to business meetings, expect you to run the shop, keep the flat, provide me with clean clothes and meals and take it all for granted. I must be one of the worst husbands in the world.'

Ourania shook her head. 'I don't think so. I'm glad you took me away from Plaka and mamma.' She shuddered. 'When I think back to how we lived then.'

Yannis smiled. 'Don't look back. We've managed to make a good life for ourselves – and I couldn't have done it without you, 'Rani.'

Giovanni spent the day exploring the hotel. By the time he sought out Orestis he knew the contents of each room, the state of the decoration and the number of guests who had slept in it during the last six months. He made copious notes and knew that despite his earlier protests he would have plans ready to put before his uncle the following day and all the information the bank manager would require.

Orestis had tried to be helpful, but his knowledge of the trade was so limited that Giovanni found the little man a tragic figure.

'Have you any receipted bills for the work that has been done in the past?'

Orestis shook his head sadly. 'Vasilis took everything with him. Said he had cleared out for me, so I could make a fresh start. It wasn't until I'd moved in that I found out the true state of the place. I'm not even sure if his books are correct. He claimed to be full up each summer and three quarters full during the rest of the year. I've not let more than fifty rooms in the last six months.'

Giovanni shook his head. 'That's not enough to cover your running costs. You've got nearly a hundred rooms, if you count those on the top floor, and you need them full the whole time to make a profit.'

Orestis spread his hands in despair. 'I cannot make people come to my hotel.'

'You can, if you have a name for being the best in the area. You leave it to my uncle and me and you'll see how it's done. He'll expect you to work hard, but he's fair and honest. I'm going out now, so if he comes in asking for me tell him I'm looking for a good hotel.'

Thoroughly puzzled the little man nodded and watched as Giovanni sauntered through the door.

'Well?' Yannis asked impatiently, once breakfast was over and the two men were sitting in the deserted room that was called a lounge.

Giovanni smiled easily. 'I've got it all here. Where do you want to start? At the top or the bottom?'

'The top. That roof is probably going to be the most expensive item.'

'We've got an option there. It needs to be stripped right back and a new roof put on, which would be fairly straight forward, just a question of putting the work in hand, but we could do better than that. What do you think about a swimming pool?'

'A what! Don't be a fool, man. What do we need a swimming pool for?'

'For people to cool off after a long, hot day of sight-seeing. Some people like an early morning swim; others would just like to spend a lazy day.' Giovanni held up his hand. 'Hear me out, uncle. The roof has to be stripped right down. If the building surveyor says the structure is sound enough to take the weight of water you have an ideal situation. A large, flat area that you could use for nothing else. During the winter it's covered and in the summer months it's cleaned out, a small bar area has cold drinks and ice creams for sale – at inflated prices due to the convenience for the patrons – and already you're making money for nothing. Think what a draw it would be in the summer. What's the first thing they ask in Crete? Where's the beach? Well, now they can come to Athens and have beach facilities. What's more, no other hotel in the city has a pool at the moment.'

Yannis scratched his ear. 'How much would it cost?'

'I don't know yet. You said you wanted my ideas before I did any costing. Now, the next thing is redecoration of all the bedrooms. A new colour scheme, whatever you fancy, and the bathrooms to tone in. They must have decent showers and that will probably mean renewing the plumbing so you might as well put in a new bath, basin and bidet at the same time. I would suggest a bath with a shower attachment. That way you give people the choice without having two separate installations. We'd probably be able to get a very good price from both the suppliers and the fitters. Carpet in the corridors would give a feeling of luxury and warmth and also make it quieter. If you fancy an early night and thirty or so people come up later the racket would be terrible on that stone floor.

Then there's the question of the lift. The whole of this area needs redesigning. I would move the reception desk over a little and knock that wall out to provide a display area for the local sites. You could have a model of the Acropolis, or a town plan of Athens. This lounge could be more open, and it could also be sunken – two or three steps down from the reception area to give the feeling of being separate – and the bar could be over there. The lift would go opposite the stairs and there is enough room on each landing to cope with people and baggage. As you come in it's almost hidden by the supporting wall of the upper floor and obviously decorated to blend in. Down in the lounge I'd keep the decoration old Athenian – rough stone walls with polished wooden tables and comfortable chairs. You could have a large open fire place that you can use in the winter, put a couple of your mother's pictures up and some prints of the city as it was years ago and you're there.'

'And the kitchen and dining room?'

'The kitchen would have to go up on the first floor. You can't bring food up from two flights down and I'm not sure if the present kitchen would pass the health inspector. There's only one window and that opens onto the dustbin area. It needs some new equipment and new china and cutlery will be a must. That would leave the basement free for storage, or it could even be turned into a night club.' Giovanni sat back with a contented smile.

'Why a night club?'

'Why not? Night clubs always charge double for their drinks, get the people to spend their money here rather than go elsewhere.'

Yannis surveyed his nephew with approval. 'You've done well. I've arranged with the building inspector to visit this afternoon and I want you to go round with him. Take note of all he says, and don't forget we have to abide by fire regulations now. Tell him we plan to put a fire escape at the back of the building and judge his reaction. Provided his verbal report is favourable you can start to get estimates for the essential repairs.'

'And the swimming pool?'

Yannis gave Giovanni a despairing look. 'If he says the building is strong enough to take it you can get an estimate, but I want one for repairing the roof in the conventional way as well.'

'Of course.' Giovanni gave a dazzling smile. 'I'll get on to everything immediately. What are you planning to do?'

'I'm taking Ourania to the Acropolis. I promised her two days ago, before all this cropped up. We'll be leaving tomorrow anyway, so this is really her last chance. Don't forget I'll need all those figures for the bank manager on Monday.' Yannis stood up, indicating that their discussion was at an end.

'You can rely on me, uncle.'

'I know. That's why you'll be coming back to oversee a good deal of the work during the winter.'

Sorrell looked up from her cheap novel as the announcement came over the loud speaker. She stuffed her book into her bag and began to follow the other passengers to the check in. She studied them carefully as she went, pushing her way through the press of bodies until she was directly behind the good looking young man who appeared to be travelling alone. She clutched at his arm, deliberately spilling the contents of her hand bag on the ground.

'I'm so sorry. Someone pushed me.' Sorrell smiled up at him.

'Not at all. Let me help you.'

They knelt together, the other passengers moving round them, as Sorrell scrabbled her possessions towards her. 'My passport? Where's my passport?' She tipped the contents of her bag back onto the ground.

'I think you'll find you have it in your hand!'

'Oh, how stupid of me. I am sorry. I'm just so nervous. I've never travelled alone before.'

He smiled easily at her. 'There's nothing to it. Once we're through passport control we'll have a drink. That will steady your nerves.'

Sorrell smiled gratefully at him. 'You're very kind.'

'Not at all. Stay with me and you'll be fine.' He tucked her hand protectively into his arm and escorted her towards the desk.

The plane taxied to a halt at Heathrow and Sorrell looked at her escort with shining eyes. 'I really did enjoy the flight, thanks to you.'

Peter smiled back at her. 'I told you there was no need for you to worry. We'll be a while getting through customs, then you'll be with your relatives and quite safe.'

'I do hope they'll be there to meet me.'

'Now, you're not to get all worried up about nothing again, are you? Of course they'll be there to meet you. Why shouldn't they be?'

Sorrell wriggled her shoulders. 'I know. I'm being silly. Of course they'll be there – but if they're not, what shall I do?'

'I'll wait with you until you see them.'

'You really are the kindest man I've ever met. Don't you have someone meeting you?'

'No, I'm on business. I'm stopping at Heathrow for the night, I have a business meeting tomorrow morning; then I'll be on a flight to Amsterdam.'

Sorrell smiled sweetly at him. 'That makes me feel better. If you do have to wait with me I'll know I'm not upsetting your plans.'

The crowds at the barriers thinned and Sorrell peered around anxiously. 'Where can they be? I cabled them to say what time I was arriving.'

'Do you have a telephone number? You could try 'phoning them.'

'Why didn't I think of that! There's a booth over there. Can you stay here and watch my luggage? I won't be a moment.' Before Peter had a chance to reply she had darted away.

Sorrell took some change from her purse and studied the instructions before dialling a number, carefully cutting herself off before it could connect. She stood, pretending to hold a conversation, watching Peter from the corner of her eye, Amsterdam sounded quite attractive. She replaced the receiver and walked dejectedly back to him.

'They've gone away,' she said, her eyes brimming with tears. 'I spoke to their cleaning lady. She said they were expecting me next week.'

Peter placed an arm round her shoulders, feeling a thrill go through his own body as she relaxed against him. 'There's no need to worry. I'll look after you. We'll take a taxi to my hotel, have a drink and work out the best thing to do.'

Sniffing gently, Sorrell allowed herself to be escorted from the airport.

Sorrell pushed her plate away from her. 'That was magnificent, Peter, thank you.'

He smiled at her. 'Now you've been fed we'll start to make some plans. Have you any other relatives in England?'

'Not that I know of. Just my uncle and his wife. What am I going to do until they return?' Tears filled her eyes again.

'Well,' Peter hesitated, 'there are a number of options open to you. You can book into a hotel and amuse yourself on your own for a week, or take the next flight back to the States; alternatively you could come to Amsterdam with me for a few days.'

'Amsterdam!' Sorrell breathed the word back at him.

'I'm going over tomorrow afternoon. I expect I'll be able to book a seat for you.'

Sorrell shook her head slowly at him. 'Peter, I'd love to, but it's impossible. I can't possibly afford it.'

'I'm not asking you to pay. It would be my treat.' He blushed to the roots of his blonde hair.

Sorrell studied him. 'What do I have to do in return?'

The flush began to spread down his neck. 'I find you terribly attractive. I thought – maybe – but you don't have to – my offer still stands.'

'I hardly know you.'

'A week would give us time to get to know one another. I wouldn't force you into anything that was – objectionable – to you.'

'When do I have to decide?'

'Well, now, really. I'll have to get on to the airport to see if I can book an extra seat.'

Sorrell appeared to hesitate. 'I don't know what to say,' she bit at her lip.

'Say yes, Sorrell, please.' Peter's hand covered hers. 'I won't be a nuisance to you. If you say no I'll respect your decision.'

'I'll come.' Sorrell relaxed back into her chair. 'This is the most crazy thing I've ever done in my life, but I trust you, Peter.'

Peter squeezed her hand. 'You'll not regret it.'

Sorrell smiled shyly at him. 'But you will, my friend,' she thought to herself.

'What do you plan to do whilst I'm at this business meeting?' Peter looked past his reflection in the shaving mirror to where Sorrell sat curled up on the bed.

'Well,' Sorrell stretched her arms above her head and Peter felt the blood pulsing through his veins. He had slept intermittently, the sofa not really accommodating his large frame. 'I thought I'd explore some of the London shops. I'd like to see if they're as good as the ones back home.'

He towelled his face and slapped at it with aftershave. 'I should be finished by two at the latest. I'll meet you back here and we can have lunch, then we'll leave for the airport about half four.'

Sorrell smiled happily and settled back into the bed. 'It's a shame you have to go to a meeting now,' she purred.

Peter moved over to her and took her in his arms. 'I could be late,' he spoke huskily as he kissed her neck.

She pressed her body against his, deliberately increasing his longing and frustration.

'There'll be plenty of time,' she whispered, nibbling gently at his ear lobe. 'A whole week in Amsterdam.'

Peter began to fumble with the thin straps of her silk nightdress and Sorrell pushed him away roughly. 'Not now. You have to go to a meeting.' She continued softly. 'I want the first time to be so special for us.'

With an effort Peter withdrew and stood by the bed. 'You're right. I'll see you back here at two.'

Sorrell nodded. 'I'll be waiting for you.'

Sorrell waited ten minutes, wanting to be quite sure Peter did not return, before she swung her legs over the side of the bed, peeled off her nightdress and walked into the shower. Once dressed, she checked her handbag. All was in order, four passports all in plain brown envelopes, her current one sitting in the zip pocket with her own credit card. She opened the zipped centre and removed a small notebook that she consulted, making a cross against a name, then began to transfer the contents from one compartment to the another. Half an hour later she took the lift down to the breakfast room and noted with pleasure the way that all heads turned to look at her as she strolled leisurely towards a table at the far end.

Mid-day saw her at the railway station with a large holdall that she deposited in the left luggage, paying for a week's storage and placing the ticket safely in her purse. She had enjoyed her visit to the shops. It was so remarkably easy provided you were not greedy and purchased items that were reasonably priced so there was no need to check with the credit company.

From the station she went to the nearest bank. This was always a gamble. If the theft she had accomplished no more than an hour before had already been notified the card would be withdrawn and she would be asked to accompany the cashier to the manager's office.

Biting her lip nervously she slipped her right arm into a sling and entered the bank where she spent some time at a side desk practising the signature on the card before going to the counter, deliberately choosing a young man. With her left hand she pushed the card towards the cashier and smiled.

'I'd like three thousand, please.'

He frowned. 'That's rather a large amount, madam. I'll have to get it checked.'

Sorrell nodded. 'Of course.' She waited as he placed the call, hoping she did not look ill at ease or nervous.

He returned almost immediately. 'It's quite in order, madam, but is it necessary for you to carry such a large amount in cash? It can be dangerous.'

'How sweet of you to be so concerned about me! I shall be quite safe. My chauffeur is waiting outside.'

'If you would just sign again for me.'

'Of course. I'm having a little difficulty at present.' She took the pen between her fingers. 'I sprained my wrist a couple of days ago. It's so inconvenient.'

The cashier counted out the notes and pushed them towards her. Without stopping to count them Sorrell put them in the zipped compartment of her hand bag and made for the door, hoping she looked like any other customer leaving the bank.

'Madam! Madam!' She could hear the cashier calling frantically to her and hurried on, elbowing her way out of the door and running down the road to jump onto a stationary bus. As they passed the bank doors she could see the cashier standing on the steps with the stolen credit card dangling from his fingers and she smiled in relief.

It was nearly three by the time Sorrell walked into the hotel foyer to find Peter waiting anxiously for her.

'What happened? I've been worried about you. You said you'd be back at two. I've been waiting ages.'

'Oh, Peter, I am sorry.' She placed her finger on his forehead and smoothed the frown he was wearing. 'I got myself hopelessly lost. I took the bus going in the wrong direction and ended up miles away.'

'Let's go upstairs,' his hand was trembling on her arm.

'What for?' asked Sorrell, her eyes wide with feigned

innocence. 'I thought we were going to have lunch? I'm starving and you said we would have to leave for the airport just after four.'

Peter dropped his hand. 'Yes, of course. I wasn't thinking.' He held the door of the restaurant open for her and she glided to the table she had occupied earlier.

Sorrell sat on the edge of the bed. 'Peter, would you mind very much if I just went to bed?' She caressed his arm gently. 'I'm terribly tired. It must be jet lag. I didn't sleep terribly well last night,' she lied.

Hiding his disappointment Peter squeezed her to him. 'You have a good sleep. I'm pretty tired myself. There's always tomorrow.'

The alarm call woke Peter with a start. He looked at Sorrell's sleeping form and felt the desire rising in him. He stroked her back, feeling her wriggle and slipped his hand onto her breast. Lazily she caught his fingers and entwined them with her own, still breathing evenly. He kissed the back of her neck, eliciting no response, and finally gave up, withdrew his hand from her grasp and slid out of bed.

Sorrell relaxed and opened her eyes as she heard him splashing in the shower. With a little more careful planning she should be able to keep his attentions at bay. As he emerged towelling himself vigorously she feigned sleep again, waiting until he was adjusting his tie before stretching languorously and smiling at him.

'I've had a wonderful sleep,' she announced.

He crossed to the bed and took her in his arms. 'I tried to wake you earlier.'

'What for? I'm not too late for breakfast, am I?'

Peter kissed her forehead. 'I wanted you to scrub my back in the shower.'

'Tomorrow, I promise.' Sorrell kissed him lingeringly. 'What a shame I slept late. I'll have to make it up to you.'

She slipped her hands beneath his jacket and ran them down his ribs, feeling him tense beneath her fingers. She grasped his lapels and pulled him down onto her. 'I can't wait for tonight,' she breathed throatily.

'We don't have to wait…' he tried to struggle away from her.

'You have a meeting to go to and I've not showered yet.' She released him and patted his face gently. 'Off you go. Waiting will make it all the more exciting.'

'Sorrell, please, let me…'

'Certainly not. You don't want people saying that your private life interferes with your business. I'll be here when you get back.'

'You won't get lost today?'

'I promise I'll be here.' She dropped her voice. 'I'll be ready and waiting for you.'

Sorrell took a leisurely shower and dressed carefully. She enquired from the reception desk where the most fashionable shopping area was situated and which area of the city she should avoid. Thanking the girl she sauntered out and hailed a taxi. She browsed for a while; then selected a credit card from her collection, purchasing whatever she fancied, which she packed carefully into one of two holdalls and deposited it at the station left luggage depot.

With her map in her hand, Sorrell walked slowly to the less salubrious area of the city and looked for a chemist. She explained how badly she was sleeping. Could they give her something that would make her go to sleep quickly and keep her slumbering peacefully until the morning? She only wanted enough for a couple of nights, being certain that her normal rhythm would return quickly. Obligingly the chemist rummaged on his shelf and took pains to explain to her the correct dosage, warned her not to mix it with alcohol and took her guilders happily.

Her purchase completed, Sorrell continued to wander along the narrow streets, ignoring the drug pushers who offered their wares and the prostitutes who lingered in the doorways. They were amateurs in her eyes.

Once back in the hotel Sorrell packed her possessions into the second holdall and began a methodical search of Peter's belongings. There was nothing of any interest to her. The usual assortment of clothing was placed neatly in the drawers, two suits hung in the wardrobe, along with half a dozen clean shirts. Pouting with annoyance she left the room for another trip to the railway station.

When Peter arrived, shortly before five, Sorrell was lying languidly on the bed reading a magazine. Her long dark hair hung loose onto her shoulders and the magenta negligee she wore enhanced its lustre. The negligee was nearly transparent, showing her every curve and Peter caught his breath. She smiled invitingly.

'I've been waiting for you, Peter.'

He swallowed nervously and licked his lips. 'You look beautiful,' he managed to stammer.

'Why don't you join me?'

He placed his briefcase on the chair and removed his jacket, moving slowly across the room towards her. She tossed the magazine to one side and looked up at him. 'I told you I'd be ready and waiting.'

'I've been thinking about you all day. I couldn't concentrate on the diamonds, or anything else for that matter.'

'Diamonds?'

'I'm a jeweller,' he muttered thickly, as he clutched her to him, burying his face in the cloud of dark hair. He could feel the excitement mounting in him as her fingers undid the buttons on his shirt and she ran her hands over his bare chest. He cupped her breast in his hand and breathed deeply to keep control of himself.

'Why don't you get out of these clothes whilst I make us a drink?' she suggested, and slipped from his grasp, allowing her negligee to ride up, permitting him an alluring glimpse of pleasure to come.

Frantically Peter struggled to divest himself until he finally stood naked before her. Sorrell eyed him up and down unashamedly as she handed him his drink. He took a sip and placed it on the table beside the bed. Sorrell stood demurely before him.

'Have some more of your drink.'

'No, I just want you, Sorrell.'

'You lay there and sip your drink.' She handed it to him. 'You need to relax and unwind. You've had a busy day. I'll give you a massage and when I've finished you'll feel much better.' She leant over and began to massage his ankles and calves, moving up to his thighs and allowing her negligee to gape, exposing her breasts.

Peter drank deeply. 'You're torturing me.' He took another gulp. 'I've finished the bloody drink.' He banged the glass down and grabbed her wrists, pulling her on top of him, fighting with her negligee.

'Peter, please, you'll tear it. I only bought it today, especially for tonight. Let me get up and take it off.'

Reluctantly he released her and watched greedily as she undid the buttons. It seemed to be taking her such a time and he was having a job to keep her in focus. He ran a trembling hand over his eyes and blinked his heavy eyelids.

'Sorrell…'

'I'm almost ready. Close your eyes and I'll surprise you.'

Peter hardly heard her as his eyelids drooped uncontrollably and he emitted a small snore.

Sorrell smiled and pulled her negligee back over her nakedness. She would just have a quick look in the briefcase he always carried before she dressed.

Retrieving her holdall from the left luggage, Sorrell visited the Ladies cloakroom for half an hour. Her hair piled high on her head, a smart trouser suit and a change of make up altered her appearance considerably. She dared not stay in the country any longer. Peter was bound to notify the police as soon as he discovered the loss of the diamonds he had been carrying. Sorrell Bartlett must disappear, possibly for ever. It was time for Madeleine Evans to return to England.

Sorrell spent two days in England under the assumed name of Madeleine Evans. Having collected the holdall she had deposited in left luggage she booked into a small, respectable hotel and studied the contents of her purse. She had five credit cards as yet untried, a small amount of Dutch currency, almost three thousand English pounds, and, of course, the diamonds.

She rolled one between her fingers speculatively. No doubt Peter would have discovered his loss by now and have alerted the police. To try to pass through customs carrying them openly would be asking for trouble and she dared not try to sell them too soon.

An hour later she was no closer to solving the problem and decided to take a chance with a jeweller. She could always disappear if there seemed to be any sign of suspicion from him. Inconspicuously dressed, she walked slowly down the main road, appearing to gaze idly into the shops as she went, but using them as a mirror to ensure no one was following her.

A pair of shoes attracted her attention and she entered to inspect them further. The sales assistant approached her and willingly went to the stock room to fetch the partner. Sorrell took the opportunity to slip three pairs of expensive tights into her bag before she returned. To Sorrell's annoyance the shoes pinched and her gaze roved round the display, her eyes alighting on a pair of black evening shoes, the heels studded with small glass stones.

'I'll try those.'

The assistant handed one to her and Sorrell studied it carefully.

'Would you like to try the other one, madam?'

'Yes,' Sorrell replied absently, as her finger nail scratched at the ornamentation.

She tried the shoe on without enthusiasm. 'No, I don't think so. Those stones would probably fall off the first time I wore them.'

'We've never had any complaints, madam.'

'How are they fixed?'

'I understand that they're glued.'

Sorrell turned the shoe back and forth in her hands. 'I'll think about it.' She handed the shoe back and left the shop deep in thought. It would be worth trying.

Having visited a shoe repairers to ask advice about replacing a lost ornament from a pair of evening shoes, she purchased a tube of glue and returned just as the shoe shop was about to close.

'I've decided to take them.'

The assistant looked at her watch surreptitiously. It was five minutes before closing time.

'Certainly, madam. I'll fetch the other one.' She almost snatched the shoe from Sorrell's hand.

Sorrell dangled a credit card in front of the assistant as she watched the shoes being hurriedly wrapped.

'You accept this card?' she asked innocently. 'I do have others.'

'Yes, madam.' The card was taken and a flimsy slip returned for her signature. After only a cursory check the card was returned to her, the bag containing the shoes pushed into her hand and she was ushered to the door.

'We are just closing, madam.'

Sorrell raised her eyebrows. 'I would have thought it would have been worth your while to stay open later if you had a customer on the premises?'

'We are not allowed to stay open. It's the law.' The girl almost slammed the door in her face and Sorrell heard the bolts shot into place.

Unconcerned, Sorrell walked on to the railway station and studied the time table. An afternoon train the next day would get her to Dover in plenty of time for the evening ferry sailing for France. Buying a newspaper from a vendor she scanned it with interest.

There was a small paragraph simply announcing that a diamond dealer had been robbed whilst he was in Holland, but no more.

Smiling contentedly Sorrell returned to her hotel room and spread the newspaper on the dressing table. She studied the heels of the shoes intently and compared the size of the diamonds with the imitation stones. The diamonds were larger, and to her eyes, obviously not glass. She removed three of the stones from each shoe and gouged the small hollows deeper, testing them at regular intervals to ensure that the diamond sat snugly, until, finally satisfied, she applied a small blob of glue and pressed each stone home. She admired her handiwork; no one but a jeweller would give them a second glance. They looked, just as she had hoped, a rather ornate pair of evening shoes.

She replaced the cap on the glue and left the shoes standing on the dressing table to dry. They would be safe enough there until the morning as she had no intention of leaving her room. Relaxing back on her bed she directed the remote control at the television screen and let the news broadcaster talk without her listening to him. She wanted to hear the weather forecast, a rough crossing did not appeal to her. An item caught her attention.

> *'Police are hunting a young woman in connection with a diamond robbery in Amsterdam. The courier in charge of the stones had met her at the airport on his journey from America to London and she had agreed to visit Amsterdam with him. Police believe she has left Holland and could be in England. All ports and airports are being watched.'*

Sorrell believed she could detect a slight smirk on the face of the news reader and smiled to herself. She could imagine how galling it had been for Peter to have to admit to having been duped so easily by a pretty face and promises. She wondered how closely the ports were being watched for Sorrell Bartlett and decided Madeleine Evans would have to take a chance. Whilst the police were scouring England she would be safely back in Europe.

As Madeleine Evans she had deposited two of her bags into the left luggage at the French railway station. She had passed through the passport check at Dover with no more than a close scrutiny of her passport and stepped onto French soil with only a cursory glance being given to her photograph.

Whilst on the ferry she had chatted innocently to a group of passengers, having her drinks supplied and managing to take a purse containing two credit cards and a wallet that contained both French and English currency. As Madeleine Evans she planned to stay above suspicion and she had given her name as Simone and adroitly changed the subject whenever a probing question had been asked regarding her past history or her future movements. There was no way she could conceal her American accent and admitted to holidaying in Europe, being indecisive about the length of time she planned to stay in Paris and whether she would travel to Germany or Italy before returning to England.

The credit cards she had used as soon as she had cleared the port, finding a bank and withdrawing the full amount available on each card. An ample supply of francs had enabled her to take a taxi to a small hotel on the outskirts of the city where she had used yet another passport to register under the name of Jean Cartwright, before taking to the fashionable streets of Paris, where a large number of shops found their stock was short at the end of the day.

She felt vaguely unsettled and ill at ease, deciding to move on after no more than four days, and left the hotel during the morning for the railway station.

In her vacated room was a holdall containing her dirty washing, and the passport in the name of Jean Cartwright sat at the reception desk. She doubted if they would realise she had left for at least a day. By that time she would be miles away and they would have no hope of billing her.

She retrieved her holdalls from the left luggage, boarded the train without a ticket and sat unconcernedly in her window seat, reading the English paper she had purchased. If she was challenged she would insist she had been in a hurry and pay the required fare without demur. She turned the pages of the paper, not really interested in English events until her own name caught her eye. This time there was half a page about the diamond robbery, describing her and giving her name. She read it a second time; then smiled in delight. The article ended with the information that the police were convinced she had not left the country and were continuing their efforts to find her. She tossed the paper to one side and settled down comfortably to enjoy her journey.

Sorrell found the casinos of Cannes to her liking. Each evening she dressed carefully and would be found sitting at a table, placing a moderate bet each time the roulette wheel was spun and usually leaving with just a little more than she had started with. During her frequent trips to the cloakroom she usually managed to return with a purse that had been left for an unguarded moment or a wallet taken from the back pocket of a gambler.

She chatted amicably to those around her, accepted invitations to dinner and the drinks that were offered to her, but did not attempt to strike up a close acquaintance with any of the men who claimed her attention. This was the kind of life she preferred to savour alone and until someone arrived who could offer her a good deal more she would keep it that way.

Yannis toured the hotel in Athens with his nephew. He had to admit the boy had done an excellent job and also managed to keep the expenditure to a minimum. The bedrooms were tastefully decorated and the remodelled bathrooms had floor covering and towels that matched or toned with the colour of the sanitary fittings. In each room the furniture was the same, two single beds, a low table, easy chair, upright chair and a desk with a mirror above it. There was a built in wardrobe in an alcove behind the door with hanging space, drawers and a shelf for shoes. On the outside of the wardrobe door was a full length mirror. Yannis nodded, satisfied. They ended up sitting in the new lounge, Orestis joining them for a celebratory drink.

'Well, what do you think?' Giovanni looked anxiously at his uncle.

'I'm pleased with everything I've seen except this lounge. There's something missing here.'

'I put up your Mamma's sketches.'

'They don't look right. They're country scenes and we're in a city here.'

'Any suggestions?' Giovanni looked at Orestis who shook his head.

'No doubt I'll have an idea. Leave it with me.' Giovanni hoped fervently that inspiration would come to him. 'I haven't touched the basement yet.' He lowered his eyes. 'I ran out of money.'

Yannis snorted. 'You overspent drastically. I've had to put my house off for at least another two years. I can't expect much return from this until then. Leave the basement; use it for storage until we begin to see some profit. What are the bookings like?'

'Not bad. We're almost half full from April to June.'

Yannis shook his head. 'Not enough to cover the running costs.'

'We need to expand our advertising campaign. I suggest we run a new brochure, like the one we did for the hotels in Heraklion some years ago. We could show the view of the Acropolis from the windows, tell them it's all newly decorated and run to the highest standards, not forgetting the added attraction of the swimming pool on the roof. We could hire a few models and make them look like guests, get some photographs taken and start flooding the travel market.'

'Have we got time before the season's under way?'

Giovanni nodded. 'If we move fast we should have. I'll need an advance, of course.'

Yannis sighed and reached for his cheque book.

'There are a couple of other things before you write a cheque.' Giovanni looked at Orestis. 'Orestis is excellent when it comes to organising the staff and supervising, and I think he's going to be invaluable when we start catering for the clients, but he only speaks Greek.'

'So? All our staff are Greek and I presume our suppliers are also.'

'We need a receptionist, preferably two, who are multi-lingual.'

'You mean you want to come over here as a receptionist?'

Giovanni shook his head. 'I don't want to leave Heraklion. I'm happy enough there. I suggest we employ two people who have attended University for languages. They would both need English, and maybe one could have French and the other German.'

Yannis frowned. 'German? We don't want Germans.'

'We want customers,' persisted Giovanni. 'We can't hope to cover every language, but English is essential and both French and Germans come over to stay. I also suggest that we take on some trainees, not only here, but in Heraklion also. They must have shown language promise at school, but not gone on to a higher education. That way we can get the more proficient to teach them and the hotel reception business whilst they improve their language skills and pay only a minimum wage.'

Yannis nodded. As usual his nephew spoke sense. 'I presume you already have someone in mind.'

Giovanni grinned. 'I have. I think they'll be ideal. They love a language, the same as I do, but they don't want to teach and there are no other openings at present.'

'Why don't they go for interpreting?'

'They're not that good! I suggest that if we do decide to take them on they have to study for a number of hours a week, become really proficient, like you made me go to classes when I first started. If we paid their fees they will have a certificate to show for it afterwards, and we make it clear that their employment depends upon results.'

Yannis looked at Orestis. 'How do you feel about this? You're a partner, too, remember.'

Orestis nodded. 'I agree. You've poured money into this place, more than I could ever have hoped to put in, however hard I worked, and you want the best. I'm too old to learn any new language properly, but it will be necessary. Giovanni's been telling me how you run your hotels in Heraklion, advertising that you speak languages, and that's what's needed here. It would give people confidence.'

'I've got it!' Giovanni slapped his knee and the other two men looked at him in surprise. 'We call the builders back, get them to make some niches in the walls, put in some lighting and show off replicas of the statues in the museum. We could always cement them to the floor to stop people walking off with them as souvenirs, and it would be different. I've been round every hotel in Athens. Their lounges are imitations of those seen in American films and we don't want that.'

Yannis looked around the walls. 'How many do you have in mind – and what size statues are we talking about?'

Giovanni half closed his eyes. 'I'd say five,' he pointed to possible locations. 'No more than a metre tall. The centre piece for that wall could be the charioteer. I'd have to get some measurements before the builders started, and we could have a little notice underneath in different languages telling people what they were.'

Yannis took his cheque book out again and signed his name with a flourish. 'That's all I can afford without taking out further loans. Be careful with it. You'll have to pay for all the advertising and your new ideas for the lounge from that. Pity you didn't think of it earlier.' Yannis handed the cheque to Giovanni who gasped.

'Is this right, uncle? You haven't put too many noughts?'

'That's right, but I'm not prepared to put any more money in until I begin to see a return, so don't get any bright ideas about turning the basement into a night club as a surprise for me. Now, I'm going over to see Dora. The typescript of uncle Yannis's memoirs is ready and I've promised to go to the publishers with her. I'll call in on my way back before I catch the night ferry, and Giovanni; I want you back in Heraklion in a fortnight. You'll be needed there.'

Giovanni frowned and was about to protest when he took another look at the size of the cheque he was holding. His frown turned to a smile.

'Whatever you say, uncle.'

Dora greeted Yannis nervously. 'The publisher sounded quite interested when I spoke to him over the 'phone.'

'That's good. Let me carry that for you.' Yannis relieved her of the cumbersome bundle of typing. 'I've brought a selection of pictures with me and if he wants something different I can go through the others at the shop. I've put them safely away for the time being. I thought I ought to wait and let him have first choice; then we'll have the others copied and start selling again.'

Dora nodded. She was very thankful that she did not have to deal with people like publishers on her own. She knew she was easily intimidated and would allow them to talk her into parting with her dead husband's memoirs for next to nothing.

'Have you had any luck with selling your flat yet?'

Dora shook her head. 'Not yet. Maybe I'm asking too much, or maybe it's just the wrong time of year.'

Yannis nodded. 'Are you managing all right?'

'Oh, yes. It doesn't cost me much to live.'

Yannis shot a quick glance at his aunt, she was definitely thinner than the last time he had seen her. 'Would you be able to do me a really big favour?'

'Of course, Yannis, if I can.'

'You know this hotel I have an interest in? Well, I've got to take Giovanni back to Heraklion in a fortnight and I wondered, no, it's too much to ask, forget it.'

'What, Yannis? You can at least ask me.'

'No, it would be a liberty.'

'Please, Yannis. I can always say no.'

Yannis appeared to consider. 'Well, I'm not sure that Orestis knows his job as well as he makes out. I could really do with someone on the spot to check up on him. I know all the time Giovanni's there he'll work hard and everything will run smoothly, but what will he do when he's left on his own? I wondered if you'd move in for a few weeks, pretend to be a guest and just let me know how things are going.'

Dora looked at him. 'Do you really think that's necessary?'

'It would certainly put my mind at rest.'

'Why didn't you just give her some money and say you've sold some more sketches?' asked Ourania.

'I'd already told her I'd put them away until the publisher had decided which ones he wanted to use. I'm sure she's not eating properly, and I thought a few weeks of hotel food might do her some good. I'll write to her and say I'm particularly interested in the quality of the food served and the variety offered.'

'Maybe we could invite her over here for a holiday?'

'I doubt she'd come, and if she did she'd probably want to stay with Anna. I don't want to put any extra burden on her. Yiorgo is quite demanding enough as it is. Anyway, let me tell you about the hotel. I've had to let Giovanni have some more money, of course, but I had budgeted for that. We'll have to put off our house for a while longer, I'm afraid.'

'Yannis, I'm not worried about this grand house you keep talking about. We have a home here.'

Yannis pulled his wife to him. 'If we had the house you'd be able to wear your Athenian suit more often. People would comment on how smart you looked and would be told 'she's the lady from the big house'.'

'Don't be silly, Yannis. Tell me more about the hotel. Why have you had to spend more money?'

'Giovanni only estimated for repair and refurbishment. I knew we'd have to advertise and that costs a good deal, photographs and printing, not to mention distribution. I must admit I hadn't thought about the receptionists needing to be bi-lingual. I suppose I'm used to Giovanni sorting out any language problems, but he can't be in Athens and Heraklion. I wish I had two more nephews like him. That could solve my problems.'

'Maybe Joseph speaks other languages?'

Yannis gave his wife a withering look. 'I wouldn't employ him if he were the last man on earth.'

'Marisa seems to think he just needs a chance.'

'Then Marisa is a fool. He's a petty crook, and I'll not give him the chance to cheat me.'

'Maybe he wouldn't – as you're family.'

'And Yiorgo's sheep might all grow wings! Giovanni came up with a good idea for the lounge.' Yannis decided to divert the subject away from his youngest nephew. Ourania listened attentively and expressed her approval.

'When it's finished can I go over to Athens to see them?'

'I should think so. When the season gets under way we could pay a surprise visit to check on the running. I'll probably have to go over fairly regularly myself and also deal with the publisher. He tried to beat Dora down unmercifully. First of all he offered her a sum for the copyright and I'm sure she would have taken it if I hadn't been there.'

Ourania frowned. 'What would that mean?'

'That after one payment she would get nothing and he would probably make a fortune. He refused to give her an advance, but at least I managed to negotiate royalties for her. He seemed quite happy with the sketches I produced and didn't ask for any others, so I'll be able to go ahead with that project now. I really could do with a few more hours in the day.'

'You won't do too much, will you, Yannis?'

Yannis kissed her tenderly. 'I suppose I'm like uncle Yannis. According to Dora he was never happy sitting still; always had to be doing something.'

Giovanni surveyed his handiwork with pleasure. The lounge was strikingly different from any other he had seen in the hotels in Athens. His uncle should be pleased with the effect.

'Well, Thalia, what do you think?' he asked her in English.

The young woman he had employed as a receptionist looked at him adoringly. Whatever Giovanni did would be wonderful in her eyes. 'Is good.'

Giovanni shook his head. 'Speak properly; otherwise my uncle will give you the sack.'

Thalia shrugged. What did it matter when she was speaking to Giovanni? 'I think you have made it look very good.'

'That's better. Now tell me in French.'

'C'est magnifique.'

Giovanni nodded. 'I think so too,' he said, reverting to Greek. He eyed the girl up and down. 'Have you been fitted for that suit yet?'

She nodded. 'I can collect it on Friday.'

'Good. Pink blouses and black court shoes, remember.'

'Do they have to be pale pink?'

'Provided they're pink and clean each day I don't mind. Remember to clean your shoes each morning when you arrive. Nothing looks worse than a smartly dressed girl with dusty shoes.'

'Do I only have one suit?'

'Why?'

'It will have to be cleaned. What will I wear then?'

Giovanni calculated quickly. 'You can order a navy blue one, same style, and wear them alternate weeks.'

'I'll need navy court shoes to go with that.'

Inwardly Giovanni cursed. He should have foreseen that. 'Then get a pair,' he said easily.

Thalia smiled at him. 'You are generous, Giovanni.'

'Mr Giovanni. And don't forget, those clothes are for when you're at work. I don't want to see you wearing them when you're not on duty.'

Thalia turned hurt eyes towards him. 'As if I would.'

'As if you wouldn't! Now, I've a job for you. I want you to take a walk around the tour operators, tell them your parents are visiting Athens and ask if they can recommend a good hotel. Find out how many give you our name.'

Thalia nodded. 'Shall I ask if they have a brochure?'

'Yes, but don't take it with you. Just write down the address each time and leave it with them. They might need it for a real customer.'

'Shall I get my shoes and blouses whilst I'm out?'

'No. They can wait until you've been back and given me the results. If you get a move on you can be finished by lunch time.'

Thalia pouted. It would be boring asking the same questions time and again, and she would have preferred to intersperse her visits to the tour operators with a browse in the shops.

Giovanni looked at his watch. 'You should be back by about one thirty.'

Giovanni waited anxiously. He had been back in Heraklion for almost a month and his uncle had made no mention of visiting Athens to check on the running of the new hotel. He wondered if he should ask to go back for a weekend, although that did not really fit in with his plans. The party who had arrived the night before had a selection of very attractive girls with them and he had not yet decided which one he would pursue. He must check their passports and see if they were travelling alone, they were always the easiest, and he would certainly avoid any who were married.

GIOVANNI

He sat in the lounge, a bottle of wine before him and waited for them to finish their meal. He would engage them in conversation, buy a couple of bottles of wine and single out the most likely one during the evening.

'I hoped I'd find you here.'

Giovanni spun round. 'Uncle Yannis – and you too, Ourania. What brings you up to Heraklion?'

'I thought it time we had a little holiday in Athens. I've heard there's a new hotel opened up which is quite good. I thought we could give it a try.'

Giovanni's eyes opened wide, then he realised his uncle was talking about the hotel he had invested in and smiled. 'I was wondering how long you would leave it before going over.'

'Dora says the publishers are ready with the proofs so I thought I could combine business with pleasure. Ourania wants another look at Athens, so here we are. Can you find us a bed for the night?'

Giovanni frowned. 'We're full, completely full.' He finished his glass of wine. 'I'll have a word at the desk and see if there have been any cancellations.'

Yannis threw back his head and laughed. 'I would never have believed it! I own a hotel and they may not have a bed for me.'

'Be thankful you're fully booked,' Ourania reminded him. 'You'd be complaining if it was otherwise.'

'Very true. You go and see what you can do, Giovanni. I presume you have a table for us to have a meal?'

'Sure to have. I'll speak to the dining room manager on my way to the desk. I'll get him to page you.'

Yannis nodded. 'We'll have a drink first. There's no hurry.' He smiled at Ourania as his nephew hurried away. 'I like to catch him unexpectedly, see how he copes. I booked a room before we came. I wasn't prepared to leave it to chance.'

Yannis parked his car on the waste ground opposite the Athenia de Luxe, which bore a notice informing car owners that the area was for patrons of the hotel only.

Thalia smiled at the couple before her. 'Certainly we have your room. How many nights, sir?'

'I'm not sure. I have some business to attend to and I'm not sure how long it will take.' Yannis eyed the smartly dressed girl up and down critically. 'I may have to entertain some English visitors. They don't speak Greek. I was wondering if you could recommend an interpreter?'

'That would depend a good deal on the nature of your business, sir. If it is a technical discussion you have in mind I would suggest you went to an agency and inquired, if you just wish to make them feel at home my colleague or myself might be able to help you if we are not on duty.'

'How much do you charge?'

Thalia blushed. 'There would be no charge. If you wished to give us a tip we would be happy to accept.'

Yannis nodded. 'I'll let you know. Nothing is definite yet.'

Thalia signalled to the porter, gave him the key to the room and indicated the luggage to be taken up. Yannis was pleased to see the man looked considerably sprightlier than the aged porter who had attended him in the past. As he was about to leave Yannis dug in his pocket for some small change.

'Before you go, I wish to make some telephone calls. Where may I use a telephone?'

'There is one in your room, sir. Just call reception, give your room number and you will be given an outside line. The cost of your call will be added to your bill.'

'Thank you, and a drink? Would we be able to have coffee in our room before we unpack?'

'Certainly. Beside the telephone you will see a list of numbers. Just call room service and they will be happy to bring you anything.'

Yannis added to the coins he gave the man. 'Thank you. You have been most helpful.'

Ourania looked at her husband puzzled. 'Who are these foreigners you're meeting?'

Yannis grinned at her. 'I've no idea. I just wanted to test the reaction to my question. She could have told me she didn't know, or told me to ask the manager. As it turned out she was constructive and helpful.'

'What else do you plan to ask?'

'I'll see what occurs to me. You just play along with me until we have to make ourselves known. Now, do you know Dora's room number? Give her a call and ask her to come here and join us, then I'll order some coffee.'

Dora entered the room with a delighted smile on her face. 'Why didn't you let me know you were coming?'

'And let the hotel know you were my aunt and had been here working as my spy? I might need you to use you again.' Yannis eyed Dora up and down. She looked no healthier than the last time he had seen her. 'How have you found living here? Is the service good?'

'Oh, Yannis, it's like a fairy tale. Whatever I've asked for has appeared within minutes, even the doctor came within half an hour.' Dora flushed.

'The doctor? What was wrong with you?'

'He couldn't find anything wrong at all. It must have been the heat and the rich food. I was perfectly all right the next day.'

Yannis nodded, unconvinced. 'Now sit down, and tell me everything. Are you pleased with your room? How's the air conditioning?'

'My room is the same as yours, the bed is comfortable and I have clean sheets every day. Nothing is too much trouble for anyone. I'm sure there couldn't be a better hotel in the whole of Athens.'

'That's my aim. To be the best. How is the food? Is the menu varied enough?'

'It's a job to know what to choose, and they give you so much! It's all so nicely served, and everyone is always smiling and happy.'

'Have you heard any complaints about anything at all?'

Dora smiled. 'Only one. An English family wanted to know why the swimming pool wasn't open. That nice girl on the desk, Thalia, she tried to explain that it was only May and would not be warm enough to swim yet, but they weren't happy.'

Yannis frowned. 'Was that their only complaint?'

Dora nodded emphatically. 'It's the only one I've heard. I've spent a lot of time sitting in the lounge listening to people and getting into conversation with them, and they all think this is a wonderful hotel.'

Yannis beamed at her. 'You really have done me a great favour. Has Orestis been working hard?'

'I haven't seen a lot of him, but whenever a guest has asked for him he has been in his office and come out to see them. All the staff appear to like him and they treat him with respect, always calling him Mr Orestis, or sir.'

'I'm glad to hear it. Now, one more thing, then we'll talk about a visit to the publisher, have you noticed any familiarity between the staff?'

'Not the way you mean. They all seem friendly with each other, but I've not seen any holding hands or sneaking away together.'

Yannis sighed with relief. 'That's good. I don't care what they do in their own time, but I don't want the guests to be aware of their private lives. Now, shall I telephone the publisher and say we'll be along tomorrow? Which would you prefer, the morning or the afternoon?'

'I really don't mind, Yannis. I'll leave all the arrangements up to you.'

Yannis nodded. He was glad his uncle had married such a sensible woman.

Having had an excellent meal Yannis and Ourania sat in the lounge. Yannis listened intently as the other guests joined them and he heard their comments, everyone seemed to be complimentary about the hotel generally, happy with the service they were receiving and their surroundings.

Yannis had seen Orestis sitting alone at the end of the dining room and deliberately ignored him. It would be interesting to see if the manager had noticed him and sought him out, or waited until they could be alone for a meeting. He did not have long to wait. Orestis bustled up to the bar and ordered a bottle of wine to be brought up from his 'special' cellar. Yannis noticed that he paid for it before asking for it to be brought to their table and wondered if that was customary or done for his benefit.

'So how are things, Orestis?'

Orestis beamed. 'It's wonderful. I would never have believed this old hotel could look so – so – magnificent. That boy, he has good ideas and he makes sure he gets a good price for everything, and it has to be the best.'

'Are you happy with the way things are running? You're a partner, remember. The way you feel counts.'

Orestis spread his hands. 'I could ask for nothing more.'

'Are the staff happy – and are you happy with your staff?'

'Yes, they all know their job and they work well.'

'Who chose them?'

Orestis shrugged. 'The chef was here before, also two of the waiters, they recommended others to me. The cleaners are the same; I took on three extra, and a new hall porter. Giovanni chose the receptionists.'

Yannis nodded. 'The one I met when I arrived seemed very pleasant and efficient. Who does the book keeping?'

'I do all of that, making up the bills for the guests and paying the tradesmen's bills and wages.'

'Good. Keep it like that. Can I have a look at the books?'

'Certainly. You'll find them entered up to last night.'

Yannis smiled easily. 'I'll have a quick look at them in the morning. Is there anything you need?'

Orestis shook his head. 'I can't think of anything. We are full for the rest of the summer and bookings are coming in for the winter months.' He leaned forward, smiling happily. 'I have heard that one or two other establishments are not in quite such a happy position.'

'And why do you think that is?'

'I learnt a great deal from your nephew. He always asked me to do something, he never told me, and he always said thank you. Before we opened I called the staff together and told them they were to treat each other the same way. They must be polite and willing, and put the customer's well being first. I reminded them that the guest is paying their wages, and if they are not happy with the staff or the service they will not come back. Your idea of giving the staff a six-month contract is very good. At first I thought it was just to give me more paper work, but now I see the reason. If someone is no good at their job we don't have to keep them for too long. They all know that if I am dissatisfied their contract will not be renewed and they will certainly not get a good reference from me.'

Yannis raised his eyebrows. He had no knowledge of the six-month contract, that had been Giovanni's own idea, and he wondered if he had instigated it at the other hotels when he took on new employees.

'Do the staff know who I am?'

Orestis shook his head. 'When I saw you in the dining room I thought it better to say nothing. If they know you are also a partner they will be trying to please you. You must see them as they are.'

Yannis raised his glass. 'To your continued success, Orestis. Keep the hotel running the way it is at present and you'll make yourself a fortune.'

Dora felt a strange surge of emotion as she picked up the first proof copy of her dead husband's book. 'Do I have to read all of it?' she asked.

'Every word,' the publisher assured her. 'If we have something wrong we need you to tell us before we run off a thousand copies.'

'A thousand copies!' Dora gasped.

'That's just the first run. I hope it will be successful, maybe four or five thousand.'

'At least. I plan to buy five hundred of the first printing.'

'Whatever will you do with five hundred, Yannis?'

'I shall have them in Ourania's shop and Manolis is going to carry some on board his boat when he takes visitors to the island. He seems to think they will sell, along with the reproductions of the prints, as souvenirs.'

The publisher cleared his throat. 'We do have copyright on the sketches.'

'Of course. We wouldn't dream of reproducing those. We have at least another three hundred to choose from.'

The publisher frowned. He had assumed those he had been offered were the only ones available. 'Maybe we could put a few more in the book?'

Yannis shook his head. 'There would be little point. Anna drew the same scenes over and over again, just different people each time.'

'I see.' He turned back to Dora. 'How quickly can you read the proof and return it to us?'

'I'm not sure. I'll be as quick as I can.'

'If there are any problems just let me know.' The publisher ushered them out. If the woman's nephew was planning to purchase five hundred of the translated copies as soon as they were printed he would raise the number he had ordered to two thousand. This could be even more profitable than he had originally envisaged.

Once outside Dora turned to Yannis timidly. 'How am I going to read this and say if anything is wrong?'

Yannis smiled at his aunt. 'Don't you worry. We'll take it to Elena. She typed it, she should know if it reads like the original.'

'Do you think she'll mind?'

'Of course she won't. She's family. Now, do you want to continue to stay at the hotel or would you rather return to live at your flat?'

One look at Dora's face gave Yannis the answer.

'I'm sure you don't need me there any longer. I ought to go home.'

'I would far rather you stayed, this time with Orestis's knowledge. He's doing very well. I have no fault to find with him at all, but it's early days. He could become slack in a few months time and I'd want to know immediately.'

Dora looked at Yannis doubtfully. 'Do you really think so?'

'It's a possibility and I prefer to be one jump ahead. I can't spare Giovanni, but you could be invaluable to me. I could put you on the pay roll – chief spy. How does that appeal to you?'

'Oh, Yannis, I could never be a spy.'

'You just be yourself and keep your eyes and ears open. Orestis will tell me what he thinks I want to hear. I know I can rely on you for the truth.'

'Well, if you're really sure,' answered Dora doubtfully, 'and if I'm being useful, then I'll stay.'

Yannis smiled to himself. Now all he had to do was ask Orestis to keep an eye on his ageing aunt and that would be another problem solved.

Orestis was more than willing to accommodate Dora. 'I'm so pleased you've told me she's your aunt. I've been quite worried about her.'

Yannis frowned. 'In what way?'

'She always seemed to be around, was rarely out for very long. I even wondered at one time if she was trying to sponge off the other guests. She was always getting into conversation with them; then I decided she was just lonely.'

'She has no need to sponge. Does she eat properly?'

Orestis frowned. 'She doesn't always take her meals here. Usually she has the breakfast and the evening meal. She says she hasn't got a very large appetite.'

'Maybe you could encourage her to eat here at lunch time as well. Ask her to join you, or to try a new item on the menu and give her opinion.'

'I'll do my best.'

Yannis smiled at him. 'I'm afraid I've just given you an added responsibility. Just let me know if any problem arises. Now I really ought to get back to my wife. I neglect her shamefully.'

On his return to Aghios Nikolaos, Yannis sought out Doctor Stavros. He bought him a drink and chatted to him generally about his recent visit to Athens.

'A beautiful city. I went there once, before the war. Was there much damage done?'

'Not to the Acropolis, I'm glad to say.' Yannis sat patiently whilst the doctor reminisced.

'Actually,' he said at last. 'I wanted the benefit of your professional advice.'

'I know I still call myself a doctor, but I haven't practised for years now. If you need a doctor I can recommend Doctor Polycratis, my successor.'

Yannis shook his head. 'It's not as simple as that. It's about my aunt.'

'Anna? Is something wrong with her?'

'No, not Anna. My aunt Dora, uncle Yannis's second wife.'

Doctor Stavros frowned. 'Do I know her?'

'You met her at uncle Yannis's funeral, the woman with the limp. I'm a bit concerned about her. When I went to Athens she looked considerably thinner than she had previously, and I knew times were a bit hard for her. I thought she was probably cutting down on her food to make ends meet. I managed to give her some money, and she should have quite a bit of extra income soon, but I don't think that's the answer. I arranged for her to stay at my hotel in Athens for a while, and she doesn't look any better. She's still there and I know the manager will keep an eye on her, but I wondered if you could give me any information.'

Doctor Stavros raised his eyebrows. 'How should I know if the lady is feeding herself properly? Surely a doctor in Athens would be the one to ask.'

'She had a doctor at the hotel once when she was sick and he said he could find nothing wrong. I know she has leprosy and I wondered if it would have any connection with weight loss.'

'It could have. Where is her seat of infection?'

'I don't know. She has a limp, so maybe her leg or hip. There's nothing visible.'

'Does she have regular check ups?'

Yannis spread his hands. 'I've no idea. We've never talked about it. She appeared fit enough until recently.'

Doctor Stavros surveyed his empty glass and Yannis hurriedly poured him another raki. 'I couldn't possibly say without giving her a thorough examination and taking samples. Her seat of infection could have spread and be causing other problems, or it could have nothing to do with leprosy. I would suggest you had her well checked over at the hospital. They should have her records regarding the disease and should be able to say if it's still active.'

Yannis nodded. 'I'll see how she is the next time I go over. If I'm still concerned I'll do my best to persuade her.'

Anna read the latest letter she had received from Annita. She described the wedding that had taken place between Helena and Gregory at length and wished Anna and Yiorgo had not declined the invitation to visit America and attend.

Andreas had found success at last. His latest play had been very well received and he had signed a contract for a television series, which, he hoped, would be offered for sale to other countries, Greece included.

Sorrell had refused to go to University and had made arrangements to go travelling, working her way around Europe. Annita could only assume that she planned to work as a waitress or behind a bar, not suitable jobs for an intelligent girl like her. Bryony had asked to stay on at the boarding school for a further year to improve her grades, but seemed to have no idea what she would eventually like to do.

Anna read the letter through a second time and sighed. She wished she had children and grandchildren to write about. If only Michael... no, she must not think about that. She must be grateful that she had Marisa and Yannis to bring up, and that Marisa had brought her children over to see her whilst they were small. She still had Yannis, of course, and Giovanni was in Heraklion, but it was not the same as having your own.

She must write back quickly to her cousin and also tell her about the book which was shortly to be published. No doubt Annita would like a copy.

Marianne sat in the garden trying hard to concentrate on her book and ignore the noises which drifted over to her from the group of young people next door. The sound of the tennis ball as it hit the racket and the accompanying squeals and laughter made her envious. A family had moved into the house next door two weeks ago and as yet there had been no opportunity to speak to them. A young man seemed to visit almost every day and she had heard him called Colin. He looked so attractive. Marianne sighed deeply. The plop of a tennis ball landing a short distance away drew her attention and she scrambled to retrieve it, pushing it beneath a bush. They would have to come and ask for it. Low voices came from the other side of the hedge and she waited with a feeling of excitement.

Colin's head appeared above the bushes and he cleared his throat. 'Excuse me. I'm afraid we've lost our tennis ball over here. Could you chuck it back, please?'

Marianne lifted her eyes from her book. 'A tennis ball?'

'Yes, we've only got the one and we're in the middle of a game.'

'You're welcome to come and look. The side gate's open.' She hoped he could not hear her heart pounding.

Colin's head disappeared from view and she waited, amazed at her own daring. Two young men rounded the corner of the house followed by a petite blonde. Marianne sat motionless.

'Look where you like. I was reading, so I really can't help you.'

The blonde girl sat down beside her. 'What are you reading?'

Marianne held out the thick volume for inspection.

'That's heavy going! Are you reading for pleasure or working?'

'Both. I enjoy political history and I'm also taking it as one of my subjects at college.'

'Yes? So did Bob. Hey, Bob, here's a kindred spirit for you. A political history freak.'

Bob loped across the lawn and sat the other side of Marianne. 'I've read that one. Have you read any of his others?'

'Not yet. I plan to when I've finished this.'

'I've got them at home. I'll lend them to you if you like.'

'That would be kind of you.'

'No problem. I majored last year so I don't really need them now. You can keep them as long as you want.'

'What do you plan to do now?'

Bob grinned lazily. 'As little as possible. My old man wants me to go into politics and is angling to get me a me a junior job. All the time he's negotiating an opening for me, as he puts it, I'm free to please myself how I spend my time. I hope it takes him all summer.' Bob lay back on the grass, his hands beneath his head. 'How about you?'

'I haven't decided yet, but I'm seriously considering international law.'

'I thought we were looking for a tennis ball.' Colin's voice cut across their conversation.

'Coming, master.' Bob rose to his feet. 'I'll see you later,' he promised.

The blonde girl looked at Marianne. 'Are you the girl who lives here?'

'Yes.'

'By the way Colin spoke I expected someone much younger. He said the stuck up kid from next door was in the garden.'

'Stuck up! I'm not stuck up.'

The girl shrugged. 'Colin seems to think you are. He says you never speak to him and look past him if you see him out.'

Marianne felt a hot flush coming to her cheeks. 'I only look past him because he never speaks to me.'

'Why should he – if you don't speak to him first?'

'Well, he's the man. He should speak first.'

'That's the most old fashioned thing I've ever heard. Do you really believe that?'

'Yes. If we were in Greece and I spoke to him first it would be considered terribly forward of me.'

'Really? But you're in America now, so you're not really Greek, are you?'

'My grandparents are Greek, my mother is Greek and my father is half Greek,' announced Marianne proudly.

'What do they do over here? Have they got a diner?'

'My grandfather is a biochemist and my grandmother helps him. My father is a doctor.'

'No wonder you're brainy! What does your mother do?'

'Organises my father. She works as his unpaid secretary. Books his appointments and writes the letters, that sort of thing. What about yours?'

'She stays at home. She found she was having a happy event when she thought it was the menopause. Julia's just over a year, so she keeps her busy. I wish they'd find that ball. They'll have forgotten the score by the time we get back, then they'll want to start again and I'm half dead. They decided it was the girls against the boys – and there's only one of me.'

'That sounds a bit unfair. Why don't you play singles?'

'Because they know I'll beat them.' She grinned wickedly. 'Do you play tennis? Come and make up a four with us. We could really show them, then.'

'I'm not very good, besides Colin hasn't asked me.'

'Oh, shucks to Colin. I've asked you.' She scrambled to her feet. 'Haven't you two found that ball yet? She's agreed to join us and make up a foursome.'

Colin scowled. 'I think we'd better give it up as lost.'

'Is this it?' Marianne strolled forward, the ball in her hand.

'Where was it?'

'Beneath that bush. It must have rolled there. I'd love to join you.'

As Marianne followed the trio to the next door garden she heard Colin talking to the girl in a low voice.

'Why did you have to ask her?'

'Don't be daft, Colin. She's seems nice, and besides, we need a fourth.'

Marianne pretended not to have heard and turned to Bob. 'Is she your sister? What's her name?'

'Elizabeth. And yours?'

'Marianne.'

'That's unusual.'

'Not really. It's customary to be called by the names that are already in your family, but mamma decided to almost break with tradition.'

Bob raised his eyebrows. 'Tell me.'

'Well, my grandmother called her children Elena, after her mother, Maria and Anna after her cousins, and Andreas after her brother. My twin is Helena, I'm Marianne and my brother is Andrew.'

Bob grinned. 'I see what you mean. Almost the same, but not quite. Now, how are we going to play? Mixed doubles or girls against the boys.'

'As we were,' answered Colin quickly.

Elizabeth smiled happily. 'Now we'll show them. Come on, Marianne. Let's see how many love games we can take.'

The next two hours passed happily for Marianne as she tried hard to match Elizabeth's game and they beat the boys handsomely.

'What did I tell you?' smiled Elizabeth. 'They really should practise harder if they want to beat a team like us.'

Marianne shook her head. 'You play magnificently. I was just happy to get my serves in.'

Bob flicked a piece of grass at his sister. 'So she should. She's a Junior Champion.'

Marianne looked at Elizabeth with admiration. 'I should have guessed. I don't think you missed a single ball.'

'The competition wasn't all that hot. Is there anything to drink?'

'Would you all like to come back next door and have a drink? I know there's some beer and fruit juice in the cooler. Dad's probably got something stronger hidden away if you fancy it.'

'Suits me, and beer would be fine.' Bob pulled his sister to her feet. 'Come on, slouch. We can't stay long. We promised Ma we'd put in an appearance this evening at dinner and we both need a shower.'

Marianne took cans of beer and fruit juice from the cooler and placed them on the worktop. 'Help yourself.' She took a fruit juice and poured it into a glass. 'Thanks for an enjoyable afternoon.'

'Maybe you'd be free again next week? We could make up a four again,' suggested Elizabeth.

'I'd like that – if it's all right with Colin.'

'Why shouldn't it be?'

Marianne looked at the young man who lounged against the wall. 'I get the impression that Colin would prefer me not to.'

Colin shrugged. 'You're welcome to play tennis with us.'
Marianne inclined her head. 'I appreciate the offer.'

To Marianne's surprise, Elizabeth telephoned her early the next day. 'Hi, there; are you doing anything special today?'

'I ought to do some work.'

'Oh! Bob and I have arranged a picnic. Dad's letting him borrow his car and I thought you might like to join us and go to the beach.'

Marianne caught her breath. 'I'd love to. Can I bring anything?'

'Just yourself. See you in half an hour.'

Before Marianne could say another word the telephone was dead. She smiled to herself and wondered if Colin had been invited, then she shook her head. What did it matter if Colin were there or not? She would enjoy herself in a way she had not been able to do since they had moved to this side of town.

At first she had attempted to keep in touch with her friends, then it had become too much effort to travel backwards and forwards and they had gradually drifted apart. She had expected to make new friends at college, but she had never become particularly friendly with any of her classmates, certainly not on visiting terms or going out in the evening. Maybe she had expected too much. When you had a twin, who always seemed to be surrounded by a host of friends and also a regular boyfriend whom she had now married, you tended to fade into the background. She shook herself. She was twenty-two and it was time she began to make her presence felt in the world rather than be content to be a shadow of Helena.

Dora lay on her bed and looked at the book that had been delivered to the hotel for her final approval. She wished her leg did not ache so much. She would try to sleep for a while; then maybe look at it before she went down to lunch. She had promised Orestis she would try a new dish created by the chef, but she really did not feel very hungry.

She carried the book down to the dining room with her and sat looking at the pictures. Despite all her late husband had told her she still found it difficult to imagine sick people living on an island, totally dependent upon each other for help and the mainlanders for food. She smiled to herself. Yannis had chosen well; the pictures were clear and showed the people as they were, their disfigurements undisguised. She pushed the book to one side as Orestis approached.

'Are you feeling brave, madam? The chef would like you to try his new sauce.'

'He hasn't poisoned me yet, Orestis. Won't you join me? I'd like you to have a look at this book and tell me what you think.'

Orestis sat at the table and took the book from her. He opened the front cover and looked at the dedication, raising his eyebrows. 'It is for you?'

Dora frowned. 'What do you mean?'

Orestis read the inscription. 'For my wife Dora, who made me laugh.'

Dora felt the tears come into her eyes. 'I do miss him,' she said sadly.

Orestis nodded sympathetically. 'Your husband wrote this book? He was a very clever man, to have such an idea and then write it as though it were he who had suffered.' Orestis was flipping through the pages quickly.

Dora shook her head. 'It is his life story,' she whispered. 'It's all true. He was sent there – and he did suffer.'

'Madam! You mean he was…'

'Yes, Orestis, he was a leper. A finer man you couldn't wish to meet, despite his illness.'

Dora began to giggle almost hysterically. 'But he didn't like sick people.'

Orestis surveyed her gravely. She might be his partner's aunt, but was she also slightly deranged? He placed the book back on the table. 'I think, maybe, if you read the book in private it would be more suitable.'

Dora controlled her laughter and shook her head. 'I know the story. I'd like you to read it. Give me your opinion.'

Orestis looked doubtful. 'Are you sure?'

'I'm quite sure. This is the first edition from the publisher. Next week it will be available in four languages for anyone who cares to buy it. I'd like to have advance notice of possible reactions.'

Orestis pursed his lips. 'I do not feel qualified to give an opinion.'

'Nonsense, man.' Dora picked up the book and thrust it into his hands. 'Now, what's this new sauce the chef wants to try on me?'

Yannis was delighted. His uncle's book was selling well. The original five hundred he had purchased were all but sold, and he was awaiting the next shipment. He approached Ourania, ostensibly to ask her advice, but really just for the confirmation of his own idea.

'Have you read it?' he asked.

She nodded. 'Every word. It brought back the visits to the island so vividly. Dora must be so proud of him.'

'It seems wrong, somehow, to make money out of his misfortune.'

Ourania raised her eyebrows. It was not like Yannis to feel guilty about making money.

'I thought,' he continued, 'It might be a gesture to send the profit I've made on selling the book to the publisher and ask him to add it to Dora's royalties. After all, she could have decided to keep the manuscript to herself, or even throw it away.'

'You don't have to justify your actions to me, Yannis.'

'No, but it's your money too, and you might have different ideas.'

'I've always left the finances to you. If that's what you want to do I'm quite happy.'

Yannis frowned. 'I was talking to Doctor Stavros the other day and he suggested Dora had a thorough check up at the hospital. That costs money. I've paid all the hotel expenses, of course, made her think she was actually working for me, but I don't think she'd accept anything for nothing.'

'When will she receive her first royalties?'

'Not for at least a year. They have to work out how many books have been sold before they pay anything. It would probably be best if I put some money aside. If it were necessary Dora could go to a private nursing home and I could tell her it was an advance on her royalties.'

Yannis scrutinized Dora carefully. 'How are you? Is hotel life still suiting you?'

'I'm fine, Yannis. What brings you over?'

'I wanted to know what my spy had to report. Is Orestis still working hard?'

'Everything seems to be going very smoothly. One or two of the staff have changed, but I expect you know that.'

Yannis nodded. 'Orestis telephoned me. He also wants to take on another receptionist.'

'He does need an extra hand,' Dora assured him. 'The three he has are very good, and that little trainee deserves upgrading, but if people are booking in and the telephone goes visitors often have to wait for attention.'

'And you think another one will solve the problem?'

'It would mean there could be three on at the busiest times.'

'And when are they?'

'First thing in the morning usually. People are deciding where to go for the day and want to know how to get there, others are trying to check out and pay their bills.

'Just in the morning?'

'No, late in the afternoon is often another time. People want to know the best places to go for entertainment, or make definite arrangements for the following day, and an extra person would relieve the pressure.'

'I'll talk to Orestis,' promised Yannis. 'Now, I want to talk to you very seriously.'

'You want me to leave the hotel?'

'Not at all. You're far too useful to me here, but you're free to go whenever you feel you've had enough.'

'I don't think that will happen, Yannis. I enjoy being here and watching all the activity. What would I do in my flat all alone? It was different when Yannis was there, but not now.'

'You've given up the idea of going to live with Daphne then?'

'I think she only asked me because she felt sorry for me. I haven't even seen her for a couple of months. I doubt if we'd really get on – two women in the kitchen.' Dora shook her head. 'What was it you wanted to talk to me about?'

Yannis hesitated. 'How are you keeping, in yourself?'

Dora shrugged. 'I get a bit tired, but I'm not as young as I was, apart from that I seem to be ticking along all right.'

'Do you have regular check ups?

'What for?'

'To see if there's any change in your condition.'

'I'm not going to get better, if that's what you mean.'

Yannis smiled. 'You could be burnt out. How do you know if you don't go for a check up?'

Dora shrugged. 'I keep taking the capsules.'

'And you feel quite well in yourself?'

For a second Dora hesitated. 'I think so.'

'Then as a big favour to me would you go and have a thorough check up?'

'What's the point if I'm feeling well?'

'It would set my mind at rest. As you say, you're not as young as you were. This is a time when little things get a hold and turn into big things. If you say you're feeling well I believe you, but I'd like to know that the doctors agreed.'

'What are you getting at, Yannis?'

'Well, I know the disease. If it isn't halted it keeps on eating away at you, often without you realising it until it's too late to do anything about it. I'd like to know yours had halted or that you were getting treatment for anything that had developed.'

Dora sighed. She had hoped her weight loss had gone unnoticed. 'I'll think about it.'

Yannis shook his head. 'I've booked you an appointment for two days time. I'll come with you, or ask Daphne if you prefer, but I do want you to keep the appointment.'

Dora looked at her nephew. 'You're too used to having your own way. Oh, I'll go along if it makes you happy, but I'm sure it will be a waste of money.'

Yannis left the hospital doctor with a grim face. He had escorted Dora and spent the day moving from one department to another whilst tests and X-rays were taken from all parts of her body. The doctor had finally smiled reassuringly at her and said they would let her know the results when they had come through, but in the meantime she should not worry.

Whilst Dora was dressing the doctor had called Yannis to one side.

'Are you her son?'

'No, her nephew; I'm her closest relative.'

'I think it might be as well if we had a little chat. How would next Wednesday suit you?'

Yannis nodded. He had not intended to stay in Athens so long, but if the doctor wanted to talk to him it must be serious.

Now having spent an hour talking to the doctor he was very concerned. 'What can I do?' he asked.

'Very little, except continue to ensure that she is well looked after. She could return to the hospital, of course, and that may be necessary eventually.'

'How long does she have?'

The doctor shrugged. 'I can't say. The disease has crept from her leg into the pelvis. We can increase her dosage, which may slow it down for a while. You have to face the fact that she will eventually be wheelchair bound and it will begin to attack the internal organs in the area. It may well have started to invade the liver. She did admit to feeling tired, having bouts of nausea and generally feeling unwell on occasions.'

'What can you do about that?'

'Nothing, unfortunately, except advise on a diet which may help in the short term and morphine later if necessary.'

Yannis felt sick. 'Suppose I took her to America? Would the hospitals there be able to do any more?'

The doctor shook his head. 'At her age and her advanced state I would think it most unlikely. Better to save your money and use it to make her as comfortable as possible later. I can give you an address to write to in America if you want further advice.'

Yannis shook his head. 'I know where to write. I have a relative in America, Doctor Kzantarou.'

The doctor raised his eyebrows. 'I'm sure he could tell you far more about the progression of the disease and what to expect. His research has helped millions.'

'When will you tell my aunt?'

'I have arranged to give her the results on Friday. I shall simply say she has regressed and we are increasing her dosage in the hope of halting it. The diet I shall advise will be to avoid any adverse effect from the medication.'

Yannis nodded. 'I'll stay a few more days so I can come with her.'

Dora listened carefully to the doctor, hardly understanding the long words that he used to describe the deterioration that was taking place in her body. Once he had finished she moved forwards on her chair.

'Now will you please tell me the truth, doctor.'

The doctor looked from his patient to her nephew. 'I have told you…'

'You've told me a lot of gibberish. Now tell me what I want to know. How far has the leprosy spread inside me and how much longer do I have to live an active life?'

'It's hard to say about the extent of the infection. To ascertain correctly we would have to do exploratory operations, which could put you through considerable discomfort, even pain, unnecessarily. As your pelvis crumbles you will obviously have more problems with your mobility. This could happen over a period of years or months. The more quickly the spread of the disease in the pelvic area, the more quickly it could move to the organs higher up, but, as you know, it is a strange disease. It could halt again for some years, or even move somewhere else and disable you rapidly. Please believe me when I say I am telling you all I know at present. Obviously we would like you to return for regular check ups and if you begin to have any pain anywhere we will do our best to alleviate it.'

Dora sat back. 'So if we look at the facts, I could live another twenty years disintegrating slowly, or I could go tomorrow if it weakens my heart?'

'I think tomorrow is being rather pessimistic.'

Dora gave the doctor a withering glance. 'My husband appeared to be perfectly fit one day and died of a heart attack the next. I think it would be as well if I made sure my affairs were in order now.'

Giovanni approached his uncle, a sheaf of plans in his hand. 'It's the ideas I have for the night club in the basement of the hotel in Athens. We've left it over a year and I think it's time we got on with it.'

Yannis smiled at the enthusiasm shown by his nephew as he unrolled the plans on the table. 'I thought if we placed the bar over there, had a small stage for live music on this side, tables and chairs at the back and left the centre free for people to dance. We'd need to put down a new floor, of course, and…'

Yannis held up his hand and stopped him. 'Giovanni, I can't afford to spend extra money on the Athens hotel at the moment.'

Giovanni gaped in astonishment. His uncle always complained that he had extravagant ideas and spent too much money, but he had never refused outright.

'What's wrong?'

'It's become a bit complicated. There's nothing wrong with the income from the hotels, but I want to redecorate the Heraklion ones this autumn. They're becoming shabby. The shop is going well and I'm even hoping to be able to continue with the new house, but it's Dora. She's very ill, far more ill than the doctor or I let her believe.'

Giovanni looked concerned. 'I don't know her very well, but she seemed a great old lady.'

'She is. That's why I want to make sure that when the time comes she'll be comfortable and well looked after. I don't want to think of her wasting away in a public ward. I want to put her into a private clinic or at the very least a private room with her own nurse.'

Giovanni whistled. 'That will cost a fortune. Can she afford it?'

'I doubt it. She has the royalties from the book, the income from Yannis's savings and the flat. For some reason she's loath to sell the flat and doesn't want to let it in case she decides to return. I just feel I must keep a very healthy bank balance and not expand any more at present.'

Giovanni's face fell. 'I understand, uncle. I'm just a bit disappointed.'

'We'll do it in a few year's time,' promised Yannis. 'By then I should know exactly where I stand financially.'

'Could I meet you tomorrow and we can talk about it again?' suggested Giovanni.

'There's no point. Nothing is going to change by tomorrow.'

'I just happen to have had an idea. I need to think it through. Meet me tomorrow afternoon and give me your opinion.'

Yannis shook his head as his nephew left the hotel office. Now what crazy scheme did he have in mind?

Giovanni greeted his uncle with a smile. 'I have a proposal to put before you and it won't cost you any money.'

Yannis raised his eyebrows. 'I'll listen, but no promises.'

'Can I rent the basement of the Athens hotel from you? No, listen,' he interposed, as Yannis was about to speak. 'I rent the basement from you and pay for all the alterations and decoration. I hire separate staff to run it and I take the profit. If it fails you still have the basement and it will have been repaired and redecorated for you. You can either use it for storage again or anything else you please.'

Yannis smiled. 'I might have guessed you wouldn't take no for an answer! Where are you going to get the money for such an undertaking?'

'I have my savings and I've also had a word with the bank manager. He would be willing to give me a loan provided you guaranteed repayment. It would only be a formality. I don't see any problem.'

'I can see plenty,' frowned Yannis. 'You have big ideas. Before you know it you'll have spent twice the amount the bank is prepared to loan you, you'll have no return until it's up and running, so you'll be coming to me to bail you out. Besides, you're needed over here and to do as you suggest you'd need to be in Athens.'

Giovanni shook his head. 'I promise before I spend a drachma of the loan I'll obtain firm prices. Once I've given instructions to the contractors I don't need to be breathing down their necks. I can go over at the weekend to see how things are progressing. I might need a week over there to finalise certain items, but if I started now I could probably take the time during our quiet season and have it up and running under a manager in six months time.'

Yannis sighed. 'Let me have a look at those plans. Then you'd better tell me the sum you have in mind. When do you have to give the bank an answer?'

Giovanni shrugged. 'They didn't say, but I think a week is reasonable. That would give you time to think about it and realise you can't lose. You'll have the rent coming in from me regularly. All I ask is a free hand in running it. What more could you want?'

'What more indeed! I can't help feeling there's a snag somewhere and I've been too slow to see it.'

Annita opened the package and looked at the book with interest. So this was Yannis's life story. She wondered how distorted it had become with Elena typing it and the publisher probably editing it himself and cutting whatever he thought to be irrelevant. She looked at the pictures curiously and read their captions. That was Yannis. Involuntarily her eyes went to the sketch above the fireplace, then she looked again at the illustration in the book. If Maria had not already been dead for some years she would have thought she was the artist. How uncanny.

She continued to look through, all the other faces unknown to her.

'So what is so interesting?' Elias looked up from his newspaper and Annita jumped.

'I was just looking at this book. It's Yannis's life story. He was writing it when he died and Dora decided to have it published. Anna has sent me a copy.'

'I'll have a look at it later. You read it and let me know what you think. What does Anna have to say in her letter?'

'Not a great deal. She and Yiorgo are still living at the farm. She says Yiorgo has a problem with his eyes and she's trying to persuade him to visit an oculist. No doubt Yiorgo is as stubborn as ever and insisting there's nothing wrong. Giovanni has started work on a nightclub in Athens. It must be in that hotel Yannis has. Anna said something about it when we were over there.'

'They seem to be doing quite well for themselves. Good luck to them. I'm off. I haven't forgotten Helena and Greg are coming for lunch. I'll be back in good time.'

'I'll ring you,' promised Annita, knowing full well her husband would forget his promise the moment he walked through the door of his laboratory. She picked up the book again. She would go out on the porch and sit and read for a while.

Helena and Greg arrived, brimming with happiness, enthusiastic about their small apartment, and full of plans for Gregory to fit out the kitchen afresh and redecorate.

'When we've finished you and grandpa will have to come over.'

'With the plans you're making we'll both be too old. It will take you years to complete all that work, Greg.'

'Not me. A couple of months and it will look entirely different.'

'Greg's not like grandpa. He gets on with things once he's started. Is he coming in for lunch?'

'Oh, dear, I forgot to 'phone him. I was so engrossed in Yannis's book that it slipped my mind. I'll do it now.'

'What book is that?'

'It's on the chair in the porch. Have a look at it and see what you think.'

Helena picked up the book and began to flip over the pages. She held out a picture for her husband to look at. 'It's written by a relative of ours. He's dead now, but he spent years on this island because he was a leper. Grandpa sent him all his research notes and he used them to convince the medical authorities that they should all be examined and given some new drugs. They decided he didn't need them and he was allowed to stay in Athens. Grandpa met him once, years ago, when he had been to a conference in Europe.'

'That's where we should have gone for our honeymoon. To Greece to look up your family.'

Helena smiled at him. 'I'd love to go one day, but we couldn't possibly have afforded a trip to Europe and the apartment.'

'That's true,' Gregory agreed. 'Maybe we should have waited a while longer before getting married.'

'I'm glad we didn't.' Helena slipped her arms round her husband and kissed him. 'In fact I don't really want you to go back to work next week. I'll be lonely.'

'Lonely or not, I have to go. Maybe we could excuse ourselves quite soon after lunch,' he squeezed her to him. 'I can think of a good deal that needs to be done.'

Helena giggled. 'We'll see.'

Annita returned. 'Well, what did you think of the book?'

'I've only flicked through it, but it looks fascinating. I'd like to read it when you've finished with it. Greg was just saying we should have gone to Greece for our honeymoon and looked up the family.'

'There aren't many of them left. Andreas never married, of course, so there are only my cousins, Anna and Yiorgo. Their nephew and his wife live locally and one of Marisa's sons works at the hotels. They haven't got a big family like us.'

'Talking of family, how are Sorrell and Bryony?'

Annita stiffened imperceptibly. 'Bryony is at college. She seems to be doing well.'

'What about Sorrell?' Helena frowned.

'She decided she wanted some time out and is travelling around.'

'And Saffron?'

Annita looked sadly at her granddaughter. 'No one has heard a word since Jeremy left. I'm sure he's looking after her well, but it would be comforting to have a letter.'

'Poor girls. They've had so many changes in their lives they must feel most confused,' commented Gregory.

'I'm glad we've always been a proper family,' remarked Helena.'

'Talking of sisters, how is yours?' asked Annita. 'Does she miss you?'

Helena shrugged. 'I think she may have done at first, but she seems to have really blossomed now. She's become friendly with the new neighbours and they're all supposed to be going off somewhere. You know, one of those long treks into the unknown where you come back with long hair and tall stories.'

A look of horror crossed Annita's face. 'Oh, no, she's not giving up her studies, is she?'

Helena smiled. 'No, it's just a few weeks vacation. She's worked hard and deserves a break. If I wasn't married I would love to join her.'

'They say twins are kindred spirits and know how the other feels,' Gregory smiled. 'You'll just have to share her feelings.'

Helena shook her head firmly. 'I'll not try to do that. She might try to do the same back, and there are some feelings I don't want to share with anyone, not even my twin sister.'

Marianne returned from her camping trip full of enthusiasm. 'We had the most wonderful time. It did me good to get away from my studies for a while. I've had time to re-think my whole career.'

Matthew looked at his daughter warily. Had she returned with some crazy idea of living in one of the shantytowns? His sister-in-law was bad enough now she had gone to live in Brazil and was 'helping the poor' under Father Jerez's guiding hand. Matthew had a nasty suspicion that the hand could guide any money Maria chose to donate away from the people and into his own the hand, and he hoped he was maligning the priest.

He smiled at his daughter. 'So what are you planning to do now?'

Marianne perched herself on the arm of the chair. 'It really depends upon you, Pappa. I'd like to go to University in England

and study international law. I think it would broaden my outlook and round me off.'

'I think it would shrink my bank balance and finish me off! Have you any idea how much it would cost?'

'I've not gone into the costing, but I thought I could try for an exchange scholarship. That way there'd only be my fare to pay.'

'And your accommodation and living expenses. I've only just paid out for your sister to get married, remember.'

Marianne placed her arm round her father's neck. 'I know you have, but that also means you have one less of us to keep now. Last year we were both at college, and if I went to England I wouldn't be eating your food or using the shower or anything, so you'd save money that way. You could even let my room if you wanted, and I'm sure I'll be able to find work during the vacations to help.'

'You've got it all worked out, haven't you? You'd better talk to your mother.'

Marianne planted a kiss on his balding head. 'Thank you, Pappa. I knew you wouldn't say no.'

Dora returned from her solicitors feeling well pleased with herself. Now she knew there would be no confusion regarding her wishes. She should never have agreed to be examined by the doctor. Ignorance had made her take each day as it came, doing her best to overcome any pain in her leg or other symptoms, but now she was conscious of every ache.

Orestis was a great help. She found him a comforting companion to spend an evening with, sometimes planning a week's menus, or watching a television programme.

Twice he had taken her to a concert at the open air theatres at the foot of the Acropolis and she had enjoyed the experience immensely. He would find out how grateful she was to him at a later date.

Yannis, of course, would have everything else, such as it was. He deserved that for the way he had looked after her. Had he been her son he could not have been more dutiful or caring. She hoped she would stay well for a long while yet. She had promised Yannis she would keep an eye on the renovations that were taking place in the basement and it was the least she could do for him. It was even quite interesting watching the work progress and seeing Giovanni's ideas take shape.

She smiled to herself. That little receptionist, Thalia, she obviously had high hopes of ensnaring him, but she would not give much for her chances. Giovanni spent so little time in Athens and when he did he shared his favours liberally. Better for Thalia to look again at the waiter who asked her out regularly, despite the snubs he received.

Dora leaned back on her pillows. It was most amusing living in a hotel and watching the actions of those around her. What a shame she was not as talented as her second husband had been or she could have written a book also.

'Well, what do you think?' Giovanni opened the doors and swept his hand across the light switch.

Yannis looked around the stark room. There was no ornamentation on the bar and the walls were whitewashed. A small stage, approached by two steps was at the far end, and most of the floor area consisted of polished wood.

'It's very plain,' he said at last.

Giovanni grinned. 'It is now, but watch this.' He went behind the bar and pressed one of a selection of switches. Immediately the lights dimmed whilst the centre light began to revolve and charioteers were seen galloping across the white walls. Another switch changed the lighting to a confusion of suffused colours.

Yannis drew in his breath. 'It's certainly different.' He could feel excitement rising in him, the combined effect of the lighting and movement before his eyes.

Giovanni adjusted a knob and the racing chariots appeared to slow, the lighting giving the effect of the horses' flanks heaving and their nostrils flaring.

'Ready for the next scene?'

Yannis nodded and watched, fascinated, as warriors appeared to be fighting to the death. 'How do you do that?'

'It's quite simple. I have a few frames of film and they're run continuously around a spindle and projected onto the centre light – except that it isn't a light, it's a mirror. I can't tell you the exact principles, it's way beyond me, but I've a friend who's well into electrical gimmicks and he set it up for me. I've half a dozen different film scenes, or I can run with just the lights if there's a floor show taking place.'

Yannis sat down on a barstool. 'Very ingenious and different. I'd like to be here for the opening to hear the reaction from your customers.'

'We'll set a date. Maybe Ourania would like to come over with you.'

'I'm sure she would. How much has this set you back?'

'My savings and most of the loan,' admitted Giovanni. 'I was wondering if you'd be willing to wait for the next six month's rent, just whilst I stock up the bar and the place gets known?'

'You never could keep within a budget,' grumbled Yannis.

'It was the special effects that took the money. There was a lot of wiring.'

'What happens when people get tired of chariots racing round them?'

'I simply ask Dimitris to buy a few more reels of film. That's the real beauty of it, uncle. I can change my décor for just a few drachmas as often as I like. If I get fed up with it I don't have to rip it all out, just switch off and forget it.'

Yannis grinned at his nephew. 'I can't keep up with you. I'll tell you what – I'll forgo the rent, return what you've paid me so far, and we'll make it a partnership. What do you say?'

Giovanni shook his head. 'I appreciate your offer, uncle, but no. I want to do this on my own. I know you've always given me credit for my ideas, but basically people think of the chain of hotels as being yours. I want to be able to claim this nightclub as mine.'

The opening of the nightclub was a success. Giovanni had printed handbills to be distributed in the city offering a free bottle of wine to every party of four who came. To his delight at the appointed opening time he had a small queue waiting outside.

'What people will do for a free drink,' remarked Yannis.

'It will be worth it if they tell their friends. Come and sit over here, that way you'll be away from the speakers, but able to see what goes on.'

Yannis took Dora's arm. She had insisted on leaving her stick in her room. 'I can't go to a nightclub with a stick!' she had remonstrated. 'That would certainly create the wrong image.'

Seated at their table Yannis waited to see what the effect of his nephew's décor would have on his wife and Orestis as well as the unsuspecting customers. Gasps were audible as the chariots appeared to race around the walls; then there was a spontaneous burst of clapping. Studying the faces of his own party, Yannis was not at all sure of their reactions, the light distorted their features; one minute they were smiling and the next they appeared to be grimacing. Loud music was coming from the speakers and before they had finished their bottle of wine couples were up and dancing.

Dora looked at Yannis. 'Is it all right for them to dance like that? The men and women together? It doesn't seem quite decent somehow.'

Yannis smiled. 'It's the fashion. What do you think of it?'

'It doesn't seem right to me.' Dora shook her head.

'I meant the décor.'

'Oh, it's incredible. I've never seen anything like it. How is it done?'

'It's to do with electricity and mirrors. What do you think, Orestis?'

'I think Mr Giovanni is going to cause a sensation. This nightclub will be the most famous in the whole of Athens. I'm sure that after tonight he'll be turning customers away.'

Yannis nodded. 'I think so too.' He kicked himself. He should have agreed to go along with the boy in the first place. That way he would have been the controlling interest, not just the landlord.

Each night Giovanni's nightclub was full. No longer did he need to offer a bottle of wine as an inducement. Word had gone around the city that there was only one place to spend the evening.

'So what do you plan to do now?' asked Yannis. 'It's obviously a success, but who's going to run it whilst you're in Heraklion?'

'I've asked Nicolas.'

'Nicolas! But he's a teacher.'

'I know, and a pretty dissatisfied one at that. I though it better to keep control within the family if possible.'

'If you were to get married there might be a chance of that in the future.'

'When I'm ready.'

'There's that receptionist upstairs who obviously finds you attractive.'

'She's only got her eye to the main chance. Thinks if she married me she could lord it over everyone and spend money like water. Nearly every month she has to ask Orestis for an advance on her wages.'

'And does he give it to her?'

'Yes, then she has to work overtime to make it up.'

'Do we need more staff on reception?' asked Yannis.

'No. We have four full-time and a trainee. If we had any more we'd have to cut their working hours and their wages otherwise they'd spend too much time being idle. Orestis has it all worked out. He's good at organisation and figures. He's also good with Aunt Dora.'

'I know, and I'm grateful. Don't look so doubtful, Giovanni. I'm sure his attention to her is no more than fulfilling his undertaking to me. How does she appear to be bearing up to you?'

'Better than I thought she would when you first spoke to me.'

'It may have halted, of course. The doctor said it could. I must make sure she has another check up before we go back to Heraklion, just to be on the safe side.'

'I hope she appreciates how good you are to her, uncle. After all, she's only a relative because she married your uncle.'

Yannis shot Giovanni a quick glance. Was there something more behind the boy's remark? 'She has no one else,' he reminded his nephew.

The doctor examined Dora thoroughly and pronounced himself pleased with her condition. 'You're doing very well. The deterioration appears to have slowed. I did think by now you could be completely crippled.'

'So did I – or worse.'

'You're taking your medication in the correct dosage?'

'Of course.'

'Then we'll leave it like that for a couple more months.'

'Aren't you going to take X-rays and tests like you did before?' asked Yannis.

'I see little point. There does not appear to be any marked change for the worse, so there would be little useful information gained from spending the time and money.'

'Money is no problem,' Yannis assured him.

'I'm pleased to hear it. With so many people it is, of course. No, leave things as they are at present. I've prescribed some painkillers to help you sleep. I imagine some nights you have considerable pain.'

Dora smiled at him gratefully. 'I hoped you would give me something. I don't like to make a fuss.'

'You make as much fuss as you like.' The doctor patted her gently on the back. 'If all my patients complained as little as you I'd be a happy man.'

'Elizabeth, I really cannot play any more. I'm exhausted.' Marianne sank down on the grassy bank and Elizabeth joined her, grinning widely.

'I'm not even out of breath yet.'

'You're in training. I only agreed to play a couple of games for pleasure!'

'Actually your game's improved tremendously since you've been playing with me.'

'I've also lost nearly a stone in weight!'

'Then it shows it's done you good. It's a pity Bob and Colin are both working now. You mark my words, give them five years and they'll look like middle-aged men with paunches. All they do is sit at their desks and munch sandwiches at lunch time.'

'I shall be doing the same in another week.' Marianne frowned at the thought.

'You're definitely going back, then?'

Marianne nodded. 'I'll go back for another year and try for my Masters. If I do well it should help me to gain a place at an English university and I can study international law.'

'And what about Bob?'

'What about him?'

'I thought you two had an understanding?'

'We do.' Marianne smiled grimly. 'He understands that I'm a career woman.'

'Oh, I thought…'

'I know what you thought, the same as everyone else, that as soon as I got my degree I would marry him. I want to do something with my life before I get tied to the kitchen sink with children hanging on my skirt.'

'You wouldn't need to have children straight away.'

'Granted, but it wouldn't be very fair to marry Bob and then announce that I'm off to England for a couple of years or more. No,' Marianne shook her head. 'It's better to leave things as they are.'

'I shall miss you. I'll have no one to thrash at tennis.'

Marianne smiled. 'You'll be starting on the circuit in a few weeks. You'll be doing plenty of thrashing then.'

'That's different. You can't practise with them like I can with you.' Elizabeth leaned back, her hands behind her head. 'If I manage to get to Wimbledon when you're in England I could look you up.'

'I may not be in London.'

'So what? England's a tiny place. You won't be far away.'

Giovanni made the trip down to Aghios Nikolaos and sought out his aunt and uncle. Yannis frowned. What was Giovanni after that had necessitated a drive down from Heraklion? They usually communicated by telephone or met when he visited the hotels in the town.

'This is an unexpected pleasure. What's brought you down to visit us?'

'I wondered how your house was going?'

Yannis glanced at him sourly. The footings had been dug and that was the extent of his new house. The land was his, but he saw no prospect of continuing with the building until the New Year at the earliest.

'I'm waiting for the end of year accounts. Then I'll have an idea how much surplus cash I have.'

Giovanni nodded. 'Very wise. Maybe you'd like to add this to it?' He handed his uncle a thick roll of notes.

'What's this?'

'The arrears of rent, and the next month's in advance. It's all there, but you're welcome to check it.'

Yannis looked at the notes in disbelief. 'Have you paid back your bank loan?'

'Not yet. I'm up to date with the repayments, but they can wait for the balance. That's a business arrangement, yours was a favour.'

Yannis pushed the money deep into his pocket. 'I appreciate it, Giovanni. I have only myself to blame for not listening to you in the first place. If I had, I'd be making the money, not you.'

Giovanni grinned. 'You're still getting your rent every month and it's money for nothing to you. No worries, no overheads, no staff problems. Just hold out your hand and I'll give it to you.'

'Have you got problems?'

'Nothing that I can't handle. I need an assistant manager for the nightclub – Nicolas can't be expected to be there every night of the week and cope with the paper work. Orestis has promised to keep his eyes open for someone suitable. When he gives me the word I'll go over and sound him out.'

Yannis frowned. 'Doesn't Nicolas know anyone?'

'He doesn't appear to. Don't worry. I'm sure I'll find someone soon. How's my favourite aunt?'

'I'm fine, Giovanni. Are you going to stay for lunch?'

Giovanni consulted his watch. 'I'd love to. How are Anna and Yiorgo? I thought I might run over and see them whilst I'm down here.'

'I'm going out myself after lunch. You could come with me, save using your car.'

Dora climbed the stairs to her apartment painfully. The lift had been out of order for a week. Once inside she eased off her shoes and sat in the armchair to rest. Maybe she was foolish not to move all her belongings to the hotel, but there could come a day when Yannis no longer wished to have her there and it would be such a trouble to bring everything back. She would have coffee before deciding which clothes she would take back with her this week. The summer was nearly over and she would be wearing her warmer dresses with cardigans very soon.

Her hip was painful today and the stairs had not helped. She would take a tablet with her coffee; then she would feel better. Finally she rose and flicked at the furniture with a duster. She would not bother to vacuum. It was much too hot and stuffy. She opened the window and looked down on the peaceful street below. It was far too quiet for her now after the bustle of the hotel.

She placed three dresses and two cardigans into a small case and tested the weight. That would be more than enough to carry down the stairs. She placed it by the door and returned to her chair. Another rest, another coffee, then she would be on her way. If only the nagging pain in her hip would stop. She swallowed another painkiller and eased herself forwards. She should not really complain, most of the time she was fine, today was just an 'off' day.

As she bent for her case her hip felt as if it were on fire, so vicious was the pain. Leaning heavily on her stick she placed the case outside the front door and turned and locked it behind her. Now for the stairs.

She hooked her stick and handbag over her arm and lifted the case, the other hand holding the rail. Almost half way down she remembered the window was still open and with a sigh she realised she would have to go back.

Somehow, as she turned, the stick became entangled between her legs, the case throwing her off balance. Wildly she groped to regain her hold on the hand rail before she fell, bumping and bruising herself on every step until she reached the small landing.

For a long while she lay still, then consciousness returned with a pounding in her head. She opened her eyes; then closed them again against the bright lights that seemed to be piercing her skull from all directions. Vaguely she acknowledged that she must move. She could not stay there all night.

Her eyes still closed she made an effort to sit up. As she tried to move her right arm it did not respond. She steeled herself to open her eyes and saw it hanging limply by her side. She must have broken it during her fall. Still struggling to sit up, her hip sent a shaft of pain through her that made her gasp and beads of sweat stood out on her forehead. There was no choice left to her, she would have to stay where she was until help came.

The concrete was hard and cold and with her left hand she tried to reach her case. If she could retrieve her clothing she could at least cover herself and be a little warmer. Had she been able to use her right arm she could have reached it easily, but short of rolling onto her right side, and any movement was impossible due to the pain in her hip, the case was inaccessible.

She felt for her handbag, at least her painkillers were in there and if she took another she might be able to move a little. Raising herself on her left arm she was able to see her bag, the clasp had opened on impact and the contents had spilled out. With a sigh of pain and impatience she lay back and closed her eyes. She would have to wait until the people who lived in the apartment below returned home.

Yannis and Giovanni returned to find Ourania waiting for them anxiously.

'Orestis 'phoned. I tried to reach you at the farm, but Anna said you had just left. He wants you to telephone him urgently.'

Yannis frowned. 'Is it the hotel?'

Ourania shook her head. 'It's Dora. He said she's in hospital.'

Yannis tapped his fingers impatiently as he waited for his call to be connected. Ourania and Giovanni listening to the one sided conversation could make out very little. Finally Yannis replaced the receiver.

'You'd better come with me, 'Rani. It doesn't sound very good.'

'What's happened?'

'According to Orestis she went to her apartment to collect some clothes. She had a fall on the stairs and lay there all night.'

'How does he know?'

'He found her this morning. When she didn't go down to breakfast he went to enquire about her. She'd obviously not been in all night so he rang her apartment. There was no answer so he took a taxi over there. He found her half frozen and in terrible pain.'

Ourania's face was full of consternation. 'Give me five minutes to pack a case.' Without waiting for Yannis to answer she left the shop and went to their apartment above.

'What would you like me to do?' asked Giovanni.

'You stay in Heraklion. Deal with any problems that might arise. If Dora looks like being in hospital for any length of time Ourania will have to stay over. Call Anna whilst I close up the shop. We must catch that ferry.'

Yannis drove straight to the hospital and asked for his aunt. The doctor shook his head sadly.

'I think, maybe, first it would be better for us to talk.'

'She's still alive?'

'Oh, yes, but I'd like to speak to you before you go to see her.'

Yannis and Ourania followed him into a small side room where he offered them seats. He pulled a sheaf of papers towards him.

'If I can just check some details with you.'

'You have all her details. She's been coming for check ups.'

'I mean the circumstances of her fall – and the results.'

'I know nothing about her fall,' Yannis answered impatiently. 'I had a telephone call from my hotel manager to say he'd found her and she was in hospital.'

'Why should your hotel manager concern himself with the whereabouts of your aunt?'

Yannis sighed. 'My aunt has an apartment, but since the death of her husband I wasn't happy about her living there alone. She lived in my hotel in Athens and my partner kept an eye on her welfare.'

'I see.' The doctor scanned the papers in front of him. 'When she was admitted she had a broken arm which we have set, but her pelvis…' The doctor shrugged. 'There is nothing we can do except keep her comfortable.'

'What do you mean? Has she broken her hip?'

'According to the X-rays we have taken her pelvis on the right side is shattered. This is obviously due to the deterioration that has taken place over the years due to her condition. There is no way we can pin it and hope for it to mend.'

'So she's going to be in a wheelchair?'

'I think it unlikely.' The doctor regarded them sympathetically. 'You have to understand that she is an elderly lady who has not enjoyed good health for a long time now. She spent the night on a cold concrete floor suffering from shock and in great pain. Pneumonia has already set in.'

'You mean she's dying?' Yannis's voice was harsh.

'I am not expecting her to rally.'

Ourania gulped and gave a little sob. 'Poor aunt Dora.'

'Can we see her? Is she conscious?'

The doctor nodded. 'Of course. I just wanted you to be prepared.'

Yannis and Ourania left the hospital sombrely.

'I'm so glad we arrived in time.' Ourania spoke quietly through her tears.

Yannis nodded. 'It was better that she died quickly than spent years in a wheelchair and watching herself disintegrate. I'll telephone Daphne when we get to the hotel. Then I suppose I'll have to arrange for her funeral. I hope she left her affairs in order.' Yannis frowned. 'I never thought to ask her.'

Ourania shrugged. 'You're her closest relative, there should be no problem.'

'Elena and Nicolas are as closely related as I am. There could be problems if she hasn't left any instructions. We'll go to the flat later and see if we can find the address of a solicitor.'

Ourania nodded. She knew she could leave everything in the capable hands of her husband.

The solicitor cleared his throat and looked at the man and woman in front of him before opening the envelope.

'I won't read the whole of it, just tell you the salient points. I can give you copies to take away with you. Now, as I understand from Mrs Christoforakis she owned the apartment after the death of her husband. The property has been left to Mr Yannis Andronicatis and Mr Orestis Lekkas.

There is rather a strange clause here, but I can assure you it is legal. Mr Andronicatis is left two thirds of the apartment, the other third is left to Mr Lekkas who is instructed to sell his share to Mr Andronicatis to clear his outstanding loan on the hotel, thus leaving Mr Andronicatis as the outright owner of the apartment and Mr Lekkas a full partner in the hotel.' The solicitor peered at Yannis above his glasses. 'Is that clear to you?'

A slow smile spread across Yannis's face. 'I knew she had a soft spot for him. Does Mr Lekkas know about this?'

The solicitor shrugged. 'Mrs Christoforakis may have told him of her intentions. She asked for it to be recorded that it was in appreciation of his kindness to her. She has left a small sum of money to her niece, Elena Christoforakis, in recognition of her secretarial services, which she gave freely, and the rest of the estate and royalties from her late husband's book passes to yourself.'

The solicitor looked at Ourania. 'I am afraid you are not mentioned, madam.'

'Are you sure you want to go to England?' asked Bob. 'I'd have thought you would have had enough of swotting and exams by now.'

'I'm a career woman,' Marianne hugged her knees and spoke seriously. 'I want to finish my education and know that I can have a good job. I want the kind of qualifications that I can fall back on for ever. I know Helena is very happy at the moment, but will it last? Although she finished her college course, she only graduated as a computer analyst. She didn't apply for a job, she has no experience. If her marriage goes sour and she has to earn her own living she'll be hopelessly out of date. Her present qualifications will count for nothing.'

'Why should her marriage go wrong? They seem very happy and they'd dated for years.'

'You never know. My aunt Maria was only married for two years before she was widowed. My aunt Anna was married for ten years; then she had a divorce.'

Bob snorted derisively. 'From what I've hard about your aunt Anna…'

Marianne frowned. 'It may not have been all her fault.'

'Well, I can't see that it was her husband's!' Bob hugged her to him. 'You're just too nice natured. What do you fancy doing tonight – disco or movie?'

'I'll leave it to you.'

'I'll ask Dad if I can borrow the car, then we could go to a drive-in.'

'You ought to get a car of your own.'

'No point. All the time I can borrow his I'm saving a packet. I put the gas in, so he doesn't complain.' Bob tilted Marianne's chin upwards. 'Cheer up. I'll still be here when you decide you're ready to settle down.'

1986

Elizabeth wrote regularly to Marianne, exulting when she had done well in a match and expressing despair and a wish to return to America when she had failed to live up to her coach's expectations. Marianne replied to each letter with alacrity, never sure if her friend would receive it before she moved on to her next venue. It was almost a relief when Elizabeth declared her intention of spending some time with her in Oxford after playing at Wimbledon.

Now they sat on Elizabeth's bed in a small hotel and gossiped as if they had never been apart.

'You should have visited me in Paris. You've never seen anything like it back home. I went to the Moulin Rouge.'

'I thought you were supposed to go to bed early and save your strength.'

'I had four days without a match and I managed to persuade my coach that I should see something of the city. He only agreed on condition that he came with me.'

'Crafty devil.'

'Not really. He could have gone anywhere he wished. All he had to do was turn up for my practice each day.'

'Does he fancy you?'

Elizabeth pulled a face. 'I hope not! He's fifty if he's a day – and married.'

'Isn't there some glamorous tennis star who wants to date you?'

'Two or three have dated me. The trouble is we've nothing to talk about except tennis. We not only bore other people, we bore each other as well. What about you? Who are you seeing?'

Marianne shrugged. 'No one in particular. I tend to go around in a group. We go to concerts and parties together, but we don't often pair off.'

'Has Bob written to you?'

'He owes me a letter.'

'He owes me a dozen! His excuse is that if I move on and don't get it he's wasted his time. What makes him think his time's so precious? All he does is sit behind a desk each day. I bet he'll look like a stuffed pig when I get home.'

'When are you going home?'

'Anxious to be rid of me? I only arrived yesterday.'

Marianne shook her head. 'Not a bit. I just feel you'll be bored to tears here.'

'Why stay here? The world is our oyster, well, Europe anyway.'

'It may be yours, but I have to budget. It cost Dad a small fortune to send me to England.' Marianne's brow puckered. 'It's a good job I was able to work at weekends.'

'Your dad gives you an allowance, doesn't he?'

'He's been very generous, but my books have cost a mint. Everyone else seemed to find them in second hand shops, but I had to buy new ones. I have a feeling they saw me coming.'

Elizabeth looked at her friend in concern. 'Are you really broke?'

'Not at all, and I know if I were I could ask Dad to cable me some money. I just don't feel I should throw money away on an expensive vacation. There might be a time when I really need it.'

'Would you have enough to come on holiday with me?'

'That would depend where you were thinking of going.'

'I'm not talking about anything extravagant. Just to Europe. I suddenly thought about it on the train up here. If I don't come up to scratch for next season I might never get the chance again and nor might you once you get back home.' Elizabeth crossed her legs beneath her. 'What about a railcard? We can both get them pretty cheap, you're a student and I'm under the age limit. Provided we keep travelling in the same direction we can go just about anywhere. We could camp or go for bed and breakfast; it doesn't have to be the best hotels. It would be fun, Marianne.'

'Would your parents let you?'

'Of course. It's only when I'm on the circuits I have to be chaperoned. There's always some mad man about who threatens to harm you if you beat the girl he's fallen in love with. Off the courts not many people recognise me. Whilst you're doing your silly exam tomorrow I'll find out the details. Just think, this time next week we could be anywhere.'

The train sped down the track for over an hour; then halted. Marianne stuck her head cautiously out of the window.

'We seem to be in the middle of nowhere.'

'I expect we're waiting for another train to pass us.'

'I can't see anything.'

'Come and sit down. It could be an express.'

Marianne resumed her seat and began to rummage in her rucksack. 'I'll write up my diary. I haven't touched it for three days.'

Elizabeth shrugged. 'I never understand why people bother to keep diaries.'

'I want to remember where we've been. I might never get the chance to come again. I don't get free trips all over Europe like some people.'

Elizabeth pulled a wry face. 'If you call spending six hours a day practising worth it. This is the first proper holiday I've had in months. I'm really looking forward to Greece. It's almost the only place I haven't visited. Are you going to telephone your grandmother and ask her the address of your relative's hotel?'

Marianne nodded. 'Maybe we could stay there and not tell them who I am until we leave,' she grinned mischievously.

'What's the point of that?'

'Well, it could be a bit difficult if I told them when we booked in. They might think we expected to stay for nothing and I'd feel really bad about that. It would be taking advantage.'

'It's up to you, they're your relatives.'

'But I don't even know them. Grandmother's cousin writes to her about twice a year and she visited Crete a few years back, but she doesn't know the ones who have the hotel.'

'Odd. I would have thought families would have wanted to keep in touch.'

'They do. When anything happens to my grandmother my mother will write to this cousin and when anything happens to her there's a niece who will write and let mother know.' Marianne searched for her pen. 'Now, where were we three days ago?

'Just entering Yugoslavia. I'd like to stay there a while on the way back. Dubrovnik looked fascinating.'

'We can. Once we've stayed our time in Greece we can start moving back towards England. We'll know how long we have and can plan accordingly.'

Marianne and Elizabeth wandered through the narrow streets that made up the Plaka district, revelling in the variety of colour, fending off the overtures of the local shopkeepers and the young men who propositioned them.

'I really feel I'm on holiday now,' remarked Elizabeth. 'All the time we were on the trains I kept expecting to wake up and find I had a match. Oh, look at the jewellery in that shop. Work out for me how much that necklace would be in dollars.'

Marianne obliged; then dragged her friend from the window. 'If you buy now you'll have no money for anything else. Besides, you don't know how good it is. If we can track down my relatives they could probably take us to a reputable shop and you'll get a guarantee.'

Reluctantly Elizabeth agreed. 'Find a telephone and ring home.'

Marianne shook her head. 'We have to go to the post office. There are very few kiosks with international lines.'

'Where is the post office? All I keep seeing are those little yellow boxes.'

'You've got the map.'

'Let's find a taverna; then we can plan our moves.'

They pored over the map together, finally deciding they would have to return towards the centre of Athens.

'Where you wish to visit?' The waiter looked over their shoulders as he placed their ice creams on the table.

'The post office.'

'Buy stamps from kiosk.'

Marianne smiled. 'I want to make an international telephone call.'

'I have telephone.'

Elizabeth's eyes sparkled. 'Could we use it? We need to find the address of some relatives who live in Athens.'

The waiter raised his eyebrows. 'You lost address? You need a bed to stay?'

'We have booked into a hotel. We just want to look up some members of my family who live here. I need to telephone my grandmother in America.'

'Please,' the waiter waved his hand. 'Use telephone when ready.'

'That's very kind of you. We'll pay for the call, of course.'

He nodded and placed their bill on the table. They would have to pay as it was in his back room and they would be unable to leave without him seeing.

The call took longer to place than Marianne had expected, although she spoke Greek to the operator in Athens. Twice the telephone appeared to connect and ring, then the line went dead. She sighed in exasperation.

'I'll have one more try, then book a call at the post office.' She dialled carefully and was rewarded with a constant ringing tone and finally the voice of her grandmother.

'What's wrong, Marianne?'

'Nothing at all. We're fine. We're in Athens and I remembered you said we had relatives here. I thought I'd like to look them up. Do you have their address?'

'Not really. Only the name of the hotel.'

'That would do. I expect we'd find it.'

'You can try. It's in the Plaka area. That's down by the Acropolis.'

'That's where we are now. It's probably round the corner from us. What's the name?'

'Athenia De Luxe.'

'Wow! I wonder if it is! Thanks. Give my love to everyone. We'll be sending postcards. Look after yourself.' Marianne replaced the receiver and let out her breath. 'Athenia De Luxe! How does that grab you? If it is de luxe we certainly can't afford to stay there.'

'It's probably a grotty bed and breakfast that we wouldn't want to stay in.'

'We'll have a look for it. It's around here.'

'We could ask the waiter.'

Marianne shook her head. 'Only if we can't find it. He might know them and it could be embarrassing.' The telephone shrilled and Marianne lifted the receiver to hear the price of her call. 'I shan't do that too often!' She took the drachmas from her purse and they returned to the sunlight where the waiter was leaning against the doorway. He greeted them with a smile.

'You find?'

'Yes, thank you. Here's the money.' She handed him the notes, then spoke rapidly in Greek. 'It is correct. I asked the operator for the charge to be relayed to me.'

His mouth fell open. 'You speak Greek?'

Marianne laughed. 'I am Greek – nearly. We'll come back another day and sample your cooking. Thank you for the use of your 'phone.'

Without counting the money he thrust it into his back pocket. 'I will make a special meal for you. You tell me all about America. One day I shall go there.'

'It's a deal.' Marianne waved her hand and steered Elizabeth away.

'What was that all about?'

'He wants us to go back and have a meal there so we can tell him all about America. Maybe we could go later in the week.'

'Maybe.' Elizabeth did not sound so certain. 'Where now?'

'To look for the Athenia De Luxe.'

Elizabeth trailed along in the wake of her friend. She felt at a distinct disadvantage. Marianne appeared to be so at home amongst the bustling Athenians, smiling at snatches of conversation and reading the road names with ease. They walked for over an hour through the narrow, winding streets, crammed with gift shops, tavernas and cafes, yet saw no sign of the hotel they were looking for.

'Couldn't we ask someone? We could be going miles out of our way – and I'm hot,' complained Elizabeth.

'We'll have a drink. Do you want to give up for today? There's no immediate rush. If I don't like the look of the place I might not even make myself known. I can always tell my grandmother I couldn't find them.'

Elizabeth sank gratefully into a chair. 'I'd like an iced coffee and one of those sticky looking cakes.'

'You'll get fat.'

'I don't care. I'll work it off as soon as I get back into training.'

They sat and watched as more visitors began to fill the eating places in the square. A boy with a basket of roses was going from table to table trying to persuade people to buy one before he was chased away by the waiters.

'Are they beggars?' asked Elizabeth.

'Probably gypsies. Just tell them to go away.'

'You tell them. They'll understand you.'

'They'll understand you just as well. Have you noticed how everyone seems able to speak the English language? If I asked a road sweeper for directions I expect he would be able to tell me.'

Elizabeth nodded. 'I feel a bit of a dumb cluck. You're all right, though.'

'I was brought up speaking Greek at home. We are Greek so we should speak our native tongue.'

'Do you still feel as Greek as you used to?'

Marianne nodded. 'I think I always will.'

'You're an odd ball. Mind you, all your family are. Must be the Greek in you.'

'No, I'm not,' frowned Marianne.

'In my book you are, but I like you, just the same. Sometimes you're so prim and well behaved it just isn't true, then when I see you at a party you're the most abandoned person there.'

Marianne shrugged. 'I believe in enjoying myself. Are we going to a disco tonight?'

'Are nicely brought up Greek girls allowed to go to discos without a chaperone?'

'You can be my chaperone, and besides, we're on holiday. Have you finished? We could walk back round to the main road and get to our hotel that way.'

Elizabeth nodded. 'I could certainly do with a shower.'

They walked through more narrow streets until finally arriving at the square where they gazed in awe at the cathedral.

'Shall we go in?'

'We're not properly dressed for church,' Marianne looked down at her legs poking from beneath her shorts. 'Let's leave it for another day.'

Unhurriedly they strolled up the road, looking into the fashionable clothes shops and calculating the cost in dollars.

'What does that say?' asked Elizabeth.

'It's only advertising. *The most unusual nightclub in the world. Come and see the chariot racing and gladiators fighting to the death whilst you dance and enjoy yourself'*, she read. 'I bet!'

'Where is it?'

Marianne studied the map, tracing the roads with her fingernail. 'Just round the corner from here. Shall we give it a go later?'

'Could do. We don't have to stay once the gladiators are dead.'

'I expect they have some fake floor show. It says the spectacle starts at ten, so we could eat first.' Marianne giggled. 'We might not feel like it afterwards with dead bodies all over the place.'

'Maybe we could ask someone at the hotel what it's like. We don't want to pay a fortune for rubbish.'

'Who do you suggest we ask? The grumpy old man on the desk or the half-witted girl who showed us up to our room?'

Elizabeth pulled a face. 'Maybe we could ask at the taverna where we eat. What are you planning to wear?'

Marianne and Elizabeth looked in apprehension at the entrance to the nightclub. It looked most unprepossessing from outside, being at the back of a large hotel and obviously situated in the basement.

'Do you think it's all right?' asked Elizabeth nervously.

Marianne shrugged. 'It should be. They spoke highly of it at the taverna. Said it was an experience not to be missed.'

'That could mean anything,' Elizabeth replied sceptically. 'You won't leave me alone, will you? Remember I don't speak a word of the language.'

'I won't leave you. You'd be safe enough, anyway.'

'I'm not so sure of that. How much do we need to get in?'

Marianne dug in her purse. 'Leave it with me. There might be a reduced charge for the natives.' She smiled sweetly at the cashier and spoke in Greek. The cashier shook her head and Marianne handed over the notes. 'It was worth a try. There are no reductions.'

Once inside, the short passage was brightly lit and they walked through the open doors into a plain room. Few people were there, mostly sitting at tables in small groups.

'Table or bar?' asked Elizabeth.

'Bar,' Marianne decided promptly. 'At least you get to speak to the bar tender. If we sit at a table we'll spend the whole evening looking at each other.' She slid onto one of the high leather stools and smiled at her companion. 'No, I'm not trying to pick anyone up. I just enjoy talking my own language after a year of nothing but English to assault my ear drums.'

She ordered ouzo for each of them and asked what time the floorshow started.

'There is no floor show tonight.'

'It was advertised,' protested Marianne. 'On a leaflet, it said there was chariot racing and gladiators.'

The bar tender grinned. 'That is not a floor show. That is the special effects.' He looked at his watch. 'About another twenty minutes. The manager will arrive and the show will start.'

'Why do we have to wait for him?'

'He's always in charge of the showing. Until he arrives people sit and drink and chat.'

'Fine. We could have saved our entrance money sat and chatted at a taverna.'

'But then you would miss the excitement, the thrill, the spectacle.'

'All I can say is that it had better be worth it!'

The bar tender grinned again and left her to serve another customer, whilst she turned to Elizabeth.

'He says it starts in about twenty minutes, when the manager arrives, and it's not a floor show, it's special effects.'

'What does that mean?'

'Search me. I suppose we'll just have to wait and see.'

The time dragged, there was nothing to look at and the bar tender became too busy to chat as more people entered and filled the tables or sat at the bar. At exactly ten, a man entered and closed the doors behind him. He strolled over to the bar and lifted the microphone.

'Good evening ladies and gentlemen,' he said in Greek. 'I should like to welcome old friends and new visitors to the most spectacular nightclub show you are ever likely to see. Feel free to dance the night away and enjoy yourselves.' He gave his audience a dazzling smile and repeated his speech in English, French and German.

'Nothing, if not versatile,' murmured Marianne.

'He's probably memorised it and doesn't really know what he's saying,' replied Elizabeth more loudly than she had intended.

The room was plunged into darkness, taking both girls by surprise; then they gasped. The sound of horses, chariot wheels and the cries of the riders seemed to be all around them. Elizabeth clutched at Marianne; then drew in her breath sharply. The walls had become alive with figures, charging chariots, the horses straining under the whips of their masters. Music became discernible in the background, gradually overtaking the noise of the race, which was deliberately muted, and almost immediately couples were up and dancing.

'Wow!' Marianne let out her breath.

Elizabeth relaxed back on her stool and took a sip from her drink. 'They'll never believe this back home.'

'And where is home, madam? I have not remembered my little speech. I speak English and French quite good and my German will get better.'

Elizabeth flushed in the darkness. 'I didn't mean you to hear.'

'I have the good ears. You would like to dance?'

'I thought you had to be here to run the show, not to enjoy it.'

'I am here to run and also to entertain.'

Elizabeth gave a slight shrug and raised her eyebrows at Marianne as she slipped off her stool and was led towards the dance floor.

Marianne watched the spectacle, fascinated and bemused. It was horrific, barbaric, yet stimulating. She felt restless and looked around hoping to catch the eye of an unattached young man, but the tables were deserted.

'You wish to dance?' asked the bartender.

'This music is certainly making me want to.'

'Then dance. Everyone dances, they do not have partners, there's no need. They just dance for pleasure.'

Marianne dragged her eyes from the walls and looked at the dance floor. The bartender had spoken truly. Few couples were actually dancing together, everyone appeared to be gyrating in their own little world. Self-consciously she joined them, finding herself moving amongst them with a smile and greeting until the music slowed, the horses doing the same, with their flanks heaving and their nostrils blowing.

She went to return to the bar only to feel her hand taken by a young man.

'Please, the next dance.'

Marianne smiled. 'If you wish,' she replied in Greek.

A look of relief came over the young man's face. 'You speak Greek?'

'I am Greek, although I live in America.'

'America, I want to go to America.'

'Everyone I meet wants to go there. What's the attraction?'

Marianne allowed him to guide her around the small dance floor whilst the walls were suffused with subdued colours and slow romantic music was played. The young man who held her in his arms was telling her of his plans and ambitions, yet he seemed unreal. She made an effort to concentrate and reply to his questions, excusing herself as the music changed and returning to her seat at the bar. She sat and watched as Elizabeth continued to dance with the manager, smiling and chatting happily until the music was almost at an end, when he came hurriedly over and flicked switches behind the bar. She watched, fascinated as the scene changed and Greeks in togas wandered amongst the Parthenon buildings and the gardens of the Agora. The pictures faded with a dream-like quality and Marianne blinked, unsure that she had really seen them a moment earlier.

Elizabeth returned and slipped onto the stool beside her. 'Isn't it fantastic?'

Marianne nodded. 'I feel quite light-headed.'

'That's probably the ouzo.'

'Who's your friend?'

'His name is Nicolas. He's the manager.'

Marianne nodded absently and sipped at her drink. The pictures were changing again.

Marianne slept late that morning and awoke to find herself alone in the room, a note from Elizabeth left on the dressing table.

'Gone to meet Nicolas. See you here for lunch.'

Marianne raised her eyebrows and yawned. She looked at her watch and was horrified to find it was already eleven. She was far too late for breakfast. She showered quickly and left the room. If she went to the café across the road she could have coffee and a roll and also see when Elizabeth returned. She bought a newspaper from the kiosk on the corner and attempted the crossword.

'Hi.'

'Hi yourself. Where've you been?'

'Nicolas took me for a drive. We went down to Piraeus.'

'Interesting?'

'Fairly. No different from any other large port.'

'And Nicolas?'

'Very interesting.'

Marianne raised her eyebrows. 'Tell me more.'

'Well, he used to be a school teacher, then his cousin opened up the nightclub and asked him to be the manager.'

'Why doesn't the cousin manage it himself?'

'He's too busy, apparently. Anyway, Nicolas loves the job.' Elizabeth reddened. 'I've told him we'll be there again tonight. You don't mind, do you?'

Marianne shrugged. 'Can we afford it?'

'We'll go in with him, so all we have to do is buy our drinks.'

'That's all right by me. What do you want to do this afternoon?'

The week passed rapidly for both the girls. Each day Nicolas took them out in his car to visit the nearest historical sites at Elizabeth's request. He had been somewhat surprised to find her so interested in the history of his country and finally she confessed that it was Marianne who had the interest.

'You should have told me earlier. I could have arranged for someone from the university to come with us. I will see if he is free tomorrow and we will go to Epidaurus.'

'What's at Epidaurus?'

'A theatre. Also the shrine of Asklepios. You will like it very much.'

Elizabeth smiled vaguely. She had enjoyed their visits to Corinth, Cape Sounion and the Acropolis, but she was not sure if she could sustain interest in the ancient site if a lecturer accompanied them and most of the dialogue was in Greek.

'When you have seen enough we can visit Nauplion and meet Marianne and Theo later.'

Still Elizabeth looked dubious.

'You will be quite safe with me, I promise. Give them their day and I will take you to Hydra on Saturday. Hydra you will love. It is the most romantic of islands.'

Elizabeth smiled. It would be churlish of her to refuse when he was obviously trying very hard to please them both.

The hydrofoil skimmed lightly over the water and eventually Hydra came into view, making both girls catch their breath.

'It's wonderful,' breathed Elizabeth.

'Everyone loves Hydra. It is one of our most beautiful islands. Everyone comes to paint here. We will climb to the top and also walk around. Today will be the day you remember.'

Elizabeth felt unaccountably sad at his words. She tried to brush the feeling aside. Maybe Marianne wanted to stay a few more days before they began their return trip. Her own desire to visit Dubrovnik had waned. She would rather stay here, and she was forced to admit, it was the company of Nicolas that added to the attraction.

'Many people come here to spend their honeymoon,' he was saying and she felt herself blushing for no reason. 'First we will have coffee; then we will walk. I have not been here for many years, so for me it will be almost new.'

The steepness of the winding roads made them breathless and their legs were aching by the time they reached the highest point of the island and were able to look over the collection of roofs to the bay below. Nicolas put his arm round Elizabeth's shoulders and turned her towards the side.

'Over there, you can just see, is another island. It is the nearest land if you have to swim.'

'Why should I have to swim?' asked Elizabeth, puzzled.

'Who knows? Maybe we have an earthquake or maybe the hydrofoil breaks down. You should know where land is.'

'Don't be silly, Nicolas.'

'Earthquakes do not always affect the land and you can be floundering in very deep water.' He looked down at her. 'I feel I could be drowning, but I do not know which way to swim to reach the land.'

Elizabeth dropped her eyes, unsure of the meaning behind his words. Her mouth felt dry and once again she felt close to tears.

'Is there anywhere up here we could get a drink?'

'Not here. We will have to go back down. We can have a drink, some food, then walk around, maybe find a secluded cove to sit.' He took Elizabeth's hand in his. 'You will find it steep as you go down,' he said. 'It is like falling in love, you start slowly, then find it happens faster and faster as you go.'

Instinctively Elizabeth gripped his hand a little tighter.

Marianne closed her eyes against the glare of the sun; then blinked rapidly. 'Nicolas, could we walk round to this cove you've talked about? I'm so sleepy that unless I lay down soon I shall fall asleep where I am.'

'If you have finished we will go.'

He led the way along by the side of the quay and round the promontory. The beach shelved inwards and there was a dried riverbed, small houses dotted around on the sides of each bank, well away from the level of the water.

'We can rest here.'

Marianne flopped down thankfully, pushed her bag beneath her head and closed her eyes. 'Wake me when it's time to leave.'

'Are you feeling all right?' Elizabeth looked at her friend in concern.

'I'm fine, just dead beat. I don't know how you're keeping going. We've been out half the night and you're still as lively as ever. Just give me an hour's sleep and I'll be fine.' She yawned hugely and settled her head more comfortably.

Elizabeth looked at Nicolas. 'Do you mind staying here for a while?'

'I do not mind. We can sit and talk.'

'What about?'

'You can tell me more about your life in America where you play tennis all the time.'

'I don't play all the time.'

'You tell me you play and each day you have to practice.'

'There is a difference. When I practise I do the same shot time and time again to try to get it perfect and it gets very boring.'

'Then why do you do it?'

'I want to get better. I need to win some major titles during the next two years or people will say I'm getting too old. Already girls who are younger than me are challenging hard. I could be lucky to last next season.' A note of seriousness had crept into Elizabeth's voice.

'What will you do when you no longer play matches?'

'I expect I'll become a coach. Most of the old players do. We trade on our past glories as long as we can, finally teaching middle aged rabbits how to hit a ball.'

Nicolas looked at her puzzled. 'Middle aged rabbits?'

'Middle aged people. We call them rabbits because they are no good at sport.'

'So I would be a rabbit?'

'Maybe. Are you good at sports?'

Nicolas shook his head. 'I never enjoy to run or jump.'

'You're a rabbit,' Elizabeth stated. 'What will you do eventually? You can't run a nightclub for ever.'

Nicolas shrugged. 'I could be a teacher again.'

'Would you want to do that?'

'No,' he admitted, 'but one cannot always do what one wants to do the most.'

'And what do you want to do most?'

'Kiss you.'

Elizabeth's eyes widened; then she laughed. 'You're not serious.'

'I am very serious. I want very much to kiss you. I want to kiss you the first night I meet you.'

'So why didn't you?'

'You would think bad things about me.'

'Why should I do that?'

'A man of my age who takes out a girl who is on holiday and begins to kiss her, she thinks he only wants one thing.'

'And you're different? Come here, you big rabbit.' Elizabeth stretched her arms round his neck and pulled his mouth down to meet hers.

Nicolas sat with his arm round Elizabeth. 'You like me, Elizabeth?'

'Of course I do. We've spent most of the week with you. We could have made excuses and moved on if we didn't like you.'

'Do you have to leave next week?'

Elizabeth nodded firmly. 'We do. I have to get back into training and Marianne has to be back at university.'

'You will come back?'

'I hope so, one day.'

'I mean, you will come back to see me?'

'If you're still at the night club of course I will.'

'No, to see me, especially to see me.'

'Nicolas, if I come back next year you'll probably wonder who I am. You must meet hundreds of girls.'

Nicolas shook his head. 'I meet hundreds of girls, yes, but only one girl I ask to come back and see me.'

'This is just a holiday romance, Nicolas.'

'I do not think so. For the first time I meet a girl who I feel comfortable with. I would like to spend more time with you, then you would see this not just a holiday romance.'

Elizabeth felt her heart fluttering. 'If I give you my address in America maybe you could visit me?'

'You would like me to do that?'

'Of course I would. You would only need your fare,' Elizabeth assured him.

'My parents would be only too happy to have you stay, that would cost you nothing.'

Nicolas frowned. 'No, that would not be right. I am not family.'

'You don't have to be family to come and stay with us.'

Nicolas looked at her. 'So you come and stay with my mamma and sister?'

'Oh, no,' Elizabeth shook her head. 'I couldn't do that. They don't know me.'

'So you understand how I feel?'

Elizabeth sighed. 'I suppose so. Do you think Marianne is going to sleep all afternoon? I'd like to go for a walk.'

'You could leave her a note to find when she awakes. She will be safe here.'

Elizabeth looked at him dubiously. 'No, anything might happen. She could be robbed, or even murdered.'

Nicolas laughed. 'You are in Greece, not America. Such things do not happen here. I will ask someone from the houses to watch over her. Will that make you happy?'

He scrambled to his feet and walked to the nearest house. Elizabeth saw a rapid interchange between the occupant and Nicolas, with smiles and nods and finally a handshake before he returned.

Nicolas pulled her to her feet. 'There is no need to leave a note. The woman will sit outside with her embroidery and when Marianne wakes she will tell her we are walking and will return.' He kissed Elizabeth on her forehead. 'There is much I want to say to you now, but I wish to be alone to say it.'

Marianne yawned and rubbed her eyes. She rolled over on her side to speak to Elizabeth and saw no sign of her. Surprised and a little annoyed she sat up and looked around. Surely they had not returned to Athens? She looked at her watch. It was after four and she was not sure at what time the hydrofoil left; maybe they had gone for a walk and forgotten the time? She rose to her feet and brushed herself down.

'Madam. Madam, please come up here. I have a message for you from your friends.'

Marianne looked in the direction of the voice and saw the woman sitting before her house, her embroidery spread on her knee. At least they had left a message. She climbed up the steep bank onto the path that ran up into the village and stood before the woman.

'Did my friends say where they were going?'

The woman nodded. 'They were going for a walk and would return in good time to catch the hydrofoil. If you are thirsty there is fruit juice in my fridge. Please go in and help yourself. I don't want to move until I've finished this tricky piece.'

Marianne looked at the shawl spread on the woman's knees. 'That is so beautiful.'

'I make ten or twelve a year. They are always my own design so you never see another exactly the same. I sell them in the shop down at the quay.'

'I admired them earlier. They have hundreds. They can't all be yours.'

'Most of us make them. Hydra is known for the beauty of her embroidery.' As she talked her needle passed in and out of the fine cloth deftly.

'I must buy one for my grandmother. How will I know if it is yours?'

'My initials are in the corner. E.A. No one else has those initials.'

'I'll remember,' promised Marianne. 'I will have a drink if you don't mind.'

'The door's open. Help yourself. You can bring one out for me at the same time.'

Elizabeth and Nicolas returned, strolling hand in hand along the beach and waved. Marianne took the empty glasses back into the kitchen and thanked the woman before she joined them.

'That was a dirty trick, going off and leaving me asleep. Where've you been?'

'Just walking,' replied Elizabeth vaguely.

Marianne gazed at her sharply, surprised by the dreamy look in her eyes and heightened colour. 'I'd like to buy a shawl before we return to Athens,' she announced.

'What for?'

'To take for my grandmother. She embroidered when she was a girl and her mother sold to the local shops. It will be a memento for her.'

'It will take time for you to choose. We have an hour before the hydrofoil, so you should return to the quay now.' Nicolas raised his hand to the woman who still sat at her needlework. 'I see she gave you the message I left.'

'She was very kind. Allowed me to help myself from her fridge to a fruit juice and we sat and chatted.'

Marianne managed to contain herself until they reached the privacy of their bedroom. 'Well?' she demanded. 'What's happened?'

'What do you mean? Nothing's happened.'

Marianne snorted. 'Don't give me that! You and Nicolas disappear off on a romantic island and come back holding hands and gazing into each other's eyes. You must think I was born yesterday.'

'You do like him, don't you, Marianne?'

'Yes, of course I do. He's good company and he's been very kind to us, taking us out and about. We've seen and done a lot more than if we'd just travelled on our own.'

'When do we have to go back?'

'We'd planned to start back in two days time. What do you have in mind?'

'Well, it was my idea to stop off in Dubrovnik for a few days. Maybe if we scrubbed that we could stay in Athens a bit longer?'

Marianne grinned. 'You could stay with Nicolas a bit longer, you mean. Beware of holiday romances. They're not what they seem.'

'That's what I said to Nicolas.'

'And?'

'He wants to visit me in America. We plan to write to each other.' Elizabeth sat down on her bed. 'I know it sounds like a holiday romance, but he says he's never bothered to ask a girl for her address before. No, don't look like that, I believe him.'

'More fool you, then. He's Greek, Elizabeth. All Greek men are charming until they've got what they want from you.'

'Don't be so sceptical. Nicolas isn't like that. We've talked a lot this afternoon.'

'I doubt if he'll even remember your name when you've been left a week.'

To Marianne's surprise Elizabeth's eyes filled with tears. 'Don't be so horrid.'

'Wow! You have got it badly. You won't do anything stupid, will you?'

'Like what?'

'Like deciding to stay and leaving me to go back on my own.'

Elizabeth shook her head. 'I'll have to go back, whether I want to or not.'

'And you don't want to?'

Elizabeth shook her head. 'You see, if I stayed we could really get to know each other, whereas being apart and writing could give us a distorted view and we could have a big let down when we met again.'

'You are serious, aren't you?'

Elizabeth nodded. 'I thought it was just me, then this afternoon Nicolas asked if he could kiss me, and we realised we both felt the same. Today has been the most wonderful day of my whole life.'

'Better than winning a championship?'

'A hundred times better.' Elizabeth frowned. 'You know, I was beginning to wonder if there was something wrong with me. All the other girls would fall in love, with the players, the coaches or someone from the press and I never did. I thought maybe I never would, that I'd go through life with no other love than tennis. Now I know I won't.'

'You seem very certain of Nicolas.'

'I am.' Elizabeth smiled happily. 'I believe him when he says he loves me, and I'm sure I love him.'

Marianne shrugged. 'I'll try not to play gooseberry. Just give me the wink when you want to be alone together. We can stay until next Friday, but there's one condition – tomorrow we go and look for this hotel that my relatives run.'

Elizabeth's face fell. 'Would you mind terribly if you went on your own? Nicolas and I had planned something else.'

'Oh? What?'

'It's a surprise.'

'Who for?'

'Me, I suppose.'

'Ha!' declared Marianne triumphantly. 'You're probably going to be whisked off to a small Greek village to be vetted by your future mother-in-law and shown where you'll be expected to live. That will curb your enthusiasm.'

Marianne entered the foyer of the hotel with butterflies in the pit of her stomach. It had taken her a considerable amount of time walking up and down the side roads before she found it above the nightclub they had frequented and now she felt distinctly out of place amongst such restrained grandeur. She waited uncertainly whilst the girl at the reception desk said farewell to a good-looking young man with a brief case in his hand.

'We will miss you, Mr Giovanni. Will you return soon?'

'In a few weeks, I expect. Look after yourself, Thalia.'

He swung out of the double doors, casting a speculative look at Marianne as he left. She looked like a tourist asking for directions, certainly not a customer.

Thalia gazed after him, adoration in her eyes, then switched her attention to Marianne.

'Can I help you?' she asked in English.

Marianne answered her in Greek. 'I am looking for Mr Yannis Andronicatis.'

Thalia shook her head. 'Mr Yannis is not here. Why do you wish to see him?'

'I believe he is a relative of mine. I'm on vacation from America and my grandmother suggested I called.'

'Oh!' Thalia was obviously at a loss with the situation. 'I will speak to Mr Orestis. Maybe he can help you. Please take a seat.'

Feeling self-conscious of her appearance, Marianne accepted her offer and sat on the beige upholstery, watching the receptionist as she rapped on a door and a rapid interchange followed with an unseen person inside. Thalia shut the door and returned to Marianne.

'Mr Orestis will see you. Please follow me.' She led the way back to the door and knocked deferentially before opening it. 'The young lady, sir.'

Orestis smiled. 'Please come in and have a seat.'

Marianne obeyed and heard the door close quietly behind her.

'Good morning. I believe you are looking for Mr Yannis? He is not here. He lives in Crete.'

Marianne's face fell. 'It was just a chance. I'm staying in Athens and my grandmother asked me to call.'

'I am sorry, madam. Mr Giovanni has just left, or maybe you could have spoken to him.'

'When will he be back?'

Orestis shook his head. 'Not for some weeks. He has returned to Crete, to the other hotels.'

'Oh, well,' Marianne shrugged. 'I can tell my grandmother I tried. Is there anyone else in Athens related to Mr Yannis? Maybe I could see them.'

Orestis considered. 'Mr Nick is also a relative. He will be here this evening if you would care to come back then.'

'What time should I come?'

'About nine-thirty. Where are you staying, madam? Maybe we could send a car?'

'I wouldn't dream of it. My friend and I are staying only about five minutes walk away. We'll come back then.'

Orestis nodded. He hoped he had done the right thing by suggesting she returned to meet Nicolas. 'Some refreshment, madam? Coffee, orange juice or ouzo?'

Marianne shook her head. 'You're very kind, but no thank you.'

Marianne waited impatiently for the return of her friend. She had spent the remainder of the morning in the museum, staying far later than she had intended and hurried back to their hotel room expecting to find Elizabeth already there. There was no sign of her and after half an hour Marianne left a note on the bed and went to a nearby taverna. She lingered over her coffee, watching Athenians and foreigners mingling together on the pavements and realised how much she would miss the country when she returned to England for her final year. She gave herself a little shake.

'Just because Elizabeth has found romance here, it doesn't follow that you will. Besides, remember Bob's in America and he's waiting for you to come home. Good, steady, reliable Bob.' The little voice in her head reminded her. 'Do I really want Bob?' she asked herself for the hundredth time. 'Of course you do,' she reassured herself. 'You know where you are with Bob.' Deep in thought she drank too deeply from her coffee and screwed up her face as the grounds felt gritty on her tongue.

'Was it really that bad?' Elizabeth slipped into the seat beside her.

'I'd got to the grounds. Have you eaten?' Marianne picked up her glass of water and rinsed her mouth.

Elizabeth nodded. 'We had lunch a couple of hours ago. I wouldn't mind a baklava, though.'

'You're a pig!'

'I know. It's being on holiday and not having to watch my weight and diet all the time. One more week of indulgence.' She sighed deeply. 'I think I'll give up proper meals next week and just eat cakes and ice cream.'

'Your coach would have a fit.'

Elizabeth giggled. 'I'd love to see his face if I turned up a stone over weight. Anyway, did you find your relatives?'

'No. I just missed him, I think.'

'Tell me.'

'As I arrived there was a gorgeous looking man just leaving. I heard the receptionist call him Mr Giovanni. I asked the manager for Mr Yannis and he told me he lives in Crete. He said I had just missed Mr Giovanni.'

'So that's that, then. At least you can tell your grandmother that you tried.'

Marianne shook her head. 'There's another member of the family at the hotel. I've arranged to go back this evening and meet him. You'll come with me, won't you? It was so intimidating walking in on my own. It really is a de luxe hotel.'

Elizabeth frowned. 'I'm supposed to be meeting Nicolas.'

'You can still meet him. We've been walking around with our eyes closed. The hotel is above the nightclub. I've arranged to meet Mr Nick there at nine thirty. We don't have to stay very long, so we'll have plenty of time to go to the club.' Marianne took another mouthful of water. 'What did you do today then? What was the surprise?'

'Well,' Elizabeth let out a deep sigh. 'I thought we were just wandering around, then Nicolas took me to the tiniest church you've ever seen in your life. It's just squashed between buildings, very small and dark. We stood there for a few minutes, then he gave me a candle and picked one up himself. He lit my candle, then lit his from mine and held them together. Then he said 'I should like to always be as close to you as our candles are to each other.' By then, of course, the wax had melted and had welded them together.' A far away look came into Elizabeth's eyes. 'Then he kissed me and asked me to marry him.'

'What!' Marianne almost choked. 'I thought you were going to write to each other and he was going to visit you in America?'

'That was yesterday.'

'So what's happened to change things?'

'We love each other. Why wait? I'm over twenty one and single.'

'He's also over twenty one, but is he single?'

'Marianne!'

'Look, Elizabeth, I know he's swept you off your feet and I admit he's charming, but he's years older than you and have you asked him about his family? For all you know he could have a wife and six children at home.'

Elizabeth smiled at her friend's concern. 'I'm sure he hasn't. We had lunch with his sister.'

Marianne was still unconvinced. 'You don't speak Greek, Elizabeth. He could have told her you were a business contact, anything.'

'I don't think so.' Elizabeth giggled. 'She speaks very good English and he introduced me as his fiancée. We also showed her my ring.'

From her handbag Elizabeth took a small blue box and opened it. 'Do you like it?'

Marianne gasped. 'It's magnificent. Why aren't you wearing it?'

'I wanted to tell you before you saw it. Nicolas is visiting his mother this afternoon to tell her and ask if he can take me there tomorrow. I get the impression that Elena had been asked to meet me first and give her approval.'

'And suppose mamma says no?'

Elizabeth shrugged. 'Why should she?'

'You're not Greek, Elizabeth. In her eyes that could be as detrimental as if you had come from Mars, and remember, in Greece the mother is the head of the family. You'll probably be expected to live in her house. She'll do the cooking, the house work and look after your children whilst you go out to work. It's a whole different way of life from ours.'

'Your parents don't live with your grandmother,' protested Elizabeth.

'Not now. When my grandmother married and went to live in America her parents followed and they lived close by. My great grandmother looked after my grandmother's children so my grandmother could return to work with my grandfather. It's the custom. For the first two years after my parents were married they lived with my grandmother until their house was built.'

'So when you and Bob get married you'll live with your mother? Helena didn't.'

Marianne shook her head. 'We've become accustomed to living as separate units now. Families have become so extended that you run out of room space, but if Helena asked to come home they'd find room for her, and her family, and they'd be pleased to have her.'

Elizabeth shook her head. 'You'll not put me off with your old wive's tales.'

Marianne dressed with care. She decided the one dress she had carried with her must take the place of her usual jeans and shirt, although it would be uncomfortable to dance in at the nightclub. She looked at Elizabeth.

'You can't wear that,' she said decisively.

'Why not?'

'We're going to the hotel first, remember. This Mr Nick is probably as old as the hills and will expect to see us decorously dressed in skirts. It's just not the place for jeans.'

Elizabeth sighed in exasperation. 'What can I wear, then?'

'The dress you brought with you.'

'I was saving that for tomorrow.'

'Then be careful you don't spill your drink down it.'

'It will be all sweaty if I wear it to dance in,' complained Elizabeth.

Marianne continued to apply her makeup carefully. 'I hope he's not too old fashioned. Grandmother nearly had a fit the first time she saw me wearing mascara. Shall I wear my hair up or down?'

Elizabeth shrugged and did not answer.

'What's wrong?'

'You're just making such a fuss. Does it matter what this old boy thinks of us? Is he likely to report back to your grandmother that we dared to enter his hotel wearing jeans? I doubt it very much.'

'It's not just him. I felt like a tramp when I walked in this morning. You could see the receptionist was about to hold her nose as I walked up to the desk. It's the kind of place where you get your jewellery out of the safe to wear it down for dinner. I just don't want to feel too self conscious and out of place.'

Elizabeth pulled off her jeans and stuffed them into a carrier bag. 'I'll wear my dress, to please you and this old uncle or whatever he is, but I'll take my jeans with me and change at the nightclub. I can leave my bag with Nicolas.'

Marianne hesitated. 'Could I leave mine too? I'll feel a fool at the nightclub dressed like this.'

Marianne and Elizabeth walked into the foyer of the Athenia De Luxe hotel; very conscious of the carrier bags they carried.

'Suppose he doesn't turn up?' hissed Elizabeth.

'We'll give him half an hour.'

Marianne went to the reception desk. The girl from earlier in the day was nowhere to be seen, nor the manager.

'I have come here to meet Mr Nick who is a relative of mine. Is it all right if we wait in the bar?'

'Certainly, madam. Would you like me to page you when he arrives?'

'Is there anyone else in the bar?'

'A couple of gentlemen.'

'Then if you could just tell him where we are. I'm sure he'll find us.' Marianne turned to Elizabeth. 'Come on, let's go and have a drink. We don't want him to think we were waiting for him to buy us one.'

Elizabeth followed her friend and sat at a table, taking in the plain décor that enhanced the statuettes placed in the niches of the walls. 'That's unusual,' she commented.

Marianne placed their drinks on the table and moved closer. 'They're copies of the museum pieces. I wonder whose clever idea that was?'

'Giovanni's, of course.'

Marianne turned to see Nicolas standing with his hand on Elizabeth's shoulder. She raised her eyebrows.

'You know Giovanni?'

'Of course. Everyone knows Giovanni. You are both looking quite ravishing tonight, may I say. Are you going somewhere special?'

Elizabeth giggled and showed the carrier bag tucked beneath her chair. 'We've brought our jeans with us. Marianne has tracked down some long lost relative of hers and he's promised to come and meet her here. She insisted we dressed up. I have to admit she was right. I would have felt terribly out of place wearing shorts or jeans.'

Nicolas looked at Marianne with interest. 'Has she now? Who exactly is this relative, Marianne?'

'I don't really know. Don't laugh, I know it sounds silly. My grandmother was betrothed to her cousin at one time, it's a long story. He had a sister who died giving birth to a son and the son now owns this hotel. I promised my grandmother I'd call in and just say hello, but Mr Yannis lives in Crete and Mr Giovanni had just left, but the manager said Mr Nick was a relative and I could meet him.'

'Really? And you have no idea how this Mr Nick is related to you?'

Marianne shook her head. 'I presume he's another cousin. I'm not very good on my family history.'

'You should know about your family. I knew nothing until my father died, then I found I had a number of very interesting relatives.' For some reason that Marianne could not fathom Nicolas seemed to be having a problem controlling his laughter.

'Why was that?' asked Marianne.

'My father had disowned his family. It was very wrong of him, but he refused to have anything at all to do with them and told my sister and I that he had no relatives. When he was on his death bed he wished to be reconciled and forgiven.'

'And was he?'

'Oh, yes. Yannis and Anna arrived in time. When we met uncle Yannis we understood why Pappa had said he had died years ago. He was a leper.'

Elizabeth caught her breath and Marianne crossed herself instinctively, then frowned.

'My grandpa researches into leprosy. That's why he left Athens and went to America.'

Nicolas nodded. 'My uncle was indebted to him. Another drink, ladies?'

Marianne looked at her watch. 'Excuse me a moment.'

She returned to the foyer and approached the reception desk. 'Excuse me, has Mr Nick arrived yet? I have another appointment to go to.'

The receptionist looked at her, a puzzled frown on her face. 'Mr Nick went into the bar a short while ago.' She came out from behind the desk and walked towards the bar with Marianne. 'There, he is talking with your friend.'

Marianne's mouth opened and closed, finally she managed to stutter thank you and returned to the table where she picked up her drink and took a long draught.

'Well, it doesn't look as if this relative of mine is going to show. I expect he's so old he's not allowed out at night.' Marianne looked very deliberately at Nicolas. 'What do you think, Mr Nick?'

Nicolas rose and bowed to her, then took her in his arms. 'I am delighted to meet you. Forgive me. I had the advantage over you.'

'When did you know?'

'Not until I walked into the bar. I, too, was expecting an elderly relative, and when I saw it was you…' Nicolas spread his hands expressively. 'I could not resist to tease.'

Elizabeth looked from one to the other, her eyes round. 'You mean, you and Nicolas, he's your relative?'

Marianne resumed her seat. 'I'm still not quite sure how.'

'I will explain. Excuse me, Elizabeth, it will be easier in Greek. There was Yannis, Maria, Anna, Yiorgo and Stelios. They were cousins to your grandmother, whose name I believe is Annita. She and Yannis were betrothed before anyone realised he was ill. Maria married a local farmer and died giving birth to her second child, Yannis. My father was Stelios. Giovanni is the second son of Mr Yannis's sister, so he is my cousin and you are my cousin also.'

'Rather far removed, I'm afraid.'

Nicolas shrugged. 'It is easier to call you a cousin than try to work out the complexities. Maybe tomorrow we can have a quiet time together and I can explain more fully.'

Marianne still looked unconvinced. 'I understood you were visiting your mother tomorrow.'

'I am, we are.' Nicolas looked at his watch. 'I have time to telephone her before I go to the nightclub. Please, go and change, so you feel more comfortable. I will meet you again in a few minutes.'

'What are you going to do?'

'Tell my mother to expect an extra visitor for lunch. She is a relative also and you should meet her whilst you can.'

Marianne drained the last of the alcohol from her glass. 'I just don't believe this. My best friend gets herself engaged to my cousin and I don't even know he is my cousin! It's ridiculous!'

Nicolas opened the door of his mother's apartment and called out 'We're here.'

'Come through, then.'

'My mother doesn't speak English,' Nicolas whispered to Elizabeth.

She looked at him in horror. 'Why didn't you tell me before?'

'What would you have done? Tried to learn Greek over night? Do not worry. You look beautiful – and I love you.'

Elizabeth looked up at him. 'Truly?'

'On my life.'

Daphne greeted them at the door of the lounge. 'Do come in. Now let me guess.' She looked from the blonde to the dark haired girl. 'It's not difficult. You have to be Marianne.'

'And this is Elizabeth.' Nicolas pushed her forward. 'Elizabeth speaks no Greek, but Marianne is fluent.'

'Are you warning me to be polite?'

'Not at all. I just don't want you to think Elizabeth rude because she cannot speak to you.'

Daphne eyed the petite blonde up and down. 'Elena told me she was beautiful, but I had not imagined she would be so small! She plays tennis? She doesn't look as though she would have the strength. You can tell her I think she is beautiful – like a little doll. Tell her I'm pleased to meet her and I hope she will look on our house as her home. Tell her…'

'Mamma, there's no need to keep saying 'tell her'. Of course I'll tell her.'

Nicolas dutifully relayed the compliments back to Elizabeth who blushed. 'Please say thank you to her for making me welcome.'

'Is Elena coming for lunch?'

Daphne nodded. 'She promised she would get away, whatever crisis occurred. She works for a shipping firm,' Daphne explained to Marianne. 'Sometimes there are problems, but please sit down.'

'That's good. She can talk to you and Elizabeth whilst I explain the family history to Marianne. When she arranged to meet me yesterday she was expecting an old man. I tried to outline the family for her last night, but I don't think she took it in. She was a bit shocked.'

'I have a copy of Yannis's book. That could help.'

Nicolas frowned. 'I don't see how.'

'If Marianne reads it she will learn about her grandmother and also about her great grandparents. Yannis included Marisa's wedding on the island and his own marriage to Dora. All sorts of interesting little pieces of information.'

'I intended to buy a copy to read on the way home.'

'Then we won't spoil it for you. What I will do is draw you a family tree. I'll draw our side and you draw yours and we'll see where we finally link up.'

'I think we should wait until your sister arrives. Elizabeth will be very bored.'

'Don't you believe it. Mamma has the photograph album out. She's going to show Elizabeth all the awful pictures of me as a child.'

'Have you any of the rest of the family?'

'Of course. They're in another album. I'll get them and we'll go through them after lunch when we've done the family tree. That way you'll get to know who everyone is.'

'There's old uncle Yannis. That's your grandmother's brother he's standing beside, he's a priest, you know, and that's aunt Anna and uncle Yiorgo outside their farm. This is my cousin Yannis who owns the hotel, and his wife. There's Giovanni. I've no idea who the girl is with him. Oh, there's cousin Ourania again with her cat, Beauty.'

'Don't they have any children?'

'No, that's why she's so besotted by the cat. Ah, there's aunt Dora. She was old uncle Yannis's second wife. She died not long ago.'

'And cousin Yannis's father? I've not seen a photo of him.'

'He was killed during the war. He and uncle Yiorgo joined the resistance, but he didn't return.'

'So your cousin Yannis was left without a father? Poor little boy.'

'He hardly remembers his father. His mother died giving birth to him and aunt Anna looked after him and his sister.'

'Is that why she never married?'

'I don't know.' Nicolas shrugged. 'Maybe she had planned to marry cousin Yannis's father when he came back from the war.'

Elena produced a camera and ushered the two girls out onto the balcony. 'We have to add you both to the family album, and I know our family in Crete will want to have copies,' Elena spoke with determination. 'You must have some of us to take back with you. Your grandmother has never seen any of us.'

'I wish I'd bothered to find the hotel before,' grumbled Marianne. 'Then I could have met Giovanni and we might have been able to go to Crete and meet the rest of the family.'

'I am very glad you did not. I might not have met Elizabeth.' Nicolas smiled down at her fondly.

'She might have preferred Giovanni,' Elena spoke mischievously.

'She might,' agreed Nicolas, refusing to be ruffled. 'Then I would be very jealous of him.'

Nicolas went to the nightclub and performed his duties mechanically. He missed Elizabeth more than he had envisaged and found it an effort to be polite and attentive to the other tourists who frequented the nightspot. Elena teased him about his moroseness and he answered her snappishly.

'What would you know about it? You always said you were a career woman and have no time for love in your life.'

'Well if you're going to carry on like this until you see her again I may have to fall in love just to get away from you. Why don't you look for that assistant you spoke about, show him the ropes and take a couple of week's holiday? If you spoke nicely to Giovanni he might even give you an advance so you could go to America.'

'What good would that do? I'd only have to come back, besides, I need to save money, not spend it.'

'You should have plenty.'

'Not as much as I need if I'm getting married. Maybe if I sold my car it would help.'

'Don't be stupid. How would you get to and from the nightclub? You'd have to take taxis and that wouldn't save you very much.'

Nicolas shrugged. He felt too tired and miserable to even think seriously about his future. He retired to write yet another long letter to Elizabeth, finding his eyelids drooping as he wrote and huge yawns destroying the flow of his thoughts. Elena was right. He must look for an assistant, besides, when he and Elizabeth were married she would not want to spend every night at home alone or in the nightclub. He leant his head down on his arms and tried to think. He must find the right man for the job, someone conscientious and trustworthy, yet extrovert enough to be able to chat to the customers and encourage them to spend their money and come again. Maybe tonight he could look over any regulars who came in. There must be someone in Athens capable of doing what amounted to a very simple job.

Nicolas looked around. There was not a familiar face to be seen. He scanned the tables where some groups sat drinking. To his surprise there was a man sitting alone, a glass of ouzo before him. He seemed to be more interested in the effects being relayed on the walls than any of the girls or the music. Provided he was no trouble Nicolas did not really care if he danced or sat alone all evening. He glanced at his watch. Nearly midnight. There was no way he could close before three in the morning, and if people chose to stay it could be later. He bent down behind the bar and yawned, willing the time to pass.

For three nights the man appeared at the nightclub, always alone, never speaking to anyone or dancing and Nicolas began to wonder what it was that he found so interesting. At regular intervals he would raise his hand to the bar tender who would hurry over with another ouzo, collect the money and return.

'The next time he calls for a drink I'll take it.'

The bar tender looked at Nicolas in surprise. 'I don't mind going.'

'I want to find out who he is. Doesn't it make you wonder why a man sits in a nightclub all evening drinking? He could sit in a taverna and drink as much for half the price.'

The bar tender shrugged. It was his job to serve drinks, not analyse why people were there.

Nicolas placed the ouzo on the table before the stranger and sat down in the vacant chair. 'Good evening,' he spoke in Greek. 'You've become quite a regular.'

The man nodded and sipped his drink.

'Are you hoping to meet some friends?'

'No.'

'Why do you come then? I don't mean to pry, but it's more expensive to sit here and drink than if you went to a taverna.'

'I like to watch the walls.'

Nicolas smiled. 'I see. You find them interesting?'

'I think they need to be changed. You use the same scenes over and over again. People are apt to get bored.'

'What scenes would you suggest?'

The man shrugged. 'It depends. You could have a high speed car chase, a sea battle, wild elephants charging. Anything for variety.'

'It can be quite difficult to find the right subject to project.'

'Rubbish. It only revolves around a cylinder and on to a reflective glass. A child could do it.'

Nicolas raised his eyebrows. 'You seem to know a good bit about it.'

'I studied electronics for a while.'

'So what are you doing now?'

'Nothing at the moment. Just enjoying myself.'

'You enjoy sitting here all night watching the walls?'

The man shook his head. 'I am not just watching the walls. I am thinking of new scenes and how they would appeal to the customers.'

Nicolas leaned forward. 'Maybe we could use some of your ideas.'

'Maybe. If I was willing to sell them to you.'

'We would have to know what they were before we paid.'

'Of course – and I would have to know more about the techniques you use. I could be suggesting the wrong type of basic module. Maybe I could have a look after you've closed and see what you're using.'

Nicolas shook his head. 'Only employees are allowed to know the techniques. You could be here to steal our ideas for a rival club.'

'I assure you I am not. I could be interested in a job, though.'

'Really?'

'All money comes to an end eventually. I sold one of my inventions recently, but the money won't last for ever. It would be quite amusing working here for a few months.'

'What did you invent?'

'I can't tell you that. When it's on the open market I'll show you. At present it's still in the developmental stage. I think you're needed to flick a switch.' The man nodded towards the bar tender who was signalling frantically to Nicolas.

'Drop in tomorrow if you're interested in a job. There just could be one for you.'

'I'll think about it.' The man drained his glass and rose. 'You think what you could offer me if I said yes.'

Joseph left the nightclub feeling well pleased with himself. Now all he had to do was continue to be careful not to trip himself up. He sat in a taverna and planned carefully over another glass of ouzo. His false identity papers were safely in his pocket and his references would not let him down if they were checked. He had made sure the electronic engineer he was impersonating had moved from his original firm.

He really had been rather clever over the last few months, managing to keep out of trouble as he moved from one country to another with a 'borrowed' car that he had the foresight to abandon every time he had arrived in a large town en route, taking a short train ride to the next town before 'borrowing' another.

Travelling light had been another advantage. His money, in the largest denominations possible, he kept in a body belt, openly visiting banks to change a note without questions being asked. His bad habit of picking a pocket whenever he was in a crowd had certainly paid off, enough to finance this little trip and a little over, even if he had to leave quickly.

He smiled to himself. He would teach his uncle a lesson for refusing to give him a job in one of his hotels. The pickings there could have been incredibly rich, making all his other nefarious acquisitions pale by comparison. He would get his own back on that smug brother of his, who lived a life of idle luxury just because he could chat up women in four different languages. He would show them, all right. Even this cousin, Nicolas, who ran the nightclub, looked as weak as water. He would show each and every one of them that he was a man to be reckoned with.

Nicolas thought carefully about the young man. He had been told he could employ an assistant. If he turned up the following day he would quiz him thoroughly about his previous employment and ask for references. Provided they proved satisfactory he could always take him on a month's trial. If Giovanni disapproved of his choice he could dismiss him when he returned from Crete. He would have a word with Orestis about the sort of questions he should ask at an interview. A couple of days to show him how to run the club, then watch him for a couple more, and then it might be possible to take some time off.

It was true that the scenes needed changing. He would have thought of that himself if he had not been so tired. He spent sleepless hours envisaging Elizabeth involved in an accident whilst travelling between venues. She could be badly injured and he was not with her, or even worse, and then he would never see her again. A vision of her face, bloody and mutilated, rose before him and he groaned and covered his eyes. If only she would telephone him to say she was safe.

Thoughts tormenting him, Nicolas finished the bottle of wine and collapsed on his bed, his good intentions about consulting Orestis fading into the background as he found oblivion in a semi-drunken sleep, waking late and finding it was time he prepared himself for work. He had slept far longer than he had intended.

He arrived at the nightclub, feeling tired and listless. Somehow a couple of hours had slipped away from him and by the time he had showered and dressed there was no time to call at the hotel, as was his custom. He opened the double doors and entered with his usual flourish, closing them behind him and surveying the occupants. Their faces seemed to swim before him as they gazed back, waiting for the spectacle to begin.

Nicolas took his place behind the bar and threw the first switch.

'Mr Nick,' the hoarse voice of the bar tender came to his ears. 'I'm so glad you've arrived. Would you mind if I went home to bed? I feel terrible. It must be this flu that is going around.'

Nicolas looked at the employee, he was certainly flushed and his breath was rasping.

'You should see a doctor. Get something for it.'

'I'll be all right.' He coughed harshly. 'I spent the day in bed and thought I'd thrown it off. It seems I was wrong.'

'Get yourself home. Ask your wife to telephone the hotel if you're not well enough to come in tomorrow.'

Gratefully the bar tender nodded. 'I expect I'll be over it by then.'

The music seemed particularly loud to Nicolas as he poured drinks and tried to make light conversation with the customers. Twice the effects ground to a halt where he had forgotten the sequence of switches. He rubbed his hand across his forehead and found he was sweating. It must be because he was trying to do two jobs at once.

'Why don't you let me give you a hand?'

Nicolas looked round to see the young man standing beside him. 'Have you ever worked a bar?'

'Of course. You concentrate on your switches and I'll serve the customers.'

Thankfully Nicolas sat back on the high bar stool. He watched the young man as he mixed cocktails and poured measures with swift efficiency. He seemed to know his job and elicited smiles and quips from all he served. A flick of the switches saw the colours muted and slower, more romantic music played. Nicolas gave a sigh of relief as people accepted the change and adapted the tempo of their dancing. There was a lull at the bar and Nicolas slid off his high stool, his legs seeming to buckle under him as he tried to stand, and with an effort he kept his balance.

'Thank you,' he said. 'I had to send my bar tender home with flu.'

'I should imagine you've got a dose yourself,' Joseph observed. 'Why don't you leave the keys with me and go home to bed? I could drop them into the hotel when I've closed up.'

Nicolas was tempted. 'No, I can't do that. You can't be expected to work the electronics and cope with the bar on your own.'

Joseph shrugged. 'I've got the job, then?'

'You can work the bar until Lakkis is well enough to return. We'll see about the electric side of things later. What's your name?'

'Kyriakos, Kyriakos Lenandraous. What's yours?'

'Nicolas Christoforakis.'

Joseph nodded. 'You must be Mr Nick, the manager.'

'That's right.'

'Well you have no need to worry. The bar will be in good hands with me to look after it. Why don't you have a brandy? Could make you feel better.'

Nicolas accepted. It could help to dull the noise of the gladiatorial fight that he would have to relay next.

As the night wore on Nicolas decided he did have flu. He felt hot and knew that his cheeks were flushed. Each breath was painful and seemed to be scraping his lungs. The pounding at his temples told him he probably had a temperature and it was unlikely he would feel any better for a few days.

'Do you really think you could work the electronics and serve?' he asked Joseph.

'Of course. It's just a question of flicking a few switches at the right time. Let me give it a go and if you're satisfied you could leave me to it.'

Nicolas relinquished his position in front of the switchboard. 'It's all marked.' He swayed slightly where he stood.

Joseph looked at the dials and switches. 'What's that for?' He pointed to an unmarked button.

'The microphone. I only use it when I first arrive.'

'You should use it more. You could tell them what's coming up next and encourage them to buy their drinks now so they don't miss any of it.'

Nicolas nodded. He really did not care. 'Where are you living?'

'I'll write my address down for you. If you don't trust me with the keys you could always ask someone from the hotel to come down and lock up,' he suggested.

A bout of harsh coughing stopped Nicolas from replying. He really was ill. If he insisted on staying he would take far longer to recover and probably give it to all his customers. He withdrew a large bunch of keys from his pocket and took four from the ring.

'That's the drinks cupboard, that turns off the electric for the special effects, and those two are the doors. I'll take the money with me. You can drop the keys and whatever's in the till off at the hotel desk when you leave.'

Joseph nodded. 'Don't you worry. I'll make sure everything is clean and tidy before I go. I'll call at the hotel tomorrow evening for the keys and open up. If you're feeling better that's fine, if not I'll run it for you for a few days.'

Nicolas hardly heard him. He was not sure if the flashing lights he saw were behind or in front of his eyes, and the pounding in his head was obliterating the sound of the music. He swayed unsteadily towards the door and out into the cool night air to his car.

Joseph looked around with satisfaction. It could hardly have worked out better for him if he had deliberately carried in the flu germs. By the look of Nicolas he would certainly be unfit to return for a week and by then he would have made himself so popular with the patrons and so indispensable that there was no way he could be asked to leave.

Joseph made good use of the week that both Lakkis and Nicolas were absent from the nightclub. The knowledge he had gleaned from his friend in electronics enabled him to purchase a few cheap rolls of film that he had enlarged and fixed to some spare spindles. Before any film was reflected onto the walls he described the events about to be seen, building up the drama that was about to unfold and capture his audience.

An added bonus in his eyes was the fact that as bar tender he was able to give short measure when he judged his customer would not notice, enabling him to drink as he pleased without there being a noticeable short fall in the stock. He would make a couple of visits to the cloakroom during the evening and in passing through the dancers he was usually able to lift a wallet or wad of notes from a pocket as he passed without suspicion falling on him. He had taken the precaution of having a spare set of keys cut, taking each one to a different locksmith and hiding them in the mean room he rented.

To his surprise he began to find the work enjoyable, although he knew his shiftless nature too well to expect the pleasure to last for more than a few months at the most. He was philosophical. All he wanted was a foothold, to make his uncle think he was a reformed character, so he could be persuaded to offer him work in one of his hotels, then he would put his master plan into action.

He felt quite downcast when Lakkis returned to work and took over the bar and he was left with the monotonous job of working the electronic switchboard of special effects. Lakkis had expressed admiration for two of the new reels of film. One showed a sports car race, which had been so edited that most of the movement was in the form of near misses and high speed crashes and the other Indians, fighting a pitched battle against a small force of cavalry who were trying to defend a stockade and protect the inhabitants.

'You're a clever man,' Lakkis had enthused. 'You should have shown the films to Mr Nick and then sold them to him.'

Joseph shook his head. 'I wanted to make sure they worked first. I know of better films than these, but I can't afford to buy them. If Mr Nick wants to invest I can get them and save him the cost of fixing them up.'

'Are you working for Mr Nick?' Lakkis could see his own job in jeopardy.

'I might work some nights, just to give him a bit of a rest, but nothing's settled. I offered to help out when both of you were sick.'

'Where've you worked before?'

'I worked a bar on a cruise ship for a few months.'

'What made you leave?'

'I wanted more time to spend with my girl,' lied Joseph. He did not need to mention that he had been asked to leave after a series of petty thefts had seemed to implicate him.

'Yes? Are you still with her?'

'No. I'd been away too much and she found someone else.'

'That was a shame.'

Joseph shrugged. 'I'm not the marrying kind, so it was probably for the best.'

Nicolas was impressed by the way the club had been run during his absence. He did not ask for references or for Orestis's advice as he had planned previously. The young man who had turned up from nowhere had done a superb job and he felt happy to have him around.

Unfortunately Nicolas was not as impressed with the reels of film as Lakkis had been. 'They're not in keeping. We want to stay Greek. You can go into any cinema and see that rubbish.'

'You still need something new. I've heard about some others, but they were too expensive for me to invest in. I didn't even know if you'd keep me on, so I couldn't be presumptuous and buy them for you.'

'I'd rather you didn't buy any more at all. Mr Giovanni says what we show. I'll pay you for the couple you've bought, but I'm not prepared to show them until Mr Giovanni has approved.'

Joseph shrugged and turned away, inwardly seething. If it wasn't his uncle Yannis it was his brother Giovanni he was up against.

'I'll know better next time,' he said docilely.

Nicolas telephoned Giovanni to tell him about the new employee and Giovanni seemed genuinely pleased. It was a relief to know that Nicolas had a reliable assistant and also to know he had been firm about which films were shown.

'I'll be over in about a month. Don't tell him I'm coming. I'd like to watch him work.'

'I'm sure you'll be more than satisfied.'

Nicolas was ecstatic; he had received a long letter from Elizabeth. It covered twelve pages of foolscap paper and described their journey back to England, her subsequent flight to America and her parents' reaction to her engagement.

They seem to think this is just a holiday romance and we'll forget each other, she complained. *That I will never do, my darling, darling Nicolas.*

My mother has said she will come with me next spring when I start on the European circuit and if you cannot come to visit us we'll take a couple of days to come to Athens. I know she just wants to see if you're suitable. It has helped with you being Marianne's cousin. They have always liked her and she and my brother have been going out together for years.

Everyone expects them to get married when Marianne comes back from England. Her sister has a dear little baby, all dark eyes and curly hair. Do you think our babies will look like that? I can't wait to see you again and tell you how much I love and miss you. I keep trying to think of a way we could get married now, but I'm under contract to play for the next year and I don't think you'd be very happy trailing around after me from place to place with nothing to do all day except watch me play tennis.

She had written on and on, describing her parents and brother, the house they lived in and the other girls she played tennis with. Nicolas read the letter over and over again. For the first time in his life he wished he had taken an interest in sport and could play tennis well enough to be on the circuit with her. That way they would be able to marry now and be together. Despite her reassurances, he was tormented by the fear that she would meet a young man during her tours that she found more attractive.

Giovanni arrived in Athens and deposited his luggage in the Athenia De Luxe. He sought out Orestis and discussed repairs and redecoration on his uncle's behalf before he asked for an up to date report on the nightclub.

'Mr Nick is doing very well. He still works very hard, even with an assistant.'

'Does he still come in here before starting?'

'Always. We usually sit and have a quick drink together, then when he closes he brings up the money to put in the safe and lets the night attendant know the club is closed.'

'Very sensible. Can't be too careful. Nicolas seems to have a business head on him, despite having been a teacher. What about this man Kyriakos? Does he do the same?'

'He comes in to collect the keys when Mr Nick has an evening off and returns them with them with the takings when he closes up.'

'He takes nothing home with him then?'

'Oh, no.' Orestis shook his head. 'Mr Nick is very strict about that. The keys and the money have to be left at the hotel.'

Giovanni nodded. It was good to hear that his instructions were obeyed to the letter.

'I'll drop in this evening. I'll give Nicolas a ring to let him know I'm here and arrange for Kyriakos to run the club tonight. I really need a pretty girl with me. Is Thalia around?'

Orestis nodded and smiled to himself. Thalia would be only too pleased to accompany Giovanni. 'I'll ask her – or will you?'

'You do it. It's only a business arrangement. I don't want her getting the wrong impression. Now, I want to go and have a look at aunt Dora's flat, just to make sure nothing needs doing, and then I've an appointment with the publishers. My uncle isn't very happy about the sales this year. He doesn't think they've printed enough – and they've put the price up. I wish he'd come and do his own haggling with them. I'll be back this evening and we could have dinner together, if you've nothing better to do.'

Orestis spread his hands. 'Nothing would please me more.'

'Good.' Giovanni rose. 'I'll leave you to persuade Thalia to go to the nightclub with me. I expect she'll claim she has nothing suitable to wear, so you'd better give her this and the afternoon off.' Giovanni placed a roll of notes in to Orestis's hands. 'That's plenty, don't let her wheedle any more out of you.'

Orestis smiled. How well Mr Giovanni knew his staff.

Nicolas greeted his cousin with pleasure when they met during the afternoon. 'I'm sure you'll be pleased with Kyriakos. He's very willing and a hard worker. The customers seem to like him and he gets on well with Lakkis.'

Giovanni nodded. 'I'm looking forward to meeting him. If he's as good as you say he's a real find.'

'I'm very happy to have him as an assistant. I wanted to ask you for some time off later in the year and I'll be relieved to know the club is in good hands.'

Giovanni raised his eyebrows. 'To visit this American girl? Are you serious about her?'

'Very,' affirmed Nicolas.

'You really intend to marry her?'

'I most certainly do. If she wasn't under contract to play tennis all over the world we could start making plans now,' Nicolas spread his hands, 'as it is we have to wait.'

'You only knew her for a few days,' remarked Giovanni scathingly.

'Ten days. It was long enough.'

'And what will happen when you're married? Do you plan to follow her around like a little dog or will she be willing to give up tennis and live here in Athens?'

'She will come to Athens. We talked about it. I'm saving hard and I want to ask a favour of Yannis. Do you think he would sell me Aunt Dora's flat?'

Giovanni shrugged. 'How would I know? You'll have to ask him yourself.'

'I intend to. The very next time he comes over.'

Giovanni ate a leisurely meal with Orestis and did not go down to the nightclub until nearly midnight, Thalia hanging appreciatively on his arm. The club was full to overflowing and he steered her to a table in the far corner and sent her up to the bar for their drinks.

'I don't want either of them to know I'm here. If Lakkis offers to bring the drinks over you must refuse and wait for them. You're not to say a word to either of them about me. If they ask who you're with just say a guest from the hotel.'

Thalia nodded. She would do anything for Mr Giovanni.

Giovanni listened to the patter that fell from the young man's lips before the next reel of film was shown. There was something familiar about his voice, but from the distance, with the lights flickering and the haze of cigarette smoke he could not see his face clearly. He hardly noticed as Thalia returned with the drinks to their table, he was riveted to the scenes taking place on the walls. Through blue and purple lights, girls could be seen twisting and gyrating provocatively as they divested themselves of their clothes. The whole tempo of the dancing had changed, seductive music was playing and Giovanni could see by the closely clinging bodies the overall effect it was having on his customers. His mouth set in a grim line.

'Shall we dance?' asked Thalia.

'We're going,' announced Giovanni, rising abruptly.

'We haven't even had our drinks,' protested Thalia.

Giovanni seized her arm and propelled her through the press of bodies and out through the double doors. Once outside he realised he was trembling with rage. If Nicolas had given permission for such films to be shown in his nightclub he was due for immediate dismissal. Thalia looked at him uncomprehending.

'What's the matter, Mr Giovanni? Don't you feel well?'

Giovanni shook himself. 'I'm sorry to spoil your evening, Thalia. I'll make it up to you. We'll go into the hotel and I'll call you a taxi.' Without waiting for her answer he pushed her along the street.

Orestis looked up in surprise when he saw the couple return to the hotel and the grimness of Giovanni's face.

'Get Thalia a taxi to take her home and then get me Nicolas on the 'phone. I'll take it in the office.'

Orestis raised his eyebrows at Thalia who shrugged. 'I think he must be feeling ill.'

Nicolas lost no time in dressing and driving to the hotel. The tone of Giovanni's voice did not encourage him to protest and he was given no chance to enquire the reason. The curt summons to get to the hotel immediately, once acknowledged by himself, was the only conversation. He walked in, expecting to find his cousin in the bar, only to be shown into the office.

Giovanni glowered at him. 'What new films have you bought to show in my nightclub?'

'None, well, whilst I was ill Kyriakos bought a couple, but I told him they weren't suitable and bought them off him.'

'So all he has down there are my originals?'

'Yes. I've got the other two at home.'

'What are they?'

'One is the car race and the other is the Indians besieging some American settlers. They're both out of keeping with the image you wanted.'

'And you don't know of any others?'

'No.' Nicolas shook his head. 'What's this all about, Giovanni?'

'I went down there, taking Thalia with me and he's showing pornography. He's showing girls stripping, not just a straightforward striptease, which might just have been acceptable, they're, they're, well – it was disgusting.'

Nicolas frowned in consternation. 'I'll go down and have a word with him.'

'You'll do no such thing. We'll go down together and I'll speak to him. He won't get away with this. I'll not have my club get a bad name and risk losing my licence.'

Giovanni walked hurriedly from the office, Nicolas following anxiously in his wake. He had never considered his cousin to be a prude, but surely he was exaggerating. Despite his haste, Giovanni opened one of the double doors silently and he and Nicolas stood just inside, their backs to the bar.

A new film was flickering on the walls and Nicolas gasped in horror. Naked bodies were writhing in ecstasy and most of the dancers appeared about to emulate them. Giovanni's hand went out and flicked on the main switch, bathing the whole of the area in pale yellow light, destroying the images and making the customers blink in bewilderment.

Giovanni strode over to the bar. 'You, Kyriakos.'

The man turned from the control panel and Giovanni drew in his breath sharply.

'You! I might have guessed you'd have a hand in this. What are you trying to do? Ruin me?'

Joseph smiled easily back at his brother. 'The customers were enjoying themselves.'

'I was here earlier and I thought that film was disgusting. This one is even worse. You're depraved if you enjoy watching filth like that.'

'Oh, I don't watch it, but it's been a tremendous draw. You'd be surprised how many people do enjoy filth, as you call it.'

'Take whatever belongs to you and get out.' Giovanni spoke between clenched teeth.

'Are you giving me the sack?'

'I'm giving you five minutes to be gone, or I'll break every bone in your body.'

Joseph picked up half a dozen reels of film and placed them in his pocket. 'I'd like my wages before I leave.'

Giovanni took a handful of notes from the till and threw them at his younger brother. 'That's probably more than you're owed and certainly more than you're worth. Get out and don't come back.'

With a nonchalant smiled Joseph pocketed the notes and pushed his way past Giovanni.

'Goodbye, Mr Nick. Goodbye, Lakkis. Nice knowing you both. Maybe we'll meet again one day.' He sauntered to the doors and passed through without a backward glance.

'Get things working, Nicolas. Be quick about it.'

Nicolas bent his head over the panel and selected the film of the Acropolis that showed the famous site as it had been in the past, populated with strolling figures, the music accompanying it restful and soothing.

'Not that one. Put on the chariot race.'

Hurriedly Nicolas complied, altering the music to suit the pictures. To Giovanni's relief the couples who had been watching the short scene at the bar began to drift back to the dance floor.

'Give me a drink,' Giovanni demanded of Lakkis. 'And one for Mr Nick. Why didn't you tell him what that degenerate character was doing?'

Lakkis hung his head. 'I'd better give you my notice now, sir.'

'Why? What else has been going on that I should know about?'

'I borrowed some money. From the takings one night. Mr Kyriakos knew about it and said if I mentioned his films to Mr Nick he would say I'd been stealing.'

'And have you?'

'No. It only happened the once. I paid it back when Mr Nick gave me my wages.'

'How much was it?'

'A thousand drachmas.'

'A thousand drachmas! A paltry sum like that! Why didn't you ask Mr Nick to lend it to you? What did you need it for?' Giovanni wondered if he had heard correctly.

'It was when I'd been sick with the flu. I asked the doctor to call on my wife; she'd caught it from me. He wouldn't go unless I paid in advance. I didn't have enough money on me, the banks were closed and Mr Nick was still away ill. I asked Mr Kyriakos and he said 'take it from the till'. I swear I paid it back as soon as Mr Nick paid me. Mr Kyriakos said if I told Mr Nick about the films he was showing he would say he had seen me helping myself from the till regularly.'

'If it only happened the once and you repaid it, why didn't you tell Mr Nick yourself? That way Joseph would have had no hold over you.'

Lakkis continued to hang his head in shame. 'It was the way he talked. He was so convincing. I didn't think Mr Nick would believe me.'

'I'd believe a rattlesnake in preference to that confidence trickster. Get yourself a drink, Lakkis. You'll not get the sack this time. If you need money in an emergency and Mr Nick isn't around, go to the hotel and ask Orestis.'

'I feel I've let you down, Mr Giovanni.'

'You have, Lakkis, but I'll not hold it against you. People are always taken in by my brother. He's a petty crook and nothing more. You couldn't be expected to see through him. If he was as skilled in a trade as he is in lying and cheating, he'd be a millionaire!'

Joseph stood outside in the cool air, clenching his fists. How he would like to smash one of them into his brother's face. He swung off down the road until he saw a taverna with the lights still burning and went inside. He ordered brandy, which he downed quickly and called for more, gazing morosely into the glass as he drank.

His plan had gone awry. Of all the nights for his brother to put in a surprise appearance! After the first showing of his films word had spread and he had found a certain element of Athenian youth had packed the club and he had creamed off the extra income. An added bonus, he reflected, was the fact that he was still in possession of the films and they had not yet been paid for. He smiled grimly. Giovanni would be very happy when he saw the size of the bill!

If only he had known Giovanni was planning a visit that night he would never have shown his 'specials' and his brother would have been impressed by his efficiency and popularity. Now he would have to start again on a plan to ingratiate himself with his family. If Giovanni mentioned his spell at the nightclub it was doubtful that his uncle would take a chance on him behaving himself in the future.

He finished his brandy and sighed. He would have to move on to somewhere new and think up a different scheme. If he only had the capital he would start up a nightclub like Giovanni's, but the films he would show would be like those he was carrying in his pocket, and he would make sure there were rooms available for rent upstairs and plenty of willing and beautiful girls. Girls. Maybe that could be Giovanni's downfall. He was known to like a pretty face.

As he felt in his pocket for some drachmas a smile twisted his face. He would stay around for a day or two, pick up a car, then remove all the alcohol and cigarettes from the bar before moving on. There were bound to be places where he could sell a few bottles without raising suspicion.

'Feeling lonely?' A soft voice spoke to him.

She slipped into the seat beside him and signalled to the man at the back who hurried over with a bottle of cheap champagne. Joseph shook his head.

'I've been drinking brandy. I'll have another and whatever the lady would like.' Joseph looked at her smooth, oval face. 'And what do you do for a living, may I ask?'

She smiled, showing white, even teeth. 'I entertain.'

'I'm sure you do.' Joseph eyed her lazily. 'Maybe tomorrow. I'm tired tonight.'

Giovanni left the nightclub, still seething with rage. He lay in his bed at the hotel and considered the implications of his brother's actions. Thank goodness he had found out and stopped him before the police had heard and closed him down. He would visit the club during the morning and search it thoroughly. He wanted nothing around that could possibly cause offence to ordinary visitors and law-abiding citizens. He must examine the reels of his original film and see if they had been tampered with. The thought of the possible scenes of debauchery he could find on the gladiators or chariot racing films made him shudder.

What had happened to make Joseph turn out the way he had? If he had resembled himself or his older brother they could have formed a successful partnership. Now he just felt sickened by him and had no wish to ever set eyes on him again. He tossed and turned until dawn broke, then gave up the unequal struggle, showered and dressed and went down to find Orestis already in the office.

'You're early, Mr Giovanni.'

'I couldn't sleep, Orestis. I found I had a problem at the club.'

Orestis raised his eyebrows and as he had hoped Giovanni was forthcoming.

'I went down last night to see how this Kyriakos was doing and I found he was showing pornography. Did you know that?'

Orestis shook his head. 'I never go down there. I'm too old for nightclubs. Did Mr Nick know?'

'He says he didn't and I believe him.'

'Mr Kyriakos seemed a nice young man,' Orestis spoke sadly.

'I'm sure he did! I'm going down there in a while and I'll take the place apart if necessary. I want to find out what else was going on that we didn't know about.'

'Would you like me to come with you?'

'No, there's no need. If Mr Nick comes in tell him where I am. Is there any chance of a coffee before I go down? I must see Thalia later. I ruined her evening, I'm afraid.'

Orestis hurried to the kitchen and stirred the staff into action, returning rapidly, bearing a pot of coffee and some croissants.

'You ought to eat something.'

Giovanni took a croissant and dipped it into his coffee. 'I'll have to start looking for a new assistant for Nicolas. I'll interview him myself and make sure Nicolas keeps a strict eye on him. We don't want a repetition of this mistake. You don't know of anyone, I suppose?'

'Well,' Orestis hesitated. 'One of the waiters here might be suitable. He's been going to the club regularly and can't stop talking about it.'

'Was that before or whilst Kyriakos worked there?'

'Before, I'm sure of that. He's hardly had any time off recently, we just can't seem to shift this flu bug from amongst the staff and he's worked overtime.'

Giovanni nodded and pushed the remainder of the croissant into his mouth. 'I'll think about it. I'll go down now and look around.'

The sight that met Giovanni's eyes was not inspiring. Everywhere there was a litter of dirty glasses, empty bottles, sticky rings on the tables and overflowing ashtrays. He had insisted that Nicolas and Lakkis had left without clearing up, saying it could be done the following day.

He sniffed suspiciously at the glasses, catching nothing but the smell of alcohol and turned his attention to the ashtrays. The stubs all appeared to be from branded cigarettes and he could smell nothing unusual about them. That was certainly a relief to him.

He examined the electric switchboard, running through all the colours of the lights and showing a blank spool to check there was nothing disguised that he could miss. Finally satisfied he took a loaded spindle of film and ran it through, watching the walls intently. After watching each reel a second time he was finally satisfied they had not been tampered with and turned his attention to the bar.

Bottles of drinks were still sealed and those that were open did not appear to have been diluted or contaminated in any way and he stacked them back neatly in the cupboard and locked it behind him. On the shelf beneath the bar he found posters and fly sheets that he leafed through and was about to replace when one caught his eye. *'SPECIAL SHOWING TONIGHT'*. There was no date and no indication of the subject; but it was certainly not a flier he had ordered to be printed. He examined them more closely and those in the middle of the pile all purported to have special attractions, whilst those at the top and bottom were his own publicity leaflets. He bundled the offending sheets together. No doubt Joseph had distributed these when he had known he was going to be in the club on his own.

Finding nothing more of an incriminating nature he turned his back on the dirty, untidy scene and returned to the hotel. He could tell Orestis to send the cleaners down now.

Joseph walked to the taverna and sat drinking, wondering if the girl from the previous night would accost him. He waited for nearly an hour before he saw her emerge from the back room and he smiled encouragingly at her. She sat beside him, her leg pressing against his.

'Are you less tired tonight?'

Joseph enjoyed her speculatively. 'Do you enjoy your work?'

She shrugged. 'It's a way of earning a living.'

'I can think of better ways.'

'Really?'

'A girl like you could be a model, a film star, even. I could introduce you to a friend of mine and he'd be sure to have a part for you.'

A spark of interest came into her eyes. 'Do you mean that?'

'I always mean what I say. Come along with me now and I'll talk to him.'

'I can't. I have to work here tonight.'

'Who says you have to work here?'

'My friend.' She nodded towards the interior of the taverna where the burly man sat watching them.

Joseph nodded. He was not prepared to oppose the heavy weight, nor was he prepared to pay to take the girl into the back room. 'That's a shame. He's only here for a day or so, looking for new talent. Why don't you ask if you could have the evening off?'

She shook her head. 'He'd not let me do that. Couldn't your friend come here?'

'You might be busy when we returned. He wouldn't want to wait.'

She bit at her lip in indecision. 'I'll go and ask him.'

Joseph watched as she argued with her pimp and finally returned to him shaking her head.

'He said no. He also said that if you're not interested, would you please leave so I can talk to someone else.'

Joseph grinned. 'I'll have a word with him.' He rose confidently and walked over to the man, seizing him by the hand. 'I'm sorry if I've offended you by taking your girl's time. I couldn't help being impressed by her beauty. I'm in Athens for a few days with a film director and I thought she would probably test out well. Still, if you have other plans for her I'll not interfere.'

'I don't blame you for trying, but she only goes into the back room, not out on the town.'

'I understand, my friend.' Joseph placed his other hand on the man's and pumping it cordially. He sauntered from the taverna, smiling at the girl as he left, then hurried round the corner before examining his prize. As he had thought, the watch the man had been wearing was gold and should fetch a good price. He fastened it on his own wrist and walked rapidly back to his lodgings.

By the end of the week Giovanni decided he could return to Crete. He had spoken severely to Nicolas, explaining the pitfalls of employing someone without checking their references and watching over them. Nicolas had hung his head.

'It will never happen again. It wouldn't have happened this time if I hadn't been sick with flu. I'd planned to interview him properly and ask for his references. He appeared to be so efficient whilst I was away that it seemed unnecessary.'

'He took advantage of you, I'm sure of that, but remember, once you've lost a nightclub licence you're not likely to get it back. Young Babbis is going to come down from the hotel and you can show him how to run the place. Orestis has vouched for him, but don't take any chances. The best of men can be tempted. Tell Lakkis to make sure he doesn't drink too much and you watch that he doesn't try to bring in his own film.'

'That's one thing I think Joseph was right about,' ventured Nicolas. 'We do need some new films.'

'Not the kind he was showing! I'll have a look around and see what I can come up with before I leave.'

'I could use the car race and the Indians, I suppose.'

'You didn't like them when you first saw them, so stick to your opinion. I thought I'd try to get something on the lines of the Labours of Hercules or the Trojan War. We want to stay Greek.'

Nicolas nodded. Giovanni was right, of course.

Joseph decided the time had come for him to depart. His landlord was harassing him for a month's back rent and he had no intention of paying for the dubious pleasure of having slept in the dingy room. He checked his belongings carefully, and packed his collection of watches securely, having ensured that he had removed any batteries that would start alarms ringing at inconvenient moments. He spent most of the day going to and from his room, removing two old shirts he espied on a local washing line and obtaining a new bag in which to pack his wardrobe.

As darkness fell he left the room, his bed was rumpled and on the floor stood his old bag with a shirt draped over the side, the other hung on the arm of the chair. At first glance it looked as if he would be returning at any minute and was a trick he had used many times before to avoid paying the rent.

He walked to Amonia Square and sat in one of the numerous cafes, reading a discarded newspaper and eating a palatable meal until he decided it was time to leave. Once into the back streets he tried the handles of the cars as he passed until he was rewarded by one opening at his touch and it took him only a second to fiddle with the wires and start the ignition. Driving with the flow of traffic he skirted the city and drove down to Piraeus, calling at a garage to fill the petrol tank on the way. He parked in a dark corner beside a warehouse and settled down to snatch a few hours sleep.

Five hours later saw him driving carefully back towards the centre of Athens where he parked the car a short distance from the nightclub. Taking the keys from his pocket he inserted one in the lock and opened the door quietly. As had guessed the place was deserted. The torch from his pocket gave him adequate light to find his way to the cupboard where the stock of alcohol and cigarettes were kept.

It took him a number of trips to empty the cupboard and stack the bottles and cartons just inside the entrance door; then he returned and locked the cupboard door behind him. He smiled triumphantly to himself. That would give them something to think about, cleaned out and all the doors locked.

He opened the door quietly and tucked some cartons of cigarettes under his arm to take to the car. He backed up and opened the rear doors and the boot, then wasting no time he loaded his spoils, placing the bottles carefully on the floor and throwing the cigarettes in haphazardly on top. Finally he locked the door of the nightclub behind him and drove steadily away towards Piraeus where he knew he would find a ready market for his goods.

Giovanni listened with growing annoyance as Nicolas told him of the raid on the nightclub.

'Get the locks changed immediately,' he rasped.

'I have,' replied Nicolas. 'I've not reported it to the police. Do you want me to?'

Giovanni sighed. 'No, we know who did it, but I doubt if we'd ever manage to prove it. I ought to have changed the locks whilst I was still there. I should have realised he would have had the keys duplicated. Well, they'll be no good to him if he decides to try again.'

'I should have thought about the locks. He took me in thoroughly.'

'Don't blame yourself, Nicolas. He saw an opportunity and exploited you. What I would really like to know is what he was doing in Athens in the first place. If he wanted to see me why didn't he come to Crete? Why hang around the nightclub?'

'Maybe he didn't know the nightclub belonged to you?'

Giovanni snorted down the telephone. 'I have a shrewd suspicion that he did, but I can't fathom out what his motive was. I won't lose any sleep over it. Make sure the bar is stocked ready for when you open and we'll just write it off as a loss. I'll not try to claim on the insurance as that could become too involved and put my premiums up. Forget about it, Nicolas, but keep an eye on that new chap. We don't want any more pilfering, not even in a small way.'

Annita laid the table for Thanksgiving with a heavy heart. Only eleven places. Her family was sadly scattered now. Maria was in Brazil, Anna had not been invited and the whereabouts of her ex-husband and Saffron were unknown. No one seemed to know where Sorrell was, but Bryony was coming. Andreas always came and now he brought Laurie with him as a matter of course. It had taken a while for Elena to get used to the idea, but Matthew had accepted him at once. Helena was so engrossed in her husband and sons that she would not have noticed who was there, and seemed quite unconcerned that her twin was in England and her brother stuck in Baltimore due to an air traffic control strike.

She should be thankful. She had more than many women of her age. She looked at Elias and smiled, the newspaper had dropped from his hand as he snored lightly. The move to America had worked out well. The only one who seemed unsettled was Marianne, and that would change once she returned and married Bob. He was a nice young man.

If she had married poor Yannis as planned she would not be here now and nor would the rest of her family. She gave a slight shudder. She would probably look rather like her cousin Anna, old and lonely, living in a tumbledown farmhouse and dependant on a relative to look after her as she became older and more incapable. At least she knew that when the time came she would be able to end her days in the care home a few miles away, her every need attended to, and no burden on her immediate family.

'Elias, do wake up. They'll be here soon and you've still got your slippers on.'

Elias opened a sleepy eye. 'I don't see why they have to come so early.'

'You asked them to come early so you would not be too late getting to bed.'

'Did I? If you say so, dear. I'll just go and change my tie, then I'll be ready.'

'And your slippers,' called Annita after him. In the last few months he had seemed to be shrinking daily before her eyes. He looked so tired and was getting so forgetful these days.

1987

Sorrell sat in the autumn sunshine. This was more to her liking. Cannes and Nice had been ideal during the summer, but in her last two weeks she had found it more difficult to find an escort for dinner or an unguarded purse as the visitors either returned to their homes or moved on to warmer climes.

She had travelled to Athens in a leisurely fashion, leaving a string of hotel bills unpaid behind her, along with items of dirty washing. Rome and Turin had yielded a supply of exclusive clothes, which so far she had resisted wearing. She planned to winter in Athens and as yet she had not decided on her life style. The hotel where she had booked in was quite unsuitable, the plumbing was both noisy and intermittent, the only other residents appeared to be long distance lorry drivers who only made one night stops. She had made a mistake and felt distinctly out of place.

She needed to find a cash supply. She sat at a taverna by the flea market and watched the crowds as they forced their way down the narrow roads. By the time they had walked a few yards they were pressed against each other and shuffling slowly. Sorrell watched intently. There must be men amongst the throng who were carrying their money in a back pocket.

She placed a few drachmas on the table and went over to the vendor who was selling apples, purchasing four, placing them in her canvas bag. Picking out the tourists to the area she pushed her way through the masses, ending up behind a young man with his arm around his girl friend. Swiftly she touched his back pockets, hoping to feel a wallet, but they were empty. She twisted and turned her way to be in front of them and picked out another likely candidate. This time she was more fortunate and slid a wad of notes into the palm of her hand that she transferred to her bag of apples without even glancing at them.

By the time she had reached the railway line her bag was quite full and she began to force her way back up the roads between the solid mass of people. It was necessary to hold her bag in front of her or it was in danger of being pulled from her hand, but it gave her no opportunity to add to the contents. Slowly she regained the square, hot and breathless, ordering an orange juice at the taverna and standing by the wall to drink it. The waiters went back and forth, serving and collecting money as the business was brisk, stuffing the notes into their back pocket. Sorrell's eyes gleamed. She finished her drink and waited for the waiter to pass her.

'Toilet?' she enquired.

He pointed to the interior. 'Up stairs.'

'Thank you.'

She entered and walked up the rough wooden staircase, avoiding the handrail that was sticky and discoloured. The smell from the toilet was disconcerting and she was decidedly pleased that she did not need to make use of the facility. She stood and looked down, biding her time until a waiter entered to remove some cakes from the cabinet. Swiftly she ran down the stairs, brushed past the waiter, deftly removing the notes from his back pocket as she did so, and hurried from the premises.

Joseph watched with a feeling of admiration. He had not seen the girl actually remove the notes. One minute the money had been there and the next it had gone. He placed a note on the table, anchored it with his glass and followed her rapidly up the hill. Sorrell rounded a corner and slowed her pace, as she did so Joseph caught hold of her elbow. She turned on him and tried to pull away, making him dig his fingers into her flesh more viciously.

'You come with me.'

'Let me go at once. I am an American citizen. You have no right to hold me.'

Joseph smiled. 'American? I speak the American. You come with me.'

'I most certainly will not! Release me.'

'No. You come.'

Sorrell tried again to wrench her arm free. 'Police! Police! This man is attacking me.' She looked desperately along the deserted street.

Joseph began to push her in front of him along the road. 'You not shout. If police come I say I arrest you as thief.'

For the first time Sorrell felt frightened. The idea of being incarcerated in a Greek jail did not appeal to her. The knowledge that many more crimes would come to light once they began to investigate her did not help.

'What do you want?'

'You come with me. No shout. I not hurt you.' The grip on her elbow did not relax as he hurried her along the street.

'Where are you taking me?'

'My room. You safe there.'

'I'm in no danger here!'

Joseph did not answer her and Sorrell succumbed to the indignity of allowing herself to be propelled along unknown alleys until she was hopelessly lost. Tears of frustration and pain stung her eyes as she was pushed through an archway and into a dark doorway. Joseph took a key from his pocket and she was hustled up the dark stairway and into a room at the top, Joseph locking the door carefully after them and placing the key back in his pocket.

Once inside he released her and smiled. 'I sorry to hurt you. You would like a drink?'

'I would like to return to my hotel.'

Joseph shook his head. 'You stay. We talk. You take drachmas, I see. Now you give to me.'

'I will not,' replied Sorrell indignantly.

'I call police. Greek police like woman.' He eyed her up and down, running his tongue round his lips suggestively. 'They keep until they tire of her. Many police in Athens.'

'I don't believe you.'

Joseph raised his eyebrows. 'You want me to call police?'

'No.' Her throat was dry with fear.

'Then you give to me.'

Reluctantly Sorrell handed over her bag and Joseph emptied the contents onto the floor. A miscellaneous collection of notes, purses and wallets fell amongst the apples. He looked at her in surprise.

'You take this morning?' He bent to pick up a wallet. As he did so Sorrell hit him on the back of his neck, knocking him off balance, but inflicting little harm. As he sprawled across the floor he caught her ankle and pulled her down with him, wrestling her into submission, finally pinning her arms and straddling her.

'You do not hit Joseph.'

Sorrell glared at him and swore in Greek. He laughed. 'Always first you learn to swear.'

'I speak Greek,' answered Sorrell through gritted teeth. 'Now let me get up. You're hurting me.'

'You will not try to hit me again?'

Sorrell did not reply.

'Then we will stay like this. I am quite comfortable.'

'I won't hit you.'

Joseph eyed her quizzically. 'If you try you will regret it.' He released his grip on her arms, but stayed astride her legs.

'Let me get up.'

'First you will answer some questions. Who are you?'

Sorrell remained silent and Joseph landed a stinging blow on her cheek. By way of an answer Sorrell raked her fingernails down his cheek, drawing blood. Joseph hit her again and before she could retaliate another stinging slap followed it. She tried to roll away from him; then reared up in an attempt to bite his shoulder.

Suddenly his hands were round her throat and his thumbs pressing on her windpipe. Desperately she fought him off, choking more with fear than the pressure on her throat. Just as suddenly he released her and in a fury she flailed at him with her fists, whilst he laughed at her, before catching her wrists, holding both of them above her head with one hand.

'Now we be friends, yes?'

Sorrell scowled. All she needed was to catch him off his guard and she would be gone. She gave a slight shiver. She pushed her hair from her eyes and directed a punch at his ribs that he deflected easily.

'You wish to fight some more? Fighting excites me.' He held her hands tightly.

'Please let me go. You're hurting me.'

Joseph shook his head. 'I want to talk to you. We can lay here on the floor and talk if you wish or sit and have a glass of wine. If you hit me again I will really hurt you. Your pretty face will never be the same again.' He ran a finger down her cheek and tilted her chin. 'Is the rest of you as beautiful? I would like to see.'

A very real fear took hold in Sorrell's heart. She realised there was no way she could overpower the man and escape. He could do as he wished with her and she was powerless to stop him.

'Please, don't touch me. I promise I won't hit you. I just want to go.'

'We will talk first.'

'I want to go now.'

Joseph shook his head. 'I want to talk; then we will make an arrangement.'

'What arrangement?'

'I know you are clever. I need a beautiful, clever woman for my plan.'

'What plan?' asked Sorrell suspiciously.

'I have an uncle and brother who are very rich. They will give me nothing, so I will make them give me my share.'

'So why do you need me?'

'My brother is susceptible to a pretty face. I need you to gain his confidence. I will not only rob him of everything I will make him look foolish also.'

Despite her fear of the young man Sorrell was intrigued. 'What would I have to do?'

'It would not be difficult.'

'I'm not agreeing to anything until I know what I have to do.'

Joseph shrugged. 'I still need to decide the details.'

'And if I say no?'

'Then you go.'

'Where?'

'That will not be my problem.'

'And if I agree to work with you?'

'You stay with me. I'll look after you.'

'I need more than that! I'm used to living in hotels and having plenty of money to spend.'

'You will have. You stay with me and you will have everything you want.' Joseph leaned forward and kissed her. 'We will be very good together.'

Sorrell shook her head. 'I don't think so. I prefer to work alone.'

Joseph released her and shrugged his shoulders.

'As you wish. Today you were lucky. I saw you and caught you. Maybe tomorrow someone else will see you. They may be the police.'

Sorrell looked at him scornfully. 'I know how to look after myself.'

'Yes?' he raised a mocking eyebrow. 'I do not think so. You are a beautiful woman. Men remember. They lose a wallet and soon the police will look for you. Very soon the most profitable areas are closed to you.'

'And how would working with you make them stop looking for me?'

'I know the police. I can look after you. Keep you safe.'

Again Sorrell shook her head. 'I don't trust you.'

Sorrell left Joseph's apartment, refusing his offer to escort her. She did not want him to know where she was staying and she also needed to recoup the money he had taken from her. To her annoyance the streets were sparsely populated with no crowds to hide her. She entered a couple of shops and browsed around, but without other customers she was unable to ascertain where the money was stored beneath the counter. Feeling decidedly unsettled by her experience she finally turned into a bar and ordered a glass of wine. There was always tomorrow. She would return to the flea market and try her luck again.

Sorrell strolled down to the market, avoiding the taverna where she had asked to use the toilet. There did not seem to be so many people about, but she managed to help herself to a wallet and a roll of notes before her wrist was seized.

'Don't try to get away.' Joseph's voice was low in her ear. 'You're being watched. Walk on with me.'

Sorrell felt a shiver go down her spine. 'I don't believe you.'

'Please yourself, but you were seen taking that wallet. There's a woman talking to the rightful owner at this moment and pointing your way. I suggest you come with me and we get lost for a while.'

'You just want to rob me again.'

'I'm telling you the truth. Hang around if you don't believe me.'

Joseph released her and began to walk on down the road. Sorrell took a swift look behind her and saw a man and woman looking in her direction. Without further hesitation she followed Joseph down the road and around the corner.

'Wait for me.'

Joseph stopped and took her hand. 'Just do as I say.'

He began to walk with her as quickly as possible until they had put a considerable distance between themselves and the main road to the market. He stopped outside a small, dirty cafe and pushed her inside.

'What do you want to drink?'

Sorrell looked at her surroundings with distaste. 'I think a bottle of lemonade would be safest – with a straw.'

Joseph called out the order and waited for the girl to bring it over to them. He waved a note in front of her. 'If anyone should come in and ask you we have been here for about half an hour. You can keep the change.'

She nodded and returned to the counter without a word of thanks. Sorrell sat silently as Joseph drank his beer. He lit a cigarette and tipped his chair back, blowing smoke towards the ceiling.

'I think it's time you and I had a proper chat. What made you go back down to the market today?'

Sorrell shrugged. 'There are plenty of tourists down there and they're pretty careless with their belongings. If you hadn't taken my money yesterday there would have been no need for me to work today.'

'There are better places than the flea market and you're a lot less likely to be spotted.'

'Where?'

'That's my business. If you agree to work with me I'll take you and show you the system. If you still want to work alone then you'll have to learn as you go along. I won't always be on hand to rescue you.'

'I didn't need rescuing today.'

Joseph raised his eyebrows. 'If that man had caught up with you and found his wallet in your bag he would have called the police. They would have made quite a scene as they arrested you; no doubt the taverna would have noticed and remembered the girl who was there just before one of them lost a large amount in notes yesterday.'

Sorrell sipped at her lemonade through the straw. 'What you want is for me to do the lifting and then give you the proceeds. I don't work that way.'

'I told you. I would look after you and keep you safe. I would expect three quarters to cover living expenses. The other quarter would be yours to spend as you pleased.'

'I'm used to having all of my takings. Why should I give any to you?'

'Protection; the cost of accommodation and food, and I am the brains behind our long term schemes.'

Sorrell shook her head. 'Half; and I shall expect it to be counted out in front of me.'

Sorrell found her relationships with Joseph satisfactory. He had introduced her to the metro system, shown her how to purchase a ticket to Piraeus and spend the remainder of the day travelling up and down the line. They would pick as many pockets as possible whilst travelling from one station to the next then leave the train. A quick visit to the toilets allowed them to dispose of any wallets or purses; then they were back on the next train to repeat the operation. One stop before Piraeus they would leave the train and wait for the next one returning to the market area; once again they would leave the train one stop before its final destination. The pickings were good and they were never on any train long enough for the passengers to become suspicious, many not realising they had lost their possessions until they had completed their journey.

They began to have a routine, moving between the flea market, the trains, the centre of Athens and general shop lifting. They never visited the same area more than once in a week and never on the same day as previously.

Occasionally they would work together, one distracting a shop keeper whilst the other raided the till. Sorrell kept a small exercise book with a note of her clothing and the way she had worn her hair to ensure that she looked as different as possible the next time she was in the vicinity.

Now Joseph had worked out a new scheme whereby she would stay at a hotel for a few days, ostensibly just passing through the city, and she put her time to good use. Each morning she would leave with as many room keys as she could manage to collect and pass them over to him. During the morning he would remove the tag giving the name of the hotel and take them to be copied. Sorrell then returned to the hotel with the originals and placed one on the desk each time she passed by. She supplemented their income by chance pilfering, whilst the keys sat, carefully labelled, in a shoebox at Joseph's small apartment. She was intrigued by the collection he was amassing, but knew he would not be forthcoming if she asked the reason.

When Joseph suggested visiting Italy for a few weeks she accepted, expecting her present life style to continue, albeit in a different country. She was not disappointed. Venice gave them rich pickings, but Naples tested her nerves. Handbags were snatched before her eyes and Joseph forbade her to carry valuables openly. He laughed at her fears, but agreed to move on to Florence, admitting that the move agreed with his own plans and there was someone he wished her to meet. Intrigued, Sorrell sat at a pavement café and waited until she saw him strolling towards her, a girl hanging on his arm.

He sat opposite and introduced Flavia with a lazy smile. 'I want you two to be friends. You are much alike.'

Sorrell raised her eyebrows. 'Really?'

'Joseph and I are old friends. Same line of business as you.' Flavia smiled at Sorrell. 'Joseph has a plan that needs two girls working together. It's just a business arrangement – and I'll earn my keep.'

'This is the first I've heard of it,' frowned Sorrell.

'I have to speak with Flavia first. If she say no, then I need to think again.' Joseph spoke in English for Flavia's benefit.

'And suppose I refuse?'

'When I tell the plan I do not think you say no.' Joseph paid for Sorrell's drink and waved the waiter away. 'You take walk in park and get to know each other. I meet you in one hour and you tell me if you work together.'

Sorrell and Flavia looked at each other and Sorrell shrugged. 'I've nothing to lose by talking.'

Joseph patted her bottom as she rose. 'Good girl, you will not regret,' he assured her.

'Well,' opened Sorrell. 'I don't know what we're supposed to be talking about, but my name's Madeleine and I'm from the States.'

Flavia nodded. 'I'm pleased to meet you. How long have you and Joseph been together?'

'A few months. Why?'

'I just wondered if he had dropped me for you.'

'And had he?'

Flavia shook her head. 'No. I haven't seen him for almost a year. Said he was going over to Athens to set himself up for life. He gave me the impression that it was a one man job.'

'I don't know his plans.'

'There's no need to be cagey with me, Madeleine. I know just how crooked Joseph is. It's part of his attraction. I was just an opportunist, but he showed me how to get organised and I'm grateful to him.'

'So what do you do?'

'Work the hotels mostly. Sit in the bar and snare some unsuspecting tourist. They give me a free meal and drinks, I promise them the earth and when we get to their bedroom I send them off for a shower, strip them of all I can and quit.'

'Don't they rumble you?'

'They're usually too embarrassed to complain.'

'Suppose they refuse to take a shower?'

'I'm mysteriously taken ill. Must be something I've eaten. Call me a taxi and I'll take myself to the hospital.'

Sorrell laughed. She found she liked this girl who obviously enjoyed her life of petty crime. 'What do you think Joseph has in mind for us?'

'I've no idea and I don't much care provided it's profitable.'

'Where did you learn your English?'

Flavia grinned mischievously. 'My father worked for the embassy. I spent ten years in London as a child.'

'So what does he do now?'

'Retired. Lives in Switzerland. What about yours?'

'I never knew him. I had a stepfather for a while; then he took off. How did you meet Joseph? He's not the kind to mix in ambassadorial circles.'

'The idiot I was living with was arrested for running drugs. I visited him in prison and met Joseph.'

'What was he in for?'

'Stealing a car that was used in a burglary. His friends shopped him. That's what first made him decide to go it alone.'

'But he's not alone if we're working with him.'

'No, but he's the boss. Calls the tune and makes sure he keeps his nose clean. If you or I get picked up there'll be nothing to link us with him.'

Sorrell fell silent. The girl was right. 'He's cleverer than I thought,' she admitted.

'Never underestimate Joseph. He's got brains.'

'And so have I,' Sorrell assured her.

Joseph joined them and they found a secluded spot beneath the trees. The two girls bent their heads to listen to him. Spending time with Sorrell had improved his English rapidly.

'I want you to do practise. You are friends on holiday. Make your story together. You must know where the other lives, what work she does, likes and dislikes. You will work with the keys the same as we did in Athens, Madeleine, but I will return both sets to you. You will work the rooms before you check out. Make sure you bring the duplicate keys with you. We do not want them to understand our system.'

'I don't see why you need two of us. I could do the job on my own,' protested Sorrell.

'I know, I know. Some hotels you will do on your own and some you will work together. When you are together Flavia can use her charm. You will have to be good, Flavia. Make sure your target is loaded and vulnerable.'

Flavia nodded. 'I don't see that it needs two of us, the other could be in the way.'

Joseph smiled at them. 'Twice the pickings, girls.'

'Not necessarily.' A stinging slap stopped Sorrell from saying any more.

'I know what I am doing,' Joseph assured her harshly. 'By the time the hotels have realised there is something wrong we will be out of town and they will not know if they are looking for one girl or two girls. You will book in and out when I say. This is to prove that my plan will work. We will then go to Crete and return to Athens for the big prize.'

'And what is that?' asked Flavia.

'You will see. So? What do you say to Joseph?'

Sorrell looked at Flavia and they nodded to each other. 'One proviso, fair shares, everything into thirds.'

Joseph nodded. 'Of course. A third share of the profits. I also have the expenses, remember.'

Sorrell enjoyed the remainder of her stay in Florence. It was amusing to have a companion some of the time and she admired Flavia's flair for seeking out a man who was lonely and unattached. They met Joseph each day and passed over to him any keys they had used and also whatever they had gleaned from the various rooms they had ransacked. Daily they scanned the local papers for any mention of crimes taking place in the city's hotels and at the first report they had left in a car that Joseph borrowed from an unsuspecting local.

The car was left on the outskirts of Rome, close to the railway station and after a short walk Joseph hailed a taxi to take them to a small hotel.

'Here we stay to rest. No work for two days,' he announced.

Sorrell sat down on the bed. She had not realised how tired she was, tired of having to be continually on the lookout for opportunity, yet on her guard against detection. Flavia sat down beside her.

'So? What do you want to do?'

'Have a long, hot bath and then sleep.'

'If this is Joseph's idea of being made for life give me another.'

'Why don't you find yourself a rich husband?'

Flavia shook her head. 'I wouldn't want to be tied down. Joseph asked me to work with him for six months, nine at the outside, then I'm free to move on if I wish or stay and take part in any further scheme he thinks up.'

'He's a strange man.'

'I've met stranger! Are you in love with him?'

Sorrell shook her head. 'That word doesn't have a place in my vocabulary.'

Sorrell, Joseph and Flavia sat in the locked hotel room. On the bed in front of them were three piles of notes. Joseph smiled broadly.

'I am proud of you two. We have managed a good haul.' He looked from one girl to another. 'I give you your share now. What you do with it is your problem. I suggest you put it somewhere safe.'

Sorrell picked up the notes and flicked through them quickly. 'Is this it, then?'

Joseph spread his hands. 'You have your share. I have changed the little trinkets you brought me into cash. Now it is for you. I will tell you my next idea. If you do not want to do you can go.'

'I'd like to hear what it is before I decide.' Sorrell held the notes firmly in her hand.

'We will go to Athens. I have a very special job for you there. I told you of my uncle and brother. They are very rich. Now is the time for them to share with me.'

'With us,' Sorrell corrected him.

'You will go to his hotel. This time I want the master keys.'

'The masters,' Sorrell frowned. 'How will I get hold of those? The chambermaid is hardly likely to have them with the room keys.'

'So where would you look to find them?'

'With the manager, or in his office.'

Joseph nodded. 'So, now you know where to look. You take. You give them to me. I give them back to you and you return them. Simple, yes?'

Sorrell shook her head. 'Simple, no. The manager is hardly likely to leave them lying around on his desk or table.'

'Of course. So you take.'

'How?'

Joseph shrugged. 'You find a way.'

Sorrell looked at Flavia. 'Are we working together?'

'Yes. Forget the rooms. I want only the master keys.'

'How long do we have?'

'A week – if you need it.'

Flavia pulled a face. 'So what's this uncle of yours like? How will we know him?'

'It is not likely he will be there. But it does not matter. In fact, it could be better if they are not there. They will not know you and we can go to another hotel they have.'

Sorrell placed the money in her handbag. 'I think Flavia and I need to have a little discussion, plan our moves. My first one is to put this somewhere safe.'

Flavia booked a single room at the Athenia De Luxe under the name of Elaine Pascale. She mingled with the other guests, extolling the wonders of Greece and comparing them with her recent tour of Yugoslavia.

'You see,' she told a small group in the bar, 'I went to Yugoslavia with my parents. They were visiting old friends. It was pretty boring. Sit by the pool and make small talk all day, barbecue in the evening and the same old boring chatter. I stuck it for three days, then I took off on my own. Decided I'd just take a bus or a train and see what else Yugoslavia had to offer. After a week I thought I'd spread my wings a little further afield, so here I am. I've even managed to convince my parents that they're stupid to stay in the one place for a month as they'd planned. They've hired a car and are motoring down to join me in a week's time. By the time they arrive I want to know Athens like a second home so I can show them around. Where have you been today? Tell me if it was worth seeing and I'll go tomorrow.'

The tourists smiled at her, included her in their talk and vied to outdo each other with traveller's tales.

Sorrell arrived the following day, wearing shorts and shirt with a backpack that she dropped thankfully on the hotel floor.

'Do you accept scruffs like me?' she asked. 'I've been walking and staying in bed and breakfasts in the villages. Now I've arrived here I'd like to treat myself to a little luxury for a few days.'

Thalia smiled at her. 'I'm sure madam will enjoy her stay here. We try to make everything comfortable. You would like a single room?'

Sorrell nodded. 'Unless you have a lonely millionaire staying here.'

Thalia handed her a key. 'Please sign the register. I will ask for your luggage to be taken up.'

Sorrell signed her name as Jane Elliott and handed over the false passport. 'I can haul this up myself.' She looked around the bar, her eyes alighting on Flavia, who she ignored. 'Is that the elevator?'

Thalia nodded. She hoped the woman would not stay long. She did not appear to be their usual class of clientele.

Sorrell emerged from her room an hour later. She had showered, donned a flowered skirt and plain top, brushed her hair and re-applied her makeup. She smiled at her reflection. She definitely preferred this vision that smiled back at her.

Sorrell returned to the foyer where Flavia was sitting with a pile of brochures advertising local tours. Sorrell stopped beside her.

'I guess you speak English?'

Flavia looked up and nodded.

'Maybe you could help me. I'm looking for somewhere to eat. I'm paying an arm and a leg to stay here for a few days; I can't afford anything too expensive.'

Flavia frowned. 'Well, there's a place down in Plaka, run by students. Their prices are reasonable and the food's good.'

'Sounds like my kind of place. How do I get there?'

'Go to the bottom of the hill, turn right and keep going until you see a gap between the shops. Turn in there and you'll see the tables.'

'Thanks. I'll see you around.' Sorrell swung out through the doors without a backward glance.

When Sorrell returned to the hotel, Flavia was sitting in the bar recounting her day to a group of fellow residents. Sorrell slipped onto the bar stool beside her and ordered a drink. She waited until Flavia stopped for breath; then tapped her on the shoulder.

'Thanks, that was a good place you directed me to for a meal.'

'Glad to hear it. What else have you done today?'

'The Acropolis. I felt that had to be my number one. I can't decide where to go tomorrow. There's a tour to Mycenae that sounds quite good or I could go to Delphi. It will make a change from walking for me whichever one I choose.'

'I've decided on Delphi. Why don't we go together? I'm travelling alone until my parents get here.'

'Yes? I'd really appreciate that.'

For two days the girls met up, pretending to get to know each other and striking up a friendship. They went on a shopping expedition into the narrow streets of Plaka and spoke quietly to each other.

'I think the time is right. I'll talk to Joseph and get him to call the hotel tomorrow morning. You go out late this afternoon and phone me and I'll fix the telephone whilst we're talking. I doubt if they can get it repaired tonight, so it will be a good excuse to ask to make a private call from the manager's office. If it doesn't work I'll have to check out and leave it up to you.'

'You'll do it, Flavia. I have every confidence in you.'

Flavia entered the dining room and took her usual place at a table by the buffet. Ten minutes later Sorrell also took her place, the girls exchanging a friendly wave.

'Telephone, please. Miss Pascale. Telephone call for Miss Pascale.'

Flavia rose. 'That's me.' She walked across to the telephone at the far end of the dining room. She scrabbled in her bag and wrote something on a piece of paper. After a few minutes she replaced the receiver and looked up with a dazed expression on her face before burying her face in her hands.

Sorrell walked over to her. 'What's wrong? Have you had bad news?'

Flavia looked up, her lip trembling. 'That was our friends in Yugoslavia. They say my parents have been involved in a car crash. They're both in hospital.'

Sorrell placed an arm round her shoulders. 'I'm so sorry. Do you know how they are? They might not be badly hurt, just cuts and bruises.'

'I must telephone the hospital. Where's the manager?' Flavia looked round wildly.

'He's at the desk.'

Flavia picked up her large bag and walked unsteadily to where Orestis was checking arrivals for the day.

'Please, I need to telephone.'

'Yes, madam. There is a telephone in your room,' answered Thalia.

Flavia passed a trembling hand over her brow. 'It's not working. I reported a fault earlier. I need to telephone the hospital. My parents, they've had an accident.'

'Of course, madam.' Thalia lifted the receiver of the telephone on the desk and handed it to her. 'If you tell me the number I will dial for you.'

'Oh, come on,' interposed Sorrell. 'She can't make a call like that out here with everyone gawping at her. Isn't there somewhere more private she could go?'

Thalia looked at Orestis and spoke to him in an undertone. He looked at the distressed girl before him.

'Please.' He took Flavia's elbow and led her to his office, indicating the telephone on the desk with his hand.

Sorrell loitered by the reception desk whilst they were gone. Hanging on hooks at the back were the keys to all the rooms and at one side hung a large bunch. They drew Sorrell like a magnet, but she knew with the receptionist there and the manager standing just outside his office door she had no chance of taking them undetected.

Flavia emerged, dabbing her eyes with a handkerchief. 'Thank you. Please can you make up my account. I have to leave at once. The news is very bad.'

With shaking shoulders Flavia walked towards the lift where Sorrell caught up with her.

'How are things?'

'They're in a critical condition. I have to leave at once.'

'Is there anything I can do? Help you pack? Just keep you company?'

Flavia smiled wanly. 'I'd appreciate having someone with me.'

The two girls entered the lift together and once in the privacy of the small compartment Flavia grinned at Sorrell. 'Perfect,' she murmured.

Half an hour later Flavia returned downstairs with her bags and paid her bill, still weeping copiously and accepting Sorrell's support and sympathy until her taxi arrived and the girls embraced in farewell.

Sorrell returned inside. 'That really was a shame. Poor girl, she was having such a good time. What a rotten thing to happen.'

'It was fortunate you had become friends, madam. You were able to help her when she needed you.'

Sorrell clapped her hand against her forehead. 'What a dumb cluck I am! I didn't even ask her for her address. I really liked her and wanted to keep in touch.'

Thalia hesitated. There was an address in Yugoslavia in the hotel register. She spoke to Orestis; then turned back to Sorrell. 'You could leave a letter here. We would be able to forward it for you.'

'Really? That would be great. I could just send her my address and ask her to write when she felt like it. It would be up to her after that.'

Orestis turned away. Thalia could continue to deal with the American woman. He could do without such drama at breakfast time. It disrupted the whole day.

Sorrell met Flavia and Joseph during the afternoon at a small hotel in Piraeus. The two girls hugged each other.

'You were marvellous,' Sorrell complimented Flavia. 'I'm sure no one suspected it was a put up job.'

'Does the manager start to look for a bunch of keys?'

'I don't think he will. Whilst Flavia was in his office I spotted a large bunch hanging up behind the desk. It stands to reason that they would have more than one set. They might not miss the one's Flavia took for months.'

'You take these back with you just the same.' Joseph dropped a heavy bunch into her lap.

'I don't know if I'll be able to get them back into the manager's office,' frowned Sorrell.

'Do not worry. Leave them at the desk at a convenient moment. Now, you would like to celebrate before you return to the hotel?'

'How much longer am I staying there?'

Joseph shrugged. 'I will pay for two more days. If you wish to stay longer you have your own money.'

'Meaning you have no more use for me?'

'I have much use for you. We need to visit hotels. We need money. This was expensive for me, and there will be more expense later when we visit Crete.'

'Are we working as we did in Italy?'

Joseph nodded. 'But you take nothing from the Athenia De Luxe. There you must leave no suspicion after you.'

Sorrell raised her eyebrows, but she had learnt better than to question Joseph.

'I'll meet you back here on Friday.'

Sorrell stayed a further two days at the hotel before checking out, her pack on her back, her skirt replaced by the pair of scruffy shorts.

'I'm off to explore the islands now,' she announced to Thalia. 'If I've any money left when I get back I'll stay here again for a couple of nights.'

'We will be pleased to see you, madam. Would you like me to call you a taxi?'

'I guess I can walk to the metro.' Sorrell swung her rucksack onto her back and with a cheerful wave she sauntered out of the doors and down the hill.

Orestis telephoned Giovanni in Crete and he listened carefully. 'You say nearly all the big hotels have suffered? Are you sure they have taken nothing from ours?'

'No more than the usual towel or ashtray. It seems strange that we should have been left alone.'

'Our security is probably better than theirs. After that little episode with Joseph I know you've been very careful to vet all new employees. Have the police any idea who's behind it?'

Orestis shook his head, despite being on the telephone to Giovanni. 'They did not say so. They claimed to have had reports over the last three months.'

Giovanni frowned. 'That sounds more like tourists taking a chance in an unlocked room. The police are probably exaggerating the extent of the problem. Don't worry, Orestis. We're insured against loss or damage of visitors' property provided they can prove it was negligence on our part.'

'If you say so. I just thought you ought to know.'

'Quite right. Let me know if the police charge anyone.'

Giovanni replaced the receiver and promptly forgot the conversation as he dressed himself with care. His shirt left open at the neck to show his bronzed chest and a gold medallion, just the right amount of after-shave, and certainly enough money in his pocket to impress whoever was the lucky lady tonight. A coach party had arrived and there were two girls who had looked available and they had noticed him, he was sure of that.

He walked into the dining room, acknowledging the deference of the waiters, his eyes roaming over the tables, ostensibly checking all was well, but in reality looking for either of the girls. Coach parties were really perfect. They spent the day travelling around the island, returning in the evening to the hotel. He had his days free to concentrate on his work and could be certain he would not have the embarrassment and inconvenience of being pursued by ardent and unwanted females for weeks or months on end.

She was sitting over by the window, her back towards him, and he walked over quietly.

'Good evening. May I join you? I don't like to see one of my guests sitting alone.'

She raised her eyebrows. 'Your guests?'

'I am the manager of this hotel. Everyone is my guest.'

Her eyes gleamed with amusement. 'I see; we all get a free meal.'

'I wish I could, but I am in business,' he spread his hands. 'My customers I have to charge, but for my friends, of course, it is different.'

'How different?'

'More than you could possibly imagine. Come with me for a drive in the moonlight, then we will walk along the sand, visit a small taverna I know, eat fresh fish caught by the light of the stars and dance the night away.'

She wrinkled her nose. 'I've had enough travelling for one day, I don't like fish and I'm too tired to go dancing.'

Giovanni frowned. He was not used to such out-right rejection.

'At least allow me to order a bottle of wine to go with our meal.'

'Our meal?'

'If you will not permit me to take you out, may I at least join you here?'

She shrugged. 'You're the manager, not me.'

Giovanni waved his hand in the air and a waiter glided to his side to take his order.

'At least the service is good with you around.'

They talked desultorily throughout the meal, Giovanni trying hard to encourage her to spend the evening with him elsewhere and her parrying his attempts by insisting that she preferred to do her sight-seeing during the hours of daylight.

'Tomorrow, you will allow me to take you out tomorrow evening?'

'Maybe, if I've nothing better to do.'

Giovanni was genuinely hurt. 'Why are you so cruel to me?'

'I'm not cruel, I'm just not one of your pick-ups.'

'You don't like foreigners?'

'I'm quite happy with them. You're not Greek, though.'

'I am half Greek. My father is Italian.'

She nodded. 'No wonder you think you can have any girl your eye alights on.' She folded her napkin and placed it on the table. 'Good night. Thank you for the wine.'

Giovanni scowled after her. This had never happened to him before.

Giovanni spent a sleepless night wondering about the girl. He realised he did not even know her name. That could be easily rectified. He would simply look at the passports that were held at reception. What was one girl anyway? By the end of the week he would have forgotten her. He rose early and was down in the foyer long before any guests had arisen, much to the annoyance of the night attendant who had been napping behind the desk. He pretended to read the morning paper whilst watching the lift door for her to emerge, but when she did so it was with another girl and she swept by him with only the briefest of smiles.

He continued to hover until they left the restaurant to return to their rooms to prepare for the day's conducted tour.

'Excuse me,' Giovanni stepped in front of them. 'May I ask if you spent a comfortable night?'

'Very, thank you.'

'And your plans for today?'

'We are joining the coach party for a tour of Knossos and the museum.'

'I'm sure you will enjoy it. A relative of mine used to work at the museum.' Giovanni bent the truth a little.

'Really. How interesting.' The polite boredom in her voice did not deter him.

'Maybe when you return you might like to visit the gift shop at the hotel? We sell many replicas of the museum pieces. A souvenir to take home, maybe?'

'Maybe. Please excuse us or we shall be keeping the rest of the party waiting.'

Giovanni watched them enter the lift and heard her companion giggle. Once in the privacy of their room Sorrell threw herself on her bed.

'Isn't he handsome?' she asked of her friend.

Flavia nodded. 'Fantastic, but why be so awful to him? You're supposed to be setting out to charm him.'

'He's obviously used to having girls fall at his feet. The only way to get him seriously interested is to pretend not to be.' A look of fierce intensity came over her face. 'I intend to have him at my feet by the end of the week.'

'He could be married,' Flavia warned her. 'Joseph didn't say.'

'Not him. He'd run a mile if you so much as stopped outside a jewellers. What a laugh, I know all about him from his brother and he has no idea who I am or what I have in mind for him.'

'And what is that?'

'You'll see.' Sorrell smiled to herself. 'You do your job and I'll do mine. Come on, or we will be keeping them waiting.'

When they returned there was no sign of Giovanni and Sorrell tried hard to conceal her disappointment.

'Maybe you've really frightened him off,' Flavia suggested.

'Not him. It's probably his afternoon off. I expect he'll be around this evening begging for some more rough treatment.'

Sorrell swept into the dining room, knowing that all heads were turning to look at her as she made her way to their table. The white, figure-hugging dress was designed to attract attention and the service at their table was excellent. Sorrell faced the door, but there was no sign of the manager, an enquiry at the reception desk was fruitless. They had no idea where he was, he may have gone to visit his family.

'I told you he could be married.'

'And pigs might fly! Let's go to the bar and get drunk.'

Settled at the bar, perched on a high stool, her back against the wall and an ouzo in her hand Sorrell watched the door to the manager's office as she sipped slowly and grimaced.

'I prefer wine to this stuff.'

'Then have some.'

'I'll probably be sick if I change drinks now.' She picked up an olive from the bowl. 'What are we doing tomorrow?'

'Drive to Aghios Nikolaos tomorrow morning. We should arrive about eleven. There will be plenty of time to look around and have some lunch, then on to Kritsa and Gournia before returning to Heraklion for the night.'

Sorrell nodded absently. The receptionist had just entered the office, a large bundle of notes in her hand. 'I wonder where he is?' She downed her drink and ordered another. 'I suppose it's not that bad after all.'

'Are we going to stay here all evening?'

Sorrell shrugged. 'There doesn't seem a lot of point. Let's go and find the night life.'

Giovanni drove steadily down to Aghios Nikolaos and sauntered into his aunt's shop.

'What brings you down here?'

Giovanni grinned. 'I've met the most fantastic girl you've ever seen. I tried to ask her out and she refused.'

Ourania raised her eyebrows. 'I doubt that often happens to you.'

'The thing is,' Giovanni frowned, 'she's travelling with a girl friend.'

'That still doesn't explain why you're here.'

'They're coming down to Aghios Nikolaos today. They're bound to come here and why shouldn't I visit my aunt?'

'Shouldn't you be working?'

'I'll do some extra hours next week,' replied Giovanni flippantly.

Giovanni saw them coming from a distance and retreated to the back of the shop. They looked in the window, pointed to articles and finally stepped inside. Ourania greeted them in halting English. Giovanni stepped forward.

'Maybe I can help? I believe both young ladies speak English.'

Sorrell removed her sunglasses. 'Well, well, well, fancy seeing you here. Shopping for a souvenir?'

'Not at all. Let me introduce you to my aunt.' Giovanni waved his hand. 'Maybe you would care to have lunch with me today as you have a chaperone with you.'

Flavia looked at Sorrell for guidance.

'I see no reason why not. I am hardly likely to succumb to your charms without you having the help of the stars and soft music.'

'There are many ways of reaching a lady's heart.'

Sorrell raised her eyebrows. 'Really? Provided you don't start using your hands I might be quite interested in counting. Where do you suggest we eat? Is the most expensive establishment the best or are we to be guided by you?'

Ourania told Anna about Giovanni's unexpected visit in pursuit of a young lady.

'Did you tell Yannis?'

Ourania shook her head. 'I didn't want to get him into trouble. I don't know how much free time he has. I've never known Giovanni chase after a girl before. He's run down here to escape from them before now.' Ourania chuckled. 'I remember one day when he had to hide in the flat upstairs all day in case she saw him.'

Anna shook her head. 'Maybe this one is different.'

'She was certainly beautiful. Come and help me unpack these new statuettes. I want to know what you think. Some of them are replicas of Roman statues. Do you think they'll sell or would I be better to stock only the Greek?'

Giovanni arrived back at the shop well pleased with himself. Ourania and Anna tackled him immediately.

'I have arranged to take a certain young lady for dinner this evening,' he declared. 'After that,' he shrugged. 'We shall see.'

'You behave yourself, Giovanni,' warned Ourania.

Giovanni gave his aunt a pained look, followed by a wink, and left the shop.

Ourania sighed. 'What do you do with a young man like that?'

Giovanni pursued Sorrell all week, waiting until the party returned from a day's sightseeing to offer her a selection of evening entertainment. Yannis had been told that his partner and manager was ardently pursuing a guest and he was not amused.

'If there are any repercussions from her family about your behaviour you are out. I'll not have my hotels get a bad name.'

'Uncle Yannis, however dishonourable my intentions I don't think I'm going to get very far,' he grumbled. 'To get what I want I would have to promise to marry the girl.'

'You've only known her a few days! Think about it. Once you're married it's for ever.'

'You haven't seen her yet. When you do you'll wish you were my age again and fancy free.'

'I'm quite happy with your aunt.'

Giovanni grinned. 'Tell me that when you've met Isabella.'

Giovanni stood with Sorrell in the moonlight. His lips brushed her hair and his hand travelled down her back and stroked her buttocks through the thin dress. He was sure she was not wearing any underwear.

'You look like a goddess. A perfect Greek statue.'

Sorrell did not answer. Her mind was frantically weaving back and forth, trying to simulate a plan whereby he would commit himself and she would have the opportunity to be in his office alone.

'It is sad when you gaze on such perfection and put out your hand to feel the delicacy and all you meet is cold, hard marble.' His hand continued to stroke her buttocks, hoping for a response.

'Maybe I am one of your Greek statues.'

'I do not see how you can be. Greek people are warm, understanding, full of love, this shows in their art.'

'Why shouldn't I be warm and full of love?'

'That is not possible. You have treated me like a stranger all the week.'

'You are a stranger.'

'The first day, maybe, but now I am your friend.'

'Are you, Giovanni?'

Giovanni placed his lips against her temple. 'I am your friend, your slave. A slave chained to a beautiful goddess.'

'You are being very Italian tonight. Chained to a goddess!'

'I am. I have seen many charming and beautiful women pass through the hotel, but never have I met one like you. From the first time I saw you I lost my heart.'

'You love me?' Sorrell turned her dark, limpid eyes on the young man beside her.

'I love you. I love you desperately. Let me show you how much I love you.' His hand began to undo the zip fastener of her dress.

Sorrell wriggled and removed his hand. 'By this time tomorrow you will be standing here with another of your guests saying the same thing.'

'I swear I will not. Stay in Crete, Isabella. Stay here with me.'

'I can't do that.'

'Why not?'

'I have to return to England.'

'Why? Why do you have to return?'

'I have to go back to work. I only took ten days leave. What would they think if I stayed here with a man I'd only known a week?'

'You could tell them you had stayed with the man you love.'

In the darkness Sorrell smiled to herself. He really was desperate for her.

Giovanni pulled her towards him and crushed her in his arms, kissing her passionately and managing to pull the zip down a little further. 'I do not know how to control myself when I am with you.' He gave a groan and the zip slid down another inch. 'I am in agony I want you so much.' He pushed himself even harder against her to leave her in no doubt of his pain. 'Do not leave. Stay here with me.'

Sorrell pulled herself away. 'I hardly know you.'

'Then stay, get to know me. I promise that you will not regret it.' His arms were round her again and she could feel the zip moving lower.

'And what am I supposed to do with myself if I stay? My friend will have returned home and I shall be alone.'

'No, you will be with me. Every minute you will be with me, every day, every night, we shall spend together.' His hand was easing the strap of her dress off her shoulder.

'And when you were tired of me? What would happen to me then?' She wriggled her body against his.

'Why should I become tired of you? Please Isabella, stay. I can make you so happy. Let me show you now, this minute, how happy I can make you.'

With an abrupt movement Sorrell pulled away and adjusted her dress. 'I'll think about it. Please take me back to the hotel now.'

Giovanni approached her as she left the dining room after breakfast. 'Excuse me, a quick word in my office, please.'

Sorrell frowned. He sounded very official. She glanced at Flavia who stood waiting for her. 'I'll be up in a few minutes.'

Giovanni opened the door and she passed through into his own small domain. Once inside he shut the door and stood with his back to it.

'Did you sleep well, Isabella?'

'Wonderfully.'

'I did not,' he shook his head sadly. 'I spent all night wondering what I could do to persuade you to stay in Crete with me.'

Sorrell felt relief sweeping over her. She smiled triumphantly. 'What do you have in mind?'

Giovanni took her in his arms. 'Anything. Anything that would convince you and make you happy. We will call at the airline office and cancel your return flight from Athens.'

'I have to go back.'

'Why? What is there in England for you? A boyfriend? Your family?'

Sorrell shook her head. 'I have no money to stay in Crete. I spent all my savings to come here. I couldn't really afford it, but Carol persuaded me,' she remembered just in time Flavia's assumed name. 'I even owe her money for some of my clothes.'

'That is no problem. I will pay for your clothes.'

'I can't leave my apartment or work in London without giving a month's notice. I would lose too much money.' Sorrell turned large, innocent eyes to Giovanni. 'And there is also my grandmother.'

'My poor little one.' He stroked her hair. 'You should not have to worry about such things. I will settle the bill for your stay in the hotel and you must tell me how much money you need to pay for your clothes. I will give it to you.'

'Oh, Giovanni,' breathed Sorrell as she nestled against him. 'Do you mean that?'

'Of course.' He tilted her chin upwards and kissed her passionately, pressing his body hard against hers and pulling at the fastenings of her dress. 'Please, Isabella. Come up to my room.'

'No, Giovanni. Carol will be waiting for me.' Sorrell caught at his hands and drew a little away from him. 'Besides, I have to go out and buy my grandmother a present. Are you free today? Maybe you could take me to a reputable jeweller.'

'Of course. We will spend the day together, and then tonight, you will come to my room and we will have a special meal.'

Sorrell was thinking frantically. This was her opportunity. All she needed was a few minutes alone in the office. She shook her head. 'I can't do that. We have to leave today.' She looked up at him coyly. 'There is always this afternoon,' she suggested.

Giovanni felt elated. At last he had broken down her defences. It had been worth the lavish promises to get what he wanted. 'Yes,' he breathed, 'this afternoon.'

'I feel quite faint and dizzy with excitement,' she murmured, leaning heavily against Giovanni and he helped her to a chair.

'Oh, dear,' she murmured. 'I need my medication. Usually I take it each day after breakfast. That's why I'm feeling ill.' Sorrell opened her bag and began to search amongst the contents. 'I haven't got it. It must be in my room; Carol can give it to you.'

Giovanni looked at her in concern. 'Are you really ill?'

Sorrell gave him a weak smile. 'Of course not; I have diabetes. I just need my medicine and I'll be fine.'

'You are all right to leave? Should I send a chambermaid or get someone to sit with you?'

'It's quite safe to leave me. I won't pass out or do anything silly. I'll just sit here quietly whilst you're gone.' Sorrell placed a trembling hand on her head and with no more hesitation Giovanni opened the door.

She could hear him hurrying across the vestibule and rose rapidly to her feet, crossed to his desk and pulled on a pair of plastic gloves before opening the drawer. As she had guessed the keys to the safe lay there at the back and it took her no more than a few seconds to open the old fashioned strongbox. The amount she saw in there almost took her breath away and she stuffed it hurriedly into the large bag she always carried, along with three jewel cases, closed and locked the door, replacing the keys where she had found them.

Giovanni did not wait for the lift, but ran up the three flights of stairs to the room Sorrell was sharing with Flavia. He banged on the door. 'Open up. Emergency.'

Flavia opened the door a crack. 'What is it? Is the hotel on fire?'

Giovanni shook his head and pushed the door wide. 'I need Isabella's medicine. She's been taken unwell and said her medicine is in her room.'

Flavia frowned. She had never heard her companion say she needed medication of any sort. Giovanni was looking in the bedside cupboard and Flavia realised this was a ruse to keep him out of the office.

'Oh, dear; I don't know where it is. Usually she has it with her first thing in the morning. Maybe she has left it in the bathroom?'

Giovanni pulled open the door and looked around. 'I can see nothing,' he shouted in exasperation.

Flavia made a pretence of looking through the drawers containing Sorrell's clothes. 'I can't find it either. I'll come down with you and ask her where she left it. I'll just get my key. Now where did I put it? I know I had it when I came up from breakfast. I wouldn't have been able to get in otherwise.'

Giovanni waited in a fever of impatience as she looked on the dressing table and then in her handbag.

'Here it is, of course. Where it should be.' She dangled it from her finger.

'Please hurry.'

Flavia followed him out of the room, down the stairs and into the office. Sorrell was sitting where he had left her with a smile on her face.

'Isabella!' he breathed.

'I am so sorry, Giovanni. I did have it with me. I just panicked for a moment. I shall be all right now.'

'You're a fine one! Where was it? In that bag of yours, I suppose. I've told you not to carry so much junk around with you.' Flavia picked up Sorrell's bag. 'Come back upstairs and turn it out. I don't want you to cause another disturbance.'

'I'm sorry, Carol. You're right. I will come up and turn out my bag.' Sorrell turned to Giovanni. 'I'll just go to my room and get rid of some of this; then I'll be ready to go out.'

Giovanni held the door open for them to pass through. 'I will be waiting for you.'

He frowned as he saw the receptionist pointing to him and a middle-aged lady made her way determinedly in his direction.

Sorrell emptied her bag onto the bed.

' 'It worked like a charm.' She placed the notes and jewel cases inside a large carrier bag and slipped them into the zipped compartment of her case. 'I can't stop. If Giovanni offers you some money just accept it. I told him I owed you money for my clothes. I'll tell you all about it later. I don't want to leave him too long in case he needs to go to the safe. I want to keep him out of the office until we're back in Piraeus. I'm packed ready to go. If I'm not here when we have to leave make sure you bring my cases and I'll see you at the ferry.'

Flavia nodded and watched as Sorrell gave a quick glance in the mirror and applied fresh lipstick to her mouth.

To her relief Giovanni was still cornered by the middle-aged woman. She smiled and leant against the reception desk until he was finally able to make his excuses.

Sorrell smiled gaily at him. 'Maybe we could go to the jewellers first? I need to get a very special present for my grandmother. She will be seventy next month and loves jewellery.' She bit at her lip. 'It will have to be something expensive. I don't usually use my credit card, but I'll make an exception for her.'

Giovanni tucked her hand into his arm. 'I know the best jeweller in town,' he assured her. 'He is sure to have something to please you and for me he will make a special price.'

Sorrell spent most of the morning examining the whole of the jeweller's stock, finally having to decide whether to have a brooch set with diamonds or emeralds. Eventually she settled for the diamonds, and gasped in horror when she converted the drachmas into English pounds.

'I can't possibly afford that. I just didn't realise the conversion rate. I had been taking two noughts off instead of one. I'll have to look again. It's such a shame. She would have loved that brooch.'

Giovanni squeezed her hand. 'I will speak to him.'

Giovanni spoke rapidly in Greek and Sorrell listened with amusement. He explained that she had misunderstood the pricing and he would be grateful if the jeweller would halve the cost to her, with Giovanni paying the rest. The jeweller shrugged. He did not care who paid for the item.

Sorrell's eyes glowed. 'I don't know how you managed to beat him down, Giovanni. My grandmother will be so thrilled. I don't know how I would have managed without you.' She held her face up for him to kiss. 'Do you know what I would like to do now?'

Giovanni smiled. 'You would like to return to the hotel and spend the afternoon in my room. An afternoon you will never forget.' He placed his arm around her waist and pulled her to him.

Sorrell shook her head. 'I need to go and have some lunch. I have to eat regularly due to my diabetes. Whilst we're eating you can tell me all about your family.'

Giovanni tried to hide his disappointment. 'And you can tell me about yours.'

Sorrell led the way to a small, but expensive restaurant that she had found during her stay. She sat as if entranced as Giovanni told her his life history and seemed quite uncomfortable when he asked for hers.

'There is so little for me to tell. My mother died when I was quite small and my father brought me to England from America and left me with my grandmother. He moved away in search of work and he, too, died whilst I was a child. My grandmother means everything to me, but,' Sorrell shrugged, 'she is an old lady. When she dies I will be quite alone in the world.' Moist eyes looked at Giovanni.

'You will never be alone again if you come back to Crete,' he promised. 'Have you calculated how much you need to repay your friend?'

Sorrell nodded and took a slip of paper from her handbag. 'I have Carol's money written down. Each time I was tempted to buy something I would look at this figure and remember that I had no money.'

Giovanni took his calculator from his pocket and turned the pounds into drachmas. It was far more than he had with him. 'We will go to the bank on our way back to the hotel. You will not have to worry about this any more.'

'You're so good to me,' murmured Sorrell.

Giovanni poured her a third glass of wine, then hesitated. 'It is all right for you to drink wine? You do not have to be careful with your food and drink?'

'Once I've taken my medicine I'm fine.' Sorrell looked down at her wrist. 'My watch! I'm sure I had it on when we left the jewellers.'

Giovanni looked at the ground beside their table. 'You are sure?'

'Positive. I looked at it before I suggested we had lunch. What is the time? I must get back to the hotel in time to collect my luggage before the coach leaves.'

'It is two thirty. We will go to the bank now and we will have time to call at the jewellers.'

'But I have the present for my grandmother.'

'And you have lost your watch. You cannot be without one.'

The bank was frustrating, Giovanni having to wait in a queue for over half an hour. He finally left with a smile on his face, despite knowing he had spent most of his savings on the girl. 'Now we buy a watch.'

'There's no time, Giovanni. I have to get back or I will miss the coach.'

'I will take you to the ferry. I'm sure your friend will arrange for your luggage. There is no need to worry. We have plenty of time.'

Sorrell protested no further and allowed Giovanni to purchase a small gold wristwatch. 'You are so kind and generous.'

He pulled her to him and kissed her hungrily. 'I so much wanted to spend this afternoon with you. You will not change your mind and stay?'

Sorrell shook her head. 'I'm sorry, too, but you know I can't stay.' She patted his face gently. 'We will have to hurry.'

Sorrell sat on the bunk in her cabin and smiled triumphantly at Flavia. 'Did I take him!'

'I was beginning to think you were going to miss the ferry.'

'And spend another week of him making eyes at me and pawing me all over whenever I was within reach?' Sorrell snorted.

'I thought he was rather nice.'

'He was just business as far as I was concerned. Now, what do you think of this?' Sorrell showed her friend the brooch. 'It's worth a mint, and with the watch and the cash we should be set up for quite a while.'

'Did you really lose your watch?'

'Of course not. I just thought I'd give it a try and it came off. How did you get on?'

'Pretty well. Mostly small pickings compared with yours, but certainly enough to cover expenses.'

'What a fool that Giovanni was! You'd never think Joseph was his brother.'

'I think Joseph took quite a chance letting you try your charms on his own brother. You might have decided you preferred him – and a regular life style.'

Sorrell shook her head impatiently. 'I like Joseph just the way he is. I know where I am with him. We're as crooked and devious as each other.'

She closed her bag with a snap. 'What shall we have to celebrate the success of our mission?'

Giovanni returned to the hotel feeling totally bemused. He had spent far too much money on the girl and had received nothing in return. He frowned. He did not usually have to spend more than the cost of a bottle of wine on the girls he fancied. He had a nasty feeling he had been taken for a ride by a professional. He banged his fist on the steering wheel. What a fool he had been!

He was totally unprepared for the way the receptionist rushed up to him, distraught and making very little sense.

'Mr Giovanni, it's gone. All gone. Two of the guests have already filed for compensation.' The small man wrung his hands.

Giovanni frowned. 'What are you talking about? What's gone?'

'Everything from the safe. It's all gone.'

'What!' Giovanni's face had whitened visibly. 'That's impossible.'

'No, Mr Giovanni, it's true. When I opened it to return the jewellery items to the Italian party who were leaving, the safe was empty.'

Giovanni almost pushed the man into his office and slammed the door. 'Sit down and tell me. From the beginning. Have you notified the police?'

Takkis shook his head miserably. 'I didn't like to until you returned.'

'Why ever not?'

'I thought, maybe, you had borrowed it, or taken it to the bank.'

'Borrowed it? Why would I borrow the hotel money?'

Takkis twisted his fingers nervously. 'The young lady, sir. I knew you planned to take her shopping, and you locked your office when you left this morning.'

Giovanni's face whitened further. He made an effort and controlled his voice. 'I can assure you I did not open the safe this morning. I did not take the money, either for myself or to pay in at the bank, and I certainly would not touch the jewellery. I wish to goodness I had. Call the police, Takkis. I'll call my uncle and let him know.'

'Yes, sir. I'm very sorry, sir.'

Giovanni managed a thin smile. 'It's not your fault, Takkis.'

Yannis drove rapidly to Heraklion. His mind was in turmoil. All he knew was that the hotel safe had been robbed and the police were there. He swept into the hotel and marched into the manager's office. He interrupted two policemen, one taking a statement and the other dusting the desk and safe for fingerprints.

'Giovanni,' he snapped. 'I want a word with you.'

'Yes, uncle.' Giovanni followed his uncle from the room and into the bar.

'Sit down and tell me the whole story.'

'I don't know very much myself. Takkis can probably tell you more. He was here.'

'Where were you?'

'It was Isabella's last day. We spent it together.'

Yannis snorted with derision. 'What time did you leave this morning?'

'About ten thirty. Isabella wanted me to take her to a jeweller to buy a present for her grandmother. We were in…' Giovanni's voice tailed away, his face ashen. He looked at his uncle with pain-filled eyes. 'It couldn't be, not Isabella.' He buried his face in his hands.

Yannis walked over to the bar and poured a stiff brandy for each of them.

'What have you remembered?'

'I met Isabella as she came out of the dining room after breakfast. I asked her to come into my office. I wanted to speak to her privately. Whilst we were talking she felt faint and asked me to fetch her medicine from her room. I was only gone a few minutes.' Giovanni raised anguished eyes to Yannis. 'It couldn't have been her.'

Yannis's lips compressed. 'What was wrong with her? What was the medicine she had to take?'

'I don't know. She's diabetic.'

'What did the medicine look like?'

'I didn't see it. I couldn't find it in her room and when I returned she said she had it in her bag all the time.'

Yannis stared at his nephew in disbelief. 'You fool! She sent you off on a wild goose chase. She's your thief, right enough. I hope you didn't spend too much on her. I doubt if you'll ever see her again.'

Giovanni felt hot with shame and embarrassment. He would never tell anyone how much money he had lavished on the girl in the course of the day.

'I hope you have her name and address in the book, and her passport number.'

'Of course I have.'

'Then we'd better get back to the police and hear what Takkis has to say.'

Takkis was full of apologies. He had not known the safe had been tampered with until two Italian women had asked for their jewellery back. He had gone to the safe and found it completely empty.

'So why didn't you call us immediately?'

Takkis looked from the policeman to Giovanni.

'Takkis waited until I returned to check I hadn't taken the money to the bank without telling him.'

'And the jewellery – would you have taken that to the bank?'

'I have done on previous occasions when the pieces have been particularly valuable.'

'I see.' His tone implied that Giovanni might be the guilty party.

Yannis interposed. 'We believe we may know the identity of the thief. There was a young lady staying here. She spent a few moments alone in the office this morning.'

The policeman raised his eyebrows and looked at Giovanni.

'She became unwell whilst she was talking to me. I left her in here whilst I fetched her medication.'

'And was the safe locked at that time?'

'As far as I know. I check that it's locked each night after the day's taking have been put in there and I'd had no reason to go to it this morning.'

'And there was nothing missing last night?'

'Nothing. I locked it behind me and put the keys in the drawer as usual.'

'Not the safest of places for them,' remarked the policeman.

'I agree, but only two receptionists, my uncle and myself have access to the office and know where the keys are kept.'

'So where is this young lady now?'

'She returned to Piraeus late this afternoon, on the overnight ferry. She flies to England tomorrow morning.'

'If you could give me her details, please. We can ask our colleagues to detain her at the airport and have a word with her.'

Giovanni nodded miserably and produced the hotel register. Painstakingly the policeman copied the information and shut his notebook.

'We'll be in touch, sir. As soon as we have any news we'll let you know.'

Takkis returned to the reception desk leaving Giovanni and Yannis alone.

'I am truly sorry, uncle.'

Yannis fixed him with a steely glare. 'I told you not to be taken in by a pretty face. Fancy leaving her in here alone!'

'Uncle, we don't know it was her, not yet.'

Yannis gave a pained sigh. 'From what I can make out when you left this morning you locked the door after you. Takkis discovered the theft when the Italians were leaving. That means you, him or this girl is the thief.'

'I'd trust Takkis.'

'So would I.' Yannis continued to look at Giovanni.

'You don't mean – no, not me, uncle. I swear I didn't touch a drachma. I used my credit card in the jewellers and drew cash from the bank. I wouldn't have needed to do that if I'd helped myself, would I?'

'You could have done that just to pull the wool over my eyes.'

'Uncle, no.' Giovanni spoke in a horrified whisper.

'You were so besotted by this girl; she could have talked you into anything.'

'I swear I didn't touch it, uncle. I wouldn't do that to you.'

'No, Giovanni, I don't think you would, but I have a nasty feeling that the police think otherwise. I just hope they can find this girl of yours and catch her with the jewellery. It could leave a nasty taste otherwise, a very nasty taste.'

Giovanni spent a sleepless night. He was wracked with guilt over the theft of the takings, despite being innocent and knowing the hotel was insured. Added to his misery was the knowledge that he had been completely deceived by Isabella. She would certainly not return to Crete and he would never see her again, unless it was to identify her as a criminal and ensure she was placed behind bars. He felt hot tears in his eyes, the shame of it all.

Joseph met Sorrell and Flavia at Piraeus. 'Any problems?'

'None.'

Joseph nodded. 'Good.'

He took their cases from them and they walked casually to the car park, ignoring the party waiting to board the coach for the airport. Once inside the privacy of the car he turned to them. 'Well? Tell me how it went?'

Sorrell held out her wrist to display the watch.

'Real?' asked Joseph.

'Of course. I've got some jewellery in my bag, along with the money from the safe.' Sorrell did not mention the money Giovanni had given her, ostensibly for Flavia.

'Good girl – and you?' he turned to Flavia.

'I'm not the ostentatious type, but I've got plenty of souvenirs.'

'Right, I'll drop you two at a taverna and go and dispose of this lot before they get on to us and start circulating descriptions.'

He held out a cloth bag and both girls dropped the jewellery into it. Sorrell took a last look at the brooch.

'I bet I'll never have one like that again.'

Joseph ignored her. 'Wait at the taverna until I get back. Don't try going back to the hotel where we were staying. We're off to Patras tonight.'

Sorrell and Flavia nodded. No doubt Joseph had decided not to pay the hotel bill.

The police returned to the hotel at mid-day. They wanted another look at the visitors' book and a list of everyone who had stayed at the hotel during the last week. All the airlines had been contacted and none of them had a Miss Isabella Chambers or Miss Carol Thompson travelling with them. The coach company was no help either. The seats for both girls had been booked in Athens, not as part of the organised tour from England.

The policeman looked from Yannis to Giovanni, but neither was able to help him further.

He shrugged and turned the page of his notebook. 'Now, if you can give me a description of the brooch and watch you say you bought this young lady. If she attempts to sell either of them we might be able to trace her.'

Giovanni's face flamed. 'I think it would be better if we visited the jeweller where we bought them. I can only tell you what they looked like; he'll be able to give you details.'

'Then if you wouldn't mind coming along with us now, sir. The sooner we have a description the better chance we have of finding her.'

Giovanni nodded miserably and followed the police out to their car.

Sorrell, Flavia and Joseph sat on the floor in the bedroom of the new hotel. Before them were a pile of notes, the result of Joseph selling on the jewellery to a fence with whom he had struck up an acquaintance.

'I probably sold at a loss, but I reckon they'll soon be on to Isabella and Carol as the likely thieves. You did very well, Madeleine. This is a little gimmick we must try again. Madeleine can be totally irresistible.' He eyed her speculatively; then squeezed her breast. 'Maybe one or two well known politicians would fall for her charms. Some rather compromising photographs could be offered to the press and the price of suppressing such material could be quite high.' He squeezed her breast harder, making her cry out in pain. 'Did you sleep with my brother?' he asked through clenched teeth.

'No, Joseph, honestly, I didn't. You're hurting me, Joseph. He wanted me to, but I swear I didn't. Joseph, please.' Tears had come into her eyes.

Joseph stoked her breast gently. 'Poor Madeleine. A whole week without a man and then Joseph hurts her pretty breast. Joseph will kiss it better.' He ripped at the halter neck of her blouse and pulled it to her waist, nuzzling and caressing her until he was fully aroused.

Sorrell tried in vain to push him away as he began to unzip his trousers. 'Not with Flavia here.'

Joseph's eyes had a wild gleam in them. 'Why not? I've had no one for a week either, so I'll have both of you. Come on, Flavia, come and join us.' He was divesting himself of his clothing frantically. 'I'll close my eyes and guess which one of you is giving me the pleasure.' He licked his lips lasciviously. 'Maybe you can think up one or two special little tricks to please me.'

Flavia rose to her feet. 'Threesomes are not my scene. I'll take my share and go. You don't need me around at the moment. I'll be back in a couple of hours.'

Joseph scowled at her; then appeared to accept her decision. 'Take your share. I've other business to attend to.' He turned his attention back to Sorrell, keeping a wary eye on the amount of money Flavia was placing in her bag.

Takkis replaced the telephone receiver and tapped on the office door. Yannis was filling in the necessary forms to claim on the insurance company for his losses and looked up with a frown.

'What is it?'

'I just thought you ought to know, sir, I've had two calls today from a travel firm. They wanted to know if we had found any jewellery when the rooms were cleaned. It seems one woman lost a pair of earrings and the other a ring. The American lady who is here was asking if her watch had been found, but she says she may have lost it when she was shopping.'

Yannis sighed. 'I wish the police would come up with something. My nephew is blaming himself, but it's beginning to look like professional criminals using a beautiful woman as the bait.'

Yannis was seriously worried. Almost every day a letter arrived from an insurance company asking him to confirm that a particular guest had stayed at the hotel between certain dates. A letter to say that the guest in question had lost an item of jewellery whilst they were there and would appreciate the article forwarded to them if it were subsequently found accompanied all of them. Each one Yannis passed to the police in the hope that it would help them in their enquiries, but they seemed no further forward.

Giovanni was miserable and spent long hours sitting in the office, recalling his week with Isabella. He had been duped. The jeweller had contacted him to ask for the balance of the money for the brooch. The credit card had not been honoured and he did not see why he should be out of pocket. Giovanni vowed he would never be taken in by a pretty face again. He continuously apologised to Yannis for his lapse until his uncle lost patience.

'For goodness sake stop apologising to me. You were only

partly to blame. At least the jewellery in the safe was covered by insurance. We only lost the cash.'

'But it wouldn't have happened if I hadn't been so foolish over that girl.'

'The guests would still have been robbed. It's taught me a lesson. The chambermaids have strict instructions never to leave a room unattended. If they've forgotten something they must lock the door whilst they go for it. I should have made that a ruling before. I knew they often stripped all the beds and then went to the linen cupboard for fresh bedding, leaving the doors open. It was just asking for a sneak thief to take advantage of the situation.'

Elizabeth slammed the ball back viciously at her coach.

'Good shot,' he called. 'Try to get the same spin, but place it deeper.'

'What do you think I'm trying to do?' Elizabeth muttered through gritted teeth as she swung her racket again.

'Better.'

The ball went back and forth between them; the momentum of the shots building up until the ball finally left the court.

'More control,' he called and Elizabeth nodded.

She picked up a ball to serve and as she swung her racket above her head a fiery shaft of pain shot up her arm and into her neck. The racket dropped and she gasped.

'What's wrong?'

'I think I've pulled a muscle.' She clutched at her right shoulder.

Her coach arrived beside her and began to feel her back and arm whilst she winced with pain beneath his hard fingers.

'We'll get the physio to look you over. You need to be fit for next week.'

Elizabeth eyed up the girl standing opposite her. She was an Amazon, but she had taken on girls twice her size before and run rings round them. She looked powerful, so she must not be given a chance to play a game of strength, better for Elizabeth to outwit her, making her run for every return and hope to wear her down.

They knocked up in a desultory fashion, each knowing the other was disguising their potential, then Elizabeth waited for the serve. It spun through the air and found its mark deep in the corner, quite impossible for her to return. Elizabeth set her mouth firmly. So that was the way the game was going to be played. From the first five serves she managed to return three, but lost the points and the first game.

'Well,' she thought to herself. 'Now I know what I'm up against.'

Refusing to be intimidated she served hard with spin and was gratified to see a flicker of annoyance cross her opponent's face as her return landed in the net. Making full use of the court she sent the girl running from side to side, then flicked a light shot over the net that caught her off balance. A ripple of applause went through the crowd, making Elizabeth feel good. The first set turned out to be a battle between them, with Elizabeth finally winning the tiebreak. She sat on her chair and mopped her face. This newcomer certainly had stamina, style and talent.

The break over, she took her place at the service line and waited. The ball barely cleared the net and she raced forward to scoop it up from the ground, only to see it flashing past her before she had time to reposition herself.

'I must play that shot deeper next time,' she vowed.

She jogged up and down on the spot, waiting for the next onslaught and made a good return shot. Once again they were fighting for every point from each other. Her opponent held her service game and Elizabeth was determined to hold her own. She raised her racket and smashed the ball soundly, hoping it would stay in the court. The ball came back and she twisted to return it to the far side. As she did so the searing pain she had suffered in her shoulder the previous week returned and she dropped her racket in agony and watched the ball pass her.

Clutching her shoulder, her racket hanging limply in her hand, she made her way to the sideline. 'I need the trainer,' she explained to the umpire. 'Can you call him?'

The umpire frowned. 'You're in the middle of a game. If you're really hurt you'll have to concede.'

Elizabeth stood and waited, hearing the speculative buzz that was coming from the spectators. The trainer hurried over to her and his fingers began to probe her taut muscles.

'Can you give me some massage and some pain killers?' Elizabeth turned her white face pleadingly towards him.

'It's not worth it. You might be able to get through the rest of the match, but you could do considerable damage to your shoulder. Better to withdraw now.'

The umpire nodded her head in agreement and miserably Elizabeth walked back to her seat. Her opponent had listened to the exchange and now came over to her.

'That was really bad luck. You were playing magnificently.'

Elizabeth managed a wan smile. 'The quality of the opposition always raises your game. You were pretty good yourself.'

Elizabeth submitted to the gruelling programme of massage and exercises her trainer organised for her, but each time he declared her shoulder ligaments mended she found they tore again after an hour of play.

She withdrew from the rest of the matches scheduled for her and determined to rebuild her strength gradually. Despite exercising and massage there seemed to be little improvement. Each time she tried to hit an overhead shot or serve the pain returned as severely as before. Finally she sought out a second opinion.

The doctor shook his head. 'I've bad news for you, I'm afraid. You should have had a complete rest for at least six weeks before attempting to play a match after the first tear. The damage you've caused is going to take a long time to heal.'

'How long?'

'A year, maybe more.'

'A year!' Elizabeth gasped. 'But I'm a tennis player.'

The doctor shrugged. 'The choice is yours. Ignore my advice and you'll be crippled in six months, never able to lift a racket again. Rest for a year, give the ligaments a chance to mend, then gentle practise for a few months, a few easy matches and within a couple of years or so you could be playing again.'

Elizabeth shook her head. 'That's impossible. I could never be out of the game for two years and expect to come back. There are too many youngsters coming along as it is. I'd never regain my position.'

'You have no alternative. You obviously cannot play at present. If you start to push yourself too soon the trouble will only return and each time it will be more severe and take longer to heal.'

Elizabeth had kept Nicolas informed regarding her injury and now he listened carefully to her as she tried to speak calmly and quietly to him over the telephone She would not be playing competitive tennis again. Her career was at an end.

'What will you do?' he asked at last.

'I haven't had time to think yet. I only found out yesterday. Oh, Nicolas, what can I do? I only know how to play tennis,' her voice broke as her self-control left her.

Nicolas felt a lump come into his own throat. 'I wish I could be with you – to comfort you.'

'I wish you could be.'

'I will come for my holiday earlier than we planned. I will come to America and we will talk. We will plan our future together. How long does it take to arrange a marriage in America?'

'Nicolas! Do you mean that?'

'Of course. You still wish to marry me?'

'You know I do.'

'Then I will telephone you when I have all my arrangements made and I will tell you when I will arrive.'

'Oh, Nicolas.' Elizabeth was sobbing over the telephone.

'Do not cry. It will not seem so bad when we are together. And, think, we will be able to get married very much sooner. If this is what you want then your injury is a good thing for us.'

Elizabeth wrote a long letter to Marianne that started sadly as she broke the news of her injury and the probability that she would never be able to play competitive tennis again.

'I was quite devastated when the doctor told me. I've no brains, you know that, so what does a broken down tennis player do for a living? I wouldn't even be able to coach without being able to demonstrate or return shots. I went home in the depths of despair. I was too miserable even to write and tell you about it then. Thank goodness Bob was at home. He talked to me for over an hour, pointing out that it wasn't the end of the world, and suggesting all sorts of awful mundane jobs that I could do, and telling me how many people had never had the opportunities I'd had and I should be grateful for those. He went on and on until I was ready to scream at him, then he suggested I 'phone Nicolas.

Nicolas was so wonderful. He had planned to come to America in three months time, but he made arrangements to come over immediately. Within a week we were together again and my shoulder didn't seem to matter any more then. He and Bob got on well together and Mum and Dad like him. I think they were expecting a really sleazy character as he runs a nightclub, so they were pleasantly surprised.

Now for the best and most wonderful news of all. I'm married. Really and truly married. Nicolas knew he couldn't stay in America, for one thing he had no work permit, but Dad pulled a few strings and we were married in the garden.

It all happened so quickly that I hardly had any time at all to make arrangements and none of my friends were there. We literally invited people by telephone. Your grandmother came, and your parents, and Helena and Greg with their baby, and Lucy from up the road, but that was all. I swore them all to secrecy until I had written you.

I wish you could have been here, then I could have had a matron of honour, but by the time Dad had arranged things we only had twenty-four hours notice and Nicolas had to leave America two days later because his visa expired. I couldn't get on the same flight as him, so I'm leaving in three days, that's why I've had time to write this long letter to you. I don't know where I'll be living in Athens, so I can't give you an address, but Nicolas has promised to meet me at the airport. I suppose we could be living with his mother, but I'd rather we were on our own.

Isn't it wonderful? I'm even glad I hurt my shoulder and can't play any more. If I'd still been going round the circuits I wouldn't be Mrs Christoforaki now. Doesn't it have a lovely ring to it? I can't quite get used to it yet, and I'm sure if anyone calls me by that name I won't answer.

I'll write to you again as soon as we're settled in Athens and you must come and see us just as soon as you can. I suppose I'll have to try to learn Greek, so I can speak to his mother. Nicolas telephoned her from here and she said she was looking forward to welcoming me into the family. Doesn't that sound stuffy and old fashioned?

I can't tell you how happy I am. I wish we weren't going to be quite so far away, but Mum and Dad have promised to come over and maybe you and Bob could come for your honeymoon? That would be really great. Almost like old times, except that we shall both be staid married women and have to behave ourselves. I miss Nicolas so much, yet he's only been gone for nine hours...'

The letter ran on for a further four pages, extolling Nicolas's virtues and saying time and again how much she loved and missed him. Marianne smiled to herself and hoped her friend would stay happy with her husband.

Nicolas was at the airport to meet the flight and greeted Elizabeth as if they had been apart for years and not just a few days.

'I have a big surprise for you. I have many surprises for you, but we will have them gently. You will be very happy in Athens.'

Elizabeth smiled gaily. Provided Nicolas was with her she would be happy anywhere.

He squeezed her hand. 'We go to our home, you have something to eat and drink, then you go to bed until this evening.'

'I don't want to go to bed, not alone.'

'You are more tired than you think. In minutes you will be sound asleep and wake ready to go out this evening.'

Elizabeth felt the tears pricking at the back of her eyelids and shook her head impatiently. If she was about to cry over being made to go to bed for a few hours she must be tired indeed!

They drew up outside an apartment building and Nicolas opened the car door and handed her out. 'Welcome to your new home.'

It was almost with a sigh of relief that she realised she was not going to live with his mother. She looked the building up and down.

'Where are we?'

'Between the city and Piraeus. It is pleasant here. The fumes of Athens do not drift so far.'

Elizabeth nodded. There would be plenty of time to get to know her way around. Nicolas opened the door and led her up a flight of steps, opening the door at the top and flinging it wide. She stepped inside, expecting to find a bare room and gasped as she saw it was fully furnished.

'When did you do this?'

'I did not. Come and sit. I have a bottle of champagne in the fridge. We will celebrate and I will tell you.'

Elizabeth sat down in a comfortable armchair and waited until Nicolas re-appeared with a bottle and two glasses. He handed her a full glass and held his up.

'This is to us. I hope we are very happy.'

Elizabeth followed suit and echoed his words. He perched on the arm of her chair and smiled down at her.

'Now I will tell you. This was the apartment my aunt left to my cousin, Yannis. He had tenants in here for some months and when they left I asked if I could buy it from him. He agreed. I had no time to decorate, but it is clean. The furniture I have not changed. In a few weeks we can make plans and you can change all that you do not like.'

Elizabeth nodded. She had sipped at her champagne and it was going to her head. Suddenly she was beginning to feel incredibly sleepy.

'Is this my surprise?'

Nicolas nodded. 'You like?'

'Very much. I thought we might live with your mother.'

'And that you would not like?'

'I think it would be difficult, being unable to speak to her,' answered Elizabeth tactfully.

'You will learn. Soon you will speak Greek.'

Elizabeth shook her head. 'I'm not very clever, Nicolas.'

'You do not have to be clever to speak Greek. Now, finish your champagne and then you must rest.'

Elizabeth opened her eyes some hours later. She did not remember undressing and going to bed. She rolled over and saw Nicolas lying beside her reading

'How long have you been there?'

'You said you did not want to go to bed alone. I keep you company.'

'And you have just been laying there reading?'

'I had a small sleep.' He smiled lazily at her. 'You had a long sleep. You feel refreshed now?'

Elizabeth nodded. 'I feel fine.'

'That is good. We have some time before we prepare to go out. What would you like to do?'

'What do you think I would like to do?'

Nicolas shrugged. 'Maybe unpack or inspect the apartment…'

Elizabeth pulled him towards her. 'You know just what I want to do. I haven't seen you for four days – and I've not been married a week yet.'

Elizabeth entered the hotel on Nicolas's arm. She giggled as he led her in. 'Do you remember the night Marianne and I came with our jeans in a carrier bag? I feel a bit like that tonight. If I blink all this will float away and I shall wake up at home with a match to play tomorrow.'

Nicolas squeezed her arm. 'You are here, in Athens, Mrs Christoforaki, and everyone wants to meet you.'

'Who? I've met your mother and your sister.'

'You have not met my cousin Yannis or Giovanni. Tonight you will meet them also.'

'Do they speak English?' asked Elizabeth suspiciously.

'Giovanni speaks English very good, uncle Yannis just a little, but you will like them, they will like you. We do not have to stay too late. They will understand that you are tired and need to have an early night.'

'But I slept most of the day.'

'So you do not want to have an early night?' He raised a quizzical eyebrow at her.

'Nicolas, you're a tease. Of course I do. I didn't want to get up, remember.'

'I remember,' he placed his lips close to her ear and whispered, making her blush. 'Now,' he announced, 'we must behave.'

Two men rose to greet them and Elizabeth was struck by the good looks of the younger man. They kissed her on both cheeks and Giovanni enquired about her flight, how she had found the apartment and what would she like to eat, whilst the older man sat quietly. She answered as best she could, feeling distinctly nervous before them, convinced they were assessing her suitability as a wife for one of their family.

Nicolas and Giovanni alternated between Greek and English, ensuring that the older man was included in the conversation. As they walked in to dinner, a considerable number of hotel staff seemed to be around and Elizabeth had a suspicion they all wanted to have a glimpse of the American woman who had married Mr Nick.

Having eaten, they returned to the hotel bar for coffee and brandy. Orestis joined them and was introduced, Nicolas explaining that he was not only the manager of the hotel, but also Yannis's partner. The two men drew a little apart and began to converse in low voices, until Yannis finally rose.

'Please excuse us. We have some business we wish to discuss. Please tell your wife she is very beautiful and charming, Nicolas. I am looking forward to you bringing her to Crete to meet Ourania.' He held out his hand to Elizabeth. 'Good night. I am happy to meet you.'

Elizabeth almost sighed with relief. She had felt very conscious of the fact that she could not converse with a man who was obviously held in great respect by her husband and his cousin. With the departure of Yannis the two men seemed more relaxed. Giovanni looked at his watch.

'Time to open, unless you'd like to do it for me? I'm sure I could entertain Elizabeth for you whilst you were working.'

'I'm sure you could, but I'm not giving you the opportunity.' Nicolas slipped a protective arm around her. He returned to speaking English for Elizabeth's benefit. 'We will go home. Elizabeth has had a tiring day. We will come one evening to see how you are managing.'

Giovanni snorted. 'I shall be managing very well. I have some new film.'

Nicolas raised his eyebrows. 'Yes? I will be interested to see.'

'I think you will like them. I have a good Hercules. Wait until you see the snakes.'

Elizabeth shuddered. 'I hope they don't look too realistic. You'll frighten your customers away.'

'Part of the attraction is a little fear. When the charioteers appear to bearing down upon them they know it is not real, but,' he spread his hands, 'suddenly they could be trampled to death and that adds to their enjoyment. When you visit I will tell you when to hide your eyes.'

Elizabeth had a distinct feeling that Giovanni was laughing at her as he left.

Giovanni joined his uncle in Orestis's office. 'Well?' he asked. 'What did you think of her?'

Yannis shrugged. 'She's very pretty. What else can I say? I only understood an occasional word when she spoke.'

'Nicolas seems happy enough with her. I think he was most relieved when I said I had to go to the club and open up. It gave them an opportunity to slip away.' Giovanni gave a slight snigger.

'They have only been married a week,' Yannis reminded him.

'I hope he has acted wisely.'

'What do you mean?'

'Well, they hardly know each other. Ten days, wasn't it? The next thing is Nicolas announcing he is betrothed to the girl.' Giovanni shook his head.

'He did go over to America for her.'

'I know, and once there the family rush him into marrying her.'

'What are you insinuating?'

Giovanni shrugged. 'Nothing, nothing at all. I just hope she will enjoy living quietly in Athens. She's been used to travelling around the world most of the year.'

'They seem very much in love.'

'I'm sure they are. I hope it lasts for them, but, who knows? Love is the most unpredictable of our emotions.'

It was two weeks before Nicolas allowed Elizabeth to visit the local grocer without him.

'You will be lost,' he warned. 'You cannot speak Greek so you cannot explain where you wish to go.'

'I know where the grocer is,' remonstrated Elizabeth mildly. 'I've been there nearly every day with you. I won't get lost. If I'm not back in half an hour you can come and look for me.'

Reluctantly Nicolas agreed to her carrying out the errand on her own and waited anxiously for her triumphant return.

'I got everything I wanted. If I didn't know the name I pointed and he told me. I hope he charged me correctly. He wrote it all down, then added it up so fast and said the figure quickly. I offered him a note and he shook his head, took two and gave me some change.'

Nicolas smiled at her concern. He had spoken to the grocer and enlisted his assistance for his wife when she was shopping and knew she would not be overcharged.

'I have good idea. One evening, when I go to work, Elena comes to be with you. She is company and also she will teach you Greek.'

'But she'll have been working all day.'

'She works in Piraeus, so she stop here as she drive home. She talk a little Greek to you while you make the meal, then she eat with us. I go to the night club and Elena talk to you more in Greek before she go home too.'

'She may not want to do that,' protested Elizabeth.

'Of course she will want,' he insisted. 'It is a good idea.'

Elizabeth began to enjoy her evenings spent with Elena. She tried very hard to remember the words her sister-in-law would try to teach her each time she came, but once Nicolas had left for work they spent most of the time chatting. Elena wanted to hear all about life in America and Elizabeth requesting details about her new family.

'It will be more easy for you to understand who is who when you have visited Crete,' Elena assured her. 'Now everyone is just a name. When you have met them you will be able to put a face.'

'Nicolas hasn't said when we're going yet. I think he's waiting until I can understand and speak a bit more Greek. I had no idea it would be so difficult. Marianne just goes from one language to another with no problem.'

'That is because she grew up with the language. Giovanni is the same. He speak Italian or Greek, no problem, his English and his French also very good.'

Elizabeth sighed. 'I begin to feel I had a deprived childhood.'

Elena frowned. 'Please?'

'No, it would be too difficult to explain. Tell me more about the family in Crete.'

'You will find Aunt Anna very kind. She is lovely lady. Always she has lived in Plaka on the farm. Uncle Yiorgo,' Elena frowned, 'he does not forgive my pappa so easily and is not so friendly, but he is a good man. Maybe you will be taken to visit friends of our cousin Yannis when you are there. Still there is Flora and Manolis, and the doctor. We visit them with my uncle Yannis before he dies on the island.'

'Do you think Nicolas would take me there?'

'To the island? Why should he not take you?'

'I thought, maybe, with his uncle dying there, it might be distressing for him.'

Elena shook her head. 'It was big shock for both of us to arrive back from a walk and find he is dead, but we did not know him well. We met him just before my pappa die, him and Aunt Anna. He had not visited his family or friends in Crete since he was sent to Athens and we ask him to take us back when Aunt

Anna returns. For one week it is very good. We visit Father Andreas in Heraklion, then Flora and Manolis in Aghios Nikolaos, we drive to Ierapetra, but Father Minos is too old and does not remember, then we go to Plaka and stay on the farm. Uncle Yannis seem very well, and we go to the island and he die.' Elena put her head close to Elizabeth's. 'I will tell you secret. Uncle Yannis still is on Spinalonga.'

Elizabeth frowned. 'But you said he was dead?'

'He is dead, but we take him back where he is happy.'

'You mean he's buried there?'

'No. He was placed in the tower. It was as Aunt Anna wish.'

'Wasn't that against the law – and what about his wife? Didn't she mind?'

'It was done in secret and Aunt Dora very pleased he had gone home.'

Elizabeth raised her eyebrows and decided it was time to change the subject. 'Tell me about the shop cousin Yannis's wife has in Aghios Nikolaos. From what Nicolas says it's quite unusual.'

Elizabeth wrote a long letter to Marianne describing her visit to their relatives who lived on Crete. She explained that they had not stopped in Heraklion to visit Father Andreas, who Nicolas had only met once and doubted if the priest would remember him. Instead they had driven straight down to Aghios Nikolaos and Elizabeth extolled the beauty of the small town, with its many colourful tavernas that surrounded the pool. She went into raptures over Ourania's shop and described in minute detail the many different sculptures and ornaments she sold, but it was the sketches, executed by Yannis's mother, that were framed and adorned the plain white walls, which had really captured her imagination.

Of Anna and Yiorgo she wrote cautiously, having no wish to offend her friend, but she had found the visit to them very difficult, Nicolas having to interpret every word that passed between them. Yiorgo, she wrote, seemed a morose man who hardly ever spoke, even to his sister, and Anna appeared sad, careworn and much older than Marianne's grandmother. Yannis wanted them to live in his house but they refused to leave the farm house where they had lived all their lives. Yannis's house was magnificent and nearly finished. They had stayed there for five days and it had been like living in a hotel.

Yannis had arranged for Manolis to take them over to Spinalonga, but his wife, Flora, had refused to accompany them to her old home. Elizabeth had tried not to look too curiously at the one-armed woman and Nicolas had told her the most wonderful love story about the couple. She repeated it to Marianne in her letter.

Apparently Flora had been sent to the island as a young girl and met Manolis when she sat on the quay asking the fishermen for building materials. Manolis had fallen in love with her and wanted to marry her, although she was a leper and had only one arm. Whilst the island was isolated from the mainland during the war neither of them knew if the other was still alive, but they never gave up hope. It wasn't until your grandfather helped your grandmother's cousin with all the information about the new drug and Flora returned from Athens that she and Manolis were finally able to get married. And guess where they live! In the little fishing cottage where your grandmother lived as a girl. I expect you know all about this, though, from your grandmother and also from the book your relative wrote.

I bought the English version of the book when we were in Aghios Nikolaos, but I didn't have a chance to read it properly until we were on the way home. We must go to Spinalonga when you are able to come over. I know you'll love it, although it does have a very 'sad' air about it. Manolis showed us where the people had lived and where the hospital was, we even looked into the tower where all the bones are laying in the bottom. It made me feel quite creepy!

Nicolas refused to toll the bell when we went past the church as he said he did that when he was over there with his uncle Yannis and shortly afterwards he died. I laughed at him and said he was superstitious, but he was adamant and wouldn't let me pull the rope. We climbed right up to the top of the fortress, which is all in ruins, and also up to the top of the island. It's surprising how high up you are. The cars on the mainland look like toys, yet you're not really very far away. You get a strange sense of being cut off from the rest of the world, quite eerie, yet very peaceful. We were over there for some hours and the time just flew. There is definitely something very strange about the atmosphere there and you must tell me if you feel the same when we go. I can't explain what it is, but there is something! Maybe that's why Flora won't go back.'

Marianne read the letter with interest. She would certainly go to Crete and visit the island before she returned to America. She might never have another opportunity.

1988

Marianne greeted Elizabeth rapturously. It was good to be back in Athens, to hear Greek spoken around her and feel thoroughly at home. She squeezed her friend's arm.

'Who would have thought we would have been back here together again? You look blooming.'

'I feel it. Athenians complain about the pollution, but it seems to suit me. Have you got everything? Nicolas is outside in the car. There was nowhere to park, of course, so he said he'd cruise around until he spotted us.'

They elbowed their way through the crowds inside the airport to the milling throng outside and took up a stance on the corner. Elizabeth looked anxiously for her husband. She waved to attract his attention and he swung in beside them. Immediately a policeman accosted him and an altercation began between them in Greek, whilst Elizabeth and Marianne placed the luggage in the boot and climbed into the back seats. Nicolas gave the policeman a friendly wave and drew away.

'What was that all about?' asked Elizabeth.

'He say I cannot park there, even if I am collecting my wife and her friend from the airport. I said I would only stay a few minutes, but he insisted I move on,' Nicolas shrugged. 'So I have done so.'

Elizabeth giggled. 'It's always the same. Whenever Nicolas picks me up he's told he can't wait there and whilst he's busy arguing I'm getting into the car.'

'Don't you drive yourself?'

Elizabeth shook her head. 'Not in Athens. I tried once and it frightened the life out of me. If we go out I wait until we've reached the outskirts before I take the wheel.'

'One day she will have to be brave. You would drive here, Marianne?'

'I've driven in London. Athens can't be worse, so I'd give it a go.'

'At least you'd know what they were shouting at you when you were in the wrong lane,' remarked Elizabeth.

Marianne smiled at her. 'I don't think you need to speak Greek to have a pretty fair idea.'

Elizabeth showed off her apartment with pride. 'I am changing things gradually,' she admitted. 'It was all very nicely decorated, but some of the furniture was rather old fashioned and worn. As we can afford it we are buying new.'

'You're very happy, aren't you?' observed Marianne.

Elizabeth nodded. 'I'm so glad I injured my shoulder. If we'd had to wait until my contract expired we wouldn't be married until next week at the earliest. We might even have changed our minds and that would have been a tragedy. Have you and Bob made any plans yet?'

'No. I thought it better to wait until I got home. Give ourselves a chance to get to know each other again. It's been almost three years with only telephone and letter contact.'

Elizabeth looked at her friend shrewdly. 'Meaning you have cold feet?'

Marianne shrugged. 'I just feel we need a bit of time together before we make up our minds. Bob may have met someone else.'

'He's not said anything to me.' Elizabeth frowned. 'Oh, I'm sure once you're back together everything will be fine. Now, what do you want to do this afternoon? Nicolas suggested we have dinner at the hotel tonight, then go to the nightclub if you're not too tired. We can spend the next few days wandering around and visiting his mother, then go off to Crete next weekend. Nicolas can't come with us, but Giovanni will meet us and we can stay in Heraklion at the hotel there. You'll like him, he's a charmer. Elena should be coming to supper tomorrow. She's still trying to teach me Greek.' Elizabeth chatted on, whilst Marianne sipped her fruit juice and relaxed.

Giovanni was not at the port to meet them and Elizabeth bit at her lip in indecision.

Marianne shrugged. 'We'll take a taxi. He probably thought we were arriving this evening. We'll turn up at the hotel and surprise him.'

'We might miss him if we don't wait.'

'So what? We'll be at the hotel and he's bound to turn up there sooner or later.'

'But Nicolas said…'

'Never mind what Nicolas said! If Giovanni thinks we're arriving this evening we could stand here all day waiting for him. We know the address so we'll just make our own way.' She indicated to the nearby taxi driver that they needed him.

'Where you go?'

Marianne answered in Greek and he loaded their cases with a smile 'You speak good Greek – for an American.'

'How do you know I'm American?'

The taxi driver touched his ear. 'I listen.'

'I've spent three years in England. I thought I'd lost my American accent.'

'Yes? What do you do there?'

'Studying.'

'I could give you a tour of Heraklion. Show you everywhere.'

'No, we're visiting relatives so they'll show us all we should see.'

'I could give you a good price.'

'I'm sure you would. Maybe another day.'

Marianne led the way into the hotel, which was not as ornate as the one in Athens, and stopped at the reception desk.

'Is Mr Giovanni here, please?'

The girl shook his head. 'Mr Giovanni is out. Can I help you?'

'There should be a room reserved for us, in the name of Christoforakis. If we go up maybe you could let us know if Mr Giovanni returns. He was supposed to meet us at the port.'

The girl nodded and handed the key to the porter. 'Room two zero two. I will telephone you if he arrives.'

'So what now?' asked Marianne. 'Do you want to sit here and wait or leave a message and go out on the town?'

'I think we ought to wait. They've a restaurant downstairs and I wouldn't mind something to eat. There was no breakfast on the ferry, remember.'

'Right. We'll give him a couple of hours to put in an appearance and make his excuses. If he's not around by then we'll go off on our own.'

Nicolas won't be very pleased when he hears.'

'So who's going to tell him?' asked Marianne. 'When we travelled to Athens before there was no one to meet us and hold our hands. You've become far too dependent on him. We're on vacation together, so forget him for a week. He'll still be there when you get back.'

Elizabeth smiled guiltily. 'Could go down to the restaurant? I really am hungry.'

Giovanni swept into the restaurant, ready with smiles and apologies. He stopped and drew in his breath sharply. It couldn't be! As he looked again he realised the dark haired girl had only a passing resemblance to Isabella. He recovered himself rapidly and walked forward, his arms outstretched.

'Elizabeth – and you must be Marianne. I am so sorry. I had to go out early on business and I was delayed. I thought I had allowed plenty of time to reach the port before the ferry docked, but,' he spread his hands, 'a little problem with my car, and I missed you. Please forgive me. You have something to eat? That is good. Now, I am at your disposal. Where would you like me to take you?'

Marianne looked at the young man, an amused smile on her lips. She did not believe for one moment he had been out on business, he had overslept and was just making an excuse.

Giovanni studied his relative from under lowered lids. She was attractive, with her cloud of dark hair and large, expressive eyes. There was something about her that reminded him of Isabella, yet she was not really like her, nowhere near as beautiful. She was very poised and sure of herself. He compared her with Nicolas's little blonde wife, who still appeared so lacking in confidence and nervous when in the company of any of the family. They were speaking in English for Elizabeth's benefit, Marianne's American accent softened after three years in England, but still unmistakable.

'I really do want to get to know you people,' she was saying. 'Grandma talked about Aghios Nikolaos and Plaka, but I guess it's all changed from when she was a girl. When she described Athens to me I had no idea it was so big. The way she spoke it was just a large town.'

'When she lived in Athens it was not so big. Now it is a very large city; big, dirty, but very good.' Giovanni smiled, showing his even white teeth. 'Aghios Nikolaos has grown also, but Plaka – there is almost nothing.'

Marianne frowned. 'I thought my grandmother's cousins still lived there?'

'They will not move. Uncle Yannis has asked them to move to his house, but they refuse. I will take you to see them at Plaka.'

'There are a lot of places I want to visit. Would it be possible for me to visit Father Andreas first? He's my great uncle and I must see him. I've brought some photographs with me. They were taken quite recently. Mamma sent them to me when she knew I was coming over. They're all of the family.'

Giovanni nodded, but he did not ask to look at them. 'I am sure he will enjoy seeing them. I will take you to him. You will talk to him and I will take Elizabeth for coffee or for shopping. He speaks only Greek and she will find it a little difficult.'

'That's up to her.' Marianne looked at her friend with raised eyebrows.

'I'll be quite happy just wandering around with Giovanni.'

'Then we will walk to the church. It is not far and we will decide a place to meet when Marianne has concluded her visit. I could take Elizabeth for a drive if she would prefer?'

Marianne and Elizabeth followed Giovanni down through the main thoroughfare before diving off into the side streets, finally halting before the house that adjoined the small, white washed church.

'In two hours we will be in the taverna down the road. You cannot miss it. Go down to the main road, cross the street and down the small road opposite. Turn to the right and you will find it.'

'Does it have a name?'

Giovanni shrugged. 'It is still known as Louisa's place. It is where old uncle Yannis lived when he was in Heraklion as a student.'

Marianne found the elderly priest very disconcerting. Having shown him the photographs, which he had clucked and tutted over, she searched for news of her grandmother and family that would interest him and he would listen intently, then ask a question that she felt bound to answer honestly and felt a sinking in her heart as she saw the look of disapproval come across his face.

'Do they ever think of returning home?'

Marianne wriggled uncomfortably. 'I think they look on America as home now. I know my grandmother enjoyed her visit a few years ago, but it would be difficult for her to return to Greece.'

'Why?'

'She would miss her children and grandchildren.'

'Why shouldn't they come also?'

'Things are different in America, uncle Andreas. We don't live together as one big family. We are all spread about, and even if we did all want to come, there's Gregory's family to consider.'

'Who is Gregory?'

'My sister's husband.'

Father Andreas nodded and sighed. 'It is not right for families to be on different sides of the world. They should be together.'

'Then why don't you go to America, uncle?'

A look of horror crossed his features. 'I couldn't possibly go to America.'

'Why not? Grandmother would love to have you to stay.'

Andreas shuddered. 'No, I am far too old for such travelling. Besides, your grandmother has told me about the way people live over there. It is not right. I could not live like that.'

'Like what?'

'The beef burgers, the fast cars, the,' his voice dropped, 'immorality.'

'Not everyone's immoral. I'm not, my brother and sister aren't.' Marianne blushed, recalling the weekends she had spent with Bob.

'That is because your mother brought you up properly, as good Greeks, but what of all the other people who are not Greek? The stories I have heard,' he raised his hands heavenwards.

'Oh, you mustn't believe everything you hear. People see a television programme or a film and think all of America is over-run by criminals.' Marianne tried to shrug the criticism aside.

Father Andreas shook his head. 'It is not only the criminals I speak about. It is also the family. You have an aunt who has gone to Brazil to do good works. That is fine, but I also hear she is not living with the women in the village, but with the priest! That is not right. To be truly a man of God you do not share your life with a woman.'

'She is much happier now she is with him. He has been a great comfort her since the loss of her husband.' Marianne defended her aunt, despite the further rush of blood to her cheeks.

'If she needs a man to be happy, then she should get married again, but you do not live with a man who has taken holy vows.'

'He has probably taken different vows from yours. Some priests are allowed to marry.'

Father Andreas ignored her comment. 'And there is your other aunt. I hope she will find it in her heart to repent of her sinful ways before her day of judgement comes.'

Marianne wriggled uncomfortably in her chair and glanced surreptitiously at her watch.

'And what about you?' he continued. 'A young woman on her own in strange countries. It should not be.'

'Greece is not strange to me. I feel quite at home here, besides, I'm not alone. I'm staying at cousin Yannis's hotel with Nicolas's wife.'

'I have heard that she is very pretty, but very American.' The priest shook his head in despair.

'I am sure you would like her. She is trying very hard to learn Greek and understand our ways.'

'Our ways?' For the first time his eyes glinted with amusement. 'You are an American.'

Marianne struggled for words. 'Yes, I am, but somehow, when I'm over here, and even in America, I feel Greek.'

'No,' he shook his head sadly. 'You do not understand what it is to be Greek, truly Greek. If you did you would not return to America.'

Marianne felt tears pricking at the back of her eyes and shook herself impatiently. Of course she was Greek and she must not let this narrow-minded old priest upset her.

'I'm sure I have a lot to learn.'

'You should stay here,' he repeated.

'What would I do here?' Marianne tried to smile.

'You would get married.'

'I'm getting married when I return to America.' Somehow the words had a hollow ring to them.

'Yes?'

'Yes,' she answered defiantly. 'To my friend's brother. I've known him for years. He's a very nice man.'

'I am sure he is, but he is not Greek.' Father Andreas gazed at his young relative piercingly. 'You should marry a Greek man.'

Marianne tried to laugh. 'If I do I'll ask you to marry me in your church.'

Father Andreas nodded solemnly. 'I would do that. It would give an old man much pleasure.' He sighed deeply. 'I have seen so much heart break, so much destruction and grief. The young people who come with high hopes for their future, then their smiles turn to frowns when they speak to each other. You make sure you choose the right man when you decide your marriage partner.'

Marianne nodded. 'I'll remember.' She rose from the hard, wooden seat. 'I really should go now. I promised to meet Giovanni and Elizabeth at Louisa's taverna and I have to find it.'

'At Louisa's?'

'Yes. You know it?'

Father Andreas nodded. 'Yes, I know it well. It was where poor Yannis stayed when he was in Heraklion.'

'So Giovanni said. I'll be interested to see it.'

'It is no different from any other small taverna in the town.'

'I'm sure it isn't, I just want to see where everyone lived. Now I'm meeting the other half of my family I really want to know them, all about them.'

'There are many things in a person's life it would be better not to know.'

Marianne laughed. 'If there are skeletons in the closets it only makes it more exciting and interesting. I'll come and visit you again before I leave. Thank you for talking to me.' Marianne kissed the wrinkled hand of her great uncle.

Father Andreas held her slim hand in his. 'Bless you, child. Your visit was a pleasure to an old man.'

He watched as she walked down the road from his house. She looked so like his sister had at that age, and was just as independent.

Marianne looked around the small taverna curiously. Plastic gingham covered the tables and counter top, the seats and backs of the chairs were of red and white plastic, and when the coffee she had ordered was brought to the table she was amused to see the red and white check reproduced on the china.

'We are trying to be upmarket,' she remarked.

Giovanni smiled at her. 'The people here are new. They try to live down the history of the place and attract customers.'

Marianne raised her eyebrows. 'Tell me.'

'This is where old uncle Yannis stayed as a student in Heraklion. His schoolteacher lodged here also and married the woman who ran the place. Pavlakis became the local Mayor, but he was a pretty stupid man. He was the friend of the German commander who came here to spy.'

'You mean he betrayed his country?' Marianne was horrified.

Giovanni shook his head. 'He was not involved. It was his wife who was the traitor. He was taken along with the rest of the government and shot, so he had no chance to defend himself.'

'And his wife?'

'She was stoned to death.'

Elizabeth choked on her coffee. 'But that's awful. Why wasn't she given a fair trial?'

'I was not around at the time, so I cannot say for certain. It was war time.'

'That's no excuse. Even during a war you're entitled to a fair trial.'

Marianne looked at her friend. 'There's only one reason a Greek will stone a woman to death and that's for adultery. I should imagine there was a good deal more to it than you know, Giovanni.'

Giovanni would not meet her eyes. 'Probably.'

Elizabeth's face had paled. 'You really mean that if a woman commits adultery she will be stoned?'

'I doubt if it would happen in the city now, only the more remote regions and islands. Why? Have you got a guilty conscience?'

'Not at all,' she answered indignantly. 'It just seems so barbaric.'

Marianne shrugged. 'It's their idea of justice. What happened after that?'

'The taverna was left until a few years ago. Then a man arrived and began to clean and decorate and then his wife came and they opened up. I have never seen more than six people in here. It will be a long while before people forget Louisa.'

'Why don't they change the name? People would soon forget about the past if they were no longer calling it "Louisa's place".'

'It is called King Minos, but everyone speaks of it as Louisa's.'

'I think it's silly of them,' announced Elizabeth. 'Do you think they have a decent loo here?'

'Follow the arrow,' advised Marianne. 'If you report back favourably I'll make the trip myself.'

Giovanni shook his head at her retreating figure. 'Poor Elizabeth. It is good she lives in Athens. She is not a Greek.'

Marianne smiled at him. 'She is trying very hard.'

'With her language, yes, but not her thoughts. She is still American.'

Elizabeth was retching miserably in the bathroom. Tentatively Marianne knocked on the door.

'Are you all right?'

'I'm not in here for fun! Of course I'm not.'

'I mean are you really ill? Do you need a doctor?'

'No, I think it was the coffee at Louisa's place. I thought it tasted funny at the time.'

'I didn't notice.'

Elizabeth pulled the door open and glared balefully at her friend. 'I'm going to bed for an hour.'

'Do you want me to stay?'

Elizabeth shrugged. 'There's no need. I've only been sick.'

Marianne picked up her book. 'I'll sit and read.'

'No, I'm just being a pig because I feel wretched. You go and have a wander round. I'll be all right when I've had a sleep.' Elizabeth smiled wanly.

'Are you sure? I'll stay if you want me to.'

Elizabeth shook her head. 'No, it's your holiday and I'm no fun to be with at the moment.' She rubbed her stomach with her hand. 'This is the first time I've been ill since I've been here.'

'You have a rest. I'll be back in about two hours; then we could have an early dinner.'

'Don't talk to me about food!' groaned Elizabeth and buried her face in her pillow.

Marianne picked up her bag and closed the door quietly behind her. She would walk down to the port and watch the fishermen, then maybe walk along the harbour arm to the Venetian port. She had gone no more than a few steps along the road when she heard her name and turned to see Giovanni.

'Where are you going?'

'For a walk. I thought I'd go down to the harbour.'

'Where is Elizabeth?'

'She is lying down. She's not feeling very well.'

Giovanni raised his eyebrows. 'What is wrong?'

'She's been sick, blames it on the coffee she had.'

Giovanni snorted. 'More likely the baklava she bought from the street vendor. I will come with you.'

'There's no need. I'll be perfectly safe on my own.'

'I am sure you will, but I would like to come with you.'

Marianne reddened. 'You're welcome. I just thought you would be busy.'

'I am never too busy to spend time with a beautiful young woman.'

'Do you say that to all the tourists?'

'I am very selective.' Giovanni took her arm. 'We will watch the fishermen, then we will have a quiet drink together, and if Elizabeth is not feeling well when we return I will take you for dinner.'

'It's very kind of you, but you don't have to, you know.'

'Marianne, I want to be with you. I want to get to know you, to hear about your family in America.'

'We're not really very interesting. You know about my grandparents, my father's a doctor. Not a specialist in anything, just an ordinary doctor. I have a twin sister who's married with a baby and a younger brother who has just started college. Now it's your turn.'

'My father is Italian, my mother is Greek. I have two brothers, Angelo is an architect and Joseph is a rogue.'

Marianne looked at Giovanni in amusement. 'Why do you say Joseph is a rogue?'

'I was being polite. It would be more truthful to say he is a criminal.'

'You're joking!'

'I wish I was. He is a disgrace to the family and has been for a number of years.'

'I'm sorry.'

'Why should you be sorry?'

'I'm sorry I asked you about him.'

Giovanni shrugged. 'He is of no consequence, not worth talking about. Tell me, your twin sister – she is very like you?'

'To look at, but we're not alike in our ways.'

Giovanni nodded. 'She has been to Greece?'

'No,' Marianne smiled. 'As soon as she left college she married Greg. She's quite happy to sit at home with her little boy. That's why I say she isn't like me. I'm glad I've lived in London and visited Europe. Tell me about Italy.'

'You have not been to Italy?'

'I've passed through on the train and I've flown over it. Does that count?'

'No. One day I will take you to see. Italy is very beautiful. A little like Greece; but different. My parents live in the city.' Giovanni shuddered. 'I hate the city. There is no sea and the countryside is miles away. That is why I prefer to live on Crete.'

'Doesn't your mother miss the countryside? She was brought up on a farm, wasn't she?'

'My mother is happy if she is with my father. I will take you to see Aunt Anna and Uncle Yiorgo; then you will see the farm where she lived.'

Marianne nodded dutifully. If they were anything like the elderly priest she had visited that morning she would rather stay in Heraklion. 'Look!' She pointed towards a fisherman who was holding up a large octopus.

'What at?'

'The octopus the man has caught.'

Giovanni nodded. 'It is a good size.' He cupped his hands round his mouth. 'Take it up to my hotel. Tell them Giovanni sent you. You will get a fair price.'

The fisherman raised his hand in acknowledgement and proceeded to bang the octopus on the rock to remove the ink sac. Marianne gave a slight shudder.

'Do you wish to stay and watch?'

The smell of fish was beginning to rise towards her. 'Let's walk out to the fort, or I'll need a bath and change of clothes when we get back.'

Slowly they walked along the broad road whilst Giovanni told her the history of the imposing Venetian fortress. She shook her head in disbelief.

'You'd never think that a handful of men could keep an invading army at bay for sixteen years. Why didn't they come overland and take Heraklion from the rear?'

'The mountains are high and dangerous if you do not know them. There were no roads, remember, no way to communicate and tell the men to advance, no way to supply them with fresh food once they had left the coast. No, that would have been far too difficult.' Giovanni's arm slipped round her waist whilst they walked.

'Can you go inside the fort?'

'In the day time and sometimes they have a theatre in the evening.'

Marianne ran her hand over the rough masonry. 'I'd like to go in. Can you see where the men lived or is it just a shell?'

'It is worth a visit,' Giovanni avoided her question, not wishing to admit he had never visited during opening hours. 'Knossos, of course, is much more magnificent.'

'I must do some planning with Elizabeth. I have to see Knossos, and I want to see that island, Spinalonga, and I have to visit my relatives.'

Giovanni adroitly moved Marianne so she had her back to the fortress wall. He placed a hand either side of her and brushed her cheek lightly with his lips.

'There is plenty of time. I will take you. I will take you wherever you wish to go.'

Marianne pushed against his chest. 'Don't be silly, Giovanni. You're not on holiday.'

'I can take a few days; besides, you are family.'

'Then don't you think you should let me go?'

'I am enjoying being so close to you. Your skin is smooth, and your hair smells of… what does it smell of?' Giovanni buried his nose in her curls. 'Lemon, very faintly of lemon.'

'Giovanni, please stop flirting with me.'

'Why? Don't you like a man to flirt with you?'

'Yes, but…'

Giovanni kissed her parted lips and to her surprise Marianne found herself responding. He drew away and smiled. 'We are both adults. We can enjoy ourselves. Now, we will find a taverna for a drink; then maybe we will flirt a little more.'

Elizabeth swung her legs over the side of the bed. She had slept for over an hour and felt fine now, just ravenously hungry. She wished Marianne would return so they could go for dinner. Within ten minutes she had washed and changed her dress, and she looked at her watch impatiently. Marianne had said she would return in a couple of hours.

Feeling unreasonably annoyed with her friend she opened the patio door and walked out onto the balcony to watch for her return. Leaning on the cool marble she looked up and down the deserted street, then at the balcony opposite where an artist at his easel caught her attention. Fascinated she watched as he daubed at the canvas then stepped back to study the effect before adding more colour. So engrossed was she that she failed to hear the bedroom door open and Marianne's voice made her start violently.

'Don't do that!' she exclaimed.

'Do what?'

'Come in quietly and frighten the life out of me.'

Marianne smiled. 'I came in quietly just in case you were still asleep. I didn't mean to make you jump. What are you watching?'

'The artist across the road. It's fascinating, he's so engrossed in his work he has no idea he's being watched.'

Marianne craned her neck. 'What's the picture?'

'I've no idea. Maybe if we called to him he'd turn it round and show us.'

'More likely to splash paint all over it and spoil it. How are you feeling now? Do you fancy anything to eat?'

Elizabeth nodded. 'I'm starving.'

Marianne grinned. 'Give me a few minutes and I'll be with you. Do you want to eat here or go and find a taverna?' she called from the bathroom.

'May as well stay here. Where have you been?'

'I wandered over to the fort with Giovanni.'

'And?'

'And nothing.' Marianne was glad she was in the privacy of the bathroom and Elizabeth could not see the blood rush to her cheeks.

The two girls ate a hearty breakfast, despite Elizabeth having had to rush to the bathroom when she first got out of bed. Giovanni joined them and helped himself to a cup of coffee.

'Now, where do I take you today?'

'Knossos,' replied Marianne firmly. 'But you don't have to take us. We can easily take a bus or a taxi.'

Giovanni covered her hand with his own. 'Of course I will take you. I will take you to Knossos, then we arrange a time and I meet you. There is a good taverna. We will have lunch, then, who knows?'

Elizabeth raised her eyebrows at Marianne. 'Who knows indeed! Can we meet you down here in about twenty minutes?'

'Of course.' Giovanni squeezed Marianne's hand. 'I will be waiting.'

Marianne found Knossos fascinating. She wandered over the site, pointing out the buildings and their original function to Elizabeth who trailed in her wake.

'Can't you just picture it? The grandeur and magnificence; all the colour and pageantry. It must have been quite awe inspiring when people came to pay their tribute to the ruler.'

Elizabeth nodded. 'It's a pity the whole of it wasn't restored. Still, there's more to see than when we went to Mycenae.'

'Let's have another look at the staircase. I just love those shields. The original wall paintings are in the museum. I'll have to go and look at those. They've got some wonderful exhibits in there according to the guidebook. You'll have to look at it later.'

'I'd be happy to sit down and look at it now,' grumbled Elizabeth.

'What's happened to your stamina? At one time you could run rings round me. Come on, we've only got another half an hour before we meet Giovanni for lunch.'

Elizabeth sighed and followed dutifully up the stone steps.

'Well? Did you enjoy your visit?' asked Giovanni.

'It was wonderful. There's so much to see. I feel I ought to go back again. I must have missed a good deal.'

'You can go back on your own,' remarked Elizabeth. 'I haven't got the same enthusiasm for archaeological sites that you have.'

'You are going back?' Giovanni looked at Marianne in surprise.

She laughed and shook her head. 'No, I'm not, not today anyway. There are other things I need to see before I start to go round a second time. When can we go to Spinalonga?'

'Tomorrow we will drive to Aghios Nikolaos, visit my uncle and aunt, maybe go to Kritsa or Gournia if you wish. The next day you can go to Spinalonga if the weather is good.'

Marianne nodded. 'That sounds fine. How about you, Elizabeth?'

Elizabeth shrugged. 'I'm happy to go along with whatever you want to do. Do they have baklava here?' She looked across at the cabinet displaying an array of gateaux and cakes.

Giovanni went up to the counter and returned with three baklavas, dripping with honey. 'This will make you grow big,' he smiled.

Marianne laughed. 'That's true, but you should say 'make you fat'.'

'Always I am ready to learn. Now, where do you wish to go?'

'Where do you suggest?'

'There are the shops in Heraklion.'

'What about the museum?'

Giovanni looked at his watch. 'It will be a little late for the museum.'

'So what else is there? What about the fort?'

'They close earlier.'

'How about a drive; to look at the countryside?'

'There is little countryside around Heraklion.'

'There must be some! Drive along the coast, then.'

Giovanni nodded. 'Very well.'

He drove them to Amnisos, then began to follow the road back along the coast and turned back into the centre of Heraklion.

'The Germans made the government walk down this road before they shot them.'

Marianne leaned forward eagerly. 'Really? Where did they do that?'

'In the gorge.'

'Can we go there?'

'There is nothing to see.'

'I'd still like to go there.'

Giovanni swung the car down a side road leading towards the beach. 'There is a new road, but this way you will see the beach. Many new hotels are built here.'

'It's a bit out of the way,' remarked Elizabeth.

'They open only in the summer time. The visitors want the beach. It is not far. There is a bus and many people hire a car.'

At the end of the road he swung to the left where the cement works barred the way forward, drove over a small bridge, looped around a side road and drew up a short distance from a farm. 'Here we walk.'

Giovanni opened a gate leading onto the farmer's land and the two girls followed him up a grassy track for a few yards before stepping into a dried riverbed. Slipping and stumbling over the worn stones they walked into a gap in the rugged hills. Marianne looked upwards.

'It's amazing. Who would have thought there was a gorge here?'

'This is very small, a crack. To see the gorge you need to visit Samaria.'

They walked deeper between the hillsides, goats and sheep grazed on the rocky ledges, following each other from one precipitous site to another. They rounded a bend and a small church stood on a slight rise.

'This is where the government met their death.' Giovanni tried the gate, which opened at his touch, stepped inside a tiny courtyard and opened the door. He waited until their eyes had become accustomed to the dark interior.

Marianne drew in her breath. The tiny church was crammed with religious artefacts; a bucket full of sand standing in the centre, held candles and Giovanni lit one automatically, Marianne doing the same. He waited patiently until they had both looked their fill; then shepherded them out, closing the door firmly behind him.

'You wish to walk on?'

'I'd like to. How about you, Elizabeth?'

'I'm happy.'

They followed the dried river's bank as it twisted and turned, moving low branches that tried to impede their progress, until Elizabeth finally sank down.

'I'm too hot to go any further. You'd never credit how much heat gets trapped in a valley.'

Giovanni and Marianne sat down beside her. 'How far into the hill does this path go?'

Giovanni waved his hand airily. 'Maybe half a mile.'

'What's at the end?'

'I have no idea.'

'Haven't you walked to the end?'

Giovanni shook his head. 'Why should I walk to the end of the valley?'

'Just to see.' Marianne scrambled to her feet. 'I'm going on.'

'You cannot go alone.'

'Why not? You and Elizabeth can stay here.'

'It may get steep. You may fall. I will come with you.'

'There really is no need.'

'Just the same – I will come.'

'Well, I'm not.' Elizabeth lay back on the grass, her hands beneath her head. 'Take as long as you like. I'm going to lay here and snooze.'

Marianne jumped down onto a flat rock in the river's bed. 'It will be easier to walk along here than on the bank. The trees grow down far too low.'

Giovanni followed her and Elizabeth watched through half closed eyes as they jumped from stone to stone.

The going became steeper than Marianne had envisaged the deeper into the gorge they walked. Before long they were helping each other and scrambling over large, precariously balanced boulders.

'Listen.' Marianne stopped and held up her hand.

'I can hear nothing.'

'That's it. There's absolute silence. I don't think I've been anywhere before where there was literally no sound at all.'

Giovanni pointed, and in the narrow strip of sky that was visible above the peaks, an eagle soared on the thermal currents, swooping suddenly to catch a meal. A shrill, distressed bleating cut through the silence.

'What was that?' Marianne felt her scalp prickle.

'A baby goat or sheep. An eagle will always take one if it has strayed from its mother.'

Marianne shuddered. 'Life is cruel. Come on, it can't be much further.'

They rounded a bend and were confronted by a wall of loose clay and stones.

'That is it. The end.'

'I'm going up. I want to see what is over the other side.'

Giovanni sighed and followed her as she made a run at the lower level. They reached the top, panting and laughing, clinging to tufts of grass and looking at almost identical scenery on the other side.

'What a waste of effort!' She turned to look at Giovanni and found his face close to her own. He released his hold on the grass and leant over and kissed her. As he did so his feet lost their hold and he began to slide relentlessly towards the valley bottom. At first Marianne watched in horror, then she realised he was totally unhurt and began to giggle. Gingerly she climbed back down and stood beside him.

'You are a mess!' she exclaimed.

Giovanni let out an enraged roar and threw out his arms, enfolding Marianne in them. 'You are wicked! Look at my suit. Look at my shoes. I try to kiss you and you push me down a mountain.'

'I didn't push you. You slipped. It just goes to show, you shouldn't try to take advantage of a situation.'

'You push.'

'I did not!'

'I say you push – now you will make it up to me.' He bent towards her and she wriggled from his grasp.

'You have to catch me first.' She took a flying leap down onto a boulder, Giovanni following her.

For some moments she kept in front of him, jumping and leaping until she found she was on top of a stone with a steep drop down to the bed of the river. She turned and Giovanni was right behind her.

'Careful,' she warned him. 'It's too high to jump.'

'I have caught you.'

'That's cheating. I couldn't jump down there.'

Giovanni took her in his arms. 'I enjoy being with you.'

'Even though you ruined your suit? Come on, we ought to get back. Elizabeth will think we've deserted her.'

Still Giovanni held her tightly to him. 'I claim my reward first for catching you.' He kissed her, lightly at first, then with more intensity.

Marianne pushed him away breathlessly. 'No, Giovanni,' she gave a little giggle. 'We'd fall over the edge.'

'When we reach the level ground.'

'When we reach level ground, we'll have level heads. Come on, help me down.'

Giovanni held out his hand and helped her to climb back to the bank. Once she stood there he pulled her to him and kissed her passionately. Marianne did not resist as she was pushed gently to the ground, Giovanni's arms still round her.

They arrived back, panting and laughing, to where Elizabeth was waiting for them. She eyed their dishevelled appearance in surprise.

'What have you been doing?'

'Giovanni slipped.'

'I did not. You push and I fall.'

Elizabeth looked from one to the other of them. 'You look as though you've both been rolling in the mud! I was just about to come and start looking for you. I'm dying of thirst, but I think you two are too dirty to be taken anywhere.'

'We will stop and buy.'

'I'd better get some bottles to bring out to the car. I don't think they'd take kindly to a couple of tramps sitting in a taverna.'

Marianne sat next to Giovanni as he drove them down to Aghios Nikolaos. She found the suburban sprawl depressing, virtually joining the outskirts of Heraklion with Malia.

'It has not always been like this,' Giovanni assured her. 'When I was a boy there was countryside. The road ran beside the sea. Sometimes, when there was a sirocco, the road could not be used.'

'Is that why they built the new road?'

Giovanni shrugged. 'Maybe. I think it was because the old road was narrow and slow. Today everyone wants to move fast from one place to another. Do you want to see the palace at Malia?'

'Is it worth seeing?'

'Of course. Do not expect to see another Knossos, but it is interesting.'

'What do you think, Elizabeth?'

'I'll go along with you.'

'They have a small restaurant, we could have coffee.' Giovanni winked at Marianne. 'Also they sell baklava.'

Elizabeth frowned. 'It's all very well for you to tease me, but I must stop eating them. My skirt was quite tight this morning.'

'Maybe their delivery has not arrived yet,' warned Giovanni.'

'In that case we'll not stop,' declared Elizabeth. 'I think I like to eat baklava with coffee because the coffee is so bitter.'

'You could have ordinary coffee.'

Elizabeth shook her head. 'It makes me feel sick when they don't use fresh milk, besides, I enjoy being able to eat whatever I fancy. All those years when I had to watch my diet and keep my weight down are behind me now.'

'Keep eating baklava and your weight will be all behind you as well! No, I didn't mean it, Elizabeth.' Marianne winced as her friend hit her on the shoulder. 'Maybe when we get to Aghios Nikolaos we could play some tennis. You'd soon shed those extra pounds.'

Elizabeth shook her head. 'I haven't played for ages now. The funny thing is I don't miss it.'

'It was probably something to do with being unfulfilled. You took your frustrations out on a poor little tennis ball,' remarked Marianne.

'Idiot! What do you take your frustrations out on then?'

'Why should I have any?'

'Tell me more,' Elizabeth sat forward.

'There's nothing to tell. I'm just well balanced.'

Elizabeth snorted and Giovanni turned off the main road towards the site of the palace. 'What do you wish to do first? Coffee or look at the site?'

'Coffee,' announced Elizabeth. 'I shall need all my strength. I know what Marianne is like once she gets on a site. She examines every stone and pokes into every corner.'

'I like to take an intelligent interest.'

Giovanni drew to a halt. 'Please, you have been talking too fast and I do not understand your meaning.'

Marianne laughed at him. 'It's called banter. It's when friends tease each other.'

They strolled slowly round the site, Marianne examining each stone for marks of the double axe, which the guidebook assured her were there.

'I can't find them,' she sighed with exasperation. 'I reckon this guidebook is so old they've worn away.'

'Does that mean we can go?' asked Elizabeth.

Marianne smiled ruefully. 'I have to admit that I find Malia a bit of a let down after Knossos. When you think of all the sites in and around Athens that are so well preserved, even the Venetian fort in Heraklion, you tend to expect a bit more substance here. Never mind, I've seen it. That's the main thing.'

Elizabeth rolled her eyes and took Giovanni's arm. 'Will we be in Aghios Nikolaos in time for lunch?'

'Easily,' he smiled. 'You are hungry again so soon?'

'I'm not, I just thought if we were going to arrive late in the afternoon it would be a good idea to buy a snack to take with us.'

The drive became more interesting having left the sprawl of Malia behind them, the road giving glimpses of the sea before retreating into the hills and emerging suddenly for the drop down into the large town.

'Oh, it's pretty,' breathed Marianne.

Giovanni beamed with pleasure. 'Many tourists visit here.'

'It's where my grandmother lived as a child.'

'You would like to see her house?'

'Is it still standing?'

'Of course. Manolis and Flora live there. You met them when you visited before, Elizabeth. Do you remember?'

'The woman who lived on Spinalonga and married a fisherman?'

Giovanni nodded.

'Do you think Manolis will take us out again?'

'It is his living now.' Giovanni drew in to the side of the road. 'What would you like to do? We can visit my uncle and his wife after lunch if you prefer.'

Elizabeth smiled. 'I think that would be a good idea. If we arrive at lunch time it looks as if we expect them to feed us.'

'They would be pleased to do so.'

'Oh, I know. I just find Greek hospitality a little overwhelming.'

Ourania greeted them with pleasure and delighted in showing Marianne her shop. She explained how she catered for tourists, being able to offer them replicas of famous works of art at reasonable prices. Her cat, Beauty, rubbed around their legs before jumping up on the chair and having a leisurely wash in the sunshine. Marianne handled the busts and ornaments with care, wondering how she could purchase an item and carry it safely back to America for her grandmother.

'What do you think she would like most?' asked Marianne of Elizabeth.

'A picture I expect.'

Marianne raised her eyes to the framed sketches. 'Yes, she probably would, but those belong to uncle Yannis and aren't for sale.'

'What about the book your uncle wrote?'

'She has a copy.'

Elizabeth shrugged. 'I don't know then.'

Marianne continued to run her fingers over various items. 'I know,' she said suddenly. 'I'll take some photos. A whole reel of Aghios Nikolaos and mount them in an album for her. I know a good deal must have changed, but if I take some of the older parts she'll remember them.'

'That's brilliant. You could take some of the farm and Spinalonga.'

'And what's more I can buy the album here. Which one do you think? A black or white?'

'Never mind the cover. Which one has white pages? I hate those horrid black ones.'

Marianne turned to Ourania and asked to be shown an album. She opened it carefully, noticing the name and address of the shop discreetly embossed in gold on the inside of the cover.

'It's ideal; just what I want. How much is it?'

Ourania shook her head. 'Please, you have it.'

'I can't do that,' Marianne replied firmly. 'It's a gift for my grandmother. If I don't pay you it isn't a gift from me.'

'Very well, but not the full price, just what I have to pay for them.'

Marianne smiled gratefully and handed over the notes, watching as Ourania wrapped it deftly.

'Where did you get the idea to have a shop like this?' she asked.

Ourania shrugged. 'I don't know. I wanted to sell something different. Giovanni's mother talked about the shops in Turin and how smart they were so we thought we'd try to sell good souvenirs. So many of the shops sell rubbish that isn't even made in Greece. If our statuettes are of Greeks, they are made in Greece, if they are of Romans they are made in Italy, and always by good craftsmen. The album you bought was made in Morocco. In it you will find a slip of paper giving the name of the manufacturer. If you find it has a fault you return the paper and the article to me and I will send you your money or another album.'

'Do you do that with everything?'

'Of course; we have a good reputation. We sell only perfect articles. The slightest flaw and we return them. Our suppliers know how particular we are and never deliberately send us anything that is damaged.'

'What a shame more shops don't follow your example.'

'Too many want to make money from the tourists. They know people will not look at their purchase until they reach home and by then it is too late to return it. I have even known some shopkeepers to offer to wrap goods, take them out to their back room and exchange them for something damaged. I always wrap the goods in front of the customer.' Ourania smiled with satisfaction.

'Doesn't your cat ever break things?'

Ourania shook her head. 'She is very good. She sits on the chair or on the floor when there are no customers. She never climbs the shelves. If she did she knows I would not let her in here.'

Marianne stroked Beauty's head absently and the cat pushed against her. 'She is lovely. Very different from most of the cats I've seen.' She turned to Elizabeth and spoke in English. 'Do you remember all those cats on Hydra? There seemed to be hundreds of them coming from nowhere when the fishing boats came in.'

Elizabeth was busy turning over a selection of sketches. 'I had no idea uncle Yannis's mother did so many.'

'Those were not made by my grandmother. They were made by Anna.'

'Your aunt?'

Giovanni shook his head. 'You remember when we were at Louisa's place?'

Elizabeth nodded.

'I told you old uncle Yannis's schoolteacher lived there with his wife. When the Germans first came he sent his wife and child to Aghios Nikolaos. He think they will be safe here. His wife returned to Heraklion and Anna is sent to Spinalonga. Uncle Yannis had boxes of her drawings.'

'Why?'

'He and his first wife looked after her.'

Elizabeth shook her head. 'No, I mean why was the girl sent to Spinalonga. Was she a leper?'

Giovanni shrugged. 'They think she is.'

'Poor little girl. Did she draw herself?'

'Only once, for uncle Yannis. It used to hang in your apartment, but after Aunt Dora died Yannis brought the portraits back to Aghios Nikolaos. If we did not have her sketches it would be as if she had not existed.'

'How sad.' Marianne felt tears in her eyes.

Giovanni squeezed her shoulders gently. 'You must not cry. It is in the past. Many bad things happen on the island – and many good things too. My mother was married there, that was a good thing.'

Marianne was forced to smile at his logic. 'I'm longing to see this island.'

'Manolis will enjoy to show you round.'

'Will his wife come with us?'

Giovanni shook his head. 'She will not go there. Only for old uncle Yannis's funeral did she agree to go back.'

'I'd like to meet her. Will she talk about her life over there?'

'She will talk of it, but she will not visit, and she will not have a picture of her sold.'

Marianne raised he eyebrows, but did not pursue her questions further. 'When will we be able to go?'

'Maybe tomorrow; if the weather is good. I will visit Manolis this evening and arrange for him to collect you from Elounda.'

'Why Elounda? Why not here?'

'I have arranged for you to stay in the hotel there. It is a good hotel and you will like it. It is better than Aghios Nikolaos. Also, you will be able to see the farm at Plaka and visit Uncle Yiorgo and Aunt Anna after you have been to the island. It will be easier for you.'

Marianne frowned. She was not sure she wanted to be so organised.

'I'd like to meet Manolis and his wife. Can I come with you tonight?'

Giovanni nodded. 'Of course. Flora speaks only Greek, and Manolis only a little English, what of Elizabeth?'

Elizabeth smiled at them. 'Don't worry about me. I'll stay at the hotel and read or write a letter to my family. I don't have to be included all the time when you want to visit people.'

Marianne looked around the tiny cottage. The whitewashed walls were hung with gaily-coloured rugs interspersed with small sketches. With unashamed curiosity she looked at them. In each there was a one-armed girl and she guessed it was Flora.

'Anna drew them,' Flora explained simply. She liked this American girl, dressed plainly in a pair of jeans and checked blouse, despite her aura of self-confidence.

'Will you tell me about your life on the island?'

Flora looked at her suspiciously. 'Why? Why should it be of any interest to you?'

'I don't know. I can't put it into words. I just feel I want to know as much as possible about my relatives over here, and you're the only one who knew old uncle Yannis well. My grandmother has talked about when they grew up together, I'm sure my aunt Anna will tell me about him, but you are the only one who lived with him on that island, the only one who knows what he was really like.'

'Yannis was a good man.'

'I know he was, everyone says so, but how? What made him different from the others who were over there?'

'Spiro was a good man, too.'

Marianne nodded. 'He was Yannis's special friend. I've read his book, but he made everything sound so easy and ordinary.'

Flora turned sad eyes on Marianne. 'I'm getting old. Sometimes it seems like a dream; then I look where my arm should be and I know it isn't. I was so frightened. I was frightened when I was sent to the hospital in Athens,' she shuddered. 'It was terrible there. The food was so bad, so many of us crowded in together – the smell!' She shuddered again. 'When they took us to the island I was even more frightened. I used to creep down to the food store at night and try to hide during the day. I was scared that one of the men might molest me, but I was never frightened of Yannis, however cross he was.'

'Why did he get cross,' prompted Marianne gently.

'When he wanted to rebuild the houses Christos refused to help him, but Yannis proved it could be done and Christos insisted he had his repaired first, whilst Yannis and Spiro were living in a damp, cold hut. Yannis nearly died that winter. He probably would have died if Phaedra hadn't looked after him when he had pneumonia. She used to try to make him rest, but it was no use. He had to keep himself busy.' Flora gave a sad smile.

'She was his wife, wasn't she?'

'He was devoted to her. After she died he didn't want to live; then Father Minos reminded him that he had Anna, and that helped, until she died too. Poor Yannis. That was when he began to drink too much. Father Andreas helped him then, and later Doctor Stavros asked him to sort out his medical mail, just to keep him occupied. That was how he found out about the cure. Yannis gave me my life with Manolis. He was such a good man.' Flora's eyes were brimming with tears.

'I'm sorry. I didn't mean to upset you.'

Flora shook her head. 'I'm not upset. I just loved Yannis. Everyone loved him, and all those on Spinalonga had reason to be grateful to him. He wanted treatment and freedom for all of us, not just himself. He made Spinalonga a wonderful place to live.'

'But you won't go back?'

Flora seemed to be struggling to explain her feelings. 'I'm so happy with Manolis. I don't want to leave him. If I went back to the island I might die there, like Yannis.' Flora crossed herself.

'Don't you mind Manolis going there?'

'Manolis could always leave. I was a prisoner.'

'Tell me more about the way you lived over there. How did you cook, do your washing and mending?'

Flora settled herself against the hard back of the upright chair. 'When we first arrived there was nothing. Everywhere was falling down and the people lived in the ruins as best they could. Then Yannis had this idea of rebuilding and...'

Marianne sat enthralled as Flora reminisced.

'You were late,' observed Elizabeth as Marianne emerged from the shower.

'I'm sorry. Did I wake you?'

'Not really. Did you have a good evening?'

'Yes. It was very strange. I'll tell you about it over breakfast.'

'Why not now?'

'It would take too long, besides, time's getting on and Manolis is taking us to Spinalonga.'

Elizabeth glanced at her watch. 'It's only half seven!'

'I know, but by the time you've showered and we've had breakfast it will be gone eight and I said we'd meet him at nine.'

'That's plenty of time.'

'I've also got to go shopping. We're going to take a picnic lunch and have it on the island, then Manolis is dropping us at Plaka so I can meet Anna and Yiorgo.'

'Oh!'

'Don't worry. Giovanni is coming to collect us and he's promised he'll be there at three, so you won't have to walk all the way back here.'

Elizabeth flung her legs over the side of the bed and stood up. 'Where are we shopping?' She sat down abruptly on the bed. 'I do feel queer. I'm going to...' She made a dash for the bathroom.

Marianne waited until she heard the sound of the toilet flushing and water being run.

'Are you all right?'

'I guess so. I'll just have a quick shower and be with you.'

Elizabeth was no more than ten minutes and certainly did not look ill as she returned to the bedroom.

'Do you want to go today, or would you like me to telephone uncle Yannis and ask him to put Manolis off?'

'I'm fine now.'

Marianne eyed her friend suspiciously. 'Are you sure? Would you like me to ask for breakfast to be sent up to you?'

'No way. I'm starving. Do you think the baker will be open?'

'I hope so, we'll need some rolls.'

'I want a baklava, and I'm sure they won't serve them for breakfast.'

Marianne looked at Elizabeth in amazement, then she began to smile, finally lying back on her bed giggling uncontrollably.

'What's wrong?'

Marianne shook her head, unable to speak. 'Wrong?' she gasped. 'Nothing's wrong. Haven't you guessed?'

Elizabeth looked at her completely mystified. 'Guessed what?'

With an effort Marianne controlled herself. 'Women who are sick, particularly in the morning, and have irresistible fancies for certain foods are usually pregnant!'

Elizabeth paled and placed a hand on her stomach. 'It can't be.'

'Have you checked up?'

'Well, no, but…'

Elizabeth scrabbled in her handbag and withdrew her diary. She flipped over the pages and looked at Marianne incredulously. 'I'm two weeks late!'

Marianne shrugged. 'That's your answer, then. Keep eating baklava and being sick in the morning. You're fine.'

Elizabeth giggled nervously. 'I can't feel anything.'

'Nor should you yet, idiot. You can keep it a secret until you get back to Athens and tell Nicolas.'

'Do you think I should 'phone him?'

'What for? It could be a false alarm. These things happen.'

'You seem to know an awful lot about it.'

'I've spent three years at University. You get a lot more than an academic education. Are you ready for breakfast? We're running out of time, particularly if we've got to take a supply of baklavas with us.'

'Are you taking costumes and a towel?'

'I certainly am. I don't know if we'll be able to swim from the island, but there must be a decent beach somewhere near.'

Manolis smiled to himself as he saw the two girls waiting on the quay at Elounda. Unlike his wife he had no qualms about visiting the island, and was looking forward to showing Marianne where her relative had lived for so much of his life. He helped them aboard and Marianne immediately began to question him.

'Is this where you used to sail from with supplies?'

'Not often. The fishermen from Elounda would take them out. I used to take the goods Father Minos had ordered and I was the ferryman for Doctor Stavros from Aghios Nikolaos. I went over every week with him and later I used to take them their money or the goods they'd ordered from the mainland.'

'What did they use their money for?'

'They eventually lived like any other village. They used to pay each other for fruit or vegetables, eggs, a hair cut, a jar of honey.'

Marianne watched fascinated as the island drew nearer. The imposing walls of the Venetian fortress frowned down on them, but here and there she could catch glimpses of roofs and walls.

'Why doesn't anyone live here now?'

'There is no need. You can see we are not overpopulated in this area; besides, everything has to be sent over by boat. It is not convenient.'

'If they had their own boat they could be independent.'

'They could, but it would be very lonely.'

'Yannis wanted to come back.'

Manolis pursed his lips. 'He was the only one.' He nosed his boat into the jetty and secured it to a large concrete bollard. Having jumped ashore he held out his hand to the girls. 'You can leave your bags. They will be safe.'

They followed him through the tunnel beneath the walls of the Venetian fortress and emerged into the sunlight that was dappling the tiny square. Marianne caught her breath. Everywhere there were signs of decay, weeds and rubbish. She felt her throat constrict and found she was fighting back her tears. Slowly she walked along the main road, peering into the empty, crumbling houses, gently tracing the ships Anna had carved on the shutters of the taverna, and marvelling that some of the decorated plaster in the rooms still survived.

Manolis was patient with her, telling her who had occupied each house, showing her the storeroom where the food had been kept and the main quay where both the lepers and the food had been off-loaded. He unlocked the church and they crept inside reverently. Leaning against the wall Marianne shuddered as she remembered how many sick people had lived in there until they had a shelter they could call their own.

'Shall I ring the bell?' asked Elizabeth mischievously, and put out her hand to the rope.

'No!' Both Marianne and Manolis answered in horrified unison.

Elizabeth smiled innocently. 'I didn't expect you to be superstitious, Marianne.'

'You know I am,' she snapped back.

'Would you like to see the hospital?' asked Manolis sensing a sudden tension between the girls.

'Yes, but most of all I want to see where Yannis lived.'

'We have passed his house. When we return you can see it properly. I want to show you the house he built first.'

They followed their guide dutifully as he showed them the hospital building, the laundry, the house where Phaedra and later Flora had lived and finally the blocks of ugly, modern flats that the government had provided. He led them carefully down the seaward side of the island and they looked down at the blue sea sucking greedily at the sheer rock, before rounding the corner and coming upon the second church and the graveyard.

'Do you want to see the tower?' asked Manolis.

Marianne nodded. 'Where in the graveyard did Yannis die?' she asked.

Elizabeth answered her. 'He was sitting by the wall, there. Nicolas and Elena climbed up to the fort and when they came back they found him.'

Marianne stepped carefully between the geometric slabs of concrete that covered the graves, passed through the gap in the wall and peered down into the darkness of the tower. As her eyes became accustomed she could make out the bones that lay at the bottom.

'How many people are in there?' she managed to ask.

Manolis shrugged. 'No one knows.'

Marianne turned away. She could not understand why she felt so indescribably sad.

Manolis took her arm. 'We will see the house Yannis built first now. There is not a great deal left.'

The two girls scrambled up the hill opposite, following the narrow path until they came to some rough stone walls standing a few feet high and showing where the window and door frames had once been. Manolis pointed proudly.

'Yannis built this. He did it to show everyone that they could rebuild houses.'

'He really was some guy, Marianne; a relative to be proud of.'

Marianne nodded soberly. 'I think everyone who lived over here can be spoken of with pride. They must have been an amazing group of people.' She began to retrace her steps down to the path below. 'Can we go and look at his other house now? I find this one depressing.'

Once back on the main path Marianne felt more comfortable and she borrowed Elizabeth's camera to take a reel of photographs. 'Your camera is so much better than mine,' she said as she looped it round her wrist. 'I really must get a new one. I want photos of Yannis's house, some of the shops and tavernas, the church, and Flora's garden. Maybe we could get them developed before we leave and she can see how it looks now.'

Manolis glanced surreptitiously at his watch. 'When you have taken the photographs we will go back on board and I will take you to the other side of big Spinalonga. You can swim there and have your picnic.'

'Can't we swim here?'

'I don't think you would enjoy it very much.' Manolis indicated with his hand towards the tunnel and both girls jumped as a group of chattering tourists emerged.

Elizabeth's eyes widened in horror. 'Hurry up, Marianne. We don't want to be here with a crowd of sightseers.'

'Five minutes,' promised Marianne. She scrambled up the steps beside the water tunnel and took a shot of Flora's garden, then raced up the crumbling steps beside the church for a view of the laundry.

Elizabeth found the visit to Anna and Yiorgo a trial. She was unable to understand a word they said, although Anna tried hard to make her feel welcome, plying her with biscuits and offering coffee or fruit juice. Marianne had no such problem, she felt comfortable sitting in the cheerless room, admiring photographs of Marisa's children when they were babies and hearing about their exploits.

'Giovanni was a little terror.' Anna shook her head and smiled. 'He would go up to the fields to see where Yiorgo was working, hide for a while and then jump out on him. Poor Yiorgo. He liked to play jokes. He put pebbles in Yiorgo's boots one day. We all had to laugh at Yiorgo, hopping around, trying to take his boots off and standing outside in the rain in his socks. He would hide his tobacco and watch whilst Yiorgo hunted everywhere. Finally Yiorgo would take out a fresh packet and within minutes his old packet would appear beside him. Giovanni would always look so innocent.'

'Did he play tricks like that on you?' asked Marianne.

Anna shook her head. 'He knew better than that. I threatened to send him to bed without any supper – and he knew I meant it. He wasn't a bad boy, just mischievous. He's a good man now. Works hard for his uncle and is always willing to help. I'm looking forward to seeing him this afternoon. He always has amusing stories to tell me about the visitors in the hotels.'

Marianne looked at her watch. 'He'll only be another half an hour. Would you think us very rude if we left now? I want to have a quick look at the village and then go up to the churchyard.'

'Of course not. You don't want to spend all your time talking to an old lady like me. Make the most of your time, who knows when you will get the opportunity to come back.'

Anna kissed Marianne affectionately. 'Say hello to your grandmother for me.'

Their walk around Plaka was disappointing. The village lay virtually in ruins; much like Spinalonga, except for the whitewashed church and tiny cemetery, where everything looked tidy and well cared for. Marianne found Yannis's grave without difficulty and tapped on it gently.

'Why do you do that?' asked Elizabeth curiously.

Marianne shrugged. 'Habit, I suppose. Greeks always tap on the tombstone to let the occupant know they have a visitor.'

Elizabeth shuddered. 'That's creepy.'

'No it isn't. Wouldn't you like to know that someone had come to see you, that you were still remembered?' Marianne was reading the inscriptions on the other stones. 'This one must be Giovanni's grandmother, and that one his great grandmother. I wonder who looks after them so well?'

Elizabeth looked out towards the island. People could be seen everywhere. 'I'm certainly glad we left there when we did.'

Marianne did not appear to hear her. 'I'd like to see inside the church.' She tried the door. 'Locked,' she announced. 'Oh, well, I suppose we'll just have to wait.'

'Can we start walking back and meet Giovanni on the way? I feel I've had enough of graveyards for one day.'

Marianne nodded. 'That's probably the most sensible thing to do. There's only the one road so he can't miss us. What must it have been like living here? It really is way out.'

'Do you want to take some photos before we go?'

Marianne looked around. 'Just the church and Yannis's grave. Give me the camera.'

'I haven't got it.'

Marianne looked at Elizabeth in horror. 'You must have it.'

Elizabeth shook her head. 'You had it on Spinalonga. Did you leave it on the boat?'

Marianne frowned. 'I'm sure I didn't. We saw the tourists were coming and I took a photo of Flora's garden; then went up the steps by the church and... that's it, that's where I left it. There was a step missing and the next one was broken, so I put the camera down by a clump of grass so I could use both hands to climb down. Oh, Elizabeth, I am sorry. I'll get you another.'

'I'm not worried about the camera. It's just the film. We'll have to take it all again.'

Marianne shook her head. 'I was the one who really wanted the photos of the island and it's my fault that they're lost.' She shrugged resignedly. 'I'm far more upset about losing your camera.'

Giovanni met the two girls as they walked along the dusty road from the churchyard. He drew up beside them and opened the door of the car.

'Have you been waiting very long for me?'

Elizabeth shook her head. 'There was so little to see at Plaka and we'd been all round the graveyard, so we thought we'd start to walk.'

The two girls climbed into the car and Elizabeth placed her bag on the floor. 'You wouldn't have a drink with you, I suppose?'

Giovanni shook his head. 'I will not be long; then we will stop at the first taverna.'

'Where are you going?' asked Marianne curiously.

'To the church.'

'It's locked.'

'Of course it is locked. I have the key.'

'Oh, good. I wanted to have a look inside.'

Giovanni drew to a halt and took a large iron key from beneath the dashboard. He inserted it into the lock and pushed back the heavy door slowly.

'Why do you keep it locked?' asked Marianne as her eyes became accustomed to the darkness of the interior. 'There's nothing in here for people to steal.'

'Visitors who come to Crete without money for a hotel stay in the church. We do not like that. They leave much mess behind them.' Giovanni took a candle from the pile by the door and handed it to Marianne.

They placed their candles into a bucket of sand before lighting them. Giovanni stood with his arm round Marianne and they stood together watching them burn down. Elizabeth stood by the door, feeling like an intruder.

With his arm still round Marianne, Giovanni escorted them both from the church and locked the door carefully behind him.

'Now we go for a drink, yes?'

Marianne spent a sleepless night. For some reason she could not forget the island she had visited earlier in the day. Each time she shut her eyes she could still see ruined houses populated by crippled men and women, and also the exact spot where she knew she had left Elizabeth's camera. The dawn found her standing at the window, straining her eyes across the bay towards Spinalonga. Elizabeth stirred in her sleep and Marianne picked up her clothes and tiptoed into the bathroom to dress. She wrote a hurried note to her friend and left the hotel.

When Elizabeth woke, almost two hours later, she read the note with a mixture of surprise and annoyance. For Marianne to want to return to the island to take another set of photographs was understandable, but the flimsy excuse of finding her camera was stupid. One of the tourists was bound to have found it. She wondered at what time she had left and looked across the bay where the waves were being whipped up by a stiff breeze. Elizabeth shrugged. She would certainly not wait for Marianne to return before she had her breakfast.

By late morning Marianne had still not returned and Elizabeth was beginning to feel concerned as the wind increased. In halting Greek she tried to ask the manager of the hotel what time Marianne had left, but either he did not know or did not understand. She had no more success with the fishermen who refused her request to be taken across to the island as the wind was increasing.

When Giovanni arrived she explained that Marianne had not yet returned and he frowned in consternation. He screwed up his eyes and looked towards the island. There was no boat tied up that he could see.

'You are sure?'

Elizabeth nodded. 'She left me a note. Said she would return on the first tourist boat, but I haven't seen one all morning.'

'They have been told not to run, it is too rough. I will ask who take her over.' Giovanni began to walk along the quay; all but one man shook his head.

'Lambros said he'd drop her off. He was going on to Aghios Nikolaos.'

'What time was that?'

'Early. Just after seven.'

'We will go to Plaka,' announced Giovanni. 'Maybe Davros will take us over.'

'Who's Davros?'

'An old man who still lives there. He used to take supplies over.'

They drove slowly, scanning the choppy sea for any sign of a boat, until they reached the almost deserted village. Giovanni drew up outside a small house and knocked on the door. An old man, supported by a crutch, opened the door a crack and peered out. Giovanni spoke to him, gesticulating towards the island and back towards Elounda. Elizabeth saw the man shake his head and she bit her lip, feeling herself near to tears. She watched as they continued to talk and finally he limped over to the car with Giovanni.

'I will go over with Davros.'

'I'll come with you.'

Giovanni shook his head. 'No. Too rough for you. Davros does not want to go. I say he has to go. He takes me over or I take his boat. You wait here. If Marianne arrives here you wave.'

'Wave what?'

Giovanni shrugged. 'Anything. Keep waving until I wave something back at you.'

'Be careful, Giovanni.'

He flashed his white teeth at her. 'Do not worry about Giovanni. Davros is a good boatman.'

Elizabeth looked to where the old man was pushing a weather worn boat down the flat stones towards the sea. He had discarded his crutch and rolled his trousers up above the knee and for the first time she saw he had a wooden leg.

'Are you sure?'

'Of course. You stay safe with the car or go to the farmhouse. We not be long. Spinalonga is close here.'

Elizabeth stayed and watched until they were safely launched then returned thankfully to the shelter of the car. The wind was blowing strongly now and she shivered. It was no day for going out on the sea and she just hoped they returned quickly.

Davros and Giovanni rowed as fast as they were able against the strong current and rising wind. 'We'll go to the old landing place,' Davros shouted to make his voice heard. 'It's more sheltered.'

Giovanni did not answer. He had not confided his fears to Elizabeth, but he knew how dangerous the island could be. If Marianne had decided to explore on her own she could have fallen down one of the many unguarded openings to the Venetian tunnels, or one of the houses could have collapsed on her. The knot of fear in the pit of his stomach seemed to contract further each time the boat gave a lurch. The sweat dripped from his forehead and made dark patches beneath the arms of his suit as he strained to keep up with Davros's strong, rhythmical stroke. He jumped ashore, leaving Davros to secure the boat and ran up through the arch to the main road.

'Marianne. Marianne. Where are you? Marianne.' He stood and listened, hearing nothing but the wind as it blew through the houses eerily. Desperately he looked to right and left. Which way should he go first? If he went up the slight incline he would reach the outcrop of rock where the narrow path led down the seaward side and at one point there was a sheer drop down to the rocks below. He hesitated no longer, calling as he hurried up the hill, he finally rounded the outcrop of rock to be buffeted by the full force of the wind. He made himself look down to the sea below as he struggled forward.

He reached the graveyard and pushed his way between the long grass and over to the tower, waiting for his eyes to become accustomed to the gloom before deciding Marianne was certainly not down there.

Returning to the path he walked back past the church to where two large drain openings could be seen and he leant over the stone surround and peered down into the murky water.

'Marianne. Marianne.' He strained his ears for the slightest sound.

'Giovanni, what are you doing?'

'Marianne,' he called down the drain. 'Are you hurt? I can't see you.'

'Turn round, then.'

Giovanni dragged his eyes away from the depths and cast a glance over his shoulder.

'Marianne!' he breathed the word. He rose rapidly to his feet and clasped her to him, covering her hair with kisses. 'Marianne, oh, Marianne, I am so worried; so frightened that harm has come to you.'

Marianne pushed back her hair from her eyes. 'I'm so glad you've come. I thought I was going to be stuck over here for ever! I was stupid to come over on my own, but the weather was wonderful when I started out. I had only planned to stay until the first tourist boat returned. I left a note for Elizabeth.'

'Why did you come today? Manolis brought you here yesterday.'

'I left Elizabeth's camera here. I can't explain, but I knew I'd be able to find it. I just had to come back, Giovanni.' Marianne shook her head. 'I'm sorry if I worried you. I didn't know there was going to be a storm. I thought I'd be back in plenty of time, but when it got rough no one came over.'

Giovanni still held her in his arms. 'You are safe. That is all that is important.'

He tilted her face upwards and kissed her full on the mouth. 'You should not have done this thing. I was frightened I would never see you again and that I could not bear.'

Giovanni pulled her close to him and she leant against him, enjoying the thrill she felt coursing through her body as his tongue began to move within her mouth.

'No, Giovanni, no,' she finally managed to gasp.

'Why do you say no? You enjoy me loving you, you tell me so the first night by the fort and again in the gorge. You say we cannot at the hotel because Elizabeth may come. She will not come now.'

He covered her mouth again with his own to stop her protests and guided her down the path to the house where Yannis had lived for so many years.

'Here we will be out of the wind,' he stated as he kissed her again and felt her body pressing urgently against his own.

Elizabeth looked at her friend petulantly. 'You still haven't told me why it took so long for Giovanni to find you. I was waiting in the car for hours.'

Marianne rolled over onto her stomach. 'I told you. I wandered around for a while after I'd found your camera and took some more photographs, then the wind began to blow and I watched the waves pounding on the sea side until I realised that no tourists would be coming over until the wind had dropped so I went back and sheltered in old uncle Yannis's house. I felt quite humble. They must have experienced conditions like that year after year.'

'Weren't you frightened?'

'No, why should I be? I knew I would be able to return when the sea calmed down. I was more annoyed with myself than anything. Giovanni said he had been calling and calling me, but the wind was blowing so hard I didn't hear him for ages.' Marianne turned large, innocent eyes on her friend.

'He was very worried about you.'

Marianne smiled to herself. 'Was he?'

'You know he was. He had relief written all over his face when you arrived back at the beach.'

'He was just happy to be back on dry land. He couldn't wait to get to Yannis's for a change of clothing.'

'It was very good of that boatman to take him over. None of the fishermen from here would go out.'

'I expect he's been out in a lot worse! I'll ask Giovanni to take us to Plaka tomorrow and I'll thank him properly. I'm sure I didn't do so today.'

Elizabeth shot her friend a shrewd glance. 'What really happened with you and Giovanni out there?'

Marianne shrugged. 'I've told you.'

'I'll ask Giovanni.'

'He'll tell you the same. What time is he coming?'

'About eight, and he said you weren't to go off anywhere.'

Marianne snorted. 'I will if I want to.'

'Oh, Marianne, please don't.'

'Why not? He's not my keeper.'

'He's just concerned about you. It was silly of you to go off alone this morning just for a camera. Anything could have happened. You could have fallen and broken your leg, and if the storm had worsened we might not have been able to get over to you for days.'

'Don't exaggerate. Anyway, I'm glad the camera was still there. I knew it would be. Don't look so worried. I won't go off again, except to have a drink before he arrives.'

'How did you get in such a mess this morning?' asked Ourania as Giovanni entered her shop.

'It's a long story. I went to Elounda to collect Marianne and Elizabeth only to find that Marianne had gone over to Spinalonga before Elizabeth was awake. The weather had turned and none of the fishermen would go out. I drove down to Plaka and helped Davros row out there. I searched the island from top to bottom before I found her, then she wondered why I was worried.'

'And why were you?'

'Anything could have happened to her. She could have fallen down one of the drains or over the cliff, besides, she's family.'

'What made her go over this morning on her own?'

'She'd left Elizabeth's camera there. Said she knew just where it was, so she went back.'

'I hope the photos are worth the trouble she put you to.'

'Oh, it was no trouble.'

Ourania smiled to herself. 'Are you coming for supper?'

Giovanni looked at his aunt in horror. 'No, I'll take them into Aghios Nikolaos for the evening. Elounda's pretty quiet at night.'

Giovanni squeezed Marianne's elbow as he helped her into the car. 'You look so beautiful. Maybe Elizabeth would like to go on ahead?' he whispered in Greek.

Marianne looked at him mockingly. 'She certainly would not.'

Giovanni shrugged. 'You owe me. Two suits I have ruined because of you.'

Marianne giggled. 'I paid you for both of them.'

'That was only the deposit, they were expensive suits!' He reverted to English. 'What would you like to do this evening? Two restaurants are very good in Aghios Nikolaos. They sell fresh fish. Then maybe you would like to dance, there is a disco, or we could sit by the pool with a bottle of wine.'

Elizabeth looked at Marianne. 'I'd rather eat first.'

'And I think maybe a drink by the pool afterwards; then we can think about the disco.'

Giovanni nodded. 'As you wish.'

'Is there anywhere here that will develop a film quickly? I asked in Elounda, but they said a week. I'd like to show Flora how her garden looks before we return to Heraklion.'

'Give it to me. I know a man. He will be very fast.'

Giovanni settled them in a restaurant on a balcony overlooking the road and took the film from Marianne. 'I will be five minutes. You choose from the menu while I am gone.'

Elizabeth smiled at Marianne. 'If I hadn't got to know Giovanni a little before you came I would have said he was falling in love with you.'

Marianne's face burned. 'Don't be silly!'

'I'm not. He can't do enough for you, but then he's always with a different girl, so I suppose it's probably become second nature to him to do all he can to please them.'

Marianne felt anger rising in her at her friend's innocent remark, mixed with a feeling of resentment towards Giovanni, who had assured her of his undying love each time she had given herself to him unreservedly.

'What are you having to eat?' she asked, trying to ignore her tumultuous feelings.

On their way to the taverna by the pool, Giovanni took them on a short detour and knocked on a shop door. He slipped inside when it was opened to him and returned bearing a packet of photographs that he handed to Marianne.

'My friend was closed, but for me he did a special job.'

Marianne smiled at him gratefully. 'How much do I owe you?'

'Now, nothing, maybe later.' He raised his eyebrows at her and she refused to meet his eyes.

They sat beside the pool, Marianne and Giovanni sharing a bottle of retzina, whilst Elizabeth sipped at a tomato juice, and Marianne began to examine her photographs.

'These are really good,' she remarked. 'Your friend certainly knows his business. The colour is superb.'

Giovanni nodded and took them from her, glancing at each one before passing it on to Elizabeth. Almost at the last one he paused and began to study it intently.

'When did you take this?' he asked.

'Which one?' He handed it back to her.

'Oh, this morning. I couldn't remember if I'd already taken one of the shutters, and the light was just right, so I took another. Stupid of me, I've got two almost identical now.'

'May I see the first one?'

Elizabeth sorted through those she held and handed it to him. Giovanni placed them on the table and then looked at Marianne.

'On the island this morning, you were alone?'

'You know I was.'

'And you took this photograph this morning?'

'I think so. Yes, it has to be. The light is coming at a different angle. Why?'

Giovanni crossed himself. 'You do not see? There, sitting in the taverna.' He indicated with his finger.

Marianne took the snapshot from him and held it up. The colour drained from her face. 'Who is it?'

Giovanni shook his head. 'I do not know. You are sure it is the photograph you took today? It could not be Elizabeth, or a tourist from the day before?'

'There's a way to find out. The negatives should be numbered.' Marianne tipped them out on the table and began to sort through them, finally holding up a couple to the light. 'There you are. That's the negative for that photo. It's number thirty, so it has to be from today.'

Elizabeth looked at the two of them in surprise. 'What are you both getting so worked up about?'

Marianne passed her the two photographs, almost identical, except in one there was an indistinct figure of a girl, dressed in white, who appeared to be sitting on a stool in the taverna.

'It's a trick of the light,' she said, handing it back.

Marianne looked at it again. 'I'm not so sure. Could there have been anyone else over there?'

Giovanni shook his head. 'There was no one on the island until I came for you. I would have seen a boat.'

'Maybe your friend muddled them if he developed them in a hurry,' suggested Marianne.

'We will ask. We will finish our drink; then we will ask him.' Giovanni drained his glass and promptly refilled it.

'I don't see what's so important about it,' remarked Elizabeth. 'It's probably only a shadow.'

Elizabeth lay back on her bed. 'Well, you certainly caused a stir.'

Marianne turned a distressed face towards her. 'I didn't mean to. I thought it had to be a trick of the light, but both Flora and Manolis were quite definite that it was Anna.'

'That's impossible. She's been dead for years.'

Marianne crossed herself. 'I know, but don't you see, it was when she carved those ships on the shutters that she cut her finger and developed blood poisoning. That's why she's still at the taverna.'

'You're being ridiculous now!'

'I'm not. You just don't understand.' Marianne felt tears coming into her eyes as she tried to understand her own feelings.

'You can't really believe in ghosts, besides, even if they did exist, why should one suddenly decide to be photographed?'

'She's trying to tell me something.'

Elizabeth snorted. 'Like what?'

'I don't know. I have to go back and find out.'

'Back to the island?'

Marianne nodded. 'You don't have to come if you don't want to.'

'You can't go on your own. You'll probably come back having photographed a whole army of ghosts.' Elizabeth buried her head in her pillow.

The hammering on their bedroom door woke both girls with a start.

'Who's there?' called Elizabeth as she sat up.

A stream of incomprehensible Greek answered her.

'What did she say?' she asked of Marianne.

'I couldn't hear properly.' Marianne opened the door as Elizabeth made her usual early morning dash for the bathroom.

'Madam, please, the telephone. It is very urgent.'

Marianne frowned and answered in Greek. 'Who is it for? Me or my friend?'

'They asked for Miss Marianne.'

'That's me. Did they say what they wanted?'

The woman shook her head. 'The call is from America and they said it was very urgent that they spoke to you immediately.'

Marianne picked up the light wrap that served as her dressing gown and began to force her arms into the sleeves as she followed the woman down the stairs. She picked up the telephone and was relieved to hear her sister's voice.

'Marianne, I'm sorry, I've no idea what time it is over there, but I had to speak to you.'

'What's wrong?'

'It's Pappa. He's had a stroke.'

'What! How bad is he?'

'They won't say. He's in the intensive care unit. Mamma's with him.'

'I'll come straight home.'

'There's no need. You might not even get here in time.' Marianne heard her sister's voice break.

'You tell Pappa to hang on. Love to Mamma. I'm on my way.' Marianne replaced the receiver and leant against the wall.

'Bad news?'

She nodded. 'My father, he's had a stroke. That was my sister in America.'

'Medicine is wonderful in America.'

Marianne nodded. 'Let's hope it's good enough.' She lifted the receiver again. 'May I make some calls? My bill, can you get that ready for me, please?'

'Of course, madam.'

Marianne dialled Yannis's number and spoke to him briefly before returning upstairs to where Elizabeth had just finished dressing.

'What was the panic?'

Marianne sank down on her bed. 'It was Helena.'

'Helena? Your sister? From America?'

Marianne nodded. 'My father's had a severe stroke. I have to get back, Elizabeth. I don't know if I'll get there in time.' She lifted her woebegone face to her friend. 'I'm sorry, but you'll be all right, Giovanni will look after you.'

Elizabeth placed her arms round Marianne. 'I'm so sorry. Don't worry about me at all. What can I do to help?'

Marianne looked around vaguely. 'Help me pack, I suppose. I 'phoned uncle Yannis and asked if Giovanni could come down and take me to the airport. He's on his way.'

'Go and shower. You'll feel a bit better then. I'll pack for both of us whilst you're in there.'

'There's no need for you to return to Athens.'

'If you're not here I'd rather be at home with Nicolas. I'm longing to tell him about the baby.'

Marianne hugged her friend back. 'Of course you are. I'll just wear jeans and my red shirt. I can carry a jumper. All the rest can be packed.'

By the time Giovanni arrived both girls were ready and waiting for him. He held Marianne in his arms.

'Believe me, I am so sorry. If you were leaving for any other reason I would do my best to stop you. You will come back, Marianne?'

'Maybe. One day. I can't make any plans at present.'

'Of course not.' He tilted her chin upwards and looked into her eyes. 'I love you, Marianne.'

Marianne returned his kiss. 'We must go. There is a flight to Athens at eleven, and I must be on it.'

Giovanni dropped his arms and picked up their cases. 'Of course.' He tried to keep the hurt from his voice. 'We can talk at the airport.'

Bob met Marianne from the airport and drove her straight to the city hospital. She was shocked when she saw her father attached to a machine that was monitoring his heartbeat and an oxygen mask over his face. A nurse sat beside him watching the screen above his head. She smiled as Marianne entered.

'You must be his other daughter,' she spoke quietly. 'Your mother said you were on your way.'

'How is he?'

'Very sick.'

'You mean he's…'

The nurse shook her head. 'He's having the best of care. Another couple of days and we hope to move him to a side ward.'

'Oh!' Marianne felt unreasonably annoyed with her sister for calling her back to America. She bent forward and kissed her father on his cheek. 'You must get better soon, Pappa. I've so much to tell you.'

Bob was waiting for her in the parking lot. 'Well? How did you find him?'

Marianne pulled a face. 'He looks terrible. He's all hitched up to machines, but the nurse said he could be moving to a side ward in a couple more days.'

'That's good, then.'

Marianne nodded. 'I suppose so, if she was telling me the truth.'

'Why shouldn't she?'

'You know what hospitals are like. Never say die until you draw your last breath. How's my mother? Have you seen her?'

Bob nodded. 'She's pretty shaken up. I think that's partly why Helena called you home.'

Marianne slumped back in her seat. 'I couldn't come back to your place for the night, could I? I'm out for the count and I can't possibly cope with my mother or anyone else for that matter.'

Bob raised his eyebrows. 'I know it's been three years, but I'd planned to take you away somewhere special for our reunion.'

Marianne shook her head. 'I just want to sleep, Bob. I've been travelling for almost two days.'

'My parents would love to have you. I'll give Helena a ring and say you're with me.'

'You are good to me, Bob.'

'That's what friends are for.' He took his hand from the steering wheel and squeezed Marianne's.

'It's good to have you back. Maybe we can have that reunion next weekend?'

Marianne wrote a brief letter to Elizabeth, simply telling her that she had arrived safely, and as much as she knew about the condition of her father who had not been moved in the prophesised two days. She spent many long hours at his bedside, relieving her mother of as much distress as she could. Helena would call in briefly, depositing her mother and taking Marianne back to her apartment for a meal.

Helena's dependence on Gregory annoyed Marianne. If he was delayed at work she would pace up and down, the baby on her hip, and at the sound of his key in the door she would run to him and declare they had been waiting for hours. She continually told Marianne what a wonderful husband he was and how she could not envisage life without him until Marianne decided she could take no more.

'I'm not coming back with you tonight, Helena. I'm visiting Bob's parents. They want to know how Pappa is getting on.'

Helena's face fell. 'But Gregory won't be back for a couple of hours.'

'What difference does that make? If I wasn't here you'd find plenty to occupy yourself.'

Helena's face crumpled. 'I don't like being on my own waiting for him to come home. I keep thinking of poor Pappa. Mamma was waiting for him to come home when the police arrived instead.'

'Pappa's a good deal older than Gregory and there's no reason to think he's going to have a stroke, now or in the future. Stop being silly, Helena. You've got two children to think about as well as Gregory.'

'I know,' Helena sniffed. 'How could I manage to bring them up if anything happened to Greg? I couldn't possibly manage without him.'

Marianne looked at her sister in disgust. 'I hope you don't go on like this in front of Mamma. You're as bad as aunt Maria used to be and with no good cause. I'm going to Bob's tonight; then I'll decide what I'm doing tomorrow. I've other friends I want to visit.'

Helena turned away. 'You just don't understand what it's like to love someone. You've only ever thought of yourself. Come on, if you want me to give you a lift.'

Marianne spent a pleasant evening with Bob's parents, assuring them that Elizabeth was very well and happy in Athens. She almost told them that Elizabeth was expecting a baby, and remembered just in time that the news was not hers to give. She could imagine their pleasure in their future grandchild and the extended holidays they would be taking to Greece. She showed them the photographs she had taken, explaining that she was planning to mount them in the album she had purchased from Ourania's shop. They looked at them with interest.

'Did your grandmother really live in that tiny house?'

'When she was a girl. She was only a fisherman's daughter.'

'You'd never know it now.'

Marianne smiled. 'That's true. She went back and visited a few years ago and said everything had changed so much that she hardly knew where she was.'

'And this is that island we've heard about.' Bob's father tapped the photo with his fingernail. 'Terrible to think of those poor sick people marooned over there.'

Marianne felt her heart constrict. Spinalonga and Giovanni. She had not written to him since her return to thank him for taking her to the airport. She should do so. Suddenly she wanted to go. To be alone to sort out her thoughts and feelings. She appeared to be the only one who accepted that her father was not going to recover.

Her mother either walked around, wringing her hands and dabbing at her eyes, or would speak cheerfully of when her husband was well again, whilst Helena clung to Gregory and either cried over him or her children. Her grandmother she had seen only once since her return and she had seemed old and shrunken, as she grieved with her daughter, reminding her of Anna.

'I really must go. I find it very tiring just sitting and looking at Pappa. I ought to write to my relatives in Greece and let them know how he is. They were very concerned when I left so hurriedly.'

'Of course. You must come over again. Come whenever you like. You know there's always a place here for you.'

Marianne kissed them both. 'I do appreciate having a bolt hole.'

Bob drove slowly, stopping the car a few doors from her house. He placed his arm round her shoulders.

'I've hardly seen you since you've been back. Could we have dinner tomorrow?'

'I'm not sure, Bob. It really depends upon Pappa.'

'I know. Let's assume there's no change in the next twenty-four hours. You can always ring me. Is it a date?'

Marianne smiled at him. 'I'd be pleased to avoid Helena again. We came very close to having a row tonight. She accused me of being selfish and thinking only of myself.'

'You wouldn't consider coming with me just because you wanted to be with me?'

'Oh, Bob, I'm sorry. I didn't mean to sound like that. It's just that everyone is being so, so – out of character. I know Pappa won't get well. If he comes out of this coma he'll be a vegetable. Why won't anyone else face facts?'

'It's just their way of coping with it.'

Marianne sighed. 'I feel so guilty. I've been away for three years studying and I could easily have come back earlier. I didn't have to visit Elizabeth. I was just being selfish. Helena was right when she said I never think of anyone but myself. If I'd come back after I graduated I could have seen Pappa and talked to him, and told him how much I appreciated all he'd done for me, and how much I loved him.'

Bob held her tightly, feeling her hot tears on his neck. 'You can't blame yourself. You could have been anywhere and unable to get back.'

Marianne did not appear to hear him. 'I wish there was some way I could make him know I'm here.'

'I'm sure he does know. They say people in a coma often know what's going on around them, they just can't respond.'

'Really? That's a comforting thought. I've been talking to him, but I felt such a fool, as if I were talking to myself.'

Bob squeezed her to him. 'You need a rest. Come out to dinner tomorrow and we'll make some plans for next week.'

Marianne kissed him lightly. 'You are a good friend, Bob. I don't know how I'd manage without you around.'

Marianne was roused in the early hours by the insistence of the telephone. She groped for it mechanically, the words she heard shocking her into instant wakefulness.

'We'll be right there.' She pulled on a pair of jeans and a jumper before knocking on her mother's bedroom door.

'What is it, dear? I thought I heard the telephone.'

'You did, Mamma. It was the hospital. They think we ought to be there. You get dressed and I'll phone Helena and wake Andrew.'

Her mother looked at her uncomprehending. 'What time is it?'

'I don't know. You just get dressed. I'll be back in a minute.'

Marianne telephoned Bob from the hospital. 'I'm afraid dinner is off. Pappa died this morning.'

'Where are you? Shall I come over?'

'I'm at the hospital. There are a few things to see to; then I'll take Mamma home.'

'Ring me again when you get there. Let me know if there's anything I can do to help.'

'Thank you, Bob. I will.'

Marianne found her time was filled with letter writing and telephoning. Despite her father having been one of a group of practitioners, every patient seemed to have been treated by him and they wrote touching letters addressed to her mother. Elena sat, most of the time twisting her handkerchief in her hands, saying nothing. Helena was equally useless when she visited. She would sit with her mother and they would both shed tears and dab at their eyes, neither of them making any attempt to help Marianne with the workload that seemed to be overwhelming her. Andrew tried to support her by running errands, but she noticed that most of his day was passed in his room or spent elsewhere.

'I'm sorry, Marianne,' he apologised. 'I'll do anything I can to help, you know that, but I just can't stand being around with Mamma and Helena being so melodramatic. I miss Pappa too.'

Marianne sensed her younger brother was near to tears. 'You do whatever suits you best. That's what Mamma and Helena are doing. It's their way of coming to terms with their grief. I'm working mine out.' She patted him on the shoulder and he left gratefully.

She surveyed the pile of unopened mail and spotted an airmail letter. Pulling it out, she saw Elizabeth's familiar handwriting and opened it eagerly. The conventional phrases she scanned until she came to the news towards the end. She was keeping well, Nicolas was thrilled with the prospect of becoming a father and they were planning to turn the spare room into a nursery. She had posted a letter containing the news to her parents the day before, so there was no need for Marianne to feign ignorance of the event. Finally she asked about Marianne's plans. When were she and Bob getting married? If it were soon, she and Nicolas would be able to come over, but she would not want to risk flying after another three months.

Marianne smiled to herself. She had not thought about any wedding plans with Bob and he had mentioned nothing further to her about their weekend. Maybe he was being patient because of her father's death. She really ought to talk to him and explain that she wanted to wait until she had carved out a career for herself. She rested her chin on her hands, realising it was a lame excuse, what she needed was time to forget Giovanni.

She had been home for six weeks now and had not thought about her future at all. She frowned. Six weeks. It couldn't be. Her last period had been in England. She took her diary from her handbag and began to count the weeks, dropping it into her lap in disbelief. She had missed two.

Bob looked at Marianne in despair. 'I just don't understand. I thought when you came back we would be married straight away. Is there someone else, Marianne?'

Marianne avoided the question. 'I just want to try and stand on my own two feet for a while. I've had a good education, and I don't want to waste it.'

'It wouldn't be a waste. You could still work after we were married. You could come into the firm as a junior partner.'

'That would be the easy way. I want to make it by my own efforts, no string pulling, no back door entry. I could have stayed in England and applied for a position. It would have meant working my way up slowly until I was finally offered a partnership, but when I was offered it I would know I'd earned it and I was worth it.'

'All right, you make your own way, but we could still get married.'

'Not at the moment, Bob,' she tilted her head defiantly.

Bob sighed. 'We could get an apartment together; then get married in a few years time. We're both young, there's no rush.'

'No, Bob. I don't want to feel I'm committed.'

'Marianne, what do you really want?'

Marianne covered her face with her hands. 'Bob, I don't know. I've some sorting out to do in my life and I have to do it on my own.'

Bob pulled Marianne's hands away from her face. 'Let me help you.'

Marianne shook her head. 'I wish I could make you understand. It would be so easy to accept your help now.'

Bob spread his hands. 'What is there to understand? You say you don't want to get married yet. All right, I can't make you. You say you have some sorting out to do in your life, but does that include me? I feel I have a right to know.'

'No, Bob. It can't include you. It's my problem, not yours.'

'What is? You're not making sense. I should never have let you go away.'

'You couldn't stop me!'

'I could have married you before you got the idea into your head about going to England.'

'It wouldn't have worked.'

'What - our marriage or stopping you going away?'

'Both. Bob, I've got to say it. I'm not sure enough of my feelings for you. I'm terribly fond of you, and I know I've relied upon you, but…'

'Marianne, I love you.'

'I know you do. That's what makes it so hard for me.'

'Is there nothing I can say that will make you change your mind?'

'Nothing, Bob.'

'How long have you felt like this?'

'I don't know.' Marianne shifted uncomfortably in her chair. 'I thought I might change my mind when I came back, but I haven't,' she finished lamely.

Bob's face was white and strained as he looked at her. 'I think maybe your sister was right when she said you were selfish and thought only of yourself. I've been sitting here, waiting for you to come home. You gave no inkling in your letters to me that you'd had a change of heart.' He rose to his feet. 'You know where I am, but I don't guarantee I'll be there if you change your mind.'

He slammed the door as he left and Marianne dropped her head into her arms. It would have been so much easier than going ahead alone. Bob loved her and in time would probably have accepted the child. She gave a small laugh. If she had not been so exhausted the first night she was back in America she might well have believed it was his and her present problem would not have arisen. Now she would have to face her mother with the news.

Anna looked around the room where she had slept for the last seventy seven years. The room held memories for her. She had shared it first with her sister, then with Yannis whilst he was a baby, and finally with Marisa. Her mattress had taken up the remaining space until Babbis and Yiorgo had built a room on at the back. Yiorgo had used the back room, giving up his bedroom to Yannis. Anna had grown used to always having someone in the room with her as Marisa had slept there until she married Victor and went to live in Italy.

During the occupation when the Italians were billeted on them, she had been able to hear them through the flimsy partition that had been erected. Their talk, laughter and snoring had become as familiar to her as Yannis's snuffling as a baby and Marisa's childhood habit of talking in her sleep.

When Marisa and Victor had visited, Anna had given up her room to them and slept down in the living room on a mattress, Yiorgo giving up his room to the children and returning to the small back room that was now used as a store room.

She had resisted leaving the farm, despite the pleading from Yannis and Ourania, but the last winter spent in the inhospitable building had finally convinced her that she had to accept their offer of a home. Yiorgo found the chopping of firewood more and more difficult as his eyesight deteriorated and she no longer had the strength do the job herself.

She knew the apartment that Yannis had designed especially for her and Yiorgo would be warmer and certainly more comfortable, but she was still loath to leave. Yannis had said she could take with her whatever possessions she wished, but there was really nothing to take except her clothes and the picture that had hung above the fireplace.

After the visit from the English girl, Michael's daughter, she knew he was not going to come back. Now there was no need for her to stay. He had intended to return. Anna gave a sad sigh and looked again at the only photograph she possessed of the man she had loved. Maybe she could ask Yannis to find a picture frame for her to put it into. It was becoming dog-eared. She smoothed it with her fingers and placed it back into the pocket of Michael's shirt. It was all she had to remember him by, an old shirt, one letter and a photograph.

1989

Joseph held Sorrell's arm as they strolled through the National Gardens in the city centre.

'Now, we check in about one thirty in the morning. There should be no one around except the night clerk. You book us in, whilst I wait in a chair. I'm a sick man,' he grinned cheerfully. 'I've just had my appendix out and I'm tired and I want to get to bed. If you have to give him any information say we're on our way to the islands for me to recuperate and our car broke down. By the time it was repaired we'd missed the ferry. Our luggage is in the car, there's no need to bring it in as we're only staying the one night. I'll wait for an hour or so and then go down to the first landing. From there I'll be able to see when they bring up the money from the nightclub. I'll give it about half an hour, by which time the night clerk will probably have nodded off, then go down to the office.'

Sorrell nodded. 'What do I do?'

'You, my dear, will be able to go to bed and sleep until I return. We will then depart and no one will be any the wiser for a few hours.'

'Suppose the night clerk doesn't go to sleep?'

'I'm not concerned about him and you don't have to be either. This is what I've been planning for years. All the other trifles we picked up on the way were just to keep us going until now.'

'What made you choose tonight?'

'What indeed! There's a trade delegation staying at the hotel with their wives. That means an official reception tomorrow. Now, what woman would dream of being seen at such a function without her jewellery, and where better to leave it until she needs it than in the hotel safe? The jewels, combined with a week's takings and the staff wages should make it quite profitable.'

Sorrell nodded. 'Then where shall we go?'

'Across the border to Albania and back to Italy. We can move up the country gradually, over to the French Riviera and down into Spain for the winter.'

Sorrell smiled contentedly. It sounded like her kind of trip.

'I'll go over, uncle Yannis. We're quiet enough here and I can have a look at the nightclub at the same time. See how the proud father is managing.' Giovanni grinned.

'It's time you settled down and thought about becoming a father,' grumbled Yannis.

'I'll let Nicolas have a few on my behalf. No woman is going to deceive me again. I learnt my lesson the hard way.' Giovanni spoke flippantly, not wishing to admit to his uncle he had been hurt a second time by Marianne's hasty departure and the brief note of thanks he had received.

Yannis shrugged. 'Find yourself a Greek girl. What about that little receptionist in Athens?'

'She gave me up and married her waiter a few months ago. She wasn't my type, anyway.'

'You surprise me. I thought all women were your type. Anyway, whilst you're over there see how Orestis feels about training an assistant manager. He's not at all fit and could do with some help. Be tactful. Don't give him the impression that I want to retire him, just ease his load a little.'

Giovanni nodded. 'You can trust me, uncle. I'll tell him you're finding it difficult in your old age, so you reckon he must be also.'

'You'll tell him no such thing!' Yannis looked at the mocking smile on Giovanni's face and realised his nephew was making fun of him. 'A touch of arthritis I may have, but I'm not in my dotage yet.'

Sorrell checked them into the hotel in the early hours, playing the part of the solicitous wife, settling Joseph into a chair by the lift where he bent forward, his hat almost hiding his face. The desk clerk had shown little interest in them and had obviously been relieved that he would not have to carry luggage up.

Once in the privacy of their room, Sorrell had opened first the wall safe, which was bare, and then the fridge.

'We may as well take advantage of their hospitality.' She selected a bottle of wine and poured a glass for both of them. 'To our success.' She lifted her glass and saluted him. 'What time are you planning to move?'

'I'll give it an hour. No point in sitting on the stairs any longer than necessary. I'll sit here and go over the details in my head.'

'I may as well get some sleep then.' She plumped up the pillows and tilted the light shade away from her eyes.

At two thirty in the morning Joseph picked up his empty glass and took it into the bathroom where he rinsed it and wiped it carefully on the towel before placing it on the shelf above the basin. The movement was enough to disturb Sorrell. She opened her eyes just enough to see him take a revolver from beneath his jacket and check the chamber.

'Joseph!' She opened her eyes wide in horror. 'What do you need a gun for?'

Joseph waved it airily at her. 'Just to frighten the old man if he becomes curious. It's not loaded.'

The waiting on the landing seemed interminable. Some late revellers passed him with a curious look and he bent hurriedly and pretended to tie his shoelace. Low voices and the sound of a key in inserted in a lock drew his attention. Two men entered the office below and Joseph sat down on the stairs and waited for them to leave. He leant his head against the ornamental uprights, feeling his eyelids grow heavy. He should not have finished the wine.

Joseph jerked himself upright. He had fallen asleep and he had no idea whether it had been for a few minutes or half an hour. He looked down at the closed door and finally decided that it was the turning of the key that had awakened him. Stealthily he began to descend the stairs. From his vantage point he could see the desk clerk's head bent over a book, his back towards the staircase.

Silently Joseph moved across to the door and inserted his own key, closing the door behind him and re-locking it. The light from his torch showed an old iron safe in the corner of the room. Biting his lips he inserted the two keys and turned them until he felt the tumblers fall before pushing down the heavy handle and allowing the door to swing open with a slight creak. He swept the contents of the top shelf into a canvas bag and began to place the jewel cases on top of the notes. His bag almost full he pulled the drawstring and swung it over his shoulder before closing the safe door. He unlocked the office door, replaced his torch in his pocket, and stepped outside.

As he did so a low laugh came to his ears and two men stepped up from the lounge, stopping in their tracks as they saw Joseph standing immobile in the door way.

'Call the police,' Giovanni called to the desk clerk as he rushed towards his brother, Nicolas following.

Without a word of warning the bullet crossed the intervening space and embedded itself in Giovanni's stomach, causing his legs to crumple beneath him.

Nicolas stared in amazement. 'You've shot him!'

The gun blasted again and Nicolas felt the sharp pain in his chest and his hand contacted a wet stickiness. 'Police,' he managed to gasp before darkness overtook him.

Andreas was already dialling as the bullet entered his skull and he slumped forward, a pool of blood spreading across the hotel register.

Joseph looked at his handiwork in horror. He had not meant to fire, only to threaten. Slowly he backed up the stairs, expecting any minute for the alarm to be raised. By the time he reached the first landing he was breathing more easily. He looked at his watch, almost four. He had an hour at least, maybe more, before the day staff began to arrive.

He ran up the next two flights of stairs and pushed open the hotel room door quietly. He cast his eyes round the room and picked up his hat that he had discarded earlier. Sorrell was sleeping peacefully, curled up in a tight ball. He calculated swiftly, then wiped his revolver with his handkerchief and placed it lightly on the bed beside her before leaving the room and making his way to the fire escape.

The sound of the door closing roused Sorrell and she opened her eyes. 'Joseph?'

She sat up in bed and heard the gun clatter to the floor. Automatically she bent down and retrieved it, then smiled. Joseph had decided to leave it behind after all. She placed it on the bedside table and turned over.

By the time it was light Joseph had driven to Piraeus. He pulled over to the side of the road and took stock of his situation. He really had been very clever. There was nothing to link him with the robbery and shooting at the hotel. True, he had not reckoned on Giovanni and Nicolas being there, but with luck they had not recognised him. It would be the story Madeleine Evans told that would be investigated.

It really had been a stroke of genius on his part to return the gun to the room where she was sure to pick it up and leave her prints on it. He decided he really had very little to worry about. A couple of hours sleep, and then he would find his usual fence in Piraeus to off-load the jewellery. He would have a good meal before continuing his drive towards the border with Albania and the following day should see him on the ferry to Brindisi.

Thalia and her husband entered the hotel and froze at the sight of the carnage.

'Stelios! What's happened?'

'Telephone for an ambulance.'

Thalia nodded and moved behind the desk, letting out a piercing scream.

'What is it?' Stelios was bending over the two men.

'Andreas. There's blood all over the desk.'

'Never mind that. Call an ambulance and then the police.'

With shaking hands Thalia did as her husband instructed. 'What's happened, Stelios?'

'I don't know! Go and wake Mr Orestis. Tell him to come down at once.'

Orestis was still shaving when Thalia hammered on his bedroom door. 'Mr Orestis. Come at once. Stelios says come now.'

Shaving cream still on his chin, Orestis opened the door. 'What's wrong, girl? Is the hotel on fire?'

'Something's happened downstairs. There's blood everywhere and Mr Giovanni and Mr Nick…'

Orestis pushed past her, not stopping to pick up his jacket or change from his slippers into his shoes. He hurried down the stairs, Thalia following him, wringing her hands and wailing.

Sorrell opened her eyes and wondered what had woken her. She looked at the bed beside her. Joseph had not returned. She swung her legs over the side. No doubt he was waiting at the car for her. She decided against a shower and had a quick wash and brushed her hair before taking a last look round the room. The gun was lying on the bedside table and she placed it inside her bag, grimacing as she did so.

She pressed the button for the lift and after some minutes without a response decided to take the stairs. As she reached the lower landing she could hear voices and see movement below. The robbery must have been discovered early, that was why Joseph had not returned for her. Unconcerned she continued down to the foyer. Standing at the bottom of the stairs was a policeman.

'Excuse me.'

The policeman turned. 'How can I help you, madam?'

'I should like to go past.'

'I'm sorry. All guests are being asked to wait in the dining room until we have spoken to them. Please be good enough to join them.'

'I can't possibly do that. My husband is waiting for me. We have a ferry to catch.'

'I'm sorry, madam. I expect your husband will be in the dining room.'

Sorrell shook her head. 'He left a short while ago to collect our car.'

The policeman looked puzzled. No one had passed out of the hotel since they had arrived. 'I'm sorry. I have to insist, madam. Please go to the dining room.'

The man watched as she retraced her steps up the marble stairs and he beckoned to another policeman on duty by the lift. 'You haven't let a man through to fetch his car, have you?'

'No. I'll check with Dimitris.' He strolled across to the main doors and turned and shook his head. Yiorgo walked across to him.

'There's something odd there. That woman said her husband had gone to fetch their car and she was going to join him. Do you reckon she was trying to avoid paying her bill?'

'Could be.'

Yiorgo looked up the stairs. 'I'll go up and keep an eye on her. Send someone up as soon as you can and we'll start checking identities and see if anyone heard anything.'

Sorrell reached the dining room and turned deliberately down the corridor in the direction of the fire escape. She pulled open the door and began to hurry down the stone steps, wrenching the door at the bottom open to come face to face with a policeman.

'I'm sorry, madam. No one is allowed to leave the hotel until the police have finished their enquiries.'

Sorrell gave him a seductive smile. 'I was just looking for my husband.'

'No one has been out this way, madam. I suggest you try the dining room. The guests have been asked to wait in there.'

Realising it would be futile to argue Sorrell climbed back up to the corridor and walked back to the dining room. It was quite possible that Joseph was waiting in there for her, having been refused leave to go to the car. She cast her eye over the people milling around or sitting at a table toying with rolls and coffee. A waiter hovered towards her.

'Would you care for some coffee, madam?'

Sorrell nodded absently. She could not see Joseph. 'What's happened?'

'A most unfortunate accident.' He poured coffee into her cup and walked away.

Yiorgo and Dimitris entered the dining room together, carrying a bundle of passports and a blood stained register. Thalia was with them, her face pale and tear stained.

Yiorgo blew his whistle and the hotel guests quietened and turned to face him. Thalia waited until she knew she would be heard.

'Ladies and gentlemen, we are very sorry to inconvenience you. There has been a most unfortunate accident to a member of the hotel staff. The police are investigating and would like your co-operation. The leader of each party will give his name, identify his passport and answer any questions. I am sure you will then be able to continue with your day.'

Thalia repeated her message in French and English, then turned to the police. 'Where do you want to start?'

'Families with children, then move on to the elderly. Start with that man over there.'

The process was painstakingly long. Sorrell was sitting too far away to hear the questions Thalia was asking on behalf of the police or to hear the replies. She looked at her watch. Eleven. No doubt Joseph had realised she had been detained at the hotel and would be waiting at their usual rendezvous in Piraeus. She accepted another cup of coffee and tried to curb her impatience.

Her turn finally came and she moved over to the table where the police sat. As she took her seat her bag bumped the arm with a hollow ring and for the first time she remembered the gun she had placed in there.

'Your name, madam?'

'Maria Panides.'

'You are Greek, madam?'

'Yes.'

'Then we will not need our interpreter. You may take a well-earned break, madam, but please do not go far. We are sure to need your services again.'

Thalia nodded and walked over to where Stelios was hovering and buried her face in his shoulder.

'And where are you from, madam?'

Sorrell racked her brains to remember the passport details. 'Thessalonica.'

'And your purpose for being in Athens?'

'I am on holiday with my husband. Our car broke down and we missed our ferry sailing.'

'And which man is your husband? Please point him out to us.'

Sorrell looked at the small number of men who were still in the dining room. 'He is not here.'

Dimitris raised his eyebrows. 'Then where is he, madam? Still in your room?'

'He went out earlier to fetch the car.'

'Ah, yes. I remember, you wanted to join him. Has he not come enquiring the reason for your delay?'

'I really don't know. I have been kept up here all morning.'

'We will check with the policeman downstairs. There is just one small matter we would like you to clarify for us. Your bill – do you have a receipt you can show us?'

Sorrell shook her head. 'My husband was going to settle it.'

'I see. And did he do so?'

'I expect he did so as he left.'

Yiorgo shook his head. 'I do not think so. You see, there is a computer at the desk. The details of all the guests are programmed in when they arrive and again when they leave. The amount, time and method of payment are also included.'

'We did not arrive until the early hours of the morning. Maybe the desk clerk did not enter our details.'

'He was very conscientious, madam. He entered your name, passport number and the time of your arrival as one thirty eight.'

'I will be quite happy to settle our account,' smiled Sorrell. She rose from the chair, her bag banging once again against the arm.

Dimitris waved her back. 'I regret we are not able to allow anyone to check out of the hotel at present.'

'Why ever not? There's only been a robbery…' Sorrell could have bitten her tongue.

'Has there, madam? Who told you there had been a robbery?'

'I don't know. I heard someone say there had been a robbery. Maybe it was the waiter. I asked him what had happened.'

'Maybe.'

'Then is that all?'

'Not quite, madam. You have something heavy in your bag. May we see what it is, please?'

'It is merely a pair of shoes.'

'Yes? If I could just have a look at them.'

Sorrell drew out a pair of black evening shoes, the heels studded with small, glittering stones. Dimitris turned them over in his hand.

'Very pretty. And what else do you have in there?'

'My hair brush, washing kit.'

'Of course. You were only staying the one night. Strange that you should bother to bring a pair of evening shoes with you.'

'I bought them earlier. I didn't bother to open my case.'

Dimitris nodded and placed them on the table at the side of him. 'If I could just see for myself.' He reached out and took a firm grip on Sorrell's bag.

'I've told you what is in there. There is no need to turn it out in front of everyone.'

Dimitris shrugged. 'It is procedure, madam. Now, please.' He pulled it from her and handed it to Yiorgo who opened the clasp and looked inside. Without a word Yiorgo showed the contents to Dimitris.

'I think, madam, a few more questions. 'Why do you carry a gun?'

'A gun? I have no need of a gun.'

'Then can you tell me why there should be one in your bag?'

'I have no idea. Someone must have put it there.'

'Really? Why should anyone want to place a gun in your bag?'

'I don't know.'

'Then I think we should find out, don't you?'

Yiorgo left the room, taking Sorrell's bag with him.

'If you would be good enough to wait just a little longer, madam. I am sure the waiter will be able to provide you with some refreshment.'

Sorrell glowered at him and he smiled, quite unperturbed.

Yannis arrived at the Athenia De Luxe in the early evening. Thalia gave him a wan smile. Having acted as interpreter for the police for a good deal of the day, she was also trying to persuade the clients that they had nothing to fear by continuing their stay in the hotel.

'Where's Orestis?'

'In the office, Mr Yannis.'

Yannis nodded curtly and opened the door. Orestis was seated at the table, a ledger spread before him and a pad of paper covered in figures. He greeted Yannis with relief.

'I came as soon as I could. How is Giovanni?'

'The hospital has operated on him and Mr Nick. They say they are stable and their condition is being continually monitored. For Andreas they could do nothing.'

Yannis sank into the chair opposite his partner and passed a trembling hand over his forehead. 'Tell me what happened, Orestis. Even more important tell me how it happened.'

Orestis spread his hands. 'I don't know. It is so terrible. To think that such a thing could happen here.'

Yannis sighed. 'Just tell me from the start.'

'I was getting dressed, no, I was shaving, I'd almost finished, and Thalia came knocking at my door. She said I was to come down straight away.'

'What was Thalia doing here so early? She doesn't come on duty until seven thirty.'

'She'd come in with Stelios. He was on breakfast shift.'

'And?' prompted Yannis.

'I came down and found them. Mr Giovanni and Mr Nick; both shot, both laying there, blood on the floor and Andreas…' Orestis shuddered. 'He had been shot through the head. There was blood and – stuff, all over the desk, the register, the computer, everything. Stelios had telephoned for an ambulance and the police. The safe had been emptied, the wages, the money and jewellery belonging to the guests, everything. All day the police have been here. They have taken statements from everyone, the staff, the guests, everyone. No one was allowed to leave until their fingerprints had been taken.' Orestis voice dropped to a whisper. 'One of the guests was arrested.'

'Why?'

'I don't know. I just saw her being taken away.'

'Her!'

'I did not know her. She arrived early in the morning with her husband.'

'Did they arrest him as well?'

'He has disappeared.'

Yannis frowned. 'I suppose I'd better let the police know I've arrived.' He reached for the telephone. 'Has anyone 'phoned my sister? She ought to know about Giovanni.'

'I'll ask Thalia. She telephoned Mr Nick's wife.'

Yannis shook his head. 'I'll do it myself when I've spoken to the hospital and had the latest news.'

Yannis found the police evasive. They confirmed Orestis's story of a robbery and shooting, but refused to admit that they had arrested anyone. A young lady was helping them with their enquiries.

Sorrell was feeling distinctly unnerved. All day she had been questioned about the gun in her bag, the same questions over and over again. She knew they were trying to trip her up and she continued to feign ignorance. They would have to release her eventually.

Dimitris and Yiorgo had gone off duty and two new men had taken their place. They had not spoken to her; they sat playing dominoes and smoking as if she did not exist.

'How much longer do I have to stay here?'

One of them had shrugged and eyed her up and down. Memories of Joseph's threats about police treatment came back to her. It was worth a try. She perched herself on the edge of the table, allowing her skirt to ride up and show an expanse of leg.

'I really haven't done anything wrong. If you let me out you could say I'd escaped.'

The policeman stretched out his hand and squeezed her knee. 'No.'

'I could make it worth your while.' Sorrell leaned a little closer.

'No.' He pushed her bottom off the table and lit another cigarette.

'Could I have a cup of coffee?'

He nodded to his companion who left the room, closing and locking the door after him.

'You're much nicer than your friend.' Sorrell tried again. 'Maybe we could talk whilst he's gone.' She ran a slim finger down his cheek.

By way of reply he took hold of her wrist and twisted it sharply. 'The answer is still no. Sit down and behave yourself.'

Sulkily Sorrell resumed her seat. To her surprise it was Dimitris who returned with the coffee.

'How are you, madam?'

'I'm getting more and more annoyed. I wish to leave. You have no reason to keep me here.'

'You still insist you do not know how the gun got into your bag?'

'Of course I don't know. How should I?'

'It would be better if you told us the truth, madam.'

'I have told you the truth. I do not know where the gun came from.'

Dimitris sighed heavily. 'I would very much like to believe you. We sent the gun for tests. The only fingerprints we found belonged to you.'

Sorrell laughed shakily. 'I expect I touched it when I took the shoes from my bag.'

Dimitris frowned. 'I could understand a smudge, but the prints are quite clear. There is an additional problem, madam. Three bullets have been fired from the chamber and they match with the bullets that were removed from the casualties. Now, would you like to tell me the truth about the gun?'

Sorrell's face whitened and her throat constricted. 'I wish to speak to someone from the American Embassy.'

Dimitris looked at her in surprise. 'Why?'

'I am American. I demand their protection.'

The telephone shrilled and Annita rose from the table to take the call. 'It could be Anna or Maria as it's Thanksgiving,' she explained to her family gathered round the table.

'More likely to be the man in the moon,' remarked Andreas dryly. 'Poor Mamma, it wouldn't hurt either of them to pick up a telephone once in a while.'

'I hope it won't have woken the boys.' Helena frowned anxiously.

'Why should it? They're upstairs.'

'They're both very light sleepers.'

Marianne walked to the bottom of the stairs and listened. 'Not a peep – and you'd certainly hear John if he'd woken.'

'He has a good pair of lungs, that one,' smiled Andreas, remembering how the child had gone scarlet and screamed when he had been removed from the lounge and taken upstairs to be changed and bedded down for the evening.

'Paul and Mark don't scream, thank goodness. They just cry quietly. I'd better go up and check them.' She dabbed at her lips with her napkin. 'Unless you'd like to go, Greg?'

'Don't fuss. They're all right.'

Helena shot her husband an annoyed glance and walked to the door, meeting her grandmother as she returned.

'Marianne, it's Bob's mother. I can't get any sense out of her. Something to do with Elizabeth and Nicolas. She's absolutely distraught.'

Marianne pushed back her chair. 'How did she know I was here? I hope there's nothing wrong with Nicola.'

'Speak slowly, Mrs Duggan. Now, why is Nicolas in hospital? He's been shot! What about Elizabeth? And the baby? Oh, thank God for that. I'll telephone her straight away. She wants me to go over? Why? What can I do to help? No, you must have misunderstood. I'll telephone her. Don't worry, Mrs Duggan. I'm sure Nicolas will be fine.' Marianne replaced the receiver and returned to the dining room. 'May I use your telephone to speak to Elizabeth in Athens?'

'Of course, what's happened?'

'I'm not very sure. Her mother said something about Nicolas having been shot and she wants me to go over.' Marianne pulled her address book from her bag and flipped through the pages until she found the number. 'I'll be as quick as I can.'

Marianne returned to the table white and shaking. Her uncle pushed the brandy bottle towards her, but she shook her head.

'It's so awful. I just can't believe it. Nicolas disturbed a burglar at the Athenia. He's in hospital seriously hurt and the desk clerk is dead.'

A shocked silence greeted her news. Andreas took the brandy bottle back and poured himself a glass and Gregory held his out for a refill.

'Elizabeth and the baby aren't hurt?'

'No, but Elizabeth's going demented. She can't understand what the doctors are telling her half the time, and the police keep asking her questions.'

'Why doesn't she get an interpreter?'

'She doesn't know when she'll need one. By the time she's phoned her sister-in-law the doctor has moved on. She has no one to leave Nicola with and she can't cope with her at the hospital.'

Helena sniffed. 'She must have some friends who'd have her for an hour or so.'

'Elizabeth doesn't speak Greek. I doubt that she's made any real friends.'

Annita looked at her granddaughter. 'You go and help your friend. Telephone her mother back and see if she's going out. You could travel together; she could help you with John – unless you'd rather leave him here.'

'Oh, Grandmother.' Marianne hugged Annita and began to cry at the same time.

'There now, no need for you to get upset. You go and monopolise the telephone and see what arrangements you can make.'

'But you can't,' Elena spoke petulantly. 'I'll be on my own if you go.'

Marianne rounded on her mother. 'You have Helena and Andrew. Elizabeth needs me for a few weeks.'

'Marianne's right, Elena.'

Andreas looked at his sister sternly. 'Don't be selfish. Marianne has spent the last year with you instead of getting on with her own life. You go and phone Mrs Duggan, my dear. Here, take this with you.' He pushed a glass of brandy into Marianne's hand and this time she did take a sip.

Marianne shifted John more comfortably on her hip.

'Would you like me to take him?' offered Mrs Duggan.

Marianne placed him in her outstretched arms and pushed the laden trolley more easily. 'I didn't realise that travelling with a baby would mean taking so much. He's got more with him than I have.'

Mrs Duggan smiled. 'I do appreciate you coming with me. Edward is in the middle of an important case or he would have come too. Will Elizabeth be there to meet us, do you think?'

'I couldn't tell her what flight we would be on. We'll go to the hotel; then I can 'phone her from there.'

'The one where…'

'Yes,' replied Marianne firmly. 'I doubt very much that they're fully booked at the moment. You wait here and I'll find a taxi.'

Orestis greeted Marianne sadly. 'It is such a terrible thing that has happened. If he had struck a little earlier or a little later, Mr Nick and Mr Giovanni would not have been here.'

'Mr Giovanni?' Marianne paled. 'He was here?'

'He too, was shot, madam.'

Marianne realised by the buzzing in her ears that she was going to faint. Orestis took her arm.

'Are you all right, madam?' He steered her into a chair and she bent her head, hot tears falling on John's head.

'Is he…?'

'In the hospital. When you visit Mr Nick you can visit him also.'

Marianne drew a deep shuddering breath. Mrs Duggan patted her shoulder.

'Do you think we could go up to our room? I think Marianne needs to rest and I certainly do.'

'Of course.' Orestis turned to Marianne. 'I have arranged for one of our suites on the top floor. I will arrange for a bed for the baby.' Orestis helped Marianne to her feet. 'Mr Yannis will be here shortly. I'm sure he will be pleased to see you. He is at the hospital at the moment with his sister.'

'His sister?'

'Mr Giovanni's mother. She arrived two days ago.'

'Of course. I'd forgotten his parents lived in Italy. How is Mr Nick's mother?'

'She is distraught; she has hardly left his bedside.'

Marianne nodded understandingly. This was probably one of the problems that Elizabeth would be asking her to sort out.

Yannis shepherded his sister into the hotel lounge. 'Wait there for a moment and I'll arrange for a meal to be sent up to your room.'

'I'm not hungry, Yannis.'

'You may not feel hungry, but you have to eat. You won't help Giovanni by starving yourself.' Yannis walked over to the desk and Orestis spoke to him rapidly. Yannis nodded and lifted the telephone. He returned to Marisa after a brief conversation. 'Elizabeth's mother has arrived. She has Marianne with her.'

Marisa followed Yannis up to the room where Marianne was desperately trying to get in touch with Elizabeth. There had been no answer from her apartment, and the hospital was now trying to find her to bring her to the telephone. Yannis knocked and Mrs

Duggan opened the door wide as Marianne beckoned them in. She replaced the receiver and shifted John more comfortably in her arms as she rose to meet them.

Marisa drew in her breath. 'The baby! He's the image of Giovanni at that age!'

Marianne's face flamed and she held John protectively against her. 'This is Elizabeth's mother,' she said unnecessarily.

Yannis nodded, looking at Marianne's baby curiously. 'This is my sister, Giovanni's mother,' he answered. 'I have ordered a meal to be sent up for us. You won't mind if we join you?'

'Not a bit. How are Giovanni and Nicolas?'

Yannis sat down on the settee. 'Does Elizabeth's mother speak Greek?'

'Not a word.' Marianne smiled at the very idea.

'Then you will have to tell her. Both Nicolas and Giovanni are seriously ill, but they should survive. Nicolas has a chest wound and Giovanni was shot in the stomach. Their conditions have been complicated because they did not receive medical attention immediately, but the surgeons are optimistic in both cases.'

Marianne moistened her dry lips. 'Are they conscious?'

Yannis shrugged. 'Sometimes. They are sedated, of course, but by the end of the week there should be some improvement. Tomorrow I will take you to see them.'

'Why not tonight?'

'They will have been settled down for the night. Visitors would not be welcomed, besides, Elizabeth would like to see her mother.'

'I've been trying to contact her.'

'She has gone back with Elena. I will telephone for you.'

Marianne turned to Mrs Duggan and repeated the information Yannis had given her. 'He's 'phoning Elena. Elizabeth went back with her this evening. There, she's on the line now.'

Yannis handed her the receiver and Marianne turned to Marisa. 'I'm so sorry about your son. He was very kind to me when I was over here and had to return so suddenly when my father was taken ill.'

Marisa nodded. 'He is a good man. He would not harm anyone.' Her eyes filled with tears. 'They say if he had not been found for another hour he would not have survived. My poor Giovanni.'

John stirred in Marianne's arms and she rocked him gently. 'Orestis said he would send a bed up for him. I'll need to feed him soon; then I'd like to put him down for the night.'

'I'll see to it.' Yannis looked at the telephone, which was obviously going to be engaged for some while. 'I'll see where our meal has got to as well.'

'May I hold him?' Marisa held out her arms.

'He's a little damp.'

Marisa smiled. 'I had three boys. They were always a little damp!'

Marianne entered the hospital with Mrs Duggan where Elizabeth was waiting for them. Her eyes widened as she saw the baby her friend was carrying.

'I'm so glad you've come, Marianne. I just can't cope any more.'

Marianne patted her shoulder. 'The doctor says Nicolas will recover. You just have to be patient.'

'It's not Nicolas. I understood what the doctor told me. It's my mother-in-law. She won't leave his side and I just feel that I'm an intruder. I'm his wife!'

'I'll have a word with her. She probably thinks she's helping you by being there all the time.'

Marianne and Mrs Duggan followed Elizabeth up to the private room where both men were being nursed. 'I'll go and have a word with Mrs Christoforaki. Where's Nicola?'

'Elena said she'd have her for an hour. She's taken her into the office so I hope she's being good. Why didn't you tell me you had a baby?'

Marianne shrugged. 'It was rather a difficult situation.'

'Is that why you wouldn't marry Bob?'

'Partly. I also realised that I wasn't in love with him.'

Elizabeth nodded and pushed open the door, leading the way to a bed where Nicolas lay swathed in bandages. Marianne looked across the room to where Giovanni lay, apparently asleep. Mrs Christoforaki did not look up as they approached.

'Mrs Christoforaki, Daphne,' Marianne touched her shoulder. 'I am so sorry about Nicolas. Elizabeth has asked me to come over and keep her company.'

'That is kind of you. She needs someone to talk to.'

'Her mother has come over also. She will be all right now. It's you I'm concerned about. Elizabeth says you've not left Nicolas's side. You must be exhausted.'

Daphne lifted anguished eyes to Marianne. 'I am waiting to hear who tried to kill my son. That policeman is waiting also.' Daphne indicated the officer who sat a short distance away from the beds. 'Wouldn't you want to know if it was your son laying there?'

Marianne felt her throat constrict. How would she feel if it was John? 'Come outside, Daphne. We can't talk in here. Elizabeth will call us if there's any change in his condition.'

Marianne returned to Elizabeth's apartment with her and her mother. They had collected Nicola from Elena's office and Marianne admired the beautiful little girl.

'She's like you, Elizabeth, except that her hair is dark. Is she good?'

'A little angel. No doubt she'll make up for her good behaviour in time. I don't know how I'll cope when she starts to crawl. Tell me about John.'

'He's pretty good. It's easier now he sleeps through the night.'

Elizabeth nodded. 'I wish you'd told me. I wouldn't have told Bob if you didn't want him to know.'

'I felt rather ashamed of myself and didn't want anyone to know outside my immediate family. I also felt pretty bad about presenting my mother with a grandson without a husband to back me up. Actually it worked out quite well. It gave her something else to think about apart from my father's death.'

'Does Giovanni know?'

'No. Why should he?'

'He is John's father, isn't he? Don't try to deny it, Marianne, he's the image of Giovanni.'

'You won't tell him, Elizabeth?'

'Not if you don't want me to, but I feel he has a right to know he has a son.'

Marianne shrugged. 'I'll think about it.' She decided to change the subject. 'I've talked to Nicolas's mother for you. She's waiting for Nicolas to be well enough to say who shot him. Now she knows he's out of danger she's just angry. I don't give much for the gunman's chances if she gets to him first. She's agreed to take a break this afternoon and I'm sure once Nicolas has been able to make a statement she'll be more reasonable. I can look after Nicola and you can go with your mother.'

Elizabeth looked at her friend gratefully. 'I thought she didn't trust me to be there on my own with him. I didn't like to ask Elena. I didn't want to offend her.'

'She's very fond of you. She kept telling me what a good wife and mother you are, and, of course, she's besotted with Nicola.'

'That I do know! For the first month I only saw the poor child when she needed feeding.'

Adam looked at the beautiful woman before him. 'I understand that you claim to be an American citizen and as such are asking for help from the Embassy.'

'That is so.'

'If we could start with the formalities, name, date of birth, address in the States, the usual things.'

Sorrell swallowed hard. 'I'm Madeleine Evans. I've been travelling Europe for a few years now so my address in the States wouldn't be relevant.'

'That's quite an expensive occupation. How have you financed your trip?'

'I saved up before I came, then a bit of casual work, cash in hand, you know.'

Adam smiled. He thought he knew the kind of casual work she meant. 'I see. Quite adventurous of you. Have you been alone?'

'Most of the time. I met people and spent a day or two here and there with them.'

'You say you met a young man a short while ago and agreed to masquerade as his wife at a hotel in Athens. Why was that?'

'I liked him.'

'I am sure he was charming, but why did you agree to pretend to be his wife?'

'He said he didn't want to check into a good hotel with a girl friend.'

'So you agreed to play a part. Why did you check into the hotel so late – or should I say so early?'

'The car broke down.'

'Where did that happen?'

Sorrell shrugged. 'I don't know Athens well enough to say.'

'Wouldn't it have been more sensible to book into a hotel where you had broken down?'

'My friend was insistent that we came here.'

'Why was that?'

'I think it was because he had promised me a night in a luxury hotel.'

'And may I ask what you did when you arrived? You don't have to be too explicit, just the general idea.'

Sorrell smiled. 'We were both rather tired. We shared a bottle of wine and he said I should go to sleep.'

Adam raised his eyebrows. 'I find it hard to believe that any young man will invite a beautiful woman to spend a night with him and then say she should go to sleep. I presume before you slept you, er, had a relationship?'

Sorrell dropped her eyes. Let the fool think whatever he wished.

'Now, you went to sleep, then what happened?'

'I woke up to find myself alone. When I went down to the foyer I was sent to the dining room and then I was arrested.' Tears filled Sorrell's eyes and spilled over onto her cheeks. 'I'm innocent, Mr Kowalski. I know nothing at all about the gun they found.'

'Rest assured, Miss Evans, I will do all in my power to uncover the facts of this unsavoury business. There is just one other thing, this young man who you agreed to spend the night with – what was his name?'

'Joseph Panides.'

'Well? What do you make of her story?'

Adam tossed his briefcase to one side. 'She's just a high class whore who bit off a bit more than she could chew. She reckons she's been travelling Europe for a couple of years, supplementing her income with casual labour.'

'A number of youngsters do.'

'Yeah, there's nothing wrong in principal, but, I don't know.' Adam scratched his ear. 'Why didn't she tell this story in the first place? According to the police she claimed she was Greek and insisted her husband had gone to fetch their car as they had a ferry to catch.'

'Maybe she was embarrassed?'

'That sort doesn't suffer from embarrassment. No, there's something more here. I suspect that if she's released she'll know exactly where to find this one night stand of hers.'

'Have you mentioned that idea to the Greek police?'

Adam shook his head. 'I came straight back here.'

'See what you can get out of her the next time you visit. It might be worth your while suggesting she could be charged with murder. That could make her open up.'

'You don't think they will?'

The ambassador shrugged. 'Circumstantial evidence. According to the police no one saw her companion, only one bed had been slept in, a bottle of wine had been consumed, but only one glass was used, her prints were on the gun, it could be made to add up.'

Adam frowned. 'She'd better be forthcoming for her own sake.'

Nicolas and Giovanni had both given brief statements to the police. Giovanni had spent the evening in his club with the manager. At closing time they had returned to the hotel together, where Andreas had been at the desk. They had entered the office and placed the evening's takings into the safe. Before going their separate ways they had decided to have a quick drink at the bar and it was as they had returned to the foyer they had seen a suspicious figure at the office door.

'Why should you assume the person was a thief?'

Giovanni shrugged. 'There was something about him. I just knew the safe had been robbed.'

'You are sure it was a man?'

'Quite definitely.'

'It couldn't have been a woman that you mistook for a man?'

'The night lights were on. It was a man.'

'Would you be able to recognise this man again if you saw him? You say the night lights were on so you must have seen his face.'

'It was too quick. I've no idea who he was.' Giovanni shut his eyes and prayed that Nicolas would also deny knowledge of the gunman's identity.

Yannis met Marianne as he arrived back at the hotel. 'You're just the person I want to talk to. Are you free this afternoon?'

'Not really,' Marianne frowned. 'I was just going over to Elizabeth's flat to look after Nicola for her.'

'Telephone her to say you will be an hour later than arranged. I'll see you in the office.' Without giving Marianne time to refuse he hurried off.

Marianne shrugged. 'May I call from here?' she asked Thalia. 'It will save me carrying this heavy lump up and down again.'

'I'll hold him for you.'

John went willingly into the outstretched arms and made a grab for a dangling earring.

Marianne knocked on the office door and entered. Yannis had a sheaf of papers before him and Orestis was looking over his shoulder and indicating with a pencil.

'I've told Elizabeth I'll be there at three. I know what you want to talk to me about and I'm sorry I've not settled it before. My bank transfer should be through by the beginning of next week if you can wait until then.'

Yannis looked at her and frowned. 'What are you talking about?'

'My bill. I've been here nearly three weeks now. When Mrs Duggan returns next Wednesday I'll move in with Elizabeth until Nicolas comes out of hospital.'

'I'm not asking for your hotel bill! I am asking for your help.'

'My help?'

Yannis nodded. 'I need some advice, legal advice. The hotel was insured for the items that were left in the safe, but it wasn't sufficient for the value that was in there on that occasion. Do I have to make the loss good? There are three travel agents asking for compensation on behalf of their clients who were staying here at the time. Can they do that?'

'It would depend why they are claiming it. Were the guests hurt or just inconvenienced? Did they miss flights home or other connections? Did the incident truly spoil their holiday?'

'I don't know!'

'Well, the first thing to do would be to check their travel arrangements with the holiday firms. If you can prove they lost nothing financially, just had a disrupted day, then a small payment, made voluntarily by you, could save a considerable amount of haggling and possibly a court case. Of course, if they missed a flight home and lost work due to that it puts a different complexion on it altogether.'

'How am I supposed to have time to do all this? I have two other hotels in Heraklion to run and Ourania's coping with the shop and my aunt and uncle on her own. I haven't time to sit here writing letters.'

Marianne looked at Orestis who shook his head. 'Mr Giovanni came over here to talk about training an assistant for me. I have angina. The doctor has told me to cut my workload as it is.'

Marianne looked doubtfully at Yannis. 'I'm willing to help if I can. I'm not a lawyer or anything. I took a degree in international law, which is more to do with politics.'

A look of profound relief spread over Yannis's face. 'You'll not find me ungrateful, Marianne. Forget about a hotel bill. If you can sort this out for me you can stay here free of charge for as long as you like.'

A week after his first visit, Adam Kowalski arrived again at the police station, where Sorrell was being held. She greeted him eagerly.

'Thank goodness you've come to tell them to let me out. I really cannot stand being here any longer. I haven't even had a change of clothing.'

Adam sat at the table opposite her. 'I'm very sorry, but I'm not here with your release papers. I need to have a few more answers from you first.'

Sorrell frowned at him. 'I don't see what more I can tell you. I keep insisting that I know nothing about the gun.'

Adam chose his words carefully. 'Miss Evans, I believe you

when you say you had nothing to do with the shooting at the hotel. Unfortunately I think it may be more difficult to convince the Greek police.'

Sorrell paled as he continued relentlessly. 'You see, I checked with the passport authorities and Miss Madeleine Evans died five years ago in Illinois. That, of course, means you must have entered the country illegally. Why should you want to enter Greece with a false passport?'

'There must be some mistake. Madeleine Evans is not an unusual name.'

'I agree, it is not, but let us assume that you were using her passport for some reason best know to yourself, you will most certainly be charged with the offence. So far you have claimed to be Maria Panides, a Greek lady from Thessalonica, and an America citizen from Illinois. Both these claims were false. In fact, the more one listens to your story the more unbelievable it sounds. Unless you are able to give me something more plausible and realistic I shall not be able to represent you at your murder trial.' Adam shook his head sadly.

'Murder?' Sorrell's head jerked upright and she looked at the lawyer with frightened eyes. 'I didn't murder anyone.'

'I would like to believe you, but so far everything you have told us has been lies, so why should we believe that?'

'But it's true. I had nothing to do with it.'

'It will be your word against the Greek police, and I have to admit that the evidence is very strongly against you. Is there anyone who can corroborate your story? This young man who you have called Joseph? If we could find him he might be able to clear your name.'

Sorrell shook her head. 'I don't know where he is.'

'I really do feel sorry for you. If your story is true this unsavoury man has left you to take all the blame on yourself, and if it is not true, then you, madam, are a cold-blooded murderess.' Adam snapped shut his briefcase.

'I'm not, no, don't go. I didn't do it. I found the gun lying on my bed.'

'I have spent many years as a lawyer, but never before have I been told by anyone that the murder weapon was found on their bed and they calmly placed it amongst their own possessions. I think it is a little late to try to convince me with a further pack of lies.'

'But it's true. I did find it there.'

'After you had used it to shoot those innocent men you went back to bed and when you awoke you found it lying there. Is that what you're saying now?'

'No, no, it wasn't like that.'

'Then what was it like, madam?'

Sorrell gave a choking sob. 'Joseph did it. He must have done. After he shot them he must have brought the gun back up to our room for me to find.'

'That lie is no more plausible than the previous one, madam.'

Sorrell watched him leave and slumped down in the chair, her head in her hands. What could she do to make him believe she had not used the gun? It was becoming clear to her now. Joseph had used her right from the start. Used her to keep him supplied with money to live an easy life and finally used her to gain his revenge on his uncle and brother. He had had no intention of taking her to Spain with him. All he had ultimately wanted was to have her accused of the murder he had committed so that he could continue to be free whilst she spent the rest of her life in prison. The knowledge as it came to her made her feel physically sick.

Adam sat for the remainder of the afternoon reading carefully, finally making a few notes before leaving the embassy and taking a taxi over to the Athenia De Luxe. He introduced himself to the desk clerk and asked for Yannis.

'I am sorry, sir. Mr Yannis has returned to Crete.'

'Who is in charge here? The manager?'

'Mr Orestis is sick. He only works in the mornings.'

'Who can I see? It's important.'

'Miss Marianne, maybe.'

'Does she speak English?'

'Miss Marianne is American.' The clerk buzzed Marianne's room and held a rapid conversation in Greek. 'Miss Marianne will see you. Please wait.'

Marianne emerged from the lift and walked over to the desk. 'Mr Kowalski, I presume? How can I help you?'

Adam frowned. Who did she remind him of? There was something in the way she walked, or was it the tilt of her head? He shook himself. 'Is there somewhere we can talk?'

'Come down to the lounge. Would you care for a drink?'

Adam sat in the deep armchair and watched as she chose a bottle of wine from the bar, opened it and brought it over.

'Now, how can I help you?'

'I am attached to the embassy staff in a legal capacity. The young woman who was arrested after the unfortunate shooting which took place here claims to be an American citizen. She also claims to have very little knowledge of the man who was her travelling companion. I was really hoping to speak to Mr Yannis Andronicatis. I wondered if he knew of any reason why his hotel should have been selected? It seems that the couple's car broke down on the outskirts of Athens and the man insisted they came on here, despite the lateness of the hour.'

Marianne frowned. 'I really don't think I'm going to be able to help you, Mr Kowalski. You see, I only came over after the event. My best friend is married to Mr Nick, one of the injured men, and I came to give her my support.'

'I had the impression you were in charge here.'

'Not really.' Marianne shook her head. 'I am a distant relative and Mr Yannis asked me just to keep an eye on things for him until he returned.'

'I see. When do you expect him back?'

'I don't know for certain. Probably when Mr Giovanni leaves the hospital.'

'Do you know when that will be?'

'We are hoping it will be the end of next week, but the doctors won't commit themselves yet.'

'I see. May I leave you my card? Maybe you would be good enough to telephone me when Mr Andronicatis returns.' Adam rose to leave. 'Thank you for sparing me your time.'

'Not at all.'

Adam left, still wondering where he had seen the young woman before.

'Well? Did you come up with anything?'

Adam shook his head. 'The owner has gone back to Crete. I spoke to a young woman who's running the place for him and she's going to call me when he returns. Where do we go from here?'

'Press the Evans woman further?'

'How? I've nothing to press her with.'

'What about the car?'

'Nothing yet. Assuming there was one it's probably been abandoned somewhere.' Adam yawned. 'I'll see her again tomorrow. I wish I could think who that woman at the hotel reminded me of. I keep almost getting it, then it slips away again.'

'Mr Kowalski, I truly do not know Joseph's name. He never told me.'

'I find it very hard to believe that you lived with a man for over a year and never knew his surname.'

'He never talked about himself at all.' Sorrell twisted her fingers nervously. 'I do know why he chose that hotel to stay in, though.'

'And why was that?'

'If I tell you will the charges against me be dropped?'

'I will only be able to persuade the Greek police to release you if we are able to find the perpetrator of this crime. Up until now you have been singularly unhelpful. I'm not even sure I should be representing you. I have no proof that you are an American citizen.'

'Joseph said the hotel belonged to his uncle and his brother. He said he wanted to have his share.'

'Are you quite sure of this?'

Sorrell nodded. 'Flavia and I managed to get the keys for him.'

'Flavia?' Adam opened his notebook. 'Who is Flavia?'

'Just a girl he introduced me to.'

'Why? Was he in the habit of introducing you to past girl friends?'

'He wanted us to become friends.'

Adam nodded. He would pursue the matter of the keys later. 'Flavia; let's start with her. Flavia what? Did she have another name?'

'She never told me.'

'Where did you meet her?'

'In Florence.'

'Florence; and you were introduced to her by this man Joseph?'

'Yes.'

'What was she like?'

'Very attractive, very Italian.'

'How long did you spend together?'

'Some months, I can't say exactly.'

'Did you get on well together?'

'Yes.'

'You speak Italian, Miss Evans?'

'No. She spoke excellent English.'

'Really? Where did she learn that – at school?'

'She'd spent her childhood in England. Her father was an ambassador.'

Adam raised his eyebrows. At last he was getting somewhere. 'And is he still an ambassador?'

'I think she said he'd retired.'

'Did you talk together about this Joseph?'

'Not really.'

'I find it surprising that two young ladies do not discuss their boyfriend.'

'He wasn't Flavia's boyfriend.'

'So why did she agree to spend her time with you?'

'I guess she just fancied a trip to Greece.'

'And what did you do when you came to Greece?'

'Just travelled around.'

'Where did the money come from? You had to eat.'

'Joseph paid.'

'Very generous of him! So where did he get the money?'

'I don't know.'

'I think you do, Miss Evans. I think you were prostituting yourself. He was a pimp.'

'That's not true.'

'Then where did he get the money from to keep two young ladies and himself for a considerable amount of time?'

'Flavia said he had left her some months earlier to come to Greece. She seemed to think he was getting money from his uncle.'

'The uncle who owns the hotel?'

'I don't know. He could have a dozen uncles.'

'He could indeed. Now, the keys. You say you and your friend managed to obtain them for Joseph. Which keys were these?'

'The master keys of the hotel.'

'Why did he want them?'

'He didn't tell me.'

'So why do you think he might have wanted them?'

Sorrell shrugged. 'I presume he had planned to rob the safe.'

'I would presume the same.'

The long telephone call to the Italian Embassy finally gave Adam a name. 'Well? Shall I telephone Switzerland and see if he knows the whereabouts of his daughter?'

The ambassador shrugged. 'You can try, but I have my doubts that he'll have any useful information for you. I think you'd do better to go to the hotel and see if there is a relative called Joseph. At least if you get his details you can put out a call for him to be picked up when he decides to surface.'

Marianne greeted Adam Kowalski with a smile and once again he tried to decide where he had seen her before. 'I'm sorry to have to bother you again, but I think we may have a lead on the murderer.'

'I'm pleased to hear it. Robbery is one thing, but deliberate murder…' Marianne shuddered.

'How well do you know Mr Andronicatis and his family?'

Marianne frowned. 'It's a little complicated. Yannis and I are second or third cousins, our grandparents were full cousins. I don't know any of them very well.'

'I see. Do you think anyone, anyone at all, would hate Mr Andronicatis enough to want to harm him or his family?'

'I wouldn't have thought so. He may have offended or upset people in his business dealings, many people do, but I wouldn't expect anyone to hate him.'

'How many hotels does he own?'

'None outright. He has a partnership in this one with Mr Orestis and he and his nephew are in partnership with two properties in Heraklion.'

'What made him decide to expand to Athens?'

Marianne shook her head. 'I have no idea. You would have to ask him.'

'The nephew he is in partnership with – that is Mr Giovanni who was shot?'

'That's so.'

'What was he doing over here?'

'He often came over on Yannis's behalf. The nightclub below the hotel is his and he quite often comes over to check that it is running efficiently.'

'I see. And Mr Nicolas?'

Marianne wrinkled her brow. 'He and Yannis are cousins.'

'I had an idea he and Mr Giovanni might be brothers?'

'Oh, no. Nicolas has a sister and Giovanni has two brothers.'

'And do any of them work for Mr Andronicatis?'

'No, Elena works for a shipping firm, Angelo is an architect and I'm not sure about Joseph.'

'Joseph?'

'His younger brother.'

Adam nodded complacently. 'Do you know where I can contact any of these people? There's just a chance they may be able to help.'

'I can give you Elena's address, but I don't know the others. I expect Giovanni has them.'

Adam shut his notebook. 'I'll not trouble him until he's discharged from the hospital. Once again, thank you for your time.'

'You're very welcome.'

'May I ask you something personal?' Marianne waited. 'Where have I met you before?'

Marianne's eyes opened wide in surprise. 'To the best of my knowledge we have never met prior to your first visit here.'

Adam shook his head. 'I'm sure I know you from somewhere.'

Adam returned to his office with a feeling akin to elation. 'I think I have a name,' he declared. 'I think the pieces are beginning to fall into place.'

The ambassador raised his eyebrows and waited for Adam to be forthcoming.

'I went to see that woman at the hotel again. I asked her about the owner, Mr Andronicatis, and her relationship with the family. She's distantly connected. I then asked about the two men who had been shot. Now,' Adam paused for effect, 'Mr Nicolas Christoforakis has a sister, and Mr Giovanni Pirenzi has two brothers, one of them is called Joseph.'

'Are you expecting me to be surprised?'

'No, I wasn't, but it gives us a name. Can we ask the police to put a call out for Joseph Pirenzi?'

'What area do you suggest we cover?'

Adam looked at the map that was pinned to the wall above the ambassador's desk. 'All countries that border Greece, obviously. There's a chance he's still around, maybe waiting for the woman to be released, but my hunch says Italy.'

'Why Italy?'

'He has a brother in Italy and another girl friend.'

The ambassador nodded. 'It might be worth while putting that call through to Switzerland.'

Marianne found the investigative work she undertook interesting. Each morning she would spend some hours in the office, either telephoning or writing replies to the travel agents. A further two had asked for financial compensation for their clients and each claim that came through for items that had been placed in the safe had to be examined and authenticated. Orestis helped her as much as he was able, but the shock he had sustained had not helped his angina and he often retired to his room for an hour's rest.

Yannis had returned to Crete, knowing his nephew was on the road to recovery, and Marianne telephoned him regularly to keep him informed regarding the latest legal developments.

'How is Orestis keeping?' asked Yannis.

'He's not at all well. He looks quite grey on occasions.'

'What can I do? He desperately needs an assistant.'

'I suppose you wouldn't consider promoting Thalia?' suggested Marianne tentatively. 'She does most of his work as it is.'

'Out of the question,' Yannis spoke firmly. 'She's a woman. Whoever heard of a woman being a hotel manager?'

'In the States there are plenty.'

'Not in Greece. No, we have to find a man.'

'What about her husband? He seems very competent.'

'He's a waiter.'

'He took charge that morning. Orestis had some bad pains and it was Stelios who dealt with the police and kept the guests and other staff from panicking.'

'I'll think about it. I'll wait until Giovanni is discharged and see how he feels.'

Each afternoon Marianne would journey down to Elizabeth's apartment and take charge of the little girl who now greeted her as an old friend.

'Come with me today. Nicolas hasn't seen her for a few days and I don't want her to forget him.'

'I'm sure she won't. I'll stay for a while; then come back here in a taxi.'

'Giovanni would like to see you.'

Marianne shrugged. She had deliberately not gone out of her way to visit him. 'I expect his mother will be there.'

'What's wrong with that?'

'I just feel a bit uncomfortable when I'm around her.'

'Why? I can't understand what she says, but she always seems pleased to see me.'

'She thinks John looks just like Giovanni did as a baby.'

'You'd have to be pretty stupid not to see the resemblance.'

'I don't want her to say anything to Giovanni.'

'I still think you should tell him.'

Marianne shook her head. 'You promised, remember.'

When they reached the ward, to Marianne's surprise both men were in wheelchairs.

'Nicolas told me yesterday. I wanted it to be a surprise for you,' exclaimed Elizabeth gleefully. 'The doctor says we can take them out in the grounds for a while.'

'You just wanted me here to push a wheelchair because you couldn't manage both of them. Hold on, Giovanni. I've never handled one of these before.'

Marianne released the brake with her foot and tried to push the chair with one hand, finding it impossible. She looked at Elizabeth for guidance and saw she had placed Nicola on her father's lap, where he held her carefully.

'Would it hurt if I sat John on you?' she asked Giovanni.

'Provided he's not on my drainage tube it should be fine.'

Marianne placed the small boy on Giovanni's legs where he looked up into the man's face and gurgled.

'I think he likes me.' Giovanni ran his hand over the boy's curls. 'He's a fine boy, Marianne.'

'Yes, he is.' Marianne could hardly trust herself to speak.

Marianne sat in the office with Yannis and Orestis. 'I've done my best, but these claims are going to have to stand. I think most of the others were just chancers.'

Yannis scrutinized the figures carefully; then picked up a second sheet of paper.

'That settles it for me, then. I'll have to sell.'

Marianne looked at him in horrified surprise. 'Sell? You don't mean the hotel?'

Yannis nodded. 'I've little choice. It's this hotel or my house. I can't send Aunt Anna and Uncle Yiorgo back to the farmhouse – and I don't think Ourania would want to live in the flat over the shop again.'

'Couldn't you sell one of the others in Heraklion?'

'They wouldn't fetch as much as this one if I sold them both. Besides, this one has a bad reputation at the moment. A new owner could give it the lift it needs.'

'But why? You do have bookings. Trade will pick up again. Give it a year and people will have forgotten.'

Yannis shook his head. 'Nicolas and Giovanni needed surgery; they had a private room and specialist nursing. I've made provision for Andreas's widow to have a pension for life as well as a lump sum now to cover her husband's funeral and immediate bills. Unfortunately there was more money and jewellery in the safe than I was insured to carry, so I've had to cover the excess. There will be other expenses as well.'

'Like letting me live here for so long without giving me a bill. Let me pay you, please.'

Yannis patted her hand. 'My dear, you have been invaluable. If you hadn't fought those travel companies I would have been paying out a most enormous sum in compensation. No, you've earned your keep and I don't want to hear any more about a bill.'

'There must be some way you can keep the hotel. It doesn't seem fair that you should be penalised. It wasn't your fault that you were robbed and the desk clerk killed.'

'To tell you the truth, I won't be sorry. Orestis is ready to retire and I'm too old to start again with a new partner. We've discussed it and it seems the most practical solution.'

'What about the nightclub?'

'I'll talk to Giovanni about that when he's fit enough. He only rents the premises from me, so it's part of the hotel.'

'So his club goes as well? What about Nicolas? It's his living.'

'We'll have to see. The new owner might want to keep a club in the basement. I'll talk to both of them when they're stronger. There's no need for you to worry over it. We'll work out a solution that keeps everyone happy; after all, they're family.'

Marianne confided her fears to Elizabeth. 'It seems so unfair on Nicolas if he loses his job.'

Elizabeth gave a small smile. 'He doesn't plan to go back to the club. We're going to the States.'

Marianne sighed with relief. 'That's wonderful. Your parents will be thrilled.'

'My mother suggested it. What about you?'

'Me? Oh, as soon as Yannis has finished dealing with compensation claims I'll be going back as well.'

Elizabeth made no comment as she changed Nicola's nappy.

Joseph sauntered into the hotel room in Florence and swept Flavia up in his arms.

'It's so good to see you again. It was perfect. It went like a dream. We're rich, Flavia.'

Flavia covered his face with kisses. 'You're wonderful, Joseph. I kept telling myself you'd do it.' She hugged him ecstatically.

'I've brought you a present.'

'A present?'

Joseph indicated the three holdalls lying by the door. 'Madeleine won't have much use for any of those for a long time.'

Flavia looked at him, a moment of doubt crossing her mind. 'What have you done with her, Joseph?'

'I've done nothing to her. She's in prison for robbing the hotel and shooting the desk clerk.'

'Joseph! Oh, Joseph, you didn't!'

'I had no choice. I only meant to threaten him if he disturbed me. I was just leaving when my brother and Nick arrived, so I had to shoot.'

'Did they recognise you?'

'I don't think so – and even if they did they've nothing to go on. Only the desk clerk saw us check in. I'd wiped my prints in the bedroom and left the gun with Madeleine. They can't prove a thing.'

'I wonder if that stunning white dress of Madeleine's is in there.' Flavia's eyes strayed towards the luggage.

'Have a look. It's all yours.'

Planting a final kiss on Joseph's cheek, Flavia descended on the three bags and began to undo the zips. She piled the assortment of clothing on a chair, exclaiming with pleasure and exhorting Joseph to look and admire the collection. She took out the final skirt and threw the bag into the corner where it landed with a solid thump.

'I thought it was empty.' She dragged the bag towards her and opened it wide, feeling inside with her hands. 'Joseph, did you know she had all this?'

Joseph looked round. 'What have you found?'

From the false bottom of the holdall Flavia pulled five passports, a collection of credit cards, a wad of money and a velvet jewellery wrap. In a flash Joseph was on his knees beside Flavia.

'The little minx! She was robbing me! She was supposed to hand it all over.'

Flavia laughed at his indignation. 'It doesn't matter. You've got it now.'

Dressed in a smart lemon suit with a paler, toning blouse, Flavia entered the jeweller's shop. She took the emerald bracelet from her bag and dangled it before the assistant. 'Do you buy jewellery?' she enquired.

He nodded guardedly. 'I will have to fetch the manager, madam.'

Flavia nodded and sat down on the wooden chair appearing quite unconcerned as the stones were examined minutely.

'This is a fine piece, madam. How much did you have in mind?'

'Ideally enough to buy an apartment.'

'I don't know that I could pay quite that amount. Shall we say twenty million liras?'

'Shall we say fifty?' Flavia leaned across the counter.

'I have to live, madam.'

'So do I.' Flavia stretched out her hand for the bracelet.

'I might be able to stretch to thirty.'

'Forty.'

'No.' He shook his head decisively. 'Thirty five is my last offer.'

'I'll take it. In cash, please.'

'I don't keep that amount on my premises, madam.'

'That's quite all right. I can wait whilst you go to the bank.' Flavia settled herself more comfortably in the chair. It was easy when you knew how. Satisfied with her first transaction she visited four more establishments before meeting Joseph on the other side of the city.

'We ought to move on by the end of this week.'

'Where do you suggest?

'Milan would be a good place. We can sell the remainder of the jewellery and you can use the credit cards before we cross into Switzerland.'

Flavia stood in the queue trying to curb her impatience. Between them they had doctored the credit cards and provided she asked for reasonable amounts she should be quite safe from detection. This would be her last visit for today.

The cashier hardly gave her a second glance as he pushed the bundle of lira across to her. Without stopping to check the amount Flavia made for the door. The cashier watched her from the corner of his eye and bent down close to the counter where he spoke quietly into a small intercom. From across the banking hall a man placed his copy of the day's stock market figures on the desk and crossed to the exit. He stood on the top step and watched as Flavia entered the small car that was waiting for her. He memorised the number and turned his back on the street as he used the telephone just inside the foyer.

Joseph and Flavia drove slowly through the build up of traffic until they reached the outskirts of Milan. Three cars back from them a Fiat driver was picking his way slowly through the congestion.

'I have them in sight. Do you want me to pick them up when they stop?'

He listened to the answer and nodded to himself, satisfied.

Flavia and Joseph drew up outside the small hotel and the Fiat continued on its way to the end of the block where it parked and waited for the unmarked police car to draw level. A rapid interchange took place between the three men before they parted.

Joseph lay back on the bed, his hands beneath his head. 'How much did you clear today?'

Flavia took a slip of paper from her handbag. 'About eighty million liras.'

'What will that be in Swiss francs?'

'I don't know. I'm not a mathematician, but I am hungry.'

'All right.' Joseph swung his feet off the bed. 'We passed a place on the way. Are you changing?'

'I'll feel more comfortable in my jeans.' She threw her jacket onto the bed and stepped out of her skirt as a knock came on the door. 'Coming.' Zipping her jeans Flavia opened the door.

'Miss Bartlett?'

Flavia shook her head. 'I'm sorry. You have the wrong room.'

'I don't think so. Miss Sorrell Bartlett.' A foot was placed in the door as Flavia tried to close it. 'We were given a very good description of you by the bank cashier.'

'I haven't been to the bank today. He must be mistaken.'

'A second man appeared behind the first, a revolver in his hand. 'If we could just come in for a moment.'

'Joseph!' Flavia turned in panic as she was pushed away from the door.

Adam Kowalski tapped his fingers together. 'They have arrested a man and woman in Milan. The Greek police have applied for extradition. They seem pretty certain that he's the one who carried out the robbery at the hotel.'

'Seems as though your Miss Evans will be off the hook.'

'She's not my Miss Evans. She still has a charge to face for entering the country illegally and the gun has only her prints on it.'

'Does she know her friends have been caught?'

'I'm just on my way to tell her; then I'll call at the hotel and let that woman know. She can telephone her uncle and friend.'

Sorrell greeted Adam cautiously. 'What do you want? I've told you all I know.'

'Not quite. I still need to know exactly who you are.'

Sorrell turned away. If she could escape prosecution for the murder of the desk clerk she did not want to be charged with a diamond theft.

'A man and woman have been arrested in Italy. The police seem to think he could be the man they want.' Adam watched for any reaction from Sorrell.

'How did you find them?'

'The woman was getting money on stolen credit cards. The bank's security system decided to put a stop to it. She finally made a mistake. She asked for money in the name of Sorrell Bartlett, a woman who's already wanted by the police.'

Sorrell's mouth dropped open, then, to Adam's alarm, she began to laugh hysterically.

'I'm pleased to hear it, Mr Kowalski. I know Mr Yannis will be relieved to know you have this man behind bars.'

Adam shifted uncomfortably. 'When will Mr Andronicatis be in Athens?'

'I'm not sure. Do you need him here?'

'I will do, but first I need to speak to him.'

'I could telephone him.'

'Would you do that for me, please?'

'You mean now?'

Adam nodded. 'Does Mr Andronicatis speak English?'

'A little.'

'This is rather difficult, but would you be willing to act as interpreter for me?'

Marianne nodded. 'It would be my pleasure.' She looked at her watch. 'At this time I would expect him to be at his house. I'll try there first.'

Yannis lifted the receiver. 'Marianne? What's wrong?'

'Nothing. I have Mr Kowalski here, from the American Embassy. A man has been arrested for robbery.'

Marianne looked at Adam for further instructions.

'Ask Mr Andronicatis how soon he can return to Athens. We need him to help us in a matter of identification.'

'He says two or three days.'

Adam nodded. 'I'll look forward to meeting him on Friday.'

Yannis let out a groan and dropped his head in his hands. 'It can't be.'

Marianne placed a consoling arm round his shoulders. 'I'll ask Mr Kowalski why they have arrested Joseph. It could be a mistake.'

She turned to Adam. 'Are you sure? He's Mr Yannis's nephew. Why would he want to do such a terrible thing?'

'According to the American woman this man Joseph arranged for her and a friend to steal the keys of the hotel. He admitted it belonged to his uncle.'

Marianne translated for Yannis's benefit. 'But he didn't shoot his brother surely?'

Adam shrugged. 'I can't say. The Evans woman insists that she did not. The two men who survived say they were shot by a man, but are unable to identify him.'

Marianne swallowed. 'What is he going to be charged with?'

'At the moment I'm not sure. He's being held for receiving and the other woman for fraud.'

'When will you know?'

'That depends on the police. Actually, you could help me there. I know it's a bit of a nerve, but would you be willing to visit the police station with me? None of the police speak English very well and it's somewhat embarrassing to have to ask the accused to translate to you.' Adam smiled wryly.

'Will it be all right for me to bring my son if my friend isn't able to look after him?'

'It's not an ideal environment for a child, but I'm sure we can cope with him if necessary.'

Marianne drove to the police station with Adam feeling distinctly nervous. 'Will I have to meet this woman?'

'There's no need. I just want to be clear about police procedure. You managed to find someone to look after your son, then?'

'I left him with Elizabeth. I'd be grateful if you could drop me back at the hospital afterwards to collect him.'

'Certainly I will.' Adam studied her profile. What was there that made her seem so familiar to him?

Dimitris spoke at length to Marianne. 'Personally I think they were all in it together. I don't think the woman we arrested shot anyone, but she's definitely an accessory. She's in the country under an assumed name and false passport which probably means she has committed a crime elsewhere and doesn't want to be discovered. We've shown her picture round to some of the hotels and her name means nothing to them, but most of them say that her face is familiar. They also say that at various times guests have reported missing property. We can't tie that to her yet, but the other woman who was arrested had been selling jewellery in Italy, and there a number of distinctive items. If we can get a positive identification that any of the pieces were taken from hotel guests we've certainly got a case. If any of those pieces were actually in the safe at the time of the robbery we would have our man. We know the woman didn't have the opportunity to leave the hotel after the shooting was discovered, so it has to be him.'

Marianne relayed the information to Adam.

'Ask him if they've checked out the other passports that were found. I'd dearly love to know who this woman really is.'

Marianne repeated the question and Dimitris opened a drawer and placed a handful of passports on the desk.

'We've sent out requests for information to the various passport offices. Three of them are American, so you might get results more quickly.' Dimitris pushed them across the table towards Adam who picked each one up and opened them in turn.

'All young women, but in each case the photograph is slightly blurred. Just enough not to arouse suspicion, but it could enable any similar woman to use it without the authorities giving her a second glance.' Adam looked at Marianne. 'Looking at this one quickly, the way passports are usually checked, you could walk through immigration with this.' Adam smiled. 'I hope you wouldn't try it – she's wanted for questioning regarding a diamond theft in Amsterdam a couple of years ago.' He turned the document towards her.

Marianne looked at the small snapshot. It did resemble her. 'They say everyone has a double,' her voice tailed away to a whisper as she read the name. 'Mr Kowalski, do you think we could go now?'

'Are you feeling ill? You've gone very pale. I shouldn't have asked you to come here.' Adam helped her to her feet and placed the three passports safely into his briefcase.

They drove to the hospital in silence and Adam pulled up at the gates. Marianne snapped open her safety belt and opened the door. Adam restrained her with his hand.

'Just a moment before you go. I've been puzzling all the way over here about your reaction to that passport photograph. You recognised that woman, didn't you?'

Marianne tried to smile. 'You said she was like me and then told me she was wanted for a jewellery theft. It just threw me for a minute.'

'What's wrong, Marianne?' asked Elizabeth.

'Nothing. Why should there be?'

'You've hardly said a word since you came back from the police station. Was it awful?'

'No, I only sat in an office.'

'What is it then?'

'Mr Kowalski was looking at some American passports that had been found with the other couple who were arrested. He said one looked a bit like me.'

'So? I expect there are a dozen or more people who look like you.'

Marianne nodded soberly. 'This one is my cousin.'

'Well, no doubt she'll be pleased to get her passport back eventually.'

'I don't think so. She's wanted in connection with a jewellery theft.'

'Oh, Marianne! That's awful!'

'It could be even worse than you think. Her passport was found amongst others in the possession of this Italian girl they've arrested. She was selling stolen jewellery and they think some of it may have come from the hotel.'

'That doesn't necessarily mean that your cousin was involved. Which one are we talking about, anyway?'

'Aunt Anna's oldest, Sorrell.'

'When did you last see her?'

Marianne thought carefully. 'About seven years ago, I think.'

'Well, she could have changed beyond recognition since then. It could be someone else's passport, just a coincidence of name. Maybe she lost it or had it stolen and someone else has used it.'

'It's possible, I suppose.'

'Of course it is. Now, cheer up. I've got some good news to tell you. Nicolas and Giovanni are being allowed home tomorrow.'

'They must be delighted. Does Yannis know?'

'He was at the hospital when the doctor came round. They'll both have to convalesce for a few months, but there's no reason why they shouldn't be perfectly fit by this time next year. Oh, Marianne, I'm so relieved.' Elizabeth burst into tears and Marianne held her in her arms.

'Come on, now. If you cry tomorrow when Nicolas comes home he'll think you're not pleased to see him.'

'When he was first in hospital and I was sent for I didn't think he'd live.' Elizabeth was sobbing uncontrollably. 'It was so awful.'

'I know. I felt the same when Pappa was dying. Everyone was talking so positively about him getting better and I didn't believe them. You must have doubted if they were telling you the truth.'

'Half the time I didn't know what they were saying. Oh, Marianne, I can't wait to go back to America. I hate living here now.'

'You only hate it because of what happened. Once Nicolas is out of hospital everything will be fine again.'

Elizabeth shook her head and dried her eyes. 'I really do want to go home.'

Adam Kowalski could not get Marianne's reaction to the passport picture out of his mind. He took it from his briefcase and studied it closely. It did resemble her in a vague way, the tilt of the head – that was it. That was what had seemed so familiar to him when he had first met her. Sorrell Bartlett – the name meant nothing to him. Why had the Evans woman laughed when he had mentioned that Bartlett was wanted in connection with a diamond theft? He tapped the picture thoughtfully. It might be worthwhile paying a surprise visit to the hotel.

'I can't possibly come down at the moment. I'm feeding John. Well, yes, I suppose Mr Kowalski can come up if it's important.'

Adam knocked and waited until the door was opened to him. 'I'm sorry to intrude, I forgot you had a child,' he lied.

'He's just about to go to bed.' Large dark eyes looked at Adam curiously whilst he continued to suck greedily at his bottle.

'Don't rush him. I can wait.'

'If you fancy a drink please help yourself from the fridge. I'll just change John; then he should settle.'

Adam opened the fridge door. 'Will you join me?'

'A glass of wine, please.' Marianne sat John up and rubbed his back until he burped loudly. 'There, that feels better, doesn't it? Come on, a nice clean diaper, then into bed.'

Adam watched as Marianne dealt swiftly with the small boy and finally settled him in his cot in the bedroom. She pulled the door almost closed, then picked up her glass of wine.

'How can I help you, Mr Kowalski?'

Adam withdrew the passport from his pocket. 'I'd like you to tell me what you know about Sorrell Bartlett.'

Marianne shrugged. 'I know nothing about her.'

'I'm sorry. I just don't believe you. I have a theory of my own – would you like to hear it?'

Hoping the trembling of her hands had not been noticed Marianne took another mouthful of wine.

'I think you are Sorrell Bartlett.'

The glass slipped from her grasp and the wine made a dark pool on the carpet. Marianne sat unmoving.

'Well? Are you Sorrell Bartlett?'

Marianne looked him directly in the eye. 'No, Mr Kowalski, I am not.'

'Are you able to prove that?'

'I can show you my passport. My friends over here can vouch for who I am and you can check me out in the States.'

'So who is Sorrell Bartlett?'

'My cousin.' Marianne's voice was a whisper.

'Did you know she was wanted by the police?'

'I had no idea. Her parents were divorced and her mother moved down to Hollywood. I haven't seen her for at least seven years, maybe a bit more. We were never close.'

Adam nodded. 'I believe you.' He finished his drink. 'You ought to mop that up before it stains,' he remarked absently. 'I'm going to see Miss Evans tomorrow and I would like you to come with me.'

Marianne looked at him unhappily.

'You're certain?'

'As certain as I can be. I told you, I haven't seen her for seven years at least.'

Adam smiled at Marianne. 'I am truly sorry I had to ask you to do this.'

'Has it helped you?'

'Yes; considerably. At last we know exactly who this young lady is and we can start to probe into her background. It's most unfortunate that she's a relative.'

Marianne gave a brittle laugh. 'She is a relative; Joseph is a relative – which one of them is going to be charged with murder?'

Adam shook his head sorrowfully. 'I can't answer that. If only one of the men could identify for certain who shot at them…' Adam spread his hands.

Adam Kowalski ate a sandwich and tried to sort out his thoughts. Maybe investigating the background of the Bartlett girl would help. He still found it hard to believe that she had actually pulled the trigger, but it was almost certain that she would be accused of murder unless some new evidence was produced.

'Aren't you going home tonight?' The ambassador looked in at the door.

Adam looked up at him. 'Do you want to know who Evans really is?'

The ambassador nodded.

'Sorrell Bartlett – the woman who's wanted for questioning regarding a diamond robbery in Amsterdam some years ago.' Adam smiled triumphantly.

'You're sure? How did you find out?'

'I went to see the woman in the hotel. I have to admit I'd read the signs wrong. I misjudged her reaction to the passport photograph and thought she was Bartlett. It turns out they're cousins. She agreed to identify her this morning.' Adam smiled complacently.

'So what are you planning to do now? It hasn't changed the evidence against her.'

'I want to do a bit of digging. See what we can come up with, starting in Amsterdam. Our office there should be able to get a lead on her. I also want to get translations of all the statements made by the guests at the hotel. There's just a chance one of them may have seen her check in with a man, which would at least confirm his presence there that night. If some of the jewellery could be positively identified he would have a lot of explaining to do.'

'Let me know how you get on. Just avoid treading on the locals' toes.'

Adam smiled. 'I will. I'll ask them to hold my hand all the way.'

Adam spoke quietly to Marianne as she took her seat in the courtroom. 'I thought you'd like to know the latest decision. All three will stand trial on the same charges.'

'What are the charges?'

'Theft, burglary, receiving stolen property, accessory to murder and murder in the first degree; and in your cousin's case the additional charge of entering the country on a false passport.'

Marianne turned horrified eyes on him. 'What happens if she is convicted?'

'She can appeal. It may depend upon the evidence given by her accomplices.'

'You mean if Joseph confesses! Do you think it likely?'

'No, I don't. I think your cousin could be staying in Greece for a considerable amount of time.'

Sorrell had pleaded not guilty on all counts except the last, and the prosecution began to reconstruct the last few years of her life whilst Marianne listened with a growing fascination.

Throughout the skilful cross questioning Sorrell maintained her innocence. She had visited Amsterdam, but of the diamonds she knew nothing. She had left the hotel as soon as Peter had fallen asleep, as he had not turned out to be the kind of person she had first taken him for. With a fluttering and lowering of her eyelashes she explained he had tried to rape her. A sceptical look was on the face of the prosecutor when he asked her to explain her subsequent hurried departure from England to France using a passport in the name of Madeleine Evans.

Sorrell appeared to hesitate. 'I lost my passport. I went to the American Embassy and whilst I was waiting a man started a conversation with me. I explained to him why I was there and he said I would have a long wait and a lot of forms to fill in to get another one. He said he was authorised to issue new ones, but he would have to charge me for jumping the queue. I decided it was worth it and agreed to meet him there the next day. I handed over the money and he gave me an envelope. I didn't check it properly until I returned to my hotel, and then I found he had given me the wrong one. I went back the following day, but there was no sign of him. I thought it was probably his day off and I would try again the next day. On the way back to my hotel I bought a newspaper which said I was wanted in connection with a diamond theft.' Sorrell's voice broke. 'I was stupid enough to panic. The passport I had looked enough like me to use and I decided to leave the country.'

The prosecutor appeared to accept her answer. 'Which hotel did you stay in whilst you were in London?'

'I really cannot remember.'

'Maybe you can remember the name you used?'

'My own, Sorrell Bartlett, of course.' Sorrell opened her eyes wide to give an innocent look.

'Would it surprise you to know that no hotel in the London area has a record of a Sorrell Bartlett staying with them on the dates we are talking about?'

Sorrell seemed to squirm. 'Well, I called it a hotel, but really it was just a bed and breakfast place.'

'I see. So when you arrived in France what did you do?'

'I took the train to Paris.'

'And how long did you stay there?'

'I can't say for certain, three weeks, maybe longer.'

'And then where did you go?'

'To St. Tropez, Nice and Cannes, along the coast.'

'And how did you finance this trip? It costs a considerable amount of money to stay in Paris for three weeks or more and then travel down to the south.'

'I did some casual work; working as a waitress, cleaner, the usual sort of thing.'

'Can you give me the names of any of the places where you worked?'

Sorrell shook her head.

'You have to say yes or no, Miss Bartlett. And from the south of France, where did you go next?'

'Italy.'

'Again doing casual work?'

'Yes.'

'Would it surprise you to know that in every large city where you spent some time there were credit card frauds and withdrawals from many of the large banks on stolen credit cards?'

'Not a bit. I imagine that kind of crime takes place in every city all the time.'

'I am sure it does.' The prosecutor looked at the judge for guidance who called for a recess.

During the afternoon the questioning continued relentlessly, with Sorrell giving plausible answers to everything.

'Now, let us talk about your visit to Greece. You stayed in Athens, I believe, and that was where you met a young man who befriended you and you agreed to work with him?'

'Yes.'

'And what was the work he wished you to undertake?'

'He asked me to obtain hotel room keys for him.'

'And what did he do with these keys?'

'I have no idea. I would take a key to him in the morning and he would return it in the afternoon to me.'

'Didn't you ask him why he wanted them?'

'No.'

'Why not? Were you frightened of this young man?'

'Yes. He said if I didn't do as he asked he would report me to the police for entering Greece under a false name.'

'And that frightened you enough to make you subservient to his wishes?'

'He said the Greek police,' Sorrell hesitated, 'didn't treat women very well.'

'Really?' The prosecutor raised his eyebrows. 'Have you any complaints about your treatment whilst you have been held?'

'No.'

'I'm glad to hear it. Now, what else did this young man ask you to do?'

'He took me to Florence to meet a friend of his. When we returned to Athens he arranged for us both to stay at the Athenia De Luxe hotel. He said he wanted us to get the master keys.'

'And why should he want these?'

'He said he wanted to get his own back on his uncle and brother.'

'And then what did you do?'

'We went to Crete.'

'All three of you?'

'No, just Flavia and I.'

'Explain to the court, please, what you were expected to do whilst you were there.'

'We were to be part of a coach party visiting the island. I was to become friendly with the manager and get whatever I could from him.'

'And did you?'

'Yes.'

'To what extent were you friendly?'

'He tried to persuade me to sleep with him.'

'And did you do so?'

'No.'

Marianne felt a sick feeling in the pit of her stomach, combined with relief that Giovanni had not slept with her cousin. She dragged her attention back to the court proceedings.

'So this young man wanted to sleep with you. What inducements did he offer?'

'He said he would repay the money that I said I owed to a friend.'

'Did you owe any money?'

'No.'

'Did he give you anything else?'

'Yes. A brooch and a watch.'

'According to the testimony of the young man, on the day when you went shopping for this jewellery you were taken unwell whilst in his office. He went to your room for some medicine. Am I correct in saying that whilst he was gone you took the opportunity to rob the safe that was in there?'

Sorrell gave the prosecutor a scornful look. 'Why should I wish to do that?'

The prosecutor raised his eyebrows. 'According to the witness you claimed to have diabetes. The medical reports carried out on you say that you have no medical condition of any sort that would require you to take medicine on a regular basis. Why should you have sent this young man to your room to collect the medication if this was not necessary?'

Sorrell thought quickly. 'I had been told to get the master keys.'

'I see. And what did you do with these keys?'

'I couldn't find them.'

The prosecutor raised his eyebrows. 'I suggest that you found them and decided to open the safe and remove the contents for yourself.'

'Objection. That is speculation. The prosecutor is leading the witness.'

'Objection upheld. Strike that remark from the records.'

'Very well.' The prosecutor consulted his papers. 'Let us return to these gifts that were from this young man whom you had duped. Where is this jewellery now?'

'Joseph sold the watch and the brooch.'

'Where did he sell these items?'

Sorrell shrugged. 'Somewhere in Piraeus, I think.'

'And your other possessions – where are they?'

'I have no idea. They were in the trunk of Joseph's car.'

The prosecutor nodded. 'Now, let us move on to the time of the shooting. I would like you to tell the court in your own words why you were at the hotel and exactly what you did from the time of your arrival until the police asked you to go to the dining room.'

'Joseph said he planned to rob the safe with the duplicates of the keys Flavia and I had taken. He said we would arrive in the early hours of the morning, say our car had broken down and we had missed a ferry. That way only the night clerk would be on duty. Joseph planned to wait until the nightclub had closed and the money had been placed in the safe. He thought there should be a great deal of money and jewellery inside as there was a trade delegation staying at the hotel. He asked me to check us

377

into the hotel as man and wife. He would feign illness so that he didn't have to go to the desk. We went up to our room where we had a bottle of wine, then Joseph said I should go to sleep and he would wake me when it was time to leave.'

The prosecutor raised his hand. 'When he said time to leave, what exactly did he mean?'

'He meant after he had robbed the safe.'

'And did you go to sleep?'

'Yes.'

'When did you awaken?'

'I think Joseph was just about to go down to the foyer.'

'What made you think that?'

'He was moving around the room.'

'And?'

'He took a gun from beneath his jacket.'

'Now, think very carefully, what did he do with the gun?'

'I thought he had left it in the room.'

'Why should you think that?'

'When I woke up again it was on my bed and fell to the floor.'

'So what did you do?'

'Picked it up and put it on the bedside table. I thought Joseph had decided to leave it behind.'

The prosecutor shook his head. 'I am sorry, but I do not believe a word of your story. I think you arranged to go downstairs with your boyfriend and keep watch whilst he robbed the safe. Unfortunately he was disturbed by the two men from the nightclub and you shot them.'

'No!' Sorrell's eyes were wide with fear. 'That's not true. I've never used a gun in my life. I swear I didn't shoot them.'

On the third day of the trial Marianne drove to the courthouse accompanied by Giovanni. She had not been able to bring herself to discuss the trial with anyone, just announcing that Sorrell was still being questioned. Today it would be different. Giovanni and

Nicolas had been called to give evidence. At the door they parted, Marianne to take her seat with the spectators and Giovanni to a small room where he would wait to be called.

Marianne studied Joseph closely. He was not unlike his brother, but instead of wide, friendly eyes, his were wary and shifted continually over the courtroom and its occupants. Giovanni did not look at him as he took his place in the witness box.

'Are you able to identify the accused?'

'He's my younger brother.'

'Before today, when was the last time you saw him?'

'When I sacked him from my nightclub.'

The prosecutor raised his eyebrows. 'Why did you sack him?'

'My night club manager was ill and he took advantage, assured him he could run the place.'

'Please tell us more.'

'He used a false name to gain employment. I turned up unexpectedly and found he was showing pornographic films. I dismissed him on the spot.'

'I see.' The prosecutor tapped his teeth with his pen. 'Do you feel that was sufficient reason to wish to take revenge on you?'

'In his eyes I expect it was.'

'I'd like to go back a while, to the summer of nineteen eighty four. Did you become enamoured of a young lady who was visiting your hotel in Crete?'

Flushing with embarrassment Giovanni answered. 'I did.'

'Did you give this lady any gifts in your attempt to persuade her to succumb to your charms?'

'I gave her a watch. She appeared to have lost hers whilst we were out shopping.'

'Anything else?'

'I paid for a brooch. She said it was a present for her grandmother. I thought she had paid half on her credit card, but the jeweller later told me the card was refused and I was responsible for the debt.'

The prosecutor picked up a box from a side table and opened it to reveal a gold watch that he showed to Giovanni. 'Do you recognise this?'

'It looks like the one I gave to Isabella.'

'Now if I showed you some photographs, would you be able to recognise the young lady you have named as Isabella?'

Giovanni nodded and took the photographs, looking through them carefully. 'That one,' he said finally, as he handed them back.

'Thank you. That will be all for the time being. Please do not leave the courthouse and remember you are still on oath.'

Giovanni stepped down, Nicolas taking his place.

'Can you identify the defendant?'

'I knew him as Kyriakos Lenandraous.'

'And when was this?'

'When I agreed to him working at Mr Giovanni's nightclub whilst I was ill.'

'And for how long did he work at this nightclub?'

'Two, maybe three months. He seemed so efficient that I employed him so I could have some time off.'

'Did the owner of the nightclub know you had employed this man?'

'He knew I had employed Kyriakos Lenandraous.'

'And what happened when the owner visited the nightclub?'

'He found this man was showing pornographic films and dismissed him instantly.'

'Did he say anything else about this man?'

'In what way, sir?'

'Did he also know him as Kyriakos Lenandraous or by some other name?'

'Mr Giovanni told me he was his brother, Joseph.'

'This was the first you knew of this?'

'Yes, sir.'

'And have you seen this young man, the one you knew as Kyriakos Lenandraous since his dismissal from the nightclub?'

'Not to the best of my knowledge.'

'Please explain yourself.'

'We may have passed in the street, but I've not noticed him.'

'Would you be able to identify him as the man who shot at you?'

Nicolas shook his head. 'It happened too fast. I didn't see his face well enough.'

'Thank you. You may step down, but please do not leave the court and remember your oath is still binding.'

'Would Mr Jackson please come to the witness box.'

The call was relayed and interpreted to a young man who looked nervously around the courtroom. Through an interpreter he was asked if he was staying at the Athenia De Luxe hotel on the night in question and confirmed he had been staying there for a week.

'And on the night in question how had you spent your evening?'

'A friend and I went to a taverna, then on to the nightclub beneath the hotel.'

'When the nightclub closed did you and your friend return immediately to your hotel room?'

'No, we'd met a couple of girls during the evening and walked them back to their hotel.'

'How far away was that?'

'A couple of roads, no more.'

'And then you returned?'

'Yes.'

'When you reached the hotel did you see anything unusual?'

'No.'

'Who was in the foyer?'

'The desk clerk.'

'No one else?'

'No.'

'You went straight up to your room?'

'Yes.'

'Did you use the lift or the stairs?'

'The stairs, we were only a couple of floors up.'

'Did you meet anyone on your way to your room?'

'There was a man on the stairs.'

'Are you quite certain it was a man you saw?'

'Yes.'

'Would you recognise this man again if you saw him?'

'Possibly.'

'Do you see the man in question in court today? If you can see him please point him out to me.'

'I think it is the accused.'

'You only think?'

'As we approached he bent down, to tie a shoelace or something. I only saw his face for a moment.'

'I see. Thank you. That will be all.'

Flavia smiled sweetly at the prosecutor and spoke through an interpreter. Yes, she had known Joseph for some years; she had met him when she was visiting her boyfriend in prison. She had no need to work, her father made her an allowance, and she also did a little translation and interpretation of Italian into English if she wanted anything extra.

She had agreed to a little masquerade at the hotel to get the keys for Joseph. He had said he wanted to surprise his uncle. Yes, she had agreed to spend a week in Crete with a girl whom Joseph introduced to her as Madeleine, although she had called herself Isabella whilst in Crete. No, she had not seen her since their return. Yes, she could explain how the watch was in her possession – Isabella had given it to her.

The prosecutor looked perplexed. 'So, you have sufficient money to live comfortably and also a valuable watch. Can you tell me how you came to be in possession of Sorrell Bartlett's passport?'

'Joseph bought a job lot from a man, three holdalls of old clothes. They looked in good condition so he was happy to give the man what he asked thinking he could sell them on. He asked me to look through them. There was a false bottom in the holdall where I found the passports and some jewellery.'

'Do you still have this jewellery?'

'No, I sold it. It was far too ostentatious for me.'

'Where did you sell this jewellery? Can you tell us the name of the establishment?'

Flavia shook her head. 'Joseph said he would deal with it for me.'

'I see. Shortly before you were arrested you were seen withdrawing money from the bank in the name of Sorrell Bartlett. Can you explain your action?'

'I was doing it as a dare. I thought I looked like her and Joseph said I looked nothing like her. I took her credit card and passport to the bank, just to prove to him that I could pass for her.'

'So why didn't you push the money straight back and hand over the credit card?'

'I had to prove to Joseph that I had actually done it. I had planned to return it the next day.'

Marianne attended each day of the trial and was sitting tensely as the judge summed up and gave his verdict.

'Miss Sorrell Bartlett, I find you guilty on all counts, including that of murder.'

Sorrell's face went white and she had to be helped back to her chair, where she appeared to be in a daze.

'Mr Joseph Pirenzi, I find you guilty of receiving stolen goods. The other charges against you are dropped. Miss Flavia Fellini, I find you guilty of obtaining money under false pretences. All three prisoners will be held until they are sentenced.'

Marianne let out a gasp of horror. 'She can't be guilty of murder!' She buried her face in her hands, feeling the tears coursing down her cheeks. She needed to leave the court but found her legs would not move. She sat immobile until she felt a hand under her arm and Adam Kowalski was helping her to her feet.

'Let me take you back to the hotel. You can do no good sitting here.'

'What will they do to her?'

'They don't have capital punishment in Greece, if that's any consolation.'

To Marianne's surprise she found Yannis waiting at the hotel when she returned. He accompanied her up to her room and took a bottle of wine from the fridge. For a while they sat in silence; then Yannis took her hand.

'This has been a most unpleasant experience for you, my dear.'

'I just want to go home.'

'I understand, maybe in a week or so.'

'A week or so? Why not now?'

'The sale of this hotel will be completed in a couple of days. I'd like you to visit Crete for a while, have a little holiday and also give me some advice regarding a few problems that have cropped up over there.'

'I ought to go home. I will have to explain to my grandmother about Sorrell. I thought I'd only be staying a week or two and I've been here three months.'

'Then another couple of weeks will make little difference. I believe your friend and her husband will be travelling back to the States at about that time so you could arrange to go together.'

Marianne hesitated. 'It would be easier if I travelled with Elizabeth. We could help each other with the children.'

'Giovanni will be returning to Crete tomorrow. You could go over with him.'

'What about you?'

'I have a few loose ends to tie up over here. I expect I'll be with you by Wednesday.'

'I ought to stay until Sorrell has been sentenced.'

'Your presence will make no difference, my dear. I can telephone you as soon as there is any news.'

Marianne passed a hand over her forehead. 'A holiday would probably do me good.'

Ourania greeted Marianne and Giovanni with delight and John was immediately whisked away to see Anna.

'That will be the last you see of him,' remarked Giovanni.

'I hope not. I've got used to having him around. I'd miss him terribly.'

Giovanni took a can of beer from the fridge. 'Will you join me?'

Marianne shook her head. 'Should you be drinking?'

'The doctors say I can eat and drink what I like in moderation. If I find something upsets me then I just have to avoid it for a while.'

'You and Nicolas were really very lucky.'

'I would not call it lucky to be shot, but I suppose it could have been worse.'

'What do you think will happen to my cousin?'

'I think it will be a good thing if your cousin is in prison for ever. If she ever came near me again...'

Marianne bit her lip. 'I'm sorry. I forgot.'

Giovanni shrugged. 'I have no feelings for her. Myself I despise for being so foolish.'

'You mustn't blame yourself. From the evidence at the trial she made a living from deceiving men.'

'That is no excuse for my stupid behaviour. Now, what would you like to do? Yannis has said you are staying here for two weeks before returning to the States with Nicolas and Elizabeth.'

'I haven't given it any thought. Maybe I could go to some of the places I missed last time.'

'I will take you.'

'What about your work at the hotel?'

Marianne could not fathom the look that crossed Giovanni's face. 'I am still recuperating. Now, this evening we will go for a meal. I will take you to a special restaurant.'

'What about John? I can't leave him for the evening.'

'Ourania and Anna will love to look after him. They'll spend the whole evening looking at him and saying how beautiful he is. I wish to spend the evening with his mother and saying how beautiful she is.'

Marianne shook her head. 'Giovanni, you don't change, do you?'

'You would not want me to change. You love me as I am.' He squeezed Marianne to him and kissed her forehead.

For the first time in over a year Marianne felt a thrill of pleasure go through her.

Giovanni drove down to Plaka with Marianne. 'I think we should visit the church. I would like to make sure all is well. No one has had time to check in the last few months.'

Marianne leaned back comfortably in the seat, secure in the knowledge that John was being well cared for by Ourania. 'I really don't mind where we go.'

Giovanni nodded and they drove in companionable silence until they reached the village. Once again Giovanni lit the candle Marianne held and they stood together watching as it burned down.

'For our relatives,' said Giovanni, and Marianne squeezed his arm sympathetically.

'Would you like to go to Spinalonga now?'

Marianne looked at Giovanni dubiously.

'You said you wanted to go back,' Giovanni reminded her. 'You could take another photograph and see if Anna is still there.'

'Do you want to climb to the top of the island?'

'Are you fit enough?' Marianne looked at Giovanni in surprise.

'Of course. I shall climb slowly. You have to be careful,' warned Giovanni. 'Some of the time we will be walking on walls and roofs.'

Gingerly Marianne followed him as he led the way up a narrow path, climbing steadily, turning back at regular intervals to help her over a steep or slippery rock. Giovanni helped her up the first few feet and they stood together on a grassy plateau. Marianne looked across the bay in amazement.

'It's incredible. We're not that high, yet everything on the mainland looks like a toy. It's sad there aren't any people living in Plaka now.'

'There is nothing to do in Plaka.'

'There could be.'

'Young people do not want to be farmers.' Giovanni sat down on the short turf and Marianne looked at him in concern.

'You shouldn't have climbed up here. You've over done it. You're as white as a sheet.'

'I'm all right. A few minutes rest is all I need. It was steeper than I remembered.' Giovanni had a look of intense concentration on his face.

Marianne sat beside him. 'This is a wonderful place. I get the feeling that we are the only two people in the world.'

Giovanni searched for her hand. 'I would be quite happy if we were.'

'I wouldn't. I'd want John with me.'

Giovanni turned her face towards him. 'Why didn't you tell me?'

'Tell you what?'

'That I had a son.'

Marianne's face flamed. 'There were a number of reasons.'

'I would have married you.'

'That's what I was frightened of.'

'What do you mean? Why should you be frightened?'

'I wouldn't want you to marry me because you felt you should.'

Giovanni pushed her back on the grass. He leant over her, twisting her hair gently between his fingers. 'If you had not returned to America so suddenly I would have asked you to marry me. With your father so ill, it wasn't the right time. You wrote and thanked me – that was all. I thought you didn't care and would marry Elizabeth's brother.'

A tear crept down Marianne's cheek. 'I kept meaning to write to you, then I realised I was having John.'

'You should have told me. I want to marry you. I could not believe it was you sitting by my bedside. I thought I had died and you were an angel.' He kissed her gently. 'I love you, Marianne. It's not too late, is it?'

'I don't know, Giovanni.'

'What do I have to do to make you say yes?'

Marianne did not answer, but she found it impossible not to respond as Giovanni kissed her.

Yannis arrived late on the Wednesday morning, looking drawn and weary. Ourania hovered over him and Marianne tried to curb her impatience to know the sentence that had been passed on her cousin. He drank almost a bottle of wine; then called Giovanni into the other room with him. Marianne looked at Ourania.

'I wish he would tell me what happened.'

'He will when he's ready. Don't worry. I'm sure everything will work out all right.'

Giovanni emerged almost an hour later. There was a grim set to his mouth and his eyes looked suspiciously moist. He walked over to where Marianne was sitting and took her hand.

'Come for a walk with me.'

Without arguing Marianne rose and walked out onto the patio. 'What's happened, Giovanni?'

'Uncle Yannis is the best man I have ever known except my father. He has sold the hotel in Athens and both of those in Heraklion.'

'But why? He explained he would have to sell the Athenia, but why the others?'

Giovanni took her hands and pulled her down on the low wall beside him. 'I knew Joseph had shot me. When I told uncle Yannis he waited until the police had arrested him. They might not have

388

found him; then he would not have had to sell the hotel to bribe the judge.'

'Giovanni!' Marianne's voice was a horrified whisper. 'He murdered the desk clerk and tried to murder you and Nicolas, yet Yannis bribed the judge so he could get away with it?'

'Think of my mother. How would she feel if she knew her son was a murderer?'

'How will my aunt feel when she hears that her daughter has been imprisoned for murder – or my grandmother and the rest of my family?' asked Marianne angrily.

Giovanni placed a finger on her lips. 'The charges against her have been dropped. She is to be sent back to the States. The only crime recorded against her in Greece is entering the country using a false passport.'

'But how?'

'Uncle Yannis sold the Heraklion hotels.'

'Sold the Heraklion hotels? You mean…'

'If we had known earlier that Sorrell was your cousin.' Giovanni spread his hands expressively. 'It was more expensive to negotiate after the trial.'

Marianne felt her head reeling. 'You mean – Sorrell won't be in prison for murder?'

'Joseph has a nine month sentence for receiving and Flavia was given six months. Sorrell is to be deported.'

'Oh, Giovanni, is it true, really true?' Tears of relief began to pour down Marianne's cheeks and Giovanni took her in his arms. 'I must go and thank Yannis.'

'There's one more thing. Marianne, I can't marry you.'

As if struck, Marianne reeled back. 'Why not?'

'I have nothing. No work, no home, nothing. I cannot ask anyone to marry me.'

'Giovanni, that makes no difference.'

'It may make no difference to you, but it does to me.' Giovanni dropped his arms and walked back into the house.

Marianne stayed where she was and sobbed bitterly. Half an hour later she went in search of Yannis and hugged him.

'Giovanni said you were the most wonderful man in the world after his father. I think you are wonderful too. Why did you do it? Why did you sell the hotels? Sorrell was nothing to you.'

Yannis shrugged aside her thanks. 'She's family,' he said simply. 'She was a scheming, wicked woman, but she was no murderess. Please, Marianne, I beg you, do not tell anyone in America about this. I am ashamed and so is Giovanni.'

'Giovanni told me he had nothing. He must have some savings.'

'He has very little. He lived well and has spent most of his savings due to his foolish behaviour with women.' Yannis sighed. 'We have the shop to provide an income, he has nothing.'

'Where is he?'

'He drove down to Plaka. I expect he has gone to the church there.'

'Would you trust me with your car? I need to speak to him urgently.'

Yannis dug in his pocket for the keys. 'You're welcome.'

Giovanni was on his knees in the tiny church. Marianne crept in and knelt beside him. He looked at her in surprise as she bowed her head and when he looked again there were dark splashes on the wooden floor in front of her. He put his arm round her and encouraged her to rise and light a candle with him before they left and locked the church.

'Why did you come?'

'I wanted to be with you.'

'I needed to think.' Giovanni took her hand. ' Come with me to look at the farmhouse.'

'There's nothing to see.'

'I want to go inside.'

They walked up the slight incline and Giovanni unlocked the padlock on the door. A stale, musty smell met them and Marianne waited until her eyes grew accustomed to the semi-darkness before she ventured inside. She walked through the living room and into the kitchen at the back. It was just as primitive as she remembered.

'What's upstairs?'

Giovanni led the way. 'Tread carefully, the stairs could be rotten.'

Testing each one, Marianne arrived at the top and peered into the two empty bedrooms.

'I told you there was nothing to see.'

'You just can't see what I can.'

Carefully Giovanni refastened the padlock whilst Marianne looked at the surrounding hills.

'Does all this land belong to Yannis?'

'Difficult to say. His father's farm adjoined this one. He and Yiorgo pulled down his old house to make more space for the sheep and goats. It could be impossible now to define a boundary between his land and Yiorgo's.'

Marianne slipped her arm through his. 'Maybe you could start the farm up again. I'd like to be a farmer's wife.'

'You couldn't live there! You saw the state of the place.'

'There's nothing wrong that a good clean and coat of paint wouldn't put right.'

'There isn't even a bathroom!'

'It was good enough for Yannis and your mother, and Yiorgo and Anna until recently. You've just been spoilt. Now, I must take Yannis's car back or he'll think I've run away with it.' Marianne whisked away from him.

Giovanni arrived back some considerable time after Marianne and she could read nothing by his expression. He excused himself from their meal and took a snack with him to his room.

'Is he feeling all right?' asked Ourania. 'His stomach isn't troubling him is it?'

'I hope he hasn't overdone it. We climbed to the top of Spinalonga yesterday and he looked quite pale afterwards.'

The following morning Giovanni had left the house by the time Marianne had finished dealing with John and he did not arrive back until the early afternoon. Once again he went straight to his room and did not emerge until Yannis and Ourania had returned from the shop.

'How's business, uncle Yannis?'

'Sales are steady.'

'Have you invested in any new stock recently?'

'I've not branched out, just the usual orders. There's no need to expand at my time of life.'

Giovanni leant forward in his chair. 'Uncle Yannis, I've had an idea.'

Yannis eyed him warily. 'I'll listen, nothing more.'

'Your land at Plaka, would you be willing to build on it?'

'Build? What would I want to build along there?'

'If you built some summer bungalows, nothing elaborate, you could rent them out to holiday makers.'

Yannis looked at Giovanni scornfully. 'What would holiday makers want to stay right along there for? There's nothing to do.'

'You could make things for them to do.'

'Like what? There isn't even a taverna.'

'We rent a portion of the beach and make it private, only the residents in our bungalows can use it. We buy some loungers and umbrellas, a few pedal boats, maybe some wind surfers or canoes. Later on we could make a proper water sports centre and you could hire out diving equipment and employ someone to teach them how to use it properly. Make a couple of tennis courts and a crazy golf. Think of the potential. The old farmhouse could be turned into a taverna and once we were up and running we could add more bungalows and equipment.'

'And where would I get the capital for such an investment?'

'You bought the apartment in Athens back from Nicolas. You could sell that. I went into the bank today and they agreed to put up a loan to match whatever capital we can raise. The manager seemed to think it was a good idea.'

'I'm sure he did! It would be years before we could pay a loan like that back and all the time he'd be earning interest on it. Besides, the farm belongs to Yiorgo and Anna, and I expect the land you have your eye on is theirs also.'

'I can't see either of them having any use for it. They've not been back once since they moved in here.'

Marianne sat with her hands clenched in her lap. It was a wonderful idea and she could visualise the potential.

'You've always made money from my ideas,' insisted Giovanni. 'At least look at the figures before you turn it down out of hand.' He tossed some sheets of paper on the table. 'It's all there. If you want anything explained just ask me.'

Yannis collected the sheets together. 'I'll look at it, but I'm not promising anything.'

As soon as Yannis had left the room Marianne rounded on Giovanni. 'Why didn't you tell me what you had in mind? It's a wonderful idea.'

Giovanni smiled at her. 'I wanted to get some figures and my idea sorted out before I spoke to anyone. I want to marry you, Marianne, but I have to be able to offer you something.'

Yannis shook his head. 'It wouldn't work. I haven't got the capital to put into it. The most suitable land is lower down, where it borders the road, and that belongs to Yiorgo and Anna, the same as the farm. I'd have to buy it off them.'

Giovanni looked at his uncle in dismay. 'We have to raise the money. This is a chance too good to be missed. I've thought of it which means that sooner or later someone else will.'

'They still can't build there. We won't sell the land.'

'There's other land along there. Yiorgo and Anna don't own it all. There'll be no point in us building a complex if someone else has one just a few hundred yards away.'

'I'm sorry, Giovanni. It is a good idea, but the amount we'd need to borrow would make it out of the question. Sit on it for a year or two, then we'll think again.'

'Without some sort of expansion we won't have any more money then than we have now. The most I can expect to get is an under manager's position at a hotel. I haven't got much in the way of savings due to my stupidity.'

Yannis shrugged. 'I'm sorry, Giovanni. I'll help you get back on your feet all I can, but I can't commit myself to this project at the moment.'

Marianne found Giovanni sitting on the patio gazing out to sea, a brooding expression on his face.

'What's wrong?'

'Uncle Yannis turned my idea down.'

'What! It's a wonderful idea. Surely he must see that? The way the tourist industry is expanding it's just what this area needs to put it on the map.'

'He agrees with the idea. He just hasn't sufficient capital to back it at the moment. The land we ought to use belongs to Yiorgo and Anna and he'd have to buy it from them.'

Marianne frowned. 'There must be some way we can do it.'

Giovanni hugged her.

'Will you wait for me? Wait until I'm back on my feet and can afford a wife and child?'

Marianne leaned her head against his chest. 'I don't think I can. I've been wondering how healed your stomach is, whether it's too soon to think of any extra exertion.' She looked up at him mischievously.

Giovanni drew in a deep breath. 'My stomach's fine. There's no one around, John's asleep, we could…'

Marianne put her finger on his lips. 'We could not! If you want me, Giovanni, this time I want a wedding ring first.'

'But, Marianne…'

'No buts, those are my terms – and I want them fulfilled as quickly as possible.' She lifted her head and kissed him. 'Think about it. I'm going to talk to Yiorgo and Anna.' She slipped from his arms and returned to the house.

It was difficult talking to the two old people, but Marianne sat with them, listening to their reminiscences and trying to extract from Yiorgo information about the extent of the farmland he owned.

'I own that road, too. That one the government insisted on putting on my land. It cuts across my fields. It was where I ran my sheep and goats.'

'But you don't run any now, Yiorgo. If you did they couldn't put a road there.' Anna was thoroughly confused and her head dropped to her chest, her eyes closing.

'You don't understand,' grumbled Yiorgo. 'The man came and said I had to sell that land or they would take it away from me. Compulsory something, they called it. Thieving I call it.'

'But you have plenty of land left,' Marianne tried to placate him.'

'Always need more when you have sheep and goats. Good job I had the use of Babbis's land or we would have run out of pasture we had so many. Yannis's idea that was; more animals, less work in the fields. Couldn't manage otherwise, just the two of us. Yannis didn't want to be a farmer anyway. He's a businessman. He has hotels and shops. He's done well for himself. When he first drove that car into Plaka – well – you should have seen the people stare…' Yiorgo rambled on and Marianne tried to steer the conversation back to the farm.

'How much land does Yannis own?'

'He has his father's farm.'

'Suppose Yannis wanted to build on his land and it wasn't sufficient. Would you let him build on yours?'

'Where would I run my sheep and goats if he built on my land?'

Marianne sighed in despair. 'You don't have any animals now, uncle Yiorgo. You live with Yannis and Ourania.'

'I do now, but when I go back I'll need it.'

She looked at the frail old man with something like amusement. 'Suppose your land was more suitable for Yannis to build on? Would you consider exchanging his for some of yours?'

'He could have the road. That's no good to me. Can't run my beasts there.'

'What about lower down, where the farm is. You wouldn't want to run animals there.'

Yiorgo fixed his almost sightless eyes on her. 'What scheme has Yannis in mind that he needs my land for?'

Marianne blushed. 'I don't think he has. I was just curious.'

'Yannis always has some scheme afoot,' grumbled Yiorgo. 'It's always been the same. Talked me into letting him have his mother's money so he could invest and buy land. Always on at me to put my money into a bank.'

'Yannis knew what he was doing.' Anna had either awakened or decided to participate in the conversation again. 'You do what Yannis says. He's a good boy, a clever boy.' Anna searched her memory. Where had she heard those words before? Oh, yes, her mother always said Yannis was a good and clever boy. Had she been talking about her brother or her nephew Yannis? Anna gave up the puzzle.

'Yannis can have my land. He can have my savings too. It will all be his soon anyway.'

'It's my land,' Yiorgo said sourly.

'Some of it is your land, the rest of it is mine, and if I want to give it to Yannis I will,' she replied querulously.

'Do you mean that, Aunt Anna?'

Anna nodded. 'What am I going to do with it? We live here. Yannis looks after us; he can have my land and savings in exchange.'

'Will you tell Yannis that, Aunt Anna?'

'You remind me when he comes home. I get forgetful these days.' Her head drooped again.

Yiorgo turned to Marianne. 'What does he want to do with the land?'

'It's for another hotel. It would still be your land, Uncle Yiorgo.'

'I'll think about it.'

Marianne left the elderly couple, hopeful that Anna would remember her promise when the time came and Yiorgo would be willing to be talked into Giovanni's idea.

Marianne sat opposite Yannis at the table. 'Giovanni says you turned his idea down.'

Yannis spread his hands. 'I had no option. I have capital and I can raise some more, but,' he shook his head, 'not the amount this would need.'

'Suppose Yiorgo and Anna were willing to give you their land to build on?'

'Why should they?'

'I was talking to them today. Anna said you could have all her land and savings in exchange for looking after her, and Yiorgo seemed willing to think about allowing you to build. It could still be their land, you would just use it.'

Yannis studied her seriously. 'You believe in this wild idea? Do you think people would want to spend their holiday in a bungalow looking after themselves?'

'I do, particularly young people, or people with families. It would be cheaper for them than staying in a hotel.'

Yannis sighed. 'Giovanni has such big ideas. It's not just the bungalows; he's talking about turning the farmhouse into a taverna, having tennis courts, crazy golf, a water sports centre. No, it's out of the question.'

'Even if you sold the flat in Athens?'

'That would probably provide enough for a couple of bungalows. You can't run a business like that.'

'If the bank is willing to lend you the same – that could make it four bungalows.'

'Four bungalows and nothing else.' Yannis shook his head.

'It could be a start. If you provided a little kitchenette in each so people could cook for themselves you could advertise them as self-catering apartments. We could convert the farmhouse into a taverna and a general store. If you built the first four by next season you could probably make enough to pay back the bank loan and have a small profit. The next year you could expand a little more. Please think about it again before you finally say no.'

Yannis pulled the papers across the table towards him. 'Maybe I'd better have another look at these figures. I did borrow money from Yiorgo once before and he didn't regret it.'

1996

'Elizabeth!' Marianne threw her arms around her friend.

'Let me look at you. You've not changed a bit!'

'That can't be Nicola! She's so big! Where's Nicolas?'

'He's getting the bags.'

Together the two girls walked into Yannis's house and Marianne led the way to the rooms that she and Giovanni considered to be their own. Nicolas deposited two heavy suitcases in the hallway and followed them. Nicola, suddenly overcome with shyness hung behind him.

'Now,' said Marianne. 'I have coffee and baklava ready; then I want to hear all your news.'

'No baklava for me,' said Elizabeth firmly.

'No baklava? Why ever not?'

'I just can't bear it. How I ever used to eat that awful sweet stuff I don't know.'

'When did you go off it?'

'A little while ago.' A flush spread gradually into Elizabeth's cheeks. 'I didn't mean to tell you yet.'

'That's wonderful. When?'

'I've only just had it confirmed.' Elizabeth looked at Nicolas. 'He nearly wouldn't let me come, just in case.'

'If I know when I book the ticket I would say no,' smiled Nicolas.

'Is there anything you would like?'

Nicolas laughed. 'Bring her a plate of olives. She eats them all day long.'

'Do you?'

'Do I what?'

'Oh, Elizabeth, have you still not learnt to speak Greek? Nicolas said you eat olives all the time.'

Elizabeth shook her head. 'I understand a few words here and there. Nicola speaks Greek. Nicolas wasn't going to bother as we live in America, but I insisted. I remembered how easily you went from one language to another. It didn't seem fair to deny her the chance.'

Marianne turned to the quiet little girl and spoke to her slowly. 'Go into the kitchen. Bring the olives for your mamma.'

Nicola looked at her father who nodded and she trotted docilely on her errand.

'So where is Giovanni?' asked Nicolas.

'Up at the taverna. He's up there most days during the season. He takes John up with him a lot of the time. I have more than enough to do here.'

'Please talk in English,' begged Elizabeth.

Marianne laughed. 'This is a good time to make you learn. Now, tell me all about everything in America.'

'Well, my father's thinking of retiring in a few months. My mother's pleased about that. Bob's still in Atlanta and Julia's become rather difficult. She's struck up a relationship with a married man. What about you?'

'Yannis has aged over the last few years, but Ourania is fine. Uncle Yiorgo is nearly blind. He spends his time messing around in the garden thinking he's being useful. He picked the heads off the flowers recently and brought them inside for Anna to cook. Aunt Anna, well, one day she's with us and the next she's in a make-believe world of her own. She spends all her time watching television and talks back to the actors. It doesn't seem to register with her that they don't reply. That's why I decided to shuffle beds around a bit and keep you in here rather than disturb them.'

'And your family in America?'

'Well, we write quite often and I telephone mamma about once a month. I don't think she has ever forgiven me for staying out here and marrying Giovanni. She comes over to visit once a year and always seems relieved when it's time for her to leave. I'm sure she comes to see John more than me. Helena and Greg came last year, but I don't think they enjoyed it. Helena was petrified the boys would be taken ill or hurt themselves. She wouldn't allow them to do anything and Greg just seems to go along with her. Andrew and Sarah love Greece. They go to a different island each year and then come over to visit us. The person I'd really like to come out is my grandmother. She wouldn't believe the change in Plaka. Nor will you when you see it.' Marianne smiled happily. 'When we've had lunch we'll drive along and relieve Giovanni of a small menace.'

Elizabeth drew in her breath as she looked at the collection of small bungalows that nestled into the foot of the hill.

'It's fantastic. You wouldn't believe this was just a ruined village when I was here last.'

Marianne pointed to the brightly coloured sails that could be seen out on the water. 'You can wind surf or snorkel. If you hold a current licence we even have scuba gear and this season we hired a speedboat for a few weeks so people could ski. There are two tennis courts and a crazy golf,' she said proudly. 'There's still an enormous amount we want to do, but it's taking shape.'

'And all this belongs to Giovanni?'

'No, none of it. The land belongs to Yannis, Anna and Yiorgo. Giovanni just had the idea and supervised the layout. He's the manager, the same as he was in the Heraklion hotels.' She swung the car off the road and parked on the waste ground beside the taverna, hooting to attract her husband's attention.

Giovanni greeted them effusively. 'Well, what do you think?'

'I think I'd like to spend a holiday here,' smiled Elizabeth. 'Maybe Marianne and I can have a game of tennis tomorrow.'

'Should you?' asked Marianne.

'Of course. I know your game. I'll stand still and make you run around for me.'

Marianne smiled grimly.

'If I remember rightly that will definitely be the way of things. Where's John?'

'Up at the crazy golf.'

'Come with me, Elizabeth, we'll find him and introduce Nicola.' Marianne held out her hand to the little girl who had not said a word.

They walked up the hill to the right of the taverna to where a six-foot high netting surrounded a piece of ground that had been levelled.

Standing with his back to them and concentrating hard was John. He swung his golf club at the ball and they watched as it negotiated the maze, stopping just short of the intended target. The oath that fell from his lips made Marianne blush and she was glad Elizabeth did not understand.

'John,' she called sharply. He swung round and she spoke to him in Greek. 'Don't ever let me hear you say that again! Come and meet Elizabeth and her little girl, Nicola.'

Meekly John walked forward. 'Hello.'

'You swore,' said Nicola, smugly.

'You wouldn't know. I said it in Greek.'

'I speak Greek.'

'Bet you don't.'

'I sure do.'

'Say something then.'

Nicola shrugged. 'What shall I say?'

'You could tell me my golf is very good.'

'I could play better than that,' she said in Greek.

'You could not,' John answered, his face darkening.

'I'll show you.' She opened the gate and walked inside the fenced area, picking up a discarded golf club.

Marianne looked at Elizabeth. 'Well! I didn't think she had a tongue in her head. I suggest we leave them to argue it out and go back down. John, look after Nicola and be down at the taverna in an hour.'

John raised his hand in acknowledgement, not taking his eyes off Nicola as she prepared to hit the golf ball.

'Don't hold your club like that,' they heard him say. 'Put your right hand here and your left there. Keep your feet apart and your back straight.'

'I don't think we'll have to worry about amusing Nicola during our stay,' smiled Elizabeth.

The two women walked back to the taverna where Giovanni and Nicolas were sitting outside at a table sharing a bottle of wine.

'Where's Nicola?' asked Nicholas.

'With John, playing golf,' Elizabeth reassured him.

'He'll look after her. He's a sensible boy. A drink for you, Elizabeth?'

Elizabeth shook her head. 'A glass of water, please. Do you serve meals at this taverna?'

'Only snacks. I can make for you if you are hungry,' offered Giovanni.

'No, I'm not hungry, thank you.'

'There are some olives behind the bar,' smiled Marianne.

'May I get them?'

'Help yourself.'

Elizabeth rose and went into the taverna where she served herself from the covered bowl that stood behind the bar.

As she turned to leave she noticed a large photograph on the wall and moved closer to examine it. She caught her breath and studied it carefully. She returned to the table feeling quite unnerved.

'Marianne, you've enlarged and mounted the photograph of your little ghost girl. Did you ever find out what she was trying to tell you?'

'Of course.'

Marianne smiled happily and took Giovanni's hand. 'She was telling me I had to come back here and marry Giovanni.'

If you have enjoyed reading *Giovanni*, you will be pleased to know that the next book in the continuing saga – *Joseph* – is planned for publication in June 2009.

See overleaf for a 'taster' of what is to come.

For up-to-date information, have a look at the author's website:

www.beryldarby.co.uk

1989

Joseph gazed morosely at the occupants of the other tables. Many of them were local people, their dress and demeanour advertising they were taking a break from their work for quick refreshment before returning to their drudgery. Joseph's lip curled derisively. What fools they were, toiling each day for a pittance. He clenched his hands in anger. How could he have known the girl was a relative when she never revealed her true name? She should be languishing in jail for a considerable number of years and he should be living comfortably, instead of which she had been deported to America and he had no chance of repeating his idea now the hotels had been sold. At least that knowledge made him smile. He had revenged himself on his uncle and cousin for refusing to accept him as part of their small consortium. It was his father's fault. If he had not sent him into the army, his uncle would have accepted and helped him as he had done Giovanni. There was no justice in the world.

Now he waited. Whilst serving his prison sentence he had done a 'favour' for Dimitris. His payment had been the promise of help to make a new start when he was released. For three days he had sat at the same taverna and he was beginning to doubt if Dimitris intended to keep to the bargain.

A man slipped into the seat beside him, placing coffee in a plastic cup on the sticky metal table. He bent over the cup, as if to blow on the contents and spoke quietly to Joseph.

'Take the underground to Piraeus. Dimitris is in Zea Marina on the *'Aegean Pride'*.'

Joseph did not reply. At last, this was the message he had been waiting for. He continued to sit in a sullen silence as the man lifted the cup to his mouth and grimaced as the heat burnt his lips. He bent his head over the cup again.

'I should get going if I were you. He won't wait all day.'

Joseph looked at his watch. It would take no more than fifteen minutes to reach Piraeus, but the Zea Marina was a considerably long walk up the hill and down the opposite side. No doubt he would be able to find the money for a taxi. He rose leisurely, strolling across the road towards the entrance to the underground station.

Without purchasing a ticket, he forced his way through the turnstile in the wake of a tourist and clattered down the stone steps to the platform. When the train arrived he entered the first carriage and pushed his way between the passengers, helping himself from their back pockets as he laid a hand on their arm or shoulder and requested they moved aside to allow him passage. Each time the train stopped he dismounted and entered the carriage lower down. One stop before Piraeus he jumped from the train, as the doors were about to close, and hurried into the toilets. He removed the cash and credit cards from each of the wallets he had purloined, placing the money in the pocket of his jacket and the cards into the back pocket of his jeans. He threw the empty wallets into the rubbish bin and returned to the platform to await the next train, which would arrive within a matter of minutes.

Piraeus was thronged with people and Joseph twisted and turned before he was able to reach the exit. He stood there for a few moments, gazing at the ships that were moored against the main road, and then turned swiftly to look behind. No one appeared to be taking the slightest notice of him. A small crowd had gathered around a police officer who was trying to understand the complaints of three men who had felt for their wallet and found it was missing when they had left the earlier train. He shrugged and smiled to himself. Tourists should take more care of their belongings, there were notices warning people of pickpockets on the underground.

The traffic was a steady stream on the road and he took his chance to weave amongst it until he reached the seaward side and was able to hail a taxi. At the beginning of Zea Marina he paid off the driver, lit a cigarette and began to look idly at the names of the ships. It occurred to him that the boat he was looking for could be at the other end of the large marina and quickened his step.

He was pleasantly surprised when he saw her. He had expected a small motorboat, but this was a cabin cruiser, gleaming white, her deck of polished wood clean and the ropes neatly coiled. As he stepped aboard, the door to the saloon opened and a voice called to him to enter.

As his eyes became accustomed to the dark interior he could see Dimitris sitting at the far side of the table and an unknown man took up a stand behind him, blocking the doorway. Joseph extended his hand.

'It's good to see you again, Dimitris.'

Dimitris ignored the hand. 'Sit down Joseph. Drink?'

'I'll have a beer.'

A can was placed before him and Dimitris raised his glass. 'To profitable times.' The two large gold rings glinted on his fat fingers.

Joseph lifted his can. 'If this is yours, times must be very profitable.'

Dimitris shrugged. 'I promised you I would contact you when the time was right; give you a helping hand, so to speak, in return for the favour you did for me.'

Joseph nodded. He would really prefer to forget the unfortunate incident when he had lured Spiro to a corner of the prison yard and left him to his fate. Dimitris had kept his word when he had said that no suspicion would fall on Joseph and no one knew who had started a brawl, which had ended in Spiro hitting his head so hard on the concrete that he had never regained consciousness.

'It is essential that if you agree to work for me there must be no way of linking us. I am a respected businessman. I could not afford to have my name linked with a petty criminal.'

Joseph's face darkened. 'I was caught up in an unfortunate situation.'

'Quite so. We do not need to discuss that. Are you interested in a lucrative occupation, which requires very little effort on your part?'

Joseph nodded.

'Very well. Tonight you will take a ferry to Rhodes. I have your documents here. Once there you will visit Lakkis. He runs a taverna, *'The Grapevine'*, and I have booked a room for you. Thalia will meet you at the harbour and show you the way.'

Joseph opened his mouth to ask a question and Dimitris held up his hand again. 'I am not prepared to disclose the nature of the work he will offer you. Needless to say, your conversations with him will be entirely confidential and I shall know nothing about them. If you decide to refuse his offer there is nothing that will link you with me.'

The small black eyes, sunken in the rolls of fat that comprised Dimitris's face, bored into Joseph, who shivered despite the heat of the day.

'If you decide not to go to Rhodes you are free to go about your business, but I will not be prepared to offer to help you in the future. I am sure you know better than to accept passage to the island and not contact Lakkis upon your arrival, as I am equally sure that you would not be so foolish as to agree to work for Lakkis and then break your agreement.' Dimitris folded his hands and his mouth curved into a grim smile. 'It is an easy matter to shake off the Greek police if they decide to follow you. It is not so easy to escape the attentions of my men.'

'I wouldn't try to cross you, Dimitris,' Joseph licked his dry lips. 'If I decided not to work for Lakkis what would happen then?'

Dimitris shrugged. 'You could stay on Rhodes or return to Athens. The choice would be yours.'

Joseph swallowed the remainder of his beer. 'I've nothing to lose by visiting Rhodes and meeting Lakkis.' He tried to smile and appear relaxed, ignoring the knot of fear that was in his stomach.

Dimitris nodded and pushed an envelope across the table. 'The ferry leaves at six. You will find a ticket and your identity papers inside. I have enclosed a small amount for travelling expenses.'

Joseph nodded and pocketed the envelope. He rose from the seat and held out his hand to Dimitris. 'I'm grateful for your help.'

Dimitris nodded and shook Joseph's hand briefly. 'I suggest you return immediately to the city and make the necessary preparations for your departure.'

The large man standing by the door of the saloon moved to one side and Joseph returned to the bright sunshine. He crossed the short plank from the boat to the shore and began the return walk to the underground. He knew better than to ignore any instructions Dimitris had given him.

Dimitris watched Joseph's progress through the saloon window and as soon as he had been swallowed up amongst the throng of people, he spoke to the man still standing by the door.

'We can leave now, Anders.'

to be continued...

Beryl Darby

YANNIS

A continuing saga

First book

The compelling story of Yannis, who comes from the village of Plaka on the island of Crete. He attends school in the town of Aghios Nikolaos and gains a scholarship to the Gymnasium in Heraklion.

Whilst in Heraklion, he is diagnosed with leprosy, shattering his dreams of becoming an archaeologist. He is admitted to the local hospital for treatment and subsequently transferred to the hospital in Athens. The conditions in the hospital are appalling: overcrowding, lack of amenities, poor food, and only basic medication. The inmates finally rebel, resulting in their exile to Spinalonga, a leper colony just across the water from Yannis's home village.

The book tells the heart-rending account of his life on the small island, his struggle for survival, his loves and losses, along with that of his family on the mainland from 1918 to 1979.